Falstaff

Also by Robert Nye

The Late Mr Shakespeare

Falstaff

Being the *Acta domini Johannis Fastolfe*,
or *Life and Valiant Deeds of Sir John Faustoff*,
or *The Hundred Days War*, as told by
Sir John Fastolf, K.G.,
to his secretaries
*William Worcester, Stephen Scrope,
Fr Brackley, Christopher Hanson,
Luke Nanton, John Bussard,
and Peter Basset;*
now first transcribed, arranged
and edited in modern spelling

By

ROBERT NYE

a&b

This edition published in Great Britain in 2001 by
Allison & Busby Limited
Suite 111, Bon Marche Centre
241-251 Ferndale Road
London SW9 8BJ
http://www.allisonandbusby.ltd.uk

A catalogue record for this book is available from
the British Library.

ISBN 0 7490 0596 3

Printed and bound in Spain by
Liberduplex, s.l. Barcelona.

TO. THE. ONLIE. BEGETTER. OF.
THESE. INSUING. FICTIONS.
MR. GILES GORDON
ALL. HAPPINESS. AND. THAT. ETERNITY
PROMISED. BY. OUR. EVER-LIVING
POET. WISHETH. THE. WELL-WISHING.
ADVENTURER. IN SETTING. FORTH.

R.N.

CONTENTS

I

About the begetting of Sir John Fastolf

I was begotten on the giant of Cerne Abbas.

That will do. It's true. Start there.

Now introduce me:

John Fastolf – Jack to my familiars, John to my brothers and my sisters, Sir John to all Europe – Knight of the most noble Order of the Garter (once removed, but I'll come to that), Lord of Lasuze, Governor of Anjou and Maine, Captain of Le Mans, Grand Butler of Normandy, Baron of Silly-le-Guillem, Constable of Bordeaux, Lieutenant of Harfleur, Keeper of the Bastille of St Anthony in Paris, master of Caister Castle and Castle Combe, owner of the Boar's Head tavern, warrior and gentleman, hey diddle diddle and hey diddle dan, fill in the details later, all the titles, Thing of Thing, This of That, all the bloody rest of it, feedum fiddledum fee – me, Fastolf, now telling you the true story of my life and the history of my valiant deeds, starting my telling today, the 25th day of March, New Year's Day of the year of our Lord 1459, which is I think the 37th year in the reign of his majesty King Henry the 6th, the prickless holy wonder, son of Harry the Prig, of Gadshill and Agincourt, and which is rather more certainly and much more vitally the 81st year of my own great march to heaven.

That will be the longest sentence in the book. Don't worry. I don't like long sentences either.

My feet itch.

PRICK

and

PRIG.

Worcester, if you really don't know the difference you must be one or the other or both yourself.

Write down every word I say, just as I say it, or I assure you I will have your balls for full-stops.

Captain of the Palace of Rouen – I am the man who built the tower there, above the river Seine on the east side. Sometime Grand Master of the Household of John, Duke of Bedford, Regent of the Kingdom of France.

GADShill, you marvellous bloody fool, an expedition as famous in its day as the one at Agincourt. I should know. I fought in both.

Everything the way I tell it, in the order I give it to you, none of your literature. When a man has scaled as many ramparts and breached as many maidenheads as I have, he doesn't need to make a sentence bob and curtsey.

Bless me, father. Bugger all. Whoops. We're off then.

It was a fig tree they lay under, my father and my mother, my father under the fig tree and my mother under my father, and the fig tree growing on the giant's sex.

A dark religious wayfarer – my uncle Hugh used to say Wiclif himself, hot down from Oxford, not yet a heretic but riding a lollardy donkey and preaching in the churchyards after Mass – this wandering Wiclif comes along shouting that the giant is the Devil's work. He recognised him no doubt as a survivor of that race descended from the 33 wicked daughters of Diocletian. He sweats in the sun with hammer and boards, disgust and nails, and builds himself a pulpit on the giant's stalk, for the purpose of delivering a sermon against it.

'Gentlemen of Dorset,' Wiclif thunders, 'I stand here on the worst part of our human nature.'

It is ten yards long, the cock of the giant of Cerne Abbas. The giant himself is a hillside high. His outline is a white chalk-filled trench as wide as my arm and two feet deep. His inside is complete in every part – ribs, nipples, eyebrows, belly-button. In his right hand he carries a knobbled club pointing up to the clouds. His left hand saws the air as he steps westward. His member is magnificently erect. Nearby is the abbey founded by St Augustine, with the silver spring that gushed up at his wink.

Don't imagine that this forked radish Wiclif got red in the face preaching to sheep. Every seven years the giant is scoured, to keep his art safe from the grass. Some that live in those valleys have an inherited obligation to repair and cleanse him. If they didn't, in time he would turn green like the rest of the hill and be forgotten. It was at the festival of the scouring that Wiclif criticised the giant's erection, and there was a good-sized crowd to listen to his opinions, after they had wrestled for silver buckles and jumped in sacks and raced for cheeses rolled down the giant's legs.

'It should be covered,' Wiclif complains.

'Cover the giant?' A great laugh goes up in the sun. 'How could you cover it?'

Wiclif considers, calling to mind his education, and then he announces: 'In Greek times, the statues were given fig leaves to hide what should not be seen by shamefast eyes.'

'Extraordinary big fig leaf you'll need here,' points out some Pythagoras of the hedgerows.

Wiclif said: 'Let it be a fig *tree* then!'

And, lo, there was a fig tree. Wiclif's disciples planted one when the greasy pole had been taken down and the seven-year scouring was over. That is why in those days, before they were called Lollards, some called his people Figgers. They dug diligently, these flesh-abhorring Figgers, and they planted their fig tree on the wick of the Cerne giant, with a purpose to obscure the terrible splendour of him from the eyes of virgins passing on the road through the valley below.

Now, life being what it is, the villagers of Cerne Abbas found that fig tree a useful and appropriate addition to their giant's attributes. In summer it was cool and shady to lie under, and a man and a woman could be secret there. In winter, it kept some of the rain off.

Glasses, glasses, is the only drinking. Tell Macbeth he can pawn or smash the plate.

My mother was a well-known wearer-out of husbands. (This is not criticism. I do not criticise. I observe.) She had been married three times before she met my father, joined to fellows of substance too, none of your Johns of Gaunt – men of pepper, ginger, cloves, my ghostly fathers, who did not fail to make me for a lack of kidneys. Yet knock as they might, I did not answer. Ferret as they did in her sweet little moss-grown coney patch, there was never a scut of a child.

Put it away, Worcester. You'll never get to heaven doing that.

My father was a man of iron will. He had a red beard and eyes like caves. He married my mother sensibly for the triple joy of her widowhood, the three estates, but he was concerned – as an

English country gentleman and an epitome of the chivalric virtues – with the making of a son.

Having heard well of the giant's child-inspiring powers, my father takes my mother by the hand and leads her up to him the night before their wedding. It had been a hot day, the hottest day that any man could remember, the skylarks swooning in the sticky air, milk turning sour in the cows' udders. At the end of that hottest day now it is suddenly Midsummer Eve and the giant stands out bold and wonderful and monstrous on his long green Dorset hill, the moon at the full above his knobbled club. My father lays my mother down on the giant's thistle, in the modest shade of Mr Wiclif's burgeoning fig tree.

'Dear heart,' says he, taking off his spurs and his liripipe hat, 'I shall require an heir.'

If ever widow woman blushed then my mother blushed hot when she saw my father unbuttoned above her in the moonlight. 'My womb,' says she, 'is empty.'

My father engages the key in the lock. It is well-oiled. He turns and enters and makes himself at home.

'I have been told,' he says,

'that any true woman,' he says,

'childless,' he adds,

'who lies,' he says,

'on the Cerne giant,' – my father

takes a shuddering juddering breath –

'conceives without fail,' he explains.

My father goes on, without need of saying.

It is sixty yards if it is an inch from the top to the toe of the giant of Cerne Abbas. The creature's club alone must be every bit of forty yards.

'O Gog,' says my mother eventually. 'O Gog, O Gog, O Gog.'

'I do believe,' says my father, 'Magog.'

Now, in the moment of my conception, as a star falls into my mother's left eye, as the wind catches its breath, as the little hills skip for joy, and the moon hides her face behind a cloud – a bit of local history. When St Augustine came calling in those parts the people of Cerne tied a tail to his coat and whipped him out of their valley. The saint was furious. He got down on his knees and prayed to God to give tails to all the children that were born in Dorset. 'Right,' said the Omnipotence. This went on, tails, tails, tails, tails, until the folk regretted their pagan manners. When

4

they expressed their regret, St Austin came back and founded the abbey, calling it Cernal because he was soon seeing his visions there – from the Latin, *cerno*, I see, and the Hebrew, *El*, God.

That's enough history. I prefer mystery.

The sun at my making was in the sign of Libra near Venus. The moon was in Capricorn. My conceptual Jupiter, so they tell me, is on Joan of Arc's Saturn, and my Mars up her Uranus.

II

About a genealogy refused

You see this fig then? My family tree has figs on it. As I was explaining eight days ago, before my autobiography was interrupted by alcohol. O times, O manners. We'll never get through hell at this rate. Courage, I'm eating the fig now. I've eaten them all my life. By the bushel I used to roll the little demons down my throat, before entering the lists of love. Half a dozen do these days. My niece Miranda comes this afternoon.

Your fig, being your *ficus*, has other properties than that sly service noticed by Pliny. Mashed, by all means, a bowl of figs works wonders in the bowels, and there's nothing like a brace of them for inspiriting a generous fart. Fig puddings on Palm Sundays. Fig-sue on Good Friday – ale, sliced figs, bread and nutmeg boiled together and supped hot like soup. Fine discharging stuff. But I'm not talking about Ajax. I am talking about Aphrodite. I am talking about your fat plum-purplish Queen Fig, your ripe and autumn forky fig, gone out to turn gold in the sun along the wall, then cherished in silk and pulled and squeezed and sleeked by a young girl's fingers. A boon to the weary warrior. Pliny himself says that the milky juice of the fig leaf and the fig stem raises blisters. It's the raising capacities and capabilities of the purple fig itself that interests me. The fat wild swelling fig, my hero. Sacred to Bacchus. Anno mundi 4483 – there was a fig tree overshadowing Romulus and Remus, where they sucked on the mother wolf's mammets.

Talking of figs and thistles, when I was a young man I used to wake up in the morning with a cock like a sword, like an iron bar. I couldn't push it down with two hands. Two strong wives couldn't push it down with four hands – Mrs Ford and her friend, they tried. I was delighting the both of them, sweet ladies

6

of Windsor. We made merry in an enormous linen-basket full of their underwear, the three of us, and all round the roots of the old oak in Windsor Park. Mrs Ford's friend had a bum like a melon. She liked me to bugger her while she sucked her neighbour's titties. Then she would have me futter Mrs Ford, while the two of them wriggled about poking their fingers up each other's arses. And so on. They couldn't get enough of it. They had to have their servants burn my buttocks with tapers to make me stop, but that only made my man the hotter and I swear I turned into a bull, a stag, a pagan god of the hunt to satisfy the pair of them. Lord, I went at it with a whopping will! I rogered and rammed and ploughed them until they thought the sky was raining potatoes and thundering to the tune of Greensleeves. When they flagged, I fed them eringoes, little candied roots of sea-holly, useful in their amatorious properties for ladies whose desires outreach their abilities. My merry mistresses divided me – a haunch each. The muscle in the middle did for both. That mid-summer night by the Herne Oak they must have had more luxury from me than their husbands had given them in all the years of their married bliss. I took them in turn, until the starlight and moonshine ran out. All the same, in the morning, even after that most extreme and thirsty intercourse – like a sword, Worcester, like an iron bar! I couldn't push it down with both hands, no matter how I tried. Even in France, when I was raising hell and raping up the Meuse and bringing great joy to all the burghers' wives in the garrisons we took, and when I was captain of Conde Norean and it was my *duty* to satisfy seven French matrons a night – still, in those dandled days, I couldn't get my cock down with both hands. But this is why I've had you call Friar Brackley. Father, I've a confession to make. A moment of truth. An instant of self-knowledge in an aging soul. Just yesterday, at the end of our New Year revels, I woke up in the morning and took stock of my stick and you know what? I realised that now I *can* push it down with both hands. Indeed, I'll tell you the truth, I can just about push it down with *one* hand. That's why I've called for you. A simple question. Worcester knows I mean it:

Father, *do you think I'm getting stronger?*

Feedum, fiddledum –

A pox of this gout!

Or, a gout of this pox!

(The one or the other plays the rogue with my great toe. . . .)

As to the other sort of family tree, I have one, as good as any now in England, somewhat superior to the shrub Plantagenet if you want to know, but I don't intend to include much here on that subject. Chaps who seek dignity in genealogy are bandits. A man is the shape that fills his own suit, not his father's, or his father's fathers. At the same time I would lie if I came pretending to have made my way single-handed in this naughty world. We Fastolfs have a history of substance.

My great great great great grandfather Fastolf is in *Domesday Book*. Page 777. You will find there written against our name that he held freely from King William the Conqueror the church in the borough of Stamford, County Lincoln. Not that my people came in with the Conqueror. We were here already. We were the chief directors of the work of the tower of Nimrod. We were with Arthur at Mons Badon. We had a seat of sorts at the Round Table. William of Normandy's companions were a low form of life in any case – the dregs of Burgundy and Flanders and the sweepings of the prisons of the Rhine – and many a family now claiming descent from them just advertises its cheap heart by the connection. The Conqueror! He even had to drill holes in his boats after crossing the channel, to prevent his army from going home again. William himself was a bastard. His mother was a tanner's daughter called Arlotta. You knew that? Bet you didn't know that his father, Robert the Devil, the last Duke of Normandy, saw this Arlotta washing her drawers in a stream one day when he was on his way home from the hunt, and that our William was conceived when the Duke jumped into the water to help her. Later, when Robert the Devil popped off on a pilgrimage to Jerusalem, his cronies told him he shouldn't leave his lands without a ruler. Robert answered: 'But I have a little bastard who, please God, will grow bigger.' Robert the Devil was stung by a gnat at the Holy Sepulchre, and never came back. God must have been pleased, because his little bastard grew up to be a big bastard.

Gurth Fastolf my ancestor fought for King Harold. The story that he obtained the Big Bastard's favour by leading a miscellany of Saxons in the wrong direction – to wit, over a cliff on an escarpment near Dover, at the time of the skirmish at Hastings – is absolutely without foundation. It is, in short, a lie put about by envious neighbours whose talents were never so complex as to catch the eye of William's wife Matilda, a dumpy woman but not beneath my great great great great grand-dad's notice. Those stupid Saxons rushed forward impetuously in the dark, as was their way, uttering unintelligible remarks, while the first of the Fastolfs was consulting a map a little to the north.

The Battle of Hastings was unfair in any case. William had a secret weapon – a hair from the head of St Peter. The Pope sent it to him. The fact that at the same time His Holiness excommunicated Harold and the entire English Army didn't help matters either.

Pass me my memory powder. It's on the shelf behind you.

April Fool you, Worcester! April bloody gob! April noddy! Don't cry – you'll make the ink run. Cheer up. I've sent Hanson and Nanton to the Friars Minor, to ask for a look at their book called *The Life of Eve's Mother*.

The famous Willy Griskin was a Fastolf too. Griskin. It's a little pig. Will's father was taxed out of existence, and he left young Will this pigling as his patrimony. Of course the boy's contemporaries laughed. The Knight of the Griskin, they called him, Little Willy Gris. So Will sold his pig and emigrated on the proceeds. In France, despite the French, he advanced himself on the back of that pigling money until he was in a position to marry a marriable woman – the widow of a banker. He was rolling in it now, and the more money he made the more the world loved him. This did not escape his notice. Sitting brooding on the fact, he had one room in his house painted and decorated by an artist called Nicholas Pisano. Will kept the key of this room on a chain which he wore about his neck, and he never let anyone in there ever, not even his wife. It was his habit, by the way, to give that lucky lady a groat every time they had marriage joys. It was his habit also, whenever he came home from seeing great men, to neglect all other business and go straight to his secret chamber. He'd stay there for hours and then come out to his family with a philosophical smile. Everyone burned to know what was in the room. His wife begged him to show them. At last, thoroughly besieged, Will Fastolf unlocked the door. The walls of the room were white and the floor was white, but on the ceiling of the room was painted a picture of a pigling and a little boy leading it by a string, and the words written:

> *Willy Gris, Willy Gris –*
> *Think what you was, and what you is!*

9

Morally impressed, no doubt, his wife had a copy of the griskin cast in bronze, and called it her piggy-bank, and she put into this piggy-bank every groat her husband gave her after their copulations. When she died, Will opened the piggy-bank with a hammer and found that it contained 140 crowns and a note wrapped round one of his groats. The note said:

> Willy Gris, Willy Gris –
> Did you think everyone's as mean as this?

I like that Griskin Fastolf tale. I'd let it stand as a complete genealogy, an explanation of my inheritance, if I hadn't mentioned the Domesday Fastolf. I brought him up to account for three things.

First, our Fastolf land. It's true that with the death of five or six or seven cousins in the engagement at the cliff, my great great great great grandfather Gurth fell heir not only to the church at Stamford, but to one or two small estates here in Norfolk.

However, to the second point – we were always accounted less than the uncouth Norman overlords in that despite or perhaps because of Queen Matilda's patronage, the Big Bastard refused my ancestor any leg up to the ranks of his so-called nobility. Gurth was told, by the burstable king himself, that he was lucky to be allowed to keep possession of his estates, and that the honours and subtleties of chivalry were not for a False Thief like him. This strange title of *False Thief* stuck to him, and has been by some illiterate annalists supposed to be the origin of our family name – corrupted, so to say, into *Fals-taff*. The declension is nonsensical, and easily refuted by the fact that not one of these same annalists can prove that my ancestor ever so much as set foot in Wales.

Which brings me to my third reason for going back this far with the family tree – that the origin of our name, as ancient as any man in England now could wish, reaches beyond the Saxon *Fel-staf*, meaning a felling-staff, or cudgel, and beyond even, as some have it, the vulgar self-command '*Fall Staff*!' meaning 'Down, weapon, down!' – much as you might cry, 'Wag, wick!' or 'Shake, spear!' on keener occasions – reaches in truth to some obscure and wonderful source in the Old Norse, where you find *Fastulfr* used as title for a pirate prince, and then again *Falst* and *Fast* who were gods in those times.

This last point is important. It is from my Scandinavian ancestors in heaven and earth that I inherit my thirst. These

Fastulfrs and *Falsts* could drink as well as they could foin or fight, and this has also been the case with me. The shape, depth, and beauty of it will be evident when we pass beyond these petty matters of where I come from to the larger matter of where I have been and what I have done.

The burstable king. The Big Bastard burst when they buried him. The grave was dug too narrow, and it had been encased with stone and lime. When they tried to get the body in, it wouldn't fit, and they had to squeeze him in sideways, three priests pushing down, and then he burst.

Of the rest of the family I'd better say only that none of them made much of a job recommending himself to history between the Conquest and my birth. There was, it's true, a Someone de Forstalff — yes, spell it that way, there are as many ways of spelling the name as pleasing a lady, for instance:

Fastolff	Fourstalf	Forestolf
Fasstolff	Fourestalf	Forrestolf
Fastolfe	Forstolfe	Forestalf
ffastolfe	fforstolfe	fforestalf
Farsstolf	Fairstolf	Forstolf
ffarsstolf	ffairstalff	fforstolf
Farstolf	Farstalff	Farestolf
Fairstelf	Forrstolf	Forlstalf
Farlstolf	Farlstalf	Farstelf
Faulstalf	Faulstellf	Faulstolf
Faustolf	Forcetalf	Forcetolf
Faustelf	Fausthalf	Faustulf
Faustoff	Faustoff	Faustoff
ffalstolf	ffalstof	ffalstaf
Falstolf	Fallstolf	Farestalf
Fallstuff	Fallstiff	Fallstealth
Fallestolf	Fallestalf	Fallestelf
Falstalfe	Fallstelf	Fairstalf
Falstaffe	Fallstalfe	Fallstelfe
Falstalffe	Falstalff	Falstalf
Falstaf	Fallstaf	Falsstaf
ffalstaff	ffallstaf	ffalsstaf
Falstafe	Falstoff	Falstaff

— they are all of them right, every one. This Someone de Forstalff is supposed to have climbed a mountain in the Alps and thrown a stone in a great puddle on the top with such force that he disturbed a dragon who had been sleeping there for a thousand years or so. The dragon immediately ate him. How the story can be true when Someone de Forstalff is the only one who could have told it, and he was inside the dragon at the only time it could have been told, I confess I don't know.

There was also a Magna Fastolfe who went with Richard Lionheart to the crusades. The story of Magna F and the 500 Turkish Lesbians being somewhat exaggerated I shall not bother to repeat it. In lower Syria he was pursued by ants as big as foxes, but escaped on a resolute camel.

Cosmas Faustolf possessed the unusual power of destroying sheep, or trees, or children, by bestowing praise upon them.

I had as well an ancestor who saw out the Albigensian heresy by standing on one foot and staring at the sun.

And in the reign of Edward the 1st there was Hannibal fforstolf, who lost his right testicle in the massacre of the Sicilian vespers, and won vast sums of money by laying bets with any man he met that, added together, their mutual equipment would come to an odd number. He amassed a small fortune. Then he met William Wallace, who was reluctant to bet with him. Hannibal kept raising the stakes until the Wallace could not refuse. William Wallace had three testicles.

This is also the place – because I *say* it is the place – to set it on record once and for all that the derivation which would have *Fastolf* mean 'son of *Fastof*' is pudding-brained. *Fastof* in such a context would have to refer to some necessity of the Church – the Fast of this, or the Fast of that, and while the members of this family have never forgotten what the inside of a church is like, or I am a peppercorn and a brewer's horse, we have never been conspicuous for our fasting. Pride, father, is not the first of the Seven Deadly Sins for nothing, eh? Pious pride – such as you get in rich libertines who abruptly give all their clothes to the poor and sing psalms naked to the scandal of young girls, or in monks who fast and pray away to skeletons and then have to put their abbots to the expense of burying them – that's the worst sort.

Let it ride then, that I am descended from a house sufficiently genteel, although without much service to the crown and the subsequent dignity of knighthood until myself. *How* and *why* I was knighted we shall come to in due course.

We are of Norfolk, we Fastolfs, and these words are set down here in Norfolk, at my Caister Castle, the building of which we shall also come to later, together for that matter with my building of the Bastille.

Eight days drunk. *Tantarra!* A happy New Year to all my ancestors.

Worcester, I should mention also my great great grandfather Alexander Fastolf, Bailiff of Yarmouth until they found out, which was in the year of God's Death 1280. And my great grandfather Thomas, who filled the same office and they never found out, 1305. Dates I like less than figs and I promise that's the last one that will disfigure your pages today. Don't underline fig in disfigure. I'm telling this for people who won't need hitting over the head to see puns.

By great great grandfather Alexander's time we had given up dragons and crusades. Dragons and crusades are neither of them very English. We Fastolfs are as English as they come.

My uncle Hugh the admiral left me a seal-ring worth £26. 13s. It is a measure of the meanness of the late Harry Monmouth – whose most loyal subject I remained ho hum – that his idea of a joke was to insist more than once that this heirloom of mine was made of copper. On the occasion when my pocket was picked at the Boar's Head tavern, this same seal-ring and four bonds of forty pounds apiece were what was stolen. The prince, informed, assessed my total loss at eightpence! But then his father had leprosy, his grandfather was a madman, and he was taught mathematics by a Scottish sheepstealer. His son has inherited the family nose. No wonder the country is in such a mess.

III

About the birth of Sir John Fastolf

2 April

I was born at three o'clock in the afternoon, with a white head and something of a round belly. The place of my birth was Wookey Hole, in Somerset, where my mother had gone at the last minute to drink water from the holy well. If you want to know why my father did not have the water brought to her in a green bottle it was because she took a fancy to go herself on a pilgrimage, and besides he was busy making preparations for the feast which was to usher in my nativity. At the same time – while my father was ordering up cheese and cherries from Norwich, and while my mother having slipped in underground and sipped the water from the holy hole was giving birth to me attended by stalagmites – there was an earthquake. I have never understood the relation between these events.

The food consumed at my baptismal feast in Caister was nothing compared with what my father ate when he arrived at Wells. News came to him at home in Norfolk of my mother being in labour – a labour which lasted for three days and three nights, so reluctant was I to put in an appearance in this world – and he jumped to horse and left the cooks and shipmen at their business. When he reached Wells he had ridden seven stallions into the ground, and his belly was giving him hell. First things first. He went straight to an inn and ordered breakfast. He told the innkeeper to lay the table for seven men.

'Seven?' said the innkeeper.

'Seven,' said my father. 'As in Deadly Sins, and Wise and Foolish Virgins, and colours of the rainbow.'

My father was a man of credit. Red beard, white hood, a key at his belt. So the innkeeper had the table set for seven, with trenchers by each plate.

No guests appeared. The innkeeper tiptoed to the window to look for my father's keeper.

'Serve up the breakfast!' cried my father.

The innkeeper decided to humour him. He served up a meal that would have suited seven hungry travellers. My father ate in one place without stopping. Then he moved eating from seat to seat.

For the first course my father had seven swans with chawdwyn – which was a mash made of chopped liver and entrails boiled with blood, bread, peppers, and wine vinegar, all the rage in those days. For titbits there were capons and a leche lombard.

For the second course my father had a black soup, then seven rabbits and a peacock that had been sewn back in its skin after roasting.

For the third course my father had a plate of sparrows seven times, a vat of baked quinces, and a fritter.

The meal was followed by a dessert of white apples, caraway, wafers, and seven jars of hippocras to drink.

My father, finished, wiped his beard and passed back his empty dishes to the innkeeper.

When the innkeeper totted up the reckoning, he said: 'How would you like this meal for free?'

My father said that he would very much like that, being about to be a father for the first time, and being himself an esquire of no great estate or prospects.

'The meal's on the house,' said the innkeeper, 'so long as you call again on your way home with your wife and child.'

My father promised that he would.

Meanwhile, I crouched in my mother in labour in Wookey Hole. The ground shivered and the earthquake came making little spider cracks along the banks of the race which roars from Wookey down to Glastonbury. By the hole's entrance is the image of a man in stone, called the Porter. The fancy of the place is this: You have to knock and ask the Porter for permission to go in. My father used to swear that when he asked him, the Porter's head nodded twice and then fell off. Perhaps it was the earthquake.

Inside Wookey Hole, my father made his way to my mother with a sheaf of reed sedge burning in his hand. Those underground caverns are as big as Westminster Hall. My mother, as I have explained, was crouched beside the place they call the holy well – which is in the chamber known as the Parlour, perfectly round, about twenty paces across. No one knows how deep that water is. It was cold enough to bring me on.

'Mary,' my father called, his voice everywhere through the caves. 'Mary, Mary, my love, love, love.'

'About time too,' said my mother. And at that moment, being three o'clock exactly, I was born.

I can vouch for the time because the earth tremor which ran from Wookey Hole with my final birth pang stopped the clock which was then not long started up in Wells Cathedral a half a mile away. The shiver of the earthquake of my coming ran through the rocks and up across the floor of the baptistry and – *ping* – checked the clock hands on the hour and the three. They buckled. Simultaneously a white flood of water flowed in spate down the race to the mere at Glastonbury. There are seven mills in use on that race, and as the flood went through them their wheels spun round with a roar so that the millers thought the mills would all fall down. One hundred fish were pumped out of Glastonbury Mere – trout, loaches, miller's thumbs, flukes, pickerel, crawfish, dewdows. These fish landed gasping on the cropped lawn of Mr Thomas Beckington the bishop, who dropped his breviary in the turkey soup upon the instant.

'It's a boy!' shouted my father.

Boy, abboy, ABBOY, abboy, a BOY, echoed through the cave.

'What else did you expect?' my mother asked quietly. 'What with that giant's *thing*!'

My father's laughter cracked a stalactite. He snipped the birth-cord with his sword and danced about the cavern with me in his arms.

'Has he cried?' called my mother.

'Not a tear,' my father said proudly.

'Then make him cry,' said my mother. 'If he doesn't start now, he'll have more than his share later.'

So my father started slapping me and shaking me, and holding me up by the heels and chucking me from hand to hand. But I kept quiet.

'The rogue won't cry,' my father said.

'Then make him laugh,' advised my mother.

Whether my father achieved this by pulling a funny face at me in the light of his reed sedge taper, or I had something else to laugh about, I soon started to make the noise they wanted. The echo must have helped augment the laughter. Yet my mother used to say that with or without the echo my original laugh was enough to set them both laughing too.

Ha, yes, wait. The earthquake that ran down from Wookey also shattered seven wine pots and seven bottles in the hostelry at Wells.

This was my birth.

My father took shawls and swaddles from his satchel, and my mother wrapped me tight in them. You'll not remember these superstitions, but a babe in the century that is gone was treated like a miniature Egyptian mummy, it being believed that if he waved or waggled his limbs about he might break one of them.

As for the white head and the round belly – I have sometimes heard wives say, when they look at a new-born child of a certain aspect, 'That one's been here before.' My white head, which I had from the moment of my coming forth in Wookey Hole, might be thought to betoken some benevolent maturity or other inheritance of experience. My round belly I had of my father, and my father's father. Fastolfs have had round bellies since eggs have joined in the middle. A Fastolf without a round belly would be like a ship without a sail.

My father and my mother now emerged with me from Wookey Hole. The earthquake subsided – the oaks no longer shaking in their sockets – and they went down quietly to the hostelry where my father had consumed his seven breakfasts.

'Take the child in by the fire, madam,' the innkeeper said, meeting us in the yard. 'Sir, now is your chance to pay for your meal.'

My father saw that the fellow was bargaining with a bandy-legged Welsh merchant, who had a load of butter in barrels on his cart. The innkeeper climbed up and kicked one of the barrels. 'How much for this little tub?' he demanded.

'That,' said the merchant, 'is a standard size barrel.'

'Keg, then,' the innkeeper conceded. 'How much?'

'That is not a keg or a tub or any other inferior condition,' the merchant hissed. 'It is a *barrel* – a standard size barrel full of best Welsh standard butter.'

The innkeeper took a measure from his hat. 'Standard size for Wales,' he said. 'Average for your leek-land, maybe. But in Somerset a man could get through the lot in one go.'

The merchant was a nationalist, of course. He jumped up and

down on the dung in the yard. 'Show me the man who can eat one of my barrels of butter in one go,' he said, 'and I will give you two of them for nothing.'

'Let's make it your cartload to my cellar full of cider,' said the innkeeper.

'A bet!'

'A bet!'

My father threw back his white hood and rolled up his sleeves and sat down there and then in the courtyard of the inn and won this wager for his host without so much a hiccup. When he had polished off the barrel of butter, in ten minutes or so, he rubbed salt into the Welshman's wound by begging for one or two half-penny rolls to scrape the staves clean.

'I've never seen anything like it,' said the merchant.

'Don't boast,' my father advised him. 'It's a decent butter, but not unique.'

My father was a man of appetite. I never knew him over-mastered by a meal, save on one occasion with a basket of raw eels, and that day he had diahorrhea.

Arrived back at Caister, I was baptized three times. My mother, you see, was persuaded to wet the baby's head at Bath and Devizes and Oxford and Banbury Cross, and when she got home, stepping towards the house, she tripped and dropped me in the ditch. I wasn't hurt, but I came out covered with mud like a coal-black imp. Taking me in, they washed me in warm water, then the priest baptized me. So I was baptized in mud, in hot water, and in the name of the Father, the Son, and the Holy Ghost.

For my christening feast they had musclade of minnows, baked herrings in sugar, gurnards, lamphreys, and a whole porpoise roasted on coals. For the second course I am told there were dates in comfit, red and white jellies, congers, salmon, dories in syrup, brett, turbot, carp, bass, mullet, and chevins. For the third they had spiced minced chicken doused in cream of almond milk, fresh young sturgeon, perch in jelly, and whelks. There was a fourth course of fruit: hot apples and pears with sugar candy, and ginger columbine.

I was too young to enjoy any of this, but my mother having put me to a wet nurse I supped well enough. My wet nurse was a young girl of Clippesby whose own suckling had just died. If there is anything in the belief that the quality of milk affects the character of the child then I can credit that the warm clear tit I had of her has done me no harm. I cannot say how long this suckling went on, but it seems to me to have been for a marvellously long time, for I can remember the pleasure of lying at her pricked pink nipple, that sweetest of thorns, with her swelling breast kneaded urgently in my little hot fist, and the good milk squirting between my lips.

Want more, Worcester? *Hey diddle diddle!* More about the wet nurse?

Her name was Jaquenetta. Her hair was jet-black and her skin white. Young breasts like fresh boiled eggs with their shells just off. Nipples like cherries. I used to nibble them with my cunning little gums, and she would moan, and then I would nibble them some more, and the milk would gush quick and quicker down my throat as she gasped above me with the shock of it.

All I can remember of that time generally is how rich and right it seemed to lead a life without thought. My young heart was set only on milk and Jaquenetta's nipples.

I can recall also the pleasure of having my wet nurse wash the part of me which pleased her most. Sometimes she would rub it while I lay sucking at her breast.

I was born with an unsatisfiable thirst.

IV

About the games of Sir John Fastolf when he was young

When I was a boy I plucked geese. It was like plucking the sky –
a snow of snapt feathers everywhere. I played truant as well. Of
course. Lord God! Who didn't? Who doesn't? And I whipped
top. So hard and fast they must be still spinning – furious little
rainbows in the corner of the granary. Nor did I escape being
whipped myself. I liked dances and robins and candles and carols,
and to hear minstrels tune their violas de gamba while the snow
was falling outside from a night sky pricked with stars.

I made a paper boat with sails. My coat and shirt got soaking
wet in the brook. My hat drifted away. For two miles I chased it.
But it went into the sea.

I made a feather fly down the wind. I stuck another feather in
my belt, like a lawyer's quill. I set more feathers in a ring about
my cap, making a crown. I was the emperor of grey-goose-feather
country.

When I went to bed at night I pulled up patchwork covers to
my chin and lay and listened to the stars falling into the water-
butt in our yard.

I rode on my father's boot.

I played at King Arthur and St George and the dragon and
Gog and Albion and Robin Hood and all the English games. I
played at marbles and Heads and Tails and Pinch Me and Follow
the Leader.

I had a swing that my father made for me in the old barn, and
I would swing and swing higher in the oaty air of summer, until
the edge of Norfolk tilted and was gone, and I was over the thin
line of green and out out out into the blue.

I was more like a monkey than a boy.

I used to silt mud from the Hundred River with a sieve. I was looking for gold.

And I had these many-coloured shells, conch shells, cowries, periwinkle shells, brought to me inland by a sailor travelling home from Yarmouth, and I'd listen to the talk of the seven seas in them. The seas spoke of treasure, and of dead men's bones.

I remember a day spent teaching grasses in my thumbs to hoot like an owl when I blew through them.

One hot afternoon I hid in an empty beehive to be cool. Thieves came and took the heaviest beehive they could find, thinking to have the most honey. But their honey was me. I came out buzzing and they jumped the gate.

When I caught butterflies, I tied threads to them. Then, with the threads on my fingers, I would run through the meadows with a cloud of my butterflies fluttering behind me.

I had a little oven of four tiles where I baked mud pies. And I liked to plunge my hand in sand: making tunnels. And I told the time by a dandelion clock.

I flew a kite from a hill above the sea. It was like holding a plug plugged into the sky. The sky was trying to get away but my kite string held it.

I had a stick which I dressed with a scarlet trailing coat and it was my horse and I called him Roan Barbary.

My cap was my helmet when it was not my crown. Sometimes, when the girls from Runham came to the barn, I would take off my shirt and fight with the other boys, and we would hit each other with our caps, because the girls looked on. We played at Hide and Seek. I remember when I found little Margaret in the linen basket and climbed in with her in the dark.

And when the girls were not there, we boys played at Piss Against the Wall, seeing who could make his piss go highest behind the dairy. I won, and Peter Pounce lost his temper and couldn't piss at all. It must have been winter. I remember the steam off our piss and the rusty mark it made in the snow, and my cousin said we'd be pissing icicles if it got any colder.

My mother gave me a chalk pipe, and a bowl of suds, and I sat blowing bubbles in the summer afternoon: one, two, three, four, bursting in the sun, five.

I started to learn Latin later, and not to pick my nose at table. Before I ate breakfast I would cross my mouth. Because my mother said my soul would be the better for it. Not to speak of my digestion. 'Don't scratch yourself at table, boy,' my father used to say. 'Only jackdaws scratch themselves at their meals.'

I remember the day my father caught a cockerel by the leg and tied it and set it up on the roof. It was red in the sun. We shot at it with bows and arrows until he knocked it into the water-butt.

Margaret in the linen basket: what a little gigglelot she was! She wore a girdle with bells and a gown of green silk.

I played cherry-stones when I should have been at confession.

Once the Hundred River froze, and the swamp round by Stokesby, and my father made me a sledge of a hunk of ice like a diamond, and my cousins formed themselves into a chain and ran along pulling me, young Fastolf, enthroned on his diamond ice-sledge. I had a horn which I held to my lips and blew like a hunter as we skimmed over the powdery fallen snow. I can still hear the *hisss* of that fine ice sledge of mine, diamond cut diamond, and see the track I made on the frozen lake. Though we all fell in the midden at the end of it.

My uncle Hugh the admiral came that Christmas. He made me skates from the thigh-bones of a hare. I strapped them to my feet, and pushed myself down the hill behind the house with long stakes tipped with iron. And once I did this jousting with my cousin – we dashed at each other across the frozen lake, striking at the ice with our iron-tipped sticks, from far apart, flying like birds or darts from a sling, crashing into each other at top speed in the driving hail. The sun was going down into the marsh like a great gooseberry. He skinned my nose but he was more bruised than I was.

I remember there was the black bear called Charlemagne, brought up from London for the Michaelmas fair, which killed all the dogs we set upon it. We starved the dogs for days to make them mad. Charlemagne shrugged them off, though he lost an eye. He escaped in Bury St Edmunds and tore up his chains and ran amuck in the cathedral.

At Easter on the Hundred River we had naval battles. A shield was fixed to the middle of a tree, and a small boat, dashed along by hard rowing and the river's current, used to have me on its high stern, holding a lance, jousting at the shield. If I struck my lance square against the shield, so as to break it, and kept my footing on the boat meanwhile, then well and good, and everyone cheered. But the art was tricky. If you struck *too* hard, and your lance didn't break, you were thrown into the river, and the boat would shoot past the mark without you. Behind the shield, though, there would be two boats at anchor, with my father and my cousins in them to pull me from the water by my hair.

I love this flat Caister country. Miles and miles and miles of bugger all.

My tutor was a chaplain from our Lady's shrine at Walsingham. He taught me to say Our Father and Hail Mary, the Creed, the Ten Commandments, and to read. He was a scholar and a man of the pen. Ink had to be made up for him before lessons, and quill-pens cut from those grey goose feathers which I have already mentioned as possessing so much enchantment for me when floated down the breeze. I recall him teaching me the lamentations of a soul in purgatory and a terrible poem called *Morte Arthure*, which seemed even longer than the lamentations of the soul in purgatory and which disappointed me because as I have said my earliest games had to do with King Arthur, and I expected the verses to unveil a mystery; but they didn't. My tutor, whose name was Ravenstone, and who went later to be master of St Paul's song school in London, used to have me construe Latin into French – with a result that I like our English tongue, and can sit here jotting down tolerable sentences of it now, the 3rd day of April, 1459, the Feast of St Richard de la Wich, whose intercession brought the salt back to the spring at Droitwich, my secretary Worcester away today to Castle Combe, and my other men Bussard, Hanson, and Nanton, also, as it happens, away about my business and out of earshot.

V

About the tutor Ravenstone & the whip

4 April

The mice are away. The cat can play.

My tutor Ravenstone was a great man for the birch. His interest in the subject was both theoretical and practical. Theory and practice have aroused my interest also, over a long life in which I have not been without opportunities for instruction. The English vice, they call it in France, where some affect to believe that no Englishman can come to a stand without the benefit of the whip across his buttocks. As I shall make clear, however, when I come to that part of my life which was spent in France, where I mixed with not a few of the lowest as well as all the highest persons of that country – the passions and persuasions inspired by the rod are not unknown in foreign places. Adam and Eve were driven from the Garden of Eden by an angel with a flaming sword.

I have something to say on this subject, but I shall not say it all in one breath today. Let no firm-buttocked virgin flinch from my report. I have been a soldier by trade and I have seen and done many things which you will not see done in an English country garden. (Although what I *have* seen and done in English country gardens would make white roses turn red and red roses go very pale indeed.) It is my intention in writing these memorials to set down *everything*. If that diet of experience proves too rich or strange a meal for some stomachs, then, Eat elsewhere, is my advice, and wish you better appetites. There is your Mr Gower for shy ladies, with his talk of Courtly Love – which most of those same ladies find so boring, if they would only admit it. (No Courtly Lover ever put out the fire between a lady's legs with one of his rhyming sighs, and most of the Courtly Lovers I have known preferred their own sex when it came to bedtime.) Those who have relished the verses of Mr Chaucer may not so spurn the

24

cunterbury tales of a plain soldier. I did not start these tellings in order to hold my tongue. I have never held my tongue in my life – it is too hot! – and I am too old now to learn how. Besides, ladies shy and hearty can have comfort of the fact that one who has been a servant of Mars has also served Venus faithfully all his days.

Mem: since I am now a servant of the Muses, and specifically Clio, better include an invocation of her soon. But today I don't feel up to that.

I remember the moment my education began. It had all gone over my head. I had not listened. My thoughts had been following those goose feathers on the wind while this bald pedant with the tic stood defining *amo amas amat*. And then, one gloomy winter afternoon, the fire banked high, the candles already lit, he turned from the window where it had started to snow, great white flakes like moths, and I heard him saying in the same dry voice:

'The rod was, at Trimalchio's banquet, a mere salt, a sweet pepper, a little seasoning, and so it can be at the temple of Love herself.'

Ravenstone must have seen my chin jerk up. Without doubt, Jack Fastolf found here a titbit of information which tickled his fancy, although in those days he could not have told you why, nor even now can I altogether explain it reasonably, after three score years and ten of researches in this and allied subjects. It remains a fire in the blood. Who, however monkish, could resist it, if a lovely woman came to him and begged him to correct her body for the good of her soul? Not I.

Of course these matters have their laughable side, which is also why I like them. My Mrs Ford, of Windsor, once confessed a great black catalogue of interesting sins to her parson, Sir Hugh Evans. This Welsh fairy advising the use of the rod, she went with him behind the font and prepared her person for it. She had been followed into the church by her jealous husband, however, and after skulking and sulking in the aisle he now burst out of hiding from behind a pillar, moved I suppose by pity of the pain which he saw about to be inflicted by a celibate arm on the most vulnerable part of his wife's anatomy. Nobly, Ford stepped out of his trousers and offered himself in the penitent's posture. My mistress, agreeing enthusiastically that her husband would be better able to bear the punishment, called out to her confessor in the act:

'Harder, harder, holy fader, for oh! oh! *oh!* I am a great sinner!'

My tutor Ravenstone preferred to promise beatings rather than perform them. He was one of that not inconsiderable tribe of men who take more pleasure in the cerebral prospect than the physical aspect. All the same, I did not go without correction in my schooldays, and my lower regions learned the language of his rod. When I failed to construe a lump of Tacitus, or let my wits wander while he explained to me the mysteries of numerals, he would demand that I consent to be horsed.

This complicated arrangement consisted of my being hoisted off the ground on the back of a manservant, with the rear portions of my person offered to my teacher. Ravenstone would then lay into them with a whippy cane which he kept in pickle. To tell you the truth, either his arm was weak, or his enthusiasm for the actual deployment of the rod indifferent, for he never hurt me much. His pleasure was rather, as I have said, in talking about the punishments which he might inflict upon my innocence if my manners were not mended or my application improved.

As for me, I observed pretty quickly that the sting of my teacher's wand, however lacking in true pedagogic zest, did wonderfully warm all the dorsal part of my flesh, and sent shivers through which communicated a preliminary stiffness to my cock.

On one occasion, requiring me to be horsed, no manservant being by, Ravenstone called into service a maid of my mother's by name of Katharina. I duly hoisted myself upon her back, bent over a desk, and was compelled to suffer the indignity of a whipping with my face pressed into a girl's plump dimpled neck for sweetener. Ravenstone did manage to lay on harder than usual that time – the monkish rogue being inspired no doubt by the proximity of female flesh to the work of his rod. Under his stripes I wriggled and writhed, more than was necessary I confess, but then Katharina's smock was made of some thin stuff, and I knew that she could feel my young member pressing harder and harder against her sweet young bum as the cane came down. When the punishment was completed we were all rather red in the face. Katharina favoured me with a look as though to say she might be more frightened of Mr Jack than of Mr Ravenstone, just as she made to curtsey and leave the schoolroom.

Before she could go, Ravenstone said: 'Kiss the rod.'

'Sir?' she said.

'You will kiss the rod,' insisted Ravenstone in a strangled

voice. And he held his cane up level with her lips.

Katharina shrugged. She was an insolent slut. However, Ravenstone was cutting swift little circles in the air with the cane, so she caught it quickly in her hands, and bent her head and kissed it. As her lips closed on the birch she looked straight at me. My spine went cold. I could not have said why.

I sat for an hour after that, bottom tingling, half-listening to my tutor's voice drone on in the summer afternoon as he rehearsed Caesar's miserable Gallic expeditions, the while I was remembering the hot spice which came off the nape of Katharina's neck where her dress rubbed it, and the exquisite trembling of her body as I was made to move upon her by the sting of the birch. It took more than an hour for my blood to forget.

However, it was not with Katharina that I first learned to pay my dues to Venus.

VI

About Sir John Fastolf's mother & the amorous vision

5 April

My mother travelled a lot when she was young. She was in Denmark and Illyria. Amongst other places she frequented the court of King Robert of Anjou, at Naples. Here she took up for a time with a crowd of penny poets. Her face made her a Muse to many; her ankles also helped. There was one of these poets, a wit called Francis Petrarch, a wearer of laurel hats, about whom in later years I heard her speak with brief affection – but otherwise she had no time for apes who write verses.

I remember an evening in winter when there were hailstones as big as my fist and I, a mere lad, sat merry as a cricket by the roaring fire, at my mother's feet – she wore red slippers – and she told me of an ambitious young Neapolitan bank clerk, John Boccaccio by name, who wrote for her a poem in 50 chapters, entitled the *Amorous Vision*. This poem was nothing less than a colossal conceit or overweening anagram opening out from my mother's name. It was prepared to a pattern cut from the *Divine Comedy* of Mr Dante, but it out-helled and out-paradised Dante by this manoeuvre: in addition to its story of a dream in which the poet, guided by a lady, sees the heroes and lovers of ancient and modern times, it contains three more poems in the shape of the initial letters of all the triplets throughout. It was in the first of these that this Italian idiot dedicated himself to my mother. He calls the heroine Fiammetta when you read the lines straightforwardly, but this was his fiction, and when you unpick the acrostic you see the identification of Fiammetta and my mother, whose name was Mary, or as he spells it M A R I A. If you don't believe me, take a look at the initial letters of the first, third, fifth, seventh, and ninth lines of the dedicatory poem in the *Amorous Vision*.

VII

About Pope Joan
(Mary Fastolf's tale)

My mother used to tell me tales by the chimneyside. My mother's tales were all of them about great queens and noble ladies.

I can remember the names of some of the ladies, but not their tales, such as Cleopatra, Queen of Egypt; Tamora, Queen of the Goths; Imogen, Princess of Britain; Hermione, Queen of Sicilia; Hippolyta, Queen of the Amazons; Marina, Princess of Tyre; and so on.

I can remember some of the tales, but not the names which should go with them, such as the tale of the magpie that had all its feathers pulled out for telling the king that the queen had eaten his brother's eel while he was away, and which ever after, when it met a bald man or a woman with a high forehead, used to say to them, 'Whose eel did you see?'

There is only one name and one tale which I can still call to mind together, from all the tales of great queens and noble ladies which my mother told me. This is the tale of Pope Joan. My mother used to act out a play of the tale, somewhat as follows, with herself as all the women and me as all the men.

Act One. Scene One. Joan is born in Magontiacum, the daughter of a money-lender.

Scene Two. She has many suitors. Chief among these is Dromio, a student. Joan loves him, but her father wishes her to marry Valentine, a fantastic.

Scene Three. Determined to discredit Valentine in the father's eyes, the lovers persuade him to come to the house and dress in the garb of a Columbine – they have told him falsely that the money-lender is an amateur of pantomime. Joan then dons Valentine's velvet doublet and crakow shoes, and while the fantastic pirouettes before the astonished money-lender, the lovers flee away to England. Joan assumes the name of John.

Act Two. Scene One. In Canterbury Joan is easily interpreted as a cleric.

Scene Two. When Dromio dies (pricked in a duel by an envenomed foil), Joan does not take off her man's dress. She keeps up her religious studies and excels all the Anglican priests in counting angels on pinheads.

Scene Three. In time she leaves England and travels to Rome.

Act Three. Scene One. In Rome, Joan, now a mature woman, although in appearance a man, lectures on the Golden Bull, the Golden Legend, the Golden Mass, the Golden Number, the Golden Rose, the Golden Rule, and the Golden Sequence. Since in addition to being as scholarly as a death-watch beetle she is also as chaste as a coffin, it doesn't cross anyone's mind that she can possibly be female. When the Pope dies – it was Leo IV, who could put out conflagrations by praying at them – Joan is elected to succeed him by an overwhelming vote of the cardinals. She refuses. They insist. She refuses again. They insist again. The third time, she accepts.

Scene Two. 'I don't know what it is about the new Pope,' says one of the cardinals, 'but he's different.' Others remark that they can't get to the bottom of it either, but they all find the new Supreme Pontiff attractive.

Joan is called John. If she *had* been a man she would have been Pope John VIII.

Now, buzz, buzz, here's the best bit. While Joan had been a common or graveyard priest, her life had been pure enough to make her seem saintly. But now that she is Pope she becomes a vast victim of lust. She proceeds (Scene Three) to debauch herself and the sacred pontificate. She finds an Ephesian cardinal more than willing to mount in secret on the surprising successor of St Peter. This cardinal, Alonso, assuages her lecherous itch. But he takes off his red hat at the crucial moment and the Pope becomes pregnant!

Act Four. Scene One. At long last, then, the game is up. The one thing a woman cannot hide, once she has it in her, betrays Pope Joan. Popes are inexperienced in pregnancy, and this one does not even know herself to be so close to the time of giving birth as in fact she is. Going from the Janiculum to the Lateran in solemn procession around the holy city, between the Colosseum and the church of Pope Clement, Joan lies down in the street and publicly gives birth to twins without any midwife present.

Scene Two. The sacred college cannot believe its 140 eyes.

Scene Three. Pope Joan is thrown into a dungeon, where she dies. Her last words are, 'Poor our sex.'

I've heard that, to the present day, if the Pope is processing around Rome, he will turn and skip down a side street when he reaches the place where his predecessor gave birth.

My mother used to act out this tale flatly and without betraying her own feelings, until she got to the point where Joan was elected by the dazzle of infatuated cardinals. Then she would fling herself up and down the gallery there, playing Pope, and make me kiss her rings and kneel before her on a plump red cushion. When it got to the pregnancy bit, she would introduce this same cushion to her belly, under her dress, and then give birth to it with many a Papal sentence and decree. Once, she took a lap dog under her dress, instead of the cushion. So one of my earlier memories of my mother, Mary Fastolf, is of her wearing a mitre and embroidered gloves and giving birth to a black-and-white puppy on the floor of Caister.

VIII

About the Duke of Hell

My lord the Black Death, the Duke of hell.

I used to think as a boy that the plague was a person. I lay in bed at night imagining him as a great duke galloping on a black horse down streets cobbled with dead men's bones, or else as a swart-skinned giant striding along, his head reaching above the roofs of the houses, every now and again leaning down to breathe a stench of death in at the upper windows.

In time, of course, I came to learn from my tutor Ravenstone that this duke of mine was born in China, where men say he started to rage early in the year of our Lord 1333. He soon killed so many that his sweat infected the middle region of the air. From China he passed into India, then into Persia, then Russia. When with evil pomp he had crossed the Alps, my lord the Black Death, he lost no time in advancing through those parts of France which are called Hesperia, and so along into Germany and Dutchland. By the time he came into England he was a past master of his art.

I remember that in my twelfth year a terrible rain started falling on the Feast of the Nativity of St John and lasted until the next midwinter, so that not a day saw the sun or a night the moon. In the same year there was this murrain of sheep everywhere in the kingdom. In one field in Norfolk more than five thousand lay dead. I saw them. I smelt it. They putrefied and even the crows wouldn't touch them.

Death brings down the cost of living. You could buy a horse for seven and six, which before the plague had been worth 40 shillings. A fat ox went for 4 shillings, a cow for 10 pence, a heifer for 6 pence, a lamb for tuppence. Cattle ran wild. There was no memory in England of death like this since the time of Vortigern.

In his day they say that there were not enough left alive to cope with the burying of the dead. It was as bad in some places in my boyhood, while the Black Duke reigned.

The symptoms of this Death consisted of pains through the whole body, boils about the size of lentils on the thighs and upper arms, with bloody vomitings. Vomiting of blood continued without intermission in most cases for three days.

Not everyone who touched a plague victim died himself – but most did. For this reason, when the Black Death came into a family, fathers rejected their own sons. As for the priests – most of them found abstruse theological reasons for not going into the houses of diseased persons. I heard one of them say it was on account of the Gratian Decretals (whatever they might be, and they don't sound very English). Dominicans and minor friars who did enter to hear the last confessions of the dying were themselves usually overcome by the plague. I knew two who went into a death room and never came out again.

Corpses lay forsaken, rotting in the houses. In the early days, servants were sometimes tempted to bury the dead by the paying of extraordinary wages. As things got worse, not even the greediest or neediest servants could be bribed to do it, and the houses of the dead lay open with all their valuables winking in the moon. Any who chose to enter met with no impediment. Death made them welcome, the perfect host.

Burn boils or burn blisters. I remember that's what they called those swellings in the thighs. Gland boils would follow in different parts of the body. Titus the wheelwright had them on his cock. The Abbot of St Benet Hulme on his legs. Seven brothers in Horsham St Faith all in identical places on their necks – like a collar, like a noose. When a burn boil started it was about the size of a hazel nut. It would grow, and at the same time you'd have violent shivering fits, until your boil was the size of a walnut, then the size of a hen's egg, then a goose's egg, excruciatingly tender and painful where it touched the sheet. The blood would rise into your throat, the sickness lasting three days as I said. Never longer.

I remember the miller in Caister, John Tregose, who died without a priest or a physician. He lay among his sacks, covered in flour. The rats watched him die. He cried at the end for his mother. His mother had been dead for 30 years.

Little Alice Prowte at Thrigby. Her parents left her in her cot and ran away when they saw the burn blisters. If I shut my eyes now I can still hear her crying:

'I'm so thirsty! Mummy, bring me just a cup of water! My hand moves, look, I'm still alive. Daddy, please don't be afraid of me.'

Her puppy dog was the only thing that would come near her. The girl and her dog were found together. They had to be shovelled up.

Because the Black Duke always took three days, at the height of the horror some people kept a linen shroud by them, so that they could sew themselves into their shrouds as soon as they saw the boils. That way, you could at least be sure of going well-dressed to your funeral.

The jails were thrown open. Condemned prisoners were let out to do the burying. Some by eating garlic by the ton managed to survive without infection, and went free after.

Day and night the dead bell sounded. At every corner you met coffins — coffins carried by hand, coffins piled on carts, coffins dragged along. I remember when the bearers stumbled with Mrs Bigot's coffin, and it flew from their shoulders and broke to pieces. The naked corpse fell out. She must have weighed twenty stones.

Wolves roamed in packs at night. In the villages round Thetford they ran into houses, tearing children from their mothers' sides.

The bishop of Bury St Edmunds, lying dead in his palace, was eaten by his dogs.

The air was thick and misty. Foul. I remember a woman's body alive with rooks. A bird had an eye on its beak.

Eventually the lucky dead were those who were dragged with a rope round their necks to a field and then burnt.

The dead bell and the sound of tears.

You were half-choked by the spicy smoke of the plague powder, burnt everywhere. The doors and lower windows of most of the houses were nailed up. Food used to be handed to the inhabitants by means of ropes and baskets.

Of the whole Town Council in Yarmouth, only two survived.

There were people in Caister who did not leave the church from mattins to compline. With a loaf of bread and a bottle of beer in their pockets, they remained all day at prayers. These folk wore deep mourning black and thought by their garb and their devotions to turn aside God's anger. They spent every hour on their knees. They wept. They prayed. They whined with such passion that it is a wonder the statues did not melt.

I have heard that there were certain warnings of the advent of my lord the Black Death, dark heralds, precursors.

A comet, God's chastising rod, appeared over London before he rode in. The moon was overcast blood-red in an eclipse. This was followed by a long unnatural frost. The comet was of black fire.

At the same time a child lying swaddled in its cradle at Cremona addressed its mother by her name, and told how it had seen the Blessed Virgin Mary beseeching her son not to destroy the world.

On Christmas Day of – I think – 1348, there stood at dawn a plume of flames above the palace of the Pope at Avignon, and on the Feast of Stephen following a ball of fire passed over Paris from east to west, and Notre Dame was struck by lightning.

The Fen country was full of stinking mists, and rainbows, and it rained snakes and frogs.

In Venice there was an earthquake which rang the bells of St Mark's before cracking the altar in three.

My uncle Hugh saved me from the plague. He was a student of the good doctor, Paracelsus. Following this master's teaching, my uncle told my parents that whatever happened they must not let my thoughts sink down to death. I was made to listen to music. I was set to the contemplation of gold and silver and precious stones that comfort the eyes and the fingers and the heart. Long tales were told to me, of Red Knights and Green Knights and Amadis de Gaul, of *Arthurus*, *rex quondam*, *rexque futurus*, and of Robin Hood. Sweet instruments were played in all my hours of sleeping. My imagination was filled up, fed, inhabited, and occupied by images of life. For as soon as the fear of death and an imagination of it obtain the upper hand, according to Paracelsus, then certainly what we dread will come to pass. 'The heart adheres to its own pitch,' my uncle taught me.

My uncle taught me to believe that I was invincible if not immortal. The Black Death could not kill me, nor any other hue of death. I was instructed also to have faith that I could not be laid low by illness, and by this belief the *Archaeus* or *Aura vitalis* was fortified – that is, the hope which is opposed to the dread inspired in us by fear and trembling.

35

In particular, that wise physician, my uncle Hugh, recommended and prescribed WINE for me – wine as a preservator, wine as a medicine, wine as a benison, and wine as a cancellor of cares.

'*Neither drunk nor yet too sober, is the way of getting over,*' he used to say, pacing the shore, with me on his back or at his heels.

My father therefore had the servants wash me every morning with wine – strong wine, clear wine, old wine, wines red and wines white, pink wine, golden wine, the wine of young lions. My hands were washed in wine, and my mouth was washed with wine, and my face was washed in wine, and my nose was washed in wine, and my ears were washed with wine, and my shoulders were washed in wine, and all the rest of my body was washed regularly with wine. Every morning also on rising I enjoyed a little vinegar of wine with toasted bread together with my breakfast, and followed it up with a wine gargle. Then during the day my father would have me drink a cup or two of wine every time I thirsted. My white wines were cooled in a jacket of water. My red wines were always as warm as my room.

I passed my childhood thus butressed with wine, and, thanks to this provision of my uncle's, I did not fall foul of the Black Death in his fury.

My father had me also, as his eldest son – Lord God, Sir, there had been other visits to the Cerne giant, and I had brothers and sisters now – sitting between two huge fires of sea-coals when the plague was at its worst. These coals we had dredged from the icy sea. I have heard since that Pope Clement VI did no less and escaped the pestilence thereby.

My mother all this while reciting tales of great queens and noble ladies who had survived far worse afflictions – mostly men – burnt incense, juniper berries, laurel leaves, beech and aloe, wormwood, balm mint, rosemary, thyme, green rue and amber, mastic, laudanum, storax, birchbark, red myrrh and sage, lavender, marjoram, camphor, and sulphur, until so thick a fug hung about the house that the canaries were suffocated in their cages. Some of these birds may have died, though, as a result of the infection of the air – I have heard that in the Alps, where you can touch clouds with your hand, the very clouds stank at that time if you poked your fingers into them.

My mother also introduced a capacious bag of spiders into the house. The spiders ran in all directions. Her thinking was that the spiders would absorb possible plague poisons, thus preserving us. They were big spiders, and speckled, as I recall.

Either because of the spiders or the wine, or both, I was spared.

I should say it was the wine.

I noticed two things of interest in these visitations of the Black Death.

First, the tanners in Yarmouth seemed from the start immune to it – whether from the wonderful properties of the tannin contained in their bark, I don't know. Those who cleaned out latrines also escaped. From this, my uncle Hugh reasoned that another good way to avoid the plague was to stand early in the morning above a latrine and inhale the stench. This might seem the opposite of his faith in wine and sweet music and imagination. How shit can be a boon in times of plague when it is a bane at other times, I confess I do not understand; unless, indeed, a man has a strange liking and secret affinity for filth, so that his heart is more completely comforted by dirt and dung than by the scent of musk and amber. I once knew a sheriff's officer called Fang who preferred the smell of pigs' dung to anything in the world, and another who was always singing the praises of stinking billy-goats, so that he could never get the upshot unless the girl's armpits had a whiff of goat about them. Paracelsus certainly teaches that in times of plague all excrements, and particularly human excrements, are healthy. Man is made in the image of God, so even his shit must have some value. My uncle Hugh lived to the age of eighty, anyway, and died singing and clapping his hands.

This brings me to the second thing I noticed. It was that the old corpse-washer in Yarmouth, who must have bathed the boils and closed the eyes of more than a thousand victims, preserved himself from the Black Death by means of his own piss. He would drink a handful of it every morning in the name of the Father, and the Son, and the Holy Ghost.

IX

About the number 100 & other numbers

Bussard is back. Bussard has a face like a pig's arse and an arse like a pig's face. Hey, Bussard! Hey, Snout-bum! This is given to Snoutbum Bussard. Grrr. A pig's arse of a day too.

Concerning Caister. Caister in the county of Norfolk is my family home. But this house was smaller in the times I have been telling of – in my childhood days. The great hall here is now 38 of my paces long, which makes about 59 feet. It is sixteen paces, or 28 feet, in width. When I was a boy you could stand with your back against one wall and aim your spits to hit the other wall without too much straining.

My ancestors were merchants of Great Yarmouth, small-time burghers, hardly wealthy. I am, to be plain, by origin the eldest son of an ordinary esquire of King Edward the 3rd's household. My uncle Hugh was an admiral, but he wasted his wages on women and relics.

My patrimony was small when I came of age. I inherited at the time a few decrepit tenements in Yarmouth and a clutch of threadbare farms between Scottow and East Somerton. No rents to speak of. And a family house that was falling down while my mother played charades and my father brooded on the construction of military machines. Tormenta, catapults, perrieres, slings, biffae, springals. The king never properly employed my father's skills. He was a great inventor of fierce and useless toys. Once in my boyhood he made a mangonel which knocked down part of the house. That house itself I have rescued from the fen and made into my castle. During the course of my career, this house has been the emblem of my fortune, the repository for my wealth. I have spent more than £7000 on this place. Reader, do you wonder how I managed it? By honest spoils, that's how. By a soldier's pay. The wages of death is no sin. I was always a believer in the right rate for the job.

Between the year of Man's Redemption 1421 then, when I became Deputy Constable of the castle and town of Bordeaux, and my final return home in (was it?) 1440, I was King Henry the 6th's councillor in France, at an annual fee of £110 sterling. I also held twenty other offices, too boring to enumerate. In my time I have been councillor to Thomas, Duke of Clarence; Thomas, Duke of Exeter; Humphrey, Duke of Gloucester; Richard, Duke of York; John, Duke of Somerset; and John, Duke of Norfolk. Not to speak of the Devil. It all adds up.

My French profits and extractions all lie invested in good rich English land. I have estates here, and in Yorkshire, and in Wiltshire. There were the tips as well, you see, and the commissions, and the side bets. O France. O ransom money.

Other capital transactions. I bought the Boar's Head tavern in Southwark in 1445. The price was £214. A bit steep, but I wanted it. The seller was my brother-in-arms, Nicholas Molyneux. Molyneux originally had it in partnership with another old campaigner from the French wars, John Winter. After Winter died, Molyneux gradually lost interest in the Boar's Head. He had married a rich widow in the expectation of her dying. When she did not oblige, despite him leaving her out of doors in all weathers, Molyneux consulted an apothecary in search of a safe poison. 'The best poison lies there between your legs,' the apothecary told him. 'Give it to her seven times a night. No woman can stand that. In seven months she'll be dead. The perfect murder.' Poor Nick. I bought the Boar's Head from him some six months after he embarked upon this master plan. He lay absolutely knackered in an upper room, covered in flakes of sweat, twitching and quaking. When I tried to shake hands with him, he yelped and pulled the sheets over his head as though I'd meant something improper. His wife meanwhile was the life and soul of the endless party downstairs, only popping up to see him every hour on the hour between midnight and dawn, tripping upstairs and down in a trance of delight. Nick's last words to me were, 'The bitch doesn't know it, but she's only got a month to live.'

Not a few of my finest hours were spent in this same Boar's Head tavern. To *own* it is a pleasure I scarcely dreamed of in my less substantial days. You will hear soon enough of my days and nights there in my prime, with Prince Hal and Mr Edward Poins and Mrs Quickly and the others.

When I came of age I was worth a beggarly £46 a year. My story is of how such a one could rise to be a baron of France, and then a gentleman landowner here in England, with a rent-roll of over £1,450 per annum clear. O brave old world, in which such things are possible. For an Englishman.

I will tell you my politics. I am a feudalist. I believe in the dead. I adhere to the ancient constitution of the state, and the apostolical hierarchy of the Church of England.

But I am running on too fast.

A pig of a cunt of a day.

What I said.

Cold, wet, and windy – like an old man's bum.

Brandy!

Let that stand too. Every word I say, Sow-face, my three-inch fool, *and* in the way that I say it.

Reader, my grand plan is this: *I shall talk to my man Bussard, or to my secretary Worcester, or to Fr Brackley, or to one of the others, even in the last resort to my stepson Scrope, or I shall write in my own hand, every day here for a hundred days. For as long as I talk they are commanded to set it down, every day, every word, without fear or favour or crossings out or any alteration. At the end of these one hundred days I shall have told the story of my life.*

This number 100 interests me.

There was lately the war in France – the wars in France – which went on for one hundred years. This began in the year of our Lord 1337, – or thereabouts, rather before my time anyway – when King Edward the 3rd woke up one morning and decided to stake his claim to that patch of God's earth which every true-born Englishman has always regarded as his happy hunting ground, or at the least back garden. Edward, I mean, added France as a jewel to the English crown. In that same year we defeated Flanders, the ally of Philip VI, at Cadsand. But the Frogs did not like belonging in our king's hat. They resisted and, with interruptions, poor peace, the war resultant went on for one hundred years. To tell you the truth, I've had so much to do with it, one way and another, that I've sometimes felt I was as old as it, and dated my birth from its beginning. My fancy, of course. It ended just six years ago, with England shamefully and disgracefully giving up all her rightful territories in France except the port of Calais. In the same year, our present monarch, King Henry the 6th, who would make a better Pope than he makes a King, went mad. Two years later he recovered his wits when eating a blancmange. How they can tell the difference I don't know.

Set it down, Snoutbum. No bloody arguing. Brandy!

Set down brandy. Yes.

The *eau de vin* which is an *eau de vie*.

Brandy: alchemy. Brandy: the elixir. *Eau d'or. Aqua auri.*

100.

There was a war for one hundred years. Between England and France. Between me and the enemies of my belly. Between Sir John Fastolf knight and the continental gnats.

Fly-swatting – that's what I did in France.

Money came back to England through my Italian banker in Paris. I made more than £13,000 in one day at the Battle of Verneuil in the year of our Preservation 1424.

A century is a not infrequent total.

This is getting out of joint, out of step, out of tune, out of time, out of chronological order. I must observe the rules and niceties of history. Clio, she's the Muse, she's the one. Tomorrow we address ourselves to Clio. Today is too late for history.

Brandy, God damn you! Brandy, you trotting turd! There is hope in brandy, none in history.

Brandy prolongs life.

Brandy sustains health.

Brandy dissipates superfluous matters in the bowels.

Brandy revives the spirits.

Brandy preserves youth.

Brandy alone, or added to some other proper golden remedy, cures colic and dropsy and ague and gravel and paralysis.

Above all, it cures Time.

Brandewine, brand wine, brandy wine. Nothing's more fine than brandy wine. *O spiritus vini gallici.*

Neither drunk nor yet too sober, is the way of getting over.

100.

Cock's passion! Just as there were ONE HUNDRED YEARS in the Hundred Years War, so I shall write these memorials of my life and valiant deeds for ONE HUNDRED DAYS exactly. I began here at Caister, my ancestral home, in the evening of New Year's Day. Today is the something or other of piggish April. I can't remember. Hell's bottom-grass, set down Fastolf can't remember. This is the something or otherst of April. Or the something or othered. And I don't care what date it was yesterday. Have I ever cared for yesterday, or yesterday cared for me? How do I know that yesterday wasn't a lie? Only now is ever true.

Cuckoo Day. Isn't it Cuckoo Day, Pigbum? The day the green lady is supposed to let all the little bleeders out of her apron, to fly up and lay their eggs in other birds' nests and sit making their idiot cry that Spring has come. To hell with their cuckoo cuckoo. Bugger Spring. Selah.

Hundred Years War. Hundred Days War.

I fought in the first war. I am fighting now in the second. I am by profession a gentleman, a soldier, and a knight. I am a knight banneret. That is my declension.

Sprinkle my glass with pure gold leaves.

I drink the Sun. *Benedicite.*

My life. So much roast beef. Who dreamt me then? Those things which I held for the truth, were they nothing? Have I been sleeping these 80 years, and didn't know it?

I am awake today. So much is certain. Brandy wine sees to that. Hail, Brand. This afternoon everything is strange and far away – mackerel fly through the trees that have turned their backs to the wind. Shit, Sir, even though yesterday those sandbanks out there were closer to me than the palms of these hands. Lords and lands, lords and lands and herring taken from the sea in season – all as hidden from me now as if they were a lie. If I set it down now about the companions of my most extreme youth – about little Margaret in the linen basket, that gigglelot – where have they gone? They run and dance and laugh and blush and are happy in my head only. Margaret is gone and green. She lies in the grave, in wet Norfolk clay, and there are worms on her fingers and in her hair. Felled is the forest. The water goes on flowing.

The Hundred River goes on flowing. The world on all sides is full of disgrace. And everything is suddener than we think. I see the bitter gall amidst the honey.

Brandy! Benedicite!

I see the bitter honey amidst the gall. 100. I was brought up in the flowing company of the Hundred River. I live now where I can stand on the banks and see my belly in it. From my windows I can watch the swans drift.

I shall live to be a hundred years old.

Shall I tell you my secret? It is this: *I, Sir John Fastolf, of*

Caister and London, of Paris and Rouen, of heaven and hell, shall most certainly and assuredly and blessedly live to be one hundred years old. I had this of a certainty from a sybil

Ergo, there was a war between England and France which lasted for a hundred years; there is a war between me and my life which shall last for a hundred days; and I, John Fastolf, knight banneret, shall of a surety live and last and endure and eat figs and prevail and drink brandy wine for a hundred years.

My uncle Hugh saved me from the Black Death by giving me a hundred cups of wine.

Thus do things go by hundreds. Down the Hundred River. Which when it was frozen I rode on on a diamond as big as a dog.

My battles. A hundred speckled spiders. I fought at Agincourt and Shrewsbury and Patay and Orleans and the Battle of the Herrings. I fought at Troyes and Meaux and Caen and St Michael's Mount. I fought at Harfleur and St Cloud, at Melun and Cravant. I was there on the five and twentieth of October in the year 1415, being then Friday, when it stopped raining, and the Feast of Crispin and Crispinian, a day fair and fortunate to the English, but most sorrowful and unlucky to the French. I was of the few, the happy few, the band of brothers.

Set down that –
Set down this –
One hundred, 100, a pissing hundred, 100, hundred.

It was hot inside that basket. The sides felt prickly. Margaret wore a gown of green silk and a girdle with little bells. She tinkled every time I touched her. Her breasts under the silk were like little apples. Or like grapes – they were so young, so tender, so beginning.

I owe my host at the sign of the Bull, in Oxford, 4d.

I owe my host Benet at Castle Combe 12d.

I borrowed from Worcester's cousin Robert Ash 3s 4d.

Also for cucumbers 5d; for shoeing of my horses 12d; for half a gallon of wine 8d.

Mem: Mr Mumford gave me 3 venison pasties.

Set down this also:

for 2 Spanish onions 1d;

and – in the same month of September – I paid for a sugarloaf weighing $2\frac{3}{4}$ lbs, at $5\frac{1}{2}$d per lb, 13d.

Not merely not Caesar, but the antithesis of Caesar.

There can be but one Caesar – *imperator mundi*, Hal, the

keeper of the universal Roman peace. Hail Hal. A Caesar who is not Caesar, a Caesar who is not the keeper of the universal Roman peace, a Hal with a halo, is no Caesar at all. The history of the world thus falls into three peaces –

1. There was the peace of Caesar;
2. There is the peace of King Henry the 6th;
3. There will be the peace of God.

And, as a consequence of spiders, it follows, as the night the day:

1. In the peace of Caesar there was the Hundred Years War;
2. In the peace of King Henry the 6th there is the Hundred Days War;
3. In the peace of God I shall live until I am exactly one hundred years old.

Big letters HUNDRED and FASTOLF.

The HUNDRED Years FASTOLF.

Brandy! Brandy! God's Nails! Brandy!

Dom Thomas Hengham, of Norwich Priory, did me this table.

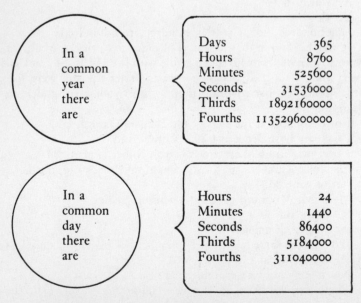

In a common year there are

Days	365
Hours	8760
Minutes	525600
Seconds	31536000
Thirds	1892160000
Fourths	113529600000

In a common day there are

Hours	24
Minutes	1440
Seconds	86400
Thirds	5184000
Fourths	311040000

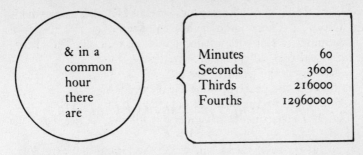

& in a common hour there are	Minutes	60
	Seconds	3600
	Thirds	216000
	Fourths	12960000

What's the time?
There's Miranda at the door. Enough for today. Amen.

X

Sir John Fastolf's invocation of Clio, Muse of History

9 *April*

Miranda is my niece. Hail, Clio, et cetera.

She's my brother Adam's daughter, a lively lovely girl, with eyes like a fire that needs poking. Her hair is black and straight. It always looks as if it's wet. Milicent had brown hair, gold in the ripples. She'd stand for hours braiding it before the glass. Miranda's gown last night was of thin white silk. Her slippers had gold threads in them. Beneath her breasts a crossed girdle, also of gold. Miranda's breasts are like handfuls of firm cream.

When she was little she liked to ride on my belly. She would sit astride it as though I were a camel. I used to hump up and down and from side to side and she would drum me with her tiny heels.

The day came when the sheet slipped off.

'I know what *that* is,' said Miranda, pouting, rubbing her cherry cheek in my crutch and looking up at me as wise as serpents.

'What is it then?' I asked her.

'Your *soldier*!' said Miranda.

You do not argue with a girl of twelve. With such an opinion, in any case, it was a matter of some ease to persuade her to give heed to bringing my eager soldier to attention. Her clever little fingers soon learned how to do this. She liked to inspect him thoroughly, lingeringly, running her fingers up and down the length of him in loops. She liked to check his equipment underneath. To deck him with ribbons from her hair. To salute him. To drill him hard. To make him march on the spot. And at last and always to play the fumbling game in which she fought with my soldier and made him die. This was all done with her hands and wrists.

46

One afternoon in the orchard I sought to persuade her otherwise.

'Miranda, my chick.'

'Yes, uncle?'

'My soldier is cold.'

Fondling me, a bright embroidery of colour in her cheeks. 'He doesn't *look* cold, uncle.'

'You little witch. He is though.'

Rolling me like pastry between her palms. 'He feels very *hot*, uncle. And oh, how *hard* he's getting.'

'Yes. Miranda . . .'

'Look: he's come to attention.'

'That's all for you, my dear.'

'Good soldier. Brave soldier. Oh, how *big* he is!'

At this, I nearly shot off in her face. I pulled her down across me. I had to make a tent of her black tresses. I could feel her hot little gasps as she bent to her task of fascinated inspection. Her cool hair was all about the throbbing subaltern.

'Miranda.'

'Yes, uncle?'

'The soldier's very cold. Pop him in your mouth and warm him up, will you?'

My nice niece flung herself away from me, rolling in the fallen apples, giggling uncontrollably. 'Oh no no, uncle, I couldn't do that!'

'Why not in heaven's name?' I cried.

Miranda's fingers flew to her mouth. She sucked them saucily as she looked at me. Her cheeks were scarlet. Her blue eyes blazed. 'I couldn't let your soldier come in my mouth, uncle,' she protested pertly, prettily, wriggling, giggling. 'Because *I don't know where he's been.*'

We put that right a few nights later in the bath. A lovely lively girl. She's fifteen years old now. I've educated her. I've brought her up to know all a soldier's ways and needs. Her little cunt is sweet and quick, brisk as a honey-bee, tender as a nut, nimble as a squirrel, tight as a glove, wide-awake, dusky, burning. Yesterday evening she sat on my knee and played with my prick, then punished it mercilessly with her little fists because she thought I was going to come to the boil before she was ready, then wanted me to tickle her as she lay face-down across my lap, finally had me fuck her on the skins in front of the fire.

'Uncle . . .'

'What is it now?'

'Wasn't I a naughty girl, playing with your whatsit?'

'Yes.'

'Wouldn't Aunt Milicent be mad if she was still alive, and found out?'

'Yes.'

'Wouldn't she be jealous that all that hot milk came shooting out of it just for me?'

'Yes.'

'Well, seeing that I've been so bad, and deserve it, I think it's only fair if you carry me up to Aunt Milicent's bed, and spank me on it – and then do it again.'

So you see, Clio, Muse as you are, I'm whacked. I spent all night invoking a lovely piece of lively girlhood, and I've nothing left for you.

XI

About Sir John Fastolf's belly & his rat

10 April

I have a biggish belly.

No doubt there have been bigger ones. There was a Roman senator I heard of who wobbled and waddled up and down the Forum needing three slaves staggering backwards in front of him to carry *his* belly. My fellow is not like that. It is not a collapsing or reluctant belly. It is not the corporation of a treacherous alderman. It is not a cormorant or a sink. It goes proudly before me, or I come modestly after it, one or the other, and one way or another I resemble a galleon in full float on the Spanish flood, or a pregnant whale. Yet neither likeness will do, for both are womanish. There is nothing like a princess about my belly. There's too much sack in it for a start.

Avoid all pickles.

My belly in size and form is something like a badger. Put it down to the short woolly hair, mixed with long straight hairs, and the general shaggy aspect. The colour of this fur is blackish-brown, darker in winter. I comb it a lot. I pomade it. I comfort it with oils. It's an inquisitive creature, my belly, and a voracious. It feeds on brewage and burnt brandy, champagne cup and puddings. That is, mutton puddings, with the occasional custard. No eggs. No eggs in custards or in sack. No pullet-sperm in my brewage.

Talking of pickles, the emperor Heliogabalus ate nothing else. This emperor had a moderately famous belly. In his garden was a forest and in this forest an elephant with tusks of fire. No one dared go near the elephant. Heliogabalus called his politicians together and asked them what was the nature of the elephant.

'The elephant approves of virgins,' said X.

'The elephant approves of musical virgins,' said Y.

49

'Virgins who can sing will please the elephant,' said Z.
WANTED: SINGING VIRGINS. Heliogabalus advertised
and got two. He had them stripped and they danced down his
garden into the forest. The first virgin carried a basin. Her name
was Scholastica. The second virgin carried a silver sword. She did
not give her name to the civil servant.

Scholastica started singing.

'I have a young sister far beyond the sea:
   Perrie, Merrie, Dixie, Domini.'

The elephant heard her and came running through the forest,
smashing the trees and beetles of course.

The unnamed virgin added her voice to the song.

'And she has sent a dowry to me:
   Petrum, Partrum, Paradisi, Temporie.'

Both were sopranoes, did I say?

The elephant stopped. It shook its head like Africa. Then it
walked slowly towards them, tusks blazing, trunk swaying. The
girls sang on. *Perrie, Merrie, Dixie, Domini.* Such nervous music!
They stroked his trunk. The elephant for his part fondled the
girls and slapped their bottoms with his ears. At last he lay down
and fell asleep with his trunk in Scholastica's lap. While he
dreamed of cherries and chickens the anonymous virgin killed the
elephant with her silver sword and the two of them filled the
basin with his blood. They took the basin back to the Emperor
Heliogabalus. He drank the blood in one go and never touched
another pickle as long as he lived, although truth to tell that was
not very long.

Now my belly, on catching sight of its enemy, death, before
determining finally on flight, will sit on its haunches and, in order
to get a more philosophical view of the danger, shade its eyes with
one of its fore-paws. Pressed for sack or sugar it grows fearless,
this same increasing belly of mine, and has been known to come
roaring on board an ice-bound vessel, and in presence of the crew
seize a barrel of beer and down it in one long suck. My belly
when I am gone will be valuable for its fur. It will make an
elegant hearth rug. Heliogabalus had an armchair made of the
elephant's skull.

'He-whore! He-whore!'

'God save the King!'

At the siege of Meaux, Horace and his ass's head. It was a
French ass. Horace was a man of Meaux. Hal busy pounding the

walls with his cannon when this Horace appears on the ramparts in his nightshirt, capering round with an ass's head the French have crowned, and going hee-haw through a trumpet. Every now and again he thumps his oracle, encouraging it to give tongue, and shouts down to us to listen to what our King has to say. (I should tell you that Henry was at that time the nickname for an ass in France.)

'*He-whore! He-whore!*'

'God save the King!'

This Horace, French patriot and comedian, the mayor of Meaux eventually awarded us, in accordance with the town's terms of surrender.

'*He-whore! He-whore!*'

We assed him good and proper. O rare.

I have a whole school of tongues in this belly of mine. I can belch in Greek, hiccup in Latin, and fart with a convocation like the fall of Babel. Fart, that is, when my belly and my bowels are on speaking terms. My bowels are laughing bowels – not a square inch of compassion in them. As for that, I can make my belly smile and sneer, as well as speak. My belly is a wise loquacious teller of stories. On winter nights it usually tells me lies. I lean back and I listen to my belly, my portly tutor, my companion in crime. And my belly reminds me of adventures past.

That time, for instance, when my belly saved me from an exorcism. It was in St George's fields, outside the city, where I had gone to play the Devil. I mean, I had taken the part of this representative in a drama of the Seven Deadly Sins, acting out Old Nick for all that it was worth and causing an embarrassing deal of conversion. The play over, the audience dispersed, I set out in the cool of the twilight to go home to my lodgings in the Inns of Court. I had no change of costume with me so I walked in the cloak and clothes I had worn for the morality: that is, a tail and two horns and various tattered silks depicting hellfire, with my face all horribly slobbered with black and green and silver. On my way across the fields I passed by a rabbit warren, belonging to my Lord the Bishop of Southwark. Now it happened that this same bishop was served in part by a very slippery priest, one Friar Puck, and that this Puck, together with a small gang of ecclesiastical scoundrels, had come to the warren that evening to pervert young rabbits. They had a horse and a ferret. The ferret in fact was loose and in the hole, and their net cast over the only exit, when I chanced upon the scene of the crime.

'Ooooh!' shrieks Puck, perceiving me loom up mighty in the gathering gloom, the moon above my horns and the night at my elbow. 'Run, girlth, run! Here comes Myth Lucifer!'

His acolytes knew no better than to take this Puck for an authority on the subject. They dropped their sticks and bolted. Puck went first, his curates after, skinny skirted virgins pursued across St George's fields (as they thought) by sevon demons with big pricks lit in hell. In fact, their own brown sins.

As for me, God's holy thistle, Madam, but I didn't see their thin net in the owl-light. My feet caught in it and I fell.

This columnar neck of mine was not quite broken on that occasion. When I came to my senses I saw that I was tangled in the net across the warren, and guessed the mean filching trade of Friar Puck, and that he and his vestals had fled for fear of me. Looking about, I saw their nag parked nearby, tethered to a bush, dripping with coneys that the sods had taken. There are no thieves in the world can rival a parcel of priests with their minds on the job. That poor horse looked like a butcher's shop, there were so many little bleeding rabbits hung about it.

I determined on morality. My performance in the Deadly Sins had shaken me to the fundament, I confess it, and I decided now in a flash of misbegotten right-thinking to ride this horse to the Bishop's house and return to him his rabbits, even if they were the worse for wear. I mounted with a couple of 'St Georges!' on the horse's back, and clapped my heels to him. The creature sagged at the middle but did its best to support me in my fool's errand.

Arrived in the full moon at the Bishop's house, I knocked at his gate. A servant opened the hatch.

'Holy Mary Mother of God, pray for us now,' he whispered, 'and at the hour of our death.'

Now on my voyage across St George's fields, and to fortify me from my fall into the net across the warren, as well as to prepare me for the pain of parting with the rabbits, I had taken one or two little sucks at my bottle. I was in no mood therefore to hear this amateur say his angelus.

'Let me in!' I instructed him plainly. 'Open the gate!'

'Do you think I'm mad?' he answered. 'Go back to hell!'

I began to feel insulted. A man does, when his morality is not appreciated. I could have wished that I had kept the coneys.

'Please yourself,' I said. 'I won't come in. You may well be mad, and it might be catching. But tell my lord the Bishop that I want to speak to him.'

The servant shut the hatch. I heard his footsteps go. They came back quick, and another's with them. But it was not the Bishop. It was his steward.

'You see!' whispers the first servant. 'It's the Devil himself perched on a black horse, with coneys hanging down about him bleeding front and back!'

'That's not coneys!' says the steward. 'I know a pack of separated souls when I see 'em. The Devil has come for our bishop's immortal part!'

I now perceived the state of the case, but before I could open my mouth the fools had slippered off inside again. I took another swig at my bottle. 'Jack Crack,' says I to myself, 'let this be a lesson to you. Doing good is not your line. Morality's a steaming heap of trouble.'

I turned my horse's head about to go, rabbits and all. But at that moment the gate groans open and out processes my lord the Bishop, complete with mitre, cope and candle and a trough of holy water. Before I can address him, he asperges me.

'In the name of the Father ✚ and of the Son ✚ and of the Holy Ghost ✚ I command and charge thee to get behind me, Satan!'

At this I parted company with my reasonableness. If there is one thing that annoys an Englishman, it is being conjured. 'You silly bishop!' I said. 'I'm not Beelzebub. I'm not even Belial or Mahomet or a cacodemon. Look! It's a *good* devil. It's Jack Fastolf, your sometimes faithful servant. I only played the Devil in the play.'

The Bishop however is into a very potent and interminable prayer in Latin. He hardly heeds me.

'Fastolf!' I roar. 'It's Fastolf, not the Devil!'

And at this point I stood up in the stirrups and Puck's horse buckled, broke, grunted and died under the weight of me and the Bishop huffs out his holy candle in a great absolution of laughter.

'It *is* Fastolf!' says he. 'He's bust the horse. By God, I'd know that belly anywhere!'

I have a pet rat. Her name is Desdemona. She is a black rat. Her skin is glossy, her tail is long. She has a stout skull, bright eyes, twelve teats. I had her from Nym, who caught her in a colander on the Isle of Dogs. She cost me five farthings. Desdemona comes when I whistle *ti-fa*. It is my pleasure to let her run up and down and round about my person, while I lie on the floor of the great hall here in Caister or on the bed now vacated for a colder one by my late sharp wife, Dame Milicent. I prefer to be naked for these exercises. I take off my red velvet jerkin and stretch out.

The drawback to your rat, as household pet, is its fecundity. Rats are deliciously prolific. A mere lick and the female conceives. Desdemona bears four or five times in the year – the fathers being rats of the castle, plausive adulterate beasts, villains, democrats, lacking her finesse, skulkers in the towers and oast houses. A usual litter is from four to ten. They come blind and bald and lecherous into the world, these wretched creatures, their tongues hanging out and with testicles like little green tomatoes. Left to their own devices they would be breeding among themselves at an age of about six months. I see to it that they are not left to their own devices.

My Desdemona has a shrewish nose, her only blot. Otherwise she is a handsome royal rat. Her tail is scaly. It stings me as she runs, for she flicks it from side to side as she scampers down my one leg and up the other. Her teeth are white and smooth and narrow, her eyes and her ears large. I have seen clumsy rats, mere spiny mice, squat web-foot things. Desdemona is not like that.

I feed her on cheeses and second-best wines.

Wine is warming.

Wine is the sun.

Avoid all water. Twice in my life, I didn't. Grr, Grr, Grrrrrrrr! I had occasion once to drink a cross section of the River Thames. My belly was as cold as if I'd swallowed snowballs for pills.

Another time I drank a mouth of Dead Sea water. That was when I was on my pilgrimage in the Holy Land. It was the most bitter thing I ever tasted – like a mouthful of piss and myrrh. That water is foul because of the five cities sunk in it. Sodom. Gomorrah. Aldama. Seboym. Segor. All were submerged on account of sodomy. Segor lasted seven years longer than the others, thanks to Lot, and being set upon a hill. When the water is clear you can see the roofs and towers. They told me no man could drink of the Dead Sea, because it was so bitter. I have sipped of it. I live to tell the tale. How? There's an essential honey in my nature, that's how – my tongue can suffer warping and unnatural elements without harm. I have also eaten the fruit of the trees that grow beside the Dead Sea. There are red apples there, as red as any roses. Bite them or break them, cut them in two: their cores are cinders. The Dead Sea land is all miracles. I saw a man once cast an iron anchor in the water there. It floated. Another dropped a feather, and it sank. These things are against kind – like the sin of Sodom. The Dead Sea tastes perverse.

O Desdemona. Desdemona.

The Seven Sacraments are these:

Matrimonium, Baptismus, Ordo, Sancta Eucharista, Penitencia, Confirmacio, Unccio summa.

That is to say, in plain English: Marriage, Baptism, Ordination, Holy Eucharist, Penitence, Confirmation, and Supreme Unction.

The Seven Gifts of the Holy Spirit are as follows:

Sapiencie, Intelligencie, Consilii, Fortitudinis, Sciencie, Pietatis, Timoris Dei,

collige dona!

These gifts are not to be translated into English. The Devil take those who have not learned by my age to translate them for themselves, and the young must go elsewhere for instruction than to an old man celebrating his belly by drowsing over a cup of hot wine beside the fire on a cold April night.

XII

About an indignity suffered by Sir John
Fastolf at the hands of the Duchess of Norfolk

11 April

When I was a few farts more than twelve years old I went to be
page to Thomas Mowbray, Duke of Norfolk. He was a tight-
arsed big-eared bastard, as slippery as they come. I could have
told you some of this right then, although if you had been King
Richard the 2nd you would not have believed me until the sod
had smothered your uncle with a feather bed, and needed bloody
banishing. A point to remember about King Richard is that he
never realised anything about anyone until he had bloody banished them. Out of sight, *into* his mind. He lived at one remove
from the throne, the world, himself. Until he had been to the
shithouse, he couldn't believe in his dinner. The royal shithouse.

As for Mowbray, he died in Venice on Holy-rood Day the
same year John of Gaunt got his – running upstairs to pack his
bags for a pilgrimage to the Holy Land. He certainly needed it.
At the time when I was in his service his thoughts never turned in
such devout directions. He had been blessed with the title of Earl
Marshal of England for arseholes rendered. He was a man on top
of the bent world.

The Devil goes nutting on Holy-rood Day.

My life in Mowbray's service was not hard. It consisted of a
kind of fostering. Being made page in a great household was
supposed to prepare you for entry to court circles later on. I
daresay the preparation lay in listening to the conversation of
one's betters, and in learning what to lick and where to crawl.

Mowbray himself was a little slit-lipped twat, with a spiky
beard like a thrush's, which he was forever tugging into a twist
while he sat trying to think of something to say. As he never
could, or did, I hardly picked up the art of conversation from

him. I daresay his tongue wagged hard enough behind the arras when he was doing his plotting with his brother-in-law, the Earl of Arundel, and other conspirators. In the end his tongue was his undoing when he rode up to London from Brentford in company with Bolingbroke (later King Henry the 4th) and chatted treason all the way, according to the written account of the conversation which Bolingbroke duly gave to Richard. Chaps with nothing to say generally are prone to say too much in particular. And Mowbray's particular was treason – he had no other hobbies.

You don't talk treason to boy pages. Whenever I saw Mowbray he seemed to be suffering from verbal constipation. He'd sit with his eyes screwed shut and furrows in his forehead, muttering ifs and buts and noes, now and again opening his eyes and his gob to spit in the fire and polish his Earl Marshal of England badge.

His wife Elizabeth, the Duchess, was another matter. After I fried the Duke's goldfish by mistake, she made something of a favourite of me, and had me wait upon her in her rosy bower. She taught me to play upon the lute, and how to dance. She taught me the usage of courts, which is to say courtesy. Courtesy came from heaven, in the first place, when the angel Gabriel greeted our Lady, *Ave Maria gratia plena*. All other virtues are contained in it.

My lady Elizabeth taught me much else. Her husband, the Duke, being so preoccupied about his plots and treasons, kidnapping someone here, putting pressure there on some rival lordling of King Richard's, she had fallen into a state of marital neglect by the time I came to serve her. I was a dreamy boy, only half-aware of a difference between the inside of my head and the world outside. Absence from the green fields of Caister, the Hundred River, and my mother and my father, made me unhappy for a while.

'Look, girls, how deliciously *melancholy* the droop of this mannikin's lower lip,' the Lady Elizabeth would say, turning me about by the shoulders for the benefit of her attendants. 'Regard also his left eyelid, with that creamy fold of flesh, and the lash that is, I swear it, longer and softer than mine.'

Then she used to twirl me about on my heels, spinning me like a top, while they all giggled and I felt dizzy.

There is nothing in this world as dangerous as the bored young wife of a rich and powerful man. While Mowbray gnawed his tongue and twisted his beard, plotting and counter-plotting, most certainly unconscious of the existence of one small Fastolf among the chapter of pages in his household, his wife the Lady Elizabeth took it into her head to have sport with me. At first this desire was shown only in teasings in her talk, or by sometimes pinching my cheek or my bottom as I stood by her, or by the playing of her long hand in my hair.

But these were mere pricking preludes.

One night in summer, the Duke away in Ireland on the King's business and his own advancement, I was brought abruptly to face with the great heat of her imagination. At that tender age, I daresay I was surprised. I cannot now swear for certain one way or the other. Life has taught me never to be surprised at what men do on the battlefield or women in the bedroom.

'His nose is wet. The truth, boy. Isn't it the prospect of my ladies in waiting which makes you hot?'

We were in her bed chamber. There were six of her ladies with us. She sat by the glass where two of them brushed her hair. I was at her feet, picking out a new tune on the lute. Two of the maids were turning down the covers on her bed.

'Cat got your tongue?' She prodded my side with her slippered foot.

I muttered something. About the evening being close. About the fact that there was thunder in the air.

The Duchess stared at me. Her eyes were green and hot. Her face was a pale and perfect oval, with high cheekbones. 'The night makes him throb,' she said. 'Girls, I think he needs a good wash to cool him down . . .'

Judging from the swiftness with which a bowl of water was produced, this conversation had already been planned by my mistress and her maids. The Duchess of Norfolk was showing that she had picked up a thing or two about plotting from her husband.

I struggled and kicked. But it was no use. Two of the girls held my arms while another pulled off my tunic and a fourth splashed water in my face. They were merry girls, and they tickled me under the arms and down my neck. I was always susceptible to tickling.

'Bring him here!' said the Duchess.

I was brought to stand before her. The two prettiest girls were still engaged in the brushing of her hair. They stopped and their eyes went wide when my mistress put her fingers in my doublet.

'Now then,' she whispered, 'let's see if our little man needs our attentions anywhere else.'

It still seemed like a game. Deftly, she unpicked my doublet. Her fingers touched my cock. I kicked out.

'Strip him!' hissed the Duchess.

Two of the girls held my arms, another two pushed me down on my back. One of them then sat astride my head – my face buried in her clothes – while half a dozen eager hands vied with each other in pulling down my hose. When I was quite naked I was allowed to stand again. The girls were flushed from their exertions. The Duchess sat quiet in her chair, fingering a fan. Her green eyes flickered up and down my person. I was on the edge of tears. I clenched my fists, determined not to cry.

A fly was in the basin. Bzzzzzz. Interminable music. Bzzzzzz. At last the Duchess spoke: 'Portia, Rosalind – wash him *properly*!'

The two girls of the hairdressing went down on their knees and addressed themselves to my private parts. They used sponges and cold water. They scrubbed me with extreme thoroughness, front and back. Their hands were gentle, but very efficient. They said nothing while they worked, but their breath came faster and faster. For my part, I gave up struggling and let them have their way. It is sweet to have your most intimate toilet performed by two lovely girls, while four others crowd round you, and your mistress sits looking on. I could not see what the Duchess thought of the reaction of my prick to the ministrations of her handmaidens, because she kept her fan across the lower half of her face. But I noticed that her eyes never strayed or swerved from the area of the washing. She spoke again just once. 'Warm rose-water,' she ordered, and the girls sprinkled me with it on the instant. Delicious.

It may be heretical, but sometimes when I have tried to picture what Paradise will be like, I have remembered that washing. The comparison is imperfect, for the washing had to come to an end, whereas we know that the joys of eternity will not. I was certainly unprepared for the *manner* in which the washing was to end, although I should have been able to foretell it.

'Bring him to me,' said the Duchess.

I was taken and held before her, my arms twisted behind my back.

'Such a pretty little page,' said the Duchess. 'Such a pretty little, dainty little, lovely little page. What do you think we should do with him, girls?'

The ladies of the bedchamber offered various suggestions.

Two of them wanted to milk me – they reckoned it was good for the complexion. One of them proposed that for sport I should be made to perform the Duke's office with his wife, while they watched. Others said I was too young for that, but not too young to be used in bed by all of them as a warmer. I didn't understand a half of the proposals – but the bits which I did understand brought a blush to my cheeks.

'See how she blushes,' said the Duchess. 'She really is an innocent.'

Portia who had washed me gave my bottom a stinging slap with the flat of her hand. 'Hardly a she, my lady,' she laughed.

'Not with that!' said her friend Rosalind, pointing.

'What?' said a third.

'This!' said Rosalind, grabbing at what she had lately washed.

The stirring of my sappy little member evidently fascinated the girl. Her grip was hard. I squealed. They crowded round –

'Let go!' the Duchess ordered.

They all fell back.

The Duchess did not touch me. She was so close, though, that I felt her breath hot on my quivering flesh.

'Far too pretty to be a boy,' she whispered. 'Tell me, little Fastolf, how would you like to be a girl?'

I shook my head. I could think of no reply.

'As dumb as my lord the Duke,' observed the lady Elizabeth. 'Never mind. Perhaps she's shy? Perhaps she'll feel better with her clothes on?'

I must have nodded my head at that.

'Very well, then,' said the Duchess. 'Portia, Rosalind, Celia – dress our new lady of the bedchamber!'

At last I realised what my mistress wanted. A dozen hands seized me and dragged me kicking and swearing and spitting to the closet. A scarlet gown, a collar of minever, various silken undergarments were applied to my person. I know no other verb for it. I fought to reject them – but there is no rejecting six determined young ladies with their minds set on one end. When they had finished dressing me my skin must have been covered in scratches under the scarlet dress.

The Duchess of Norfolk clapped her hands.

'A woman's face,' she said, 'with nature's own hand painted!'

My face, I know, was red as my apparel. The girls laughed.

'No more laughing!' said the Duchess. She took three strides across the room and spun me round in her hands. 'Now, girls, I want you to meet your new companion. This is Joan Fastolf. Joan is my new maid. She has come to wait upon me. Joan will be dealing with my most intimate requirements.'

And then the six ladies in waiting had to take it in turns to curtsey to me, and I to them, awkwardly, all under the direction of the hot and not-to-be-resisted imagination of this same Elizabeth, Duchess of Norfolk. Nor did the masquerade end with that. It was my lady Norfolk's pleasure to keep me thus captive and caparisoned as a girl for *three whole years*. My boy's clothes were removed and I was not allowed access to them. Instead, I had to wear a gown at all times, and women's shoes and stockings. And I had to dance attendance on the Duchess every minute, day and night, behaving without fail in a manner that befitted my changed gender and condition. If I once threatened to betray my sex by catching up my skirts and striding, or in any lesser manner, I was given a poke in the balls or a wicked sharp pinch by one or other of that unholy six who knew who I was and what had been forced upon me. As for the other members of the household – no doubt those who turned their minds to it wondered where little Jack Fastolf had gone, but in the vast household of an ambitious political animal there cannot have been many who bothered to turn their minds in any such direction. My worst moments came when queer gentlemen of the court came visiting, favouring me with beastly interested looks as I passed, tripping along untidily in my skirts and slippers. But for the most part I was ignored save by the six ladies in waiting, and by the Duchess herself.

She came eventually to profess herself pleased with me in my new role. She let me eat from her table, and brush her hair in company with either Portia or Rosalind, and assist her in her dressing and undressing. So you see I discovered compensations in being a girl, although truth to tell my proximity to the person of my mistress never exceeded that of her other ladies in waiting. She seemed satisfied by my transformation or transmutation, and did not touch or fondle me more than she would any of her truly female retainers. My pleasure was in being admitted to intimacies which most men only dream of. I attended my mistress in the bedroom, in her dressing chamber, and at her toilet. I slept in a dormitory with the other girls, and had innumerable opportunities for observing them half-dressed, half-undressed, or the latter entirely, for they quickly came to forget who or rather *what* I really was, though I believe some took a cruel delight in provoking me.

At first, at night, lying close between two girlish bodies softer and bigger than my own, half-fearful of falling asleep lest one or the other of them should take it into her head to toss me off, I'd comfort myself towards sleep with the thought that the great Achilles had suffered such a fate as this. I remembered his story from the lips of my tutor Ravenstone – how as a boy he had been compelled to live among women, where he assumed a name which no one knew, and where he remained for seven years in bondage. But after a while I accepted my own condition without heroic comparison, and then grew reconciled to it, and to feeling either Rosalind or Portia or both of them together groping for me in their sleep. It was my first education in the ways of women.

Of course I lived in a state of half-arousal all the time, from the nearness to so many female bodies, and especially from my intimacy with the lady Elizabeth, who had me nearly always to hand. Yet she never suffered to touch me other than she touched Portia and Celia and the others, as I have explained, and looking back on that curious time now – it is like a long sugary summer dream! – from the wisdom of age, I hazard the guess that having trapped and contained me in female garb and reduced the burgeoning and inadequate threat of my tiny manhood, she was well content to leave things at that. Her pleasure was in seeing me so daintily emasculate, and having me stand by impotent at moments when it was most piquant to her to feel my impotency there. Thus, once I was in womanish apparel there was no longer any of the horseplay which she had allowed her ladies to inflict upon me in the evening of my change. You hardened lovers who read this will find my reaction difficult to understand, but I advise you only to remember your own fear and confusion when *you* were boys and inexperienced – anyway, I was glad of my lady Elizabeth's cool established temper towards me, and found that I could better enjoy the strange and silken dream of my being a girl in her service because I was now aware that she did not intend to press me into odder intimacies.

So I remained for those three years in skirts. At the end of them the Duke came back from Ireland. One morning I woke and found my doublet returned, my gowns all gone. Whether my mistress feared that her husband would notice my disguise, and

62

suspect her of perversion in having a boy-page in girl's clothes by her in her chamber, I do not know. I had to assume boy's garb again and be once more Jack Fastolf. I was growing quickly, and I was called therefore soon into more manly affairs of the household – such as learning how to groom my master's dogs, and how to polish his armour.

I enjoyed being young Jack, the Duke's page. But I had enjoyed also being Joan, my lady the Duchess of Norfolk's seventh maid.

XIII

About a menu

The hell with Clio. The girl's a whore. Muse, you do not amuse
me. You're a pain in the imagination, less than a bubble in the
wine, more than I can bear. I'm glad I never married you.

God damn it all – there have to be times when a man does not
care to fare back further than his last dinner. Worcester, get the
boy to fetch the menu from the cook, and you set down what we
did tonight at table. That should make war enough for today.

MENU

An olive, stoned, inside a warbler;
the warbler in an ortolan;
the ortolan inside a lark;
the lark inside a thrush;
the thrush inside a quail;
the quail, in vine-leaves, in a golden plover;
the plover inside a lapwing;
the lapwing inside a partridge;
the partridge inside a woodcock;
the woodcock inside a teal;
the teal inside a guinea-fowl;
the guinea-fowl, well larded, inside a duck;
the duck inside a pheasant;
the pheasant in a goose;
the goose inside a turkey;
the turkey inside a swan;
the swan inside a bustard.

This bird served with onions stuffed with
cloves, with carrots, with celery, with coriander

64

seeds, with garlic, for Mr Worcester, Mr Scrope, Mr Hanson, Mr Nanton, Mr Bussard, and Fr Brackley.

For the second course of the same
Four yards of black pudding, London measure;
13 lbs of cherries;
custards;
a dozen wheaten loaves;
two pounds of sweet butter.

For the third course ditto
Twelve apples piping hot and twelve cold pears with sugar candy.

For Sir John Fastolf
Piment, claret, hippocras, Vernage, Greek, malmsey, Candia, ribolla, rumney, Provence, Montross, Rivere, muscatel, rosette, Oseye, Rhenish, Beaune, Saint-Emilion, Chablis, Epernay, Sézanne, Saint-Pourçain of Auvergne. NB: No wines of Gascony, which parch the blood. No wines of Bordeaux, which block the bowels. No wines of Orleans or Château-Thierry, which fly to the head. The malmsey is your natural wine from Madeira, mulled and spiced, and not the concoction some make to that name – which is mere water, honey, clary juice, beer grounds, and brandy.

PS FROM THE COOK
The butcher wants paying £7 15s. 8d.
The taverner wants paying £70 10s. 6d.
I want my wages for the last five months.
The undercook wants his flute back, and his marmoset.
There is also the matter of the £13 9s. 11d. outstanding from our deliberations with the dice.

XIV

*How Sir John Fastolf went to war
& about the sea fight at Slugs*

13 April (Friday too)

As you will have gathered from my successful impersonation of a
girl, my figure in those days was shapely. I had no trouble in
seeing my toes. I could even have touched them, if I'd wanted to.
I was so thin in the waist, I could have slipped through an
alderman's ring. I was assiduous also, and eager, and athletic. So,
from being Mowbray's page I progressed to being Mowbray's
squire. Oh my ambitions were limited enough in those innocent
days. I thought it a very great thing to wear a liripipe hat.

When Mowbray went to the wars, young Jack (just-lately-
Joan) went with him.

To tell you the truth, that puking treacherous Duke of
Norfolk never stumbled out with blue fire in his belly towards
even a brawl in a tavern yard. He was hardly a warrior by nature.
He preferred to sit and plot and plait his beard. But King Dick –
remembering no doubt how his grand-dad had once responded to
a French invitation to do homage with the remark that he would
only ever go to Paris with his helmet on his head and sixty
thousand men behind him – King Dick was beginning to make
anxious noises about France. (The English kings have a habit of
doing this when things are going badly with their wives. Richard
was no good in bed with Isabella.) My master Norfolk, as Earl
Marshal, knew that he would have to make a move to preserve his
own credit. He went through the motions of an expedition up and
down the Channel. King Dick cheered up. Isabella imported a
Turkish dildoe.

We had seven ships when we sailed out of Yarmouth. It was
the first time I had been to sea. The wind blew and the rain fell
and the waves slopped up and down. I did not care for it. One

part of the sea is much the same as another, take my word.

We met the French at Slugs. It was a Sunday, a day of thick fog, about the feast of the Trinity, and they had been burning our port of Rye and other mischief, and then dashing off again always before we could get at them. At Slugs, though, they made a stand, on account as we thought of the weather.

This was the order of the battle. We had seven vessels. The French had nine. We saw them a mile away, the fog drifting off awhile like spindrift, and as they saw us at the same time there was nothing for it but a fight.

Mowbray paced up and down, gnawing at a rotten apple.

'Not too close, gentlemen. Not too close.'

I stress: This was my introduction to the noble and ancient art of war. I was fifteen years old. The behaviour of my superiors did not impress me. Our seven English ships pursued through the water a zig-zag which had nothing to do with advancing on the enemy. The Frogs meanwhile seemed undecided. It is well known that in these situations the favoured tactic of the French navy is to send word to stir up their friends the Scots, encouraging a few diversionary northern battles of passionate local ferocity while they retire to review things from the brothels of Flanders. No one could believe that such diplomacy was on the cards this time. Because of the fog the two fleets had come too close together for either to withdraw without disgrace. But while we bore down on them at a rate of knots (even if sideways) through deep seas, the French vessels had stopped moving altogether. They looked indeed remarkably low in the water.

'They have great weapons!' Mowbray shouted, like a nun about to be raped by monkeys. How he knew they had any weapons at all when his eyes were shut I can't begin to tell you. 'To port!' he cried. And then: 'To starboard!'

I perceived that my captain's master plan was to shoot past the French fleet as amazingly and irretrievably as possible. In this manner he would be seen by history to be *not retreating*. Possibly he might even fire a few hundred arrows into the foam as we vanished into the shrugging sun. The important thing was that he had no intention of engaging the enemy direct, if he could help it.

Nor, to be truthful, and despite my resemblances to Achilles, had I. The prospect of a noble death may be said to appeal to you at fifteen with rather more force than it does at 25 or 105. The imagination is picturesque at that age, you might say, and reaches after adventures with both hands. But the prospect of death in any guise has never made appeal to me. I like the sun on my back, my shadow on the ground. For that reason I busied myself in the rigging aft. It was not aft enough for my liking. But it was aft.

We met (O navigation, O my stars) the French.

I still do not understand how it came about that we met them. Our progress was, roughly, south-south-west. Theirs, so far as they had any progress, was south-south-east. Students of geometry and metaphysics might well suppose the two fleets could have travelled alongside each other on endless small divergence until shortly before the day of doom. So it should have been. So I am convinced my costive lord of Norfolk would have liked it. But at some point south of Grongue, on that foggy afternoon of intermittent sunshine, we met. Rather, our ship, the *St George*, collided with the biggest of theirs, the *St Denis*.

A sickening crunch. A splintering of timber. Sails suddenly collapsed, flapping against the masts like swans nailed up.

'O God,' remarked Mowbray. 'O merciful Mary, mother of us, pray for me now at the hour of my death. Down! We're going down!'

'French warship engaged, sir,' reported his first lieutenant, a great skulking hammer of a man, with an axe to swing. 'Permission to board.'

'Do what?' shrieked Mowbray.

'Permission to go aboard and defeat the enemy, sir,' requested the lieutenant.

Mowbray was halfway down the ladder to his cabin. 'Oh very well,' he muttered. 'If you insist. I'm just going to fetch my sword. Don't let me make you late.'

The reader might well suppose that this conduct on the part of the Earl Marshal of all England was not altogether what was expected of a warrior in the wars in France. If every great captain had behaved as Mowbray did, in his country's behalf, would we have won the battle of Agincourt? Ah, reader, the question betrays your innocence of the ins and outs of war. Agincourt, as you shall come to learn from one who fought there, was not the clearcut nonsense imagined by a generation of armchair soldiers since. It was random, bizarre, bloody, absurd. It was a parcel of chaos imperfectly given shape by its survivors, who looked back on the events of the day, counted the dead, and said: 'We won this; you lost that. I'm still alive – so I am victor.' I have been a professional soldier, and I know what I am talking about. Mowbray's mean demeanour that day at Slugs was admittedly extreme. He took small care to mask his cowardice. He made his determination to survive apparent to the youngest squire up his aft rigging. In this, he was more brazen than most, but typical of what many felt and thought. Oh certainly, by the Devil's thin belly, Sir, there *were* those in France who thought and fought about higher things, such as glory. All of those madmen are still in France. About six feet in.

Our men were swarming and tumbling into the French vessel where she lay fast beside us, held by long grappling hooks. There was a lot of hacking about with swords. The odd arm flew. An ear. A hand. A head on a marlin spike.

Bone smashed.

Gristle torn.

Skull bashed in.

Brains and blood on the deck. Thick and thin. Grey stuff and red stuff. Men falling face-forwards, fighting.

The enemy offered little real opposition, though – even my inexperienced eye could tell that. Those who did fight seemed unable to control or co-ordinate their movements. Did all Frenchmen walk like this? I wondered. Was every Frenchman so casual, so careless of self-defence? I could not believe it. A surprising number of them seemed to have lost all interest in life. They moved about with contented smiles, awaiting the eventual buffet which sent them pitching straight down the salty gap between the boats.

This desultory brutal brawling went on for perhaps a quarter of an hour. The swirling fog made everything vague – time as well as place. I busied myself higher and higher in the rigging. It was interesting how high you could get, once the necessity presented itself. There was no view to speak of. Occasional splinter of sun on the sea. Mostly fog. But I was above the battle.

A gull drifted past. I reached out my hand and touched it as it flew. The poor thing nearly turned inside-out with fright.

I began to sing to myself a song which I had heard the girls sing behind the barn at Caister:

> *When I was a young maid, and*
> *Washt my mammy's dishes,*
> *I put my finger up my cunt and*
> *Pluckt out little fishes.*

TRUMPETS! Lord God! The ship lurched violently. Reared. Plunged. Lurched again. I clung to the mast. I was suddenly drenched with spray. We had been hit! We were on fire!

There was smoke everywhere. As much smoke as fog. Below me, a foggy inferno. The flames licked higher. I would be cooked on my spit, if it didn't snap first with the heat. I heard a deal of shouting and screaming. Men caught fire and jumped into the sea.

The gull floated back across my vision, unconcerned, and flapped to rest in a cloud. Only it was not a cloud. It could not be, since the gull folded its wings, and sat as gulls sit when they have a solid perch.

I screwed up my eyes, tears in them from the smoke, and made out the tracery of another set of rigging just to my right. I swung out. I attached myself to this, sending the gull off downwind again with an irritable scream. A moment later my former home collapsed like a blown-through spider's web.

Thus, Jack Fastolf came to board the troopship of the Duc de Aquitaine!

Sir, – (I do hope your pox is giving you no trouble today?) – I had climbed into the rigging of the enemy vessel. I was not frightened, not at all. I considered my vantage point in the battle. (Perspective is everything in warfare.) I could hear French voices cursing down below me in the fog. I tried to climb higher – but there was no higher. I was right atop the Frenchman's mast, next to the fleur de lys!

I determined to do what any Englishman would do, in that position. I would capture the enemy flag and then return to my master, the Duke of Norfolk. I reached for the fleur de lys – I had it in my grasp –

Fig me!

I fell!

Either a swing of the vessel, or a stray volley of arrows, or a sudden explosion of sun through fog to dazzle my eyes – I don't know which. One or the other made me fall. Down, down, down, like Humpty Dumpty – to land smack bang on the Duc de Aquitaine!

It was said later that I fought like ten men. This may well have been true. I always fight like at least seven men. But as a matter of fact the Duc's neck snapped cleanly when I landed on his head, and he was dead before his body hit the deck. As for his

70

crew, they ran from me as from an avenging angel. Only later did I work it out that this was probably because I dropped out of heaven close-wrapped in the flag – and appeared to those shit-scared drunken Frenchmen as their own national colours come to life, exacting a terrible final vengeance on the commander who had led them to their doom.

By God's damsons, Madam, I swear that that was what they were, to a man: *drunk*.

The boat was loaded to the gunnels with sack, pillaged from English cellars, and those Frenchmen had been drinking it all the way home from Rye. They were pissed as newts. I had only to pop my face out of the fleur de lys and shout 'Death!' and they fell over their swords to surrender.

Such was the manner in which I went to war and took my first French prisoners. By this time, Mowbray's men, my companions, were all around me, and when they saw me extricating myself from the flag, bent over Aquitaine's corpse, I was set up on their shoulders as a hero.

Mowbray came up scowling. The fire on the *St George* had to be extinguished, and while that was being done he had trans-ferred to the enemy vessel. I am sure he deplored my part in its capture, but the men were adopting me as the mascot of a great victory, and he was diplomat enough to fall in with their wishes.

'Well, sir squire,' he said, chewing his beard, 'I hear that you elected to *drop in* for the coup de grace.'

Men have gone down to history with witty cracks like that. I avoid them like the plague. Speaking of the plague, we English fell to and drank up a great many more gallons of our own sack in accordance with my uncle Hugh's prescription. There never was a better antidote to death. Besides, nothing tastes as sweet as stolen wine regained.

I drank my share and I sang my round of the chorus in the victory party which followed. But it was the next day's engage-ment, when the bulk of the French fleet came back and bumped into us again in the fog, which made the name of Fastolf so terrible to the enemy.

XV

*About the sea fight continued, & how
Sir John Fastolf made his name terrible
to the enemy*

The next morning the French came back. Perhaps they had never been away? It was hard to tell. The weather was so foggy. You breathed out and it disappeared. What is certain is that at about eight bells the enemy loomed up nasty on the starboard bow, firing burning arrows and parlez-vousing away fifteen to the dozen across a sea as calm and pale as milk. You could smell the garlic on their breath. Distance seemed discredited by such a day.

The crew of our bonny half-burnt vessel, the *St George*, were gigantically drunk. We lay alongside that captured ship of the French fleet, the *St Denis*, from which sufficient quantities of sack had been removed to make our night memorable. Now the time of reckoning had come. These foreign waiters were at hand to present the bill.

What was to be done?

To Mowbray's mind, forked as his beard, only one thing *could* be done in a situation like this: surrender. He ordered the hauling down of our English ensign and the running up of a white flag.

Here a problem presented itself. We didn't have a white flag handy. Locker after locker was ransacked. Not a white flag. Not a snotrag. A man might wonder how many other battles have been won for lack of the necessary equipment with which to surrender in the first place.

Mowbray was determined not to be put off by a little detail like this. 'Tear up a shirt!' he said.

I do not know whether it is true that the English crew of the *St George*, and our prisoners of war aboard the *St Denis*, had not a single clean white shirt between them. Certainly when a man sets

72

out to war, white linen is not the best of stuff to take along. Certainly it was a time of appalling fashions, when men went in for shoes that curled at the toes, and the wearing of meaningless little cloaks known outside the tailoring trade as bum-freezers. Again, the night's hilarity might be mentioned as the reason why whatever clean linen there could ever have been aboard those vessels was now in a state of dirt and disrepair. For this reason, or that, or none, nothing could be found that was really suitable to be used as the white flag with which my lord Thomas, Duke of noble Norfolk, could bring about his wished-for surrender.

'Well, the Devil take you all!' his grace proposed, jumping up and down on the poop deck in his cork-heeled shoes. 'However, he's not having me – and neither are the Frogs. . . .'

So saying, he fell down a rope-ladder and launched himself in a coracle to the best of what remained of his sobriety. He disappeared into the fog to leeward, watched with some disfavour and bewilderment by his crew. One fellow drank a toast to him, fell overboard (or was pushed), and was eaten by a basking shark.

The French, without hesitation, rammed us amidships. Half a dozen of their soldiers leapt aboard with enthusiastic cries. The rest hung back and waited. This was usually the procedure in naval engagements – the idiots and the valiant went first, the rest tended to postpone things a little, watching to see if the enemy intended to make much of a struggle of it.

Your English soldier, or sailor for that matter, fights best with a gallon of sour sack in his bladder, and a roaring hangover in his head. When they saw these nimble Frenchkins coming, our gallant lads laid hands on a belaying pin or two, and struck out hugely. Few of the blows went home, and one or two English hearts were suddenly filled up with sword thrusts, but our general air of wild resistance was sufficient to prompt the enemy to take a quick sprint through our ranks and round the stern. They assembled then under the rear mast, panting, doubtful. Fog was again descending, or rather seeming to well up thick and grey out of the indifferent silence of the sea.

I decided to take a hand.

Why had I not done so earlier? Couldn't I have been heaving a cudgel with my companions at the time of the first French attack? Certainly, I could, Sir. The reason why I did not was that I was not on board the *St George*. I was on the *St Denis*.

So great and glorious a cargo of alcohol had drawn me like a chick to a nest, a hand to a wallet, an iron filing to a mighty magnet. My night had been spent in the hold of the French vessel, in the embrace of Dionysus. I emerged now, at eight and a bit bells, fifteen years old, as brave as a young bull, and very, very drunk.

Madam, I took in the state of battle at a glance.

Our gallant lads were looking round half-wittedly for the French. The French were massing for a second attack.

I swung into action. I seized a hogshead of sack in each hand and launched myself upon the foe. I was standing at the time in the rigging of the *St Denis*, and from where I was I could see three of every Frenchman on the *St George*. This, however, I took and take to be no less than fair. Three Frenchmen have ever been about the equivalent of one Englishman.

I fought that morning, in the sweet fog, in the day so foul and fair, like a man inspired. I used my sword, my cudgel, and my belaying pin. But mostly I used the great hogsheads of sack. I swung and clashed them round and round and round. Skulls cracked, blood spilled, men fell, panic reigned. And all the while I fought, I kept up the single roaring two-note chant:

'Fastolf! Faust off! Faust off! FASTOLF!'

(I made the *Fast* or *Faust* sound like a verb, you understand, and the *olf* or *off* what the French could do.)

The English, with their backs to the wall, or when their blood is up, are a musical nation. The crew of the *St George*, drunk as pancakes, still knew a good tune when they heard one. And there is no tune sweeter than the chanting of a warrior's name, and the cracking of enemy bones to accompany it.

'Fastolf! Faust off!' they cried, – and falling to the hogsheads they went like all hell at the enemy, swinging and banging and breaking skulls as if skulls were no more than eggshells.

The French, I think, were taken aback by this novel method of warfare, our secret and surprising weapon. There was no coping with anything like this in their manuals of instruction, the *etudes* of their *guerre*. Your French soldier is a methodical animal. His courage consists in standing up. Or, at the most, in going slightly forward. He fights well enough when his flag is in the breeze, and the foe comes marching along in a straight line towards him with *his* flag in the breeze, and all the common courtesies of killing properly observed. But confront him with a drunken young boy fighting like a pocket Hercules, and a boatload of disoriented sailors tossing great hogsheads of sack about, and no one caring to advance in straight lines except occasionally to stop to be sick over the side, and believe me your Frenchman is perplexed.

Those Frenchmen soon found themselves about half perplexed to death, and the other half not at all sure what had hit them and was going on hit-hit-hitting them.

The fog had come up thick as soup again, giving me a useful accomplice. I was able (thanks to my nimbleness of foot and lightness and smallness of person) to hop in and out with my hogsheads, darting to attack when least expected, vanishing as soon as more than a couple of the enemy realised where I was, or what I was about. Those who half saw me must have taken me for an imp or a hobgoblin. For the better to break bones, I strung half-a-dozen of the hogsheads together, and swung them round and round my head as I ran the decks.

And all my bone-breaking I punctuated with the same roaring chant, which the English crew echoed and redoubled as they came to my assistance:

'Fastolf! Faust off! *Faust off!* FASTOLF!'

The god of battles tilted things our way. The French blundered about like concussed billygoats, and a confounded Frenchman is only half a creature. They shouted at each other. They cursed. They cried. They referred to witchcraft to account for their failure to cope with one of the rattling skeleton-smashing sallies of this puckish little ghostly rival – myself. Thus, I heard:

'Allez, allez!'

'Le diable!'

'Mais oui. C'est un petit diable.'

'Un esprit de vin!'

'Mais magnifique!'

'Oh mon Dieu, mon Dieu, mais j'ai peur de le petit diable de vin!'.

These remarks provided fresh inspiration for my sorties. I took to climbing into the rigging above the gaggle of the French, and pouring whole hogsheads of sack down on them.

'Il pleut!'

'Il pleut vin!'

'C'est un miracle!'

'Un coup de diable!'

The frightened little Froggies fancied that some great god of grapes was pissing wine down on them, I believe. They sensed a something still and unnatural in the day – what with the sweet fog and the sudden shafts of sun. My appearance, my unheard-of mode of martial behaviour, and the suddenness of my sorties matched with their swift and unpredictable changes of direction – all combined to cause an extraordinary consternation amongst them. Add to this the encouragement which my example gave to our English crew. They fought like heroes now, swigging more sack when not smashing enemy skulls with the hogsheads, tossing Frenchmen to left and to right, but always overboard.

Io Fastolf! Io triumph!

The day was ours. *Benedicite*. Pass the brandy.

Imagining no doubt that some vast host of the English fleet was upon them, so doubly and redoubtably did the cry of 'Fastolf! A Fastolf!' ring from English ship to English ship, the whole French fleet turned tail and sailed for Portugal. We were left in possession of the *St Denis*, the flagship which had rammed us, and two other minor vessels. My personal pleasure in the victory was enhanced when our scouts reported that the minor vessels were as heavy laden with a cargo of wine as the first boat we had captured.

All that long glorious afternoon we counted the dead and opened the hogsheads. The day was given over to abrupt sea-burial and the invention of toasts:

'To the squire of sack!'

'To young Captain Jack!'

'To the elf and staff that felled the French!'

'To the pisspot of wine!'

'To the little Cupid who peed on the French navy from a great height!'

'To Fastolf!'

'Faust off!'

'A Fastolf!'

'To fast or fall, to olf 'em all!'

'To Jack!'

'To Jack!'

'To Jack!'

'To crack Jack smack-their-heads and leave-'em-dead FAS-TOLF!'

It was a merry day. We played on fifes and flutes. We buried French and fished for flounders. I was captain of the flagship until the time came to turn and sail for home. We took our French bounty in tow.

An hour towards Yarmouth we pulled alongside the Duke of Norfolk, shivering in his coracle. It is the mark of a wise soldier to remember in the hour of his triumph the little details and accidents which led up to his victory. My master's failure to find a white flag and his subsequent desertion of the ship had been prime factors in my need to carry the day. So – I ordered the rescue of the Duke, and had him hauled aboard in a fishing net although the men were all for leaving him to the whims of the English channel.

Once safe aboard, Norfolk suffered the usual change of heart and style. It is true that when a battle is done there is nothing like imagination for assessing the rôle which you have played in it. By the time we reached the sound off Yarmouth harbour, Thomas Mowbray, Duke of Norfolk, bestrode history as the man who defeated the French fleet at Slugs and recaptured a quantity of sack in the doing of it. As for the crew – they were all too drunk to care or remember, I daresay, and besides who would have believed them, or me, if anyone should have told the truth, insisting that the victory had been achieved by a young and inexperienced squire, in his first martial engagement, who having slain the Duc de Aquitaine with a single blow of his arse, had gone on to break the skulls of two dozen men by a novel use of hogsheads?

No one would have believed it, is the answer. But I set down the truth of the Battle of Slugs now, so that history eventually will know.

Clio, are you listening? You strumpet! You trull! You puzzell!

I often wonder if some of the battles of former times, pried open, might be found to have similar causes and stories hidden inside them. Remove the official despatches, the Homer Line, and who knows what really happened at Troy, or at Thermopylae, or Marathon? I cannot concern myself with such antiquities. I am a plain soldier, and I tell a plain soldier's straight unvarnished tale. Not the affairs of the past, but the actualities of the present age concern me. Be sure, by Clio's little clack-dish, Sir, before this War of my Hundred Days is done, you will be acquainted with the truth of many another skirmish in which John Fastolf aquitted himself well and his country not ill. I have been a man who has left a certain discreet but definite mark on history, and the time has come to disclose it, so that Englishmen, true Englishmen of the time to come, may know why my name struck terror in the enemy, and would still be terrible to him, should he hear it anew in these mincing nancy days of Harry the 6th's poor peace.

I was pissing bloody sack as we sailed into harbour.

As for Norfolk, my master, all he could mutter, as we came, fifes and flutes playing, into Yarmouth water, to a heroes' welcome, were the same words, over and over:

'White! White underwear! The boy was wearing white beneath his doublet all the time. That would have made an excellent flag, a noble flag, a sweet persuasive flag!'

XVI

Sir John Fastolf's cursing of the cook

15 April

Cook the cook.

The cook's a crook.

He can go and persuade himself otherwise with a sausage.

He can fig off.

I'll bet you've never seen him licking his own fingers.

Bugger the cook with damsons.

What's his name again?

Macbeth. I knew it. His father was a thane, some kind of Scotch goat. I heard about it. There was this papal legate hot for the mother. He tucks his bull under his arm and goes up where they hold court and capers on the blasted heath. 'I'm sorry,' he says. 'A new rule has come through from Rome. All you thanes are to be buggered, by the Pope's command.'

'O holy father,' wheedles our fellow, 'can't you make an exception in my favour?'

'I regret not. Remove your leggings, please.'

Macbeth goes down on his knees. 'Excellency, for pity's sake,' he begs, 'I have a wife –'

The legate picks his teeth. 'Oh, very well. For a small fee in addition. But no one must know.'

Consider this sweet Hibernian scene – Macbeth's father putting aside the plaid and lying face down across the throne. Lady Macbeth lying on her husband's back.

The legate mounts and does his duty, so that it looks as though he's buggering the thane

Got it Worcester?

Macbeth face down.

Lady M face up.

Lady M's dress up.

Legate's papal bull up.

It's a long moisty fuck in the misty Scottish morning. A born cuckold, our squashed thane gets excited. His own prick knocks a hole in the bottom of the throne and pokes out red on the other side.

'Look!' cries young Macbeth, a lad wise beyond his years. 'Look what a pizzle that legate's got on him! It's gone through my mother and my father and the tip's still waggling!'

The cook's a cunt.

Listen: far from owing him five months' wages, he owes *me* for five months' pilfering of supplies. I know the price my partridge fetch in Yarmouth. I know the difference between his books and what we have to eat.

I hope an onion grows out of his belly.

When he drops dead of dysentery in the soup, or of his own soup in the dysentery, I want the undercook to chop off the Macbeth prick and stuff it up the Macbeth arse. That's the only hole in Norfolk the thing's not been in.

As for his sack – he says it is very old. I say it is in its second bleeding childhood.

You know why Hal's sceptre was so long? When he was a boy he was on all the time at his father to let him marry. 'Wait, wait,' said old Henry the 4th, 'your thing's not big enough. When it's long enough for you to sit on it – then I'll find a wife for you.' So our prince takes the future of England in his hands and he pulls it as hard as he can, and he sees that what the king says is right enough – it won't reach his royal arse. He waits a year or two, and every spare minute he's busy lengthening his member, pulling it and stretching it and schooling it and generally making it fit for any carnal Agincourt. At last, the day dawns when his princely instrument not only reaches his arse, it surpasses it.

'Jack,' he tells me, 'now I can marry without bringing shame on the house of Plantagenet.'

'Ho hum,' says I. 'Why bother? Seeing your prick's grown so long it reaches your arse – *just fuck yourself*!'

Macbeth! Macbeth! Macbeth!

Macbeth has murdered sleep, and my digestion.

Macbeth deserves to BE cooked slowly on an open fire, with two crab-apples in his gob and garlic up his bum-gut. Not that such garnishing could make him edible.

The Marshal de Retz had a servant who'd been excommunicated. When he died the local priory refused the body Christian burial.

Bluebeard says: 'Give me a week. I'll have him safe in holy ground.'

Then he invites to his castle at Tiffauges all the monks of Poitou, and he has his cook slice up a special dish and season it and pepper it. The rashers come curled on a great silver platter.

The monks eat as monks do.

The monks say how sweet and salt and tender and thank you very much.

'Sirs,' says de Retz, 'it is I who should thank you. That man of mine you refused to have in your graveyard – you have just admitted him to the holier ground of your bellies. Let us give thanks for what we have received.'

The father prior had hiccups for a month.

As for Mr Macbeth's dice – effects of gravity and gravy – they were *loaded*.

XVII

How Sir John Fastolf was apprenticed monk

16 April

Back from the wars, I cut quite a figure as a summer boy of fashion. This did not last long. My master Mowbray was jealous as a toad. I think he suspected me also of standing too high in his wife's favour. He determined to take me down a peg or two. In fact, if it had been his express intention to ruin my pride after the glory that had settled upon me at the Battle of Slugs he could not have chosen his next move better.

I was apprenticed to be a monk!

Pious readers stop here. I have met few Christians in my life whose faith was stout or deep enough to survive many tales of the truth of the monastic life. What goes on behind abbey walls is better left to religious imaginations. I shall have more to say on this subject when I come to tell you of that later period in my story where I had recourse to going as a man into a monastery, and indeed of that other occasion when I was obliged to go as a woman into a nunnery. At the time of which I am now speaking, remember, I was still a boy, solidly ignorant of the ways of the world, fifteen years old and green as grass – although, as I've explained, something of a temporary hero on account of that single encounter with the French.

That I was not to be allowed to advance my career on the back of that victory was made clear to me when my master the Duke started deploring my part in it. 'The boy fell out of the rigging by mistake,' he said. 'Then there were these accidents with the hogsheads. He was drunk. Disgraceful in one so young. I blame myself. He was in my care. I am looking for ways to atone, and to mend his reputation.'

Mowbray took this version of that event, and he repeated it in the right ears until it was believed. In case the reader is pursuing

82

these annals for moral instruction, I will add from time to time certain aphorisms of my own which have been distilled from a lifetime's experience, taking care not to introduce the really profound ones at any stage in my narrative before their merit is out of proportion to my growth. Know then that after hearing Mowbray's version of the Battle of Slugs I began to learn that truth is not a goddess or any other manner of immutable or immortal, but simply what men of power repeat long enough in the ears of other men of power. Certainly there are times when truth is more than that, but there has never been a time in the history of the world when it has been less.

Mowbray started to rabbit on about my welfare. He tugged at his twattish beard and ogled the corners of the room. 'The boy needs discipline,' he said. 'He should have been an oblate.'

The word *oblate* sent a shiver down my spine. In this enlightened century, the institution of oblates has been almost forgotten. Four Popes in the last two hundred years have spoken against it, and the trade is dead. But when I was a boy it was common enough. Your oblate was a child – a child offered by its parents or guardians to be a monk or a nun. The age of seven was generally considered the earliest at which this gift could be accepted by the Church, although the generous Canons Regular of Porto admitted children three or four years after they had been weaned.

I seized these usual tendernesses as my line of defence. 'I'm too old to be an oblate,' I protested.

'Don't be so modest,' said Mowbray. 'The Supreme Pontiff is very concerned about all this business, of course. As a matter of fact, I hear he's just gone on record that it is the oblate's right to make his own final and irrevocable choice at the end of his fifteenth year.'

This sounded promising. Reasonable.

Too reasonable.

'Logically,' said Mowbray, 'it must follow from what the Holy Father has recommended, that a boy can be made an oblate *up to and including the age of fifteen*. Pack your bags. Your father agrees. You leave for Hulme abbey in the morning.'

So it was, in the winter of my fifteenth year, that I found myself a nightly grasshopper *ad monasterium Hulme ordinis Sancti Benedicti diocesis Norwicensis* – that's to say, at the abbey of Hulme, of the order of St Benedict, in the diocese of Norwich. I mean that I had to stridulate prayer all night long. I had also to fast daily – a terrible combination. To lift up my soul to God. To adore. To be contrite. To give thanks. To supplicate. My fare was black bread and little beans and potherbs. Cabbage without salt. O my throat. O those anthems. All I had to drink was slops and water.

There was the Litany of the Holy Name, the Litany of the Holy Ghost, the Litany of the Blessed Virgin Mary, the Litany of the Saints, and the Litany of St Joseph. There was of course the Angelus and the Vespers of our Lady, and then there was the prayer of Manasses and the prayer of St Richard. There was the prayer for all things necessary to salvation. There was the Litany of Penitence and the Litany of the Blessed Sacrament. There were the anthems of our Lady, *Alma Redemptoris* (from Advent Sunday until the Feast of Purification), *Ave Regina Caelorum* (from the Feast of Purification until Wednesday in Holy Week), *Regina Caeli* (from Easter to the Saturday before Trinity Sunday), and *Salve Regina* (from Trinity Sunday until Advent).

My favourite was the *Canticum Trium Puerorum* – the Song of the Three Children, which the saints sang in the flaming fiery furnace, blessing the Lord:

Benedicite, omnia opera Domini, Domino. . . . O all ye works of the Lord, bless ye the Lord. *Benedicite, sol et luna, Domino.* . . . O ye sun and moon, bless ye the Lord. . . . O ye showers and dew, bless ye the Lord. . . . O ye fire and heat, bless ye the Lord. . . . O ye dews and frosts, O ye ice and snow, light and darkness, seas and floods, whales, fowls, beasts, cattle, priests, O Ananias, Azarias, and Misael. . . . BENEDICITE!

I've always shouted *Benedicite* with all my heart, given half a chance. But it's not so very easy on slops and water and potherbs.

What else? At Nocturns, let's see, hey diddle diddle, and indeed at all the Hours, if we made mistakes, or nodded off, or were noticed whispering to each other in the choir stalls, we were stripped of frock and cowl, and stretched on the flogging block, and beaten soundly in our shirts. There was a Brother Mikal, who kept a smooth and pliant osier rod for this especial purpose. He used to wake us in the mornings just by touching us softly with that rod. We had then to leap out of bed, and trot down from the dormitory, and wash and comb and start in at our prayers. O the place was a windmill of prayer all right.

When I say 'we' I mean myself and the other oblates. There were a dozen of us. The youngest was eight, the oldest were myself and a long sickly boy called – what was his name? –

Duncan. *Benedicite!* It is strange how some part of the mind, called upon, suddenly remembers. I would have thought that that boy's name was gone from my head for ever. I could have called up for you his pasty washed-out face, and his hair the colour of tow, and the way his shoulders stooped, but until I began to speak of him a minute ago, I would have sworn that his name was something I had long forgotten.

At night, we slept two by two, and there would be a monkish master between each pair of us. Tallow candles were fixed on spikes in all the lanterns, so that these overlords could observe the least unruly movement of our souls or other parts. They used to come among us also, the monks, with rods in one hand and candles in the other, and if your Latin sounded vague you'd be smartly touched.

'Boys need custody with discipline, and discipline with custody,' Brother Mikal used to say, in his peculiar whining voice, which all came down his nose, so that every word was like a blob of snot.

Discipline with custard.

The oblates had one other litany, all our own, which we sometimes sang under our breath to the traditional tunes:

> *Sordidum mappale*
> *Olus sine sale*
> *Stratum lapidale*
> *Stabulum sordidale*
> *Kyrie eleison*

and so on, all about Hulme abbey of course, for in good English this would go something like:

> *Dirty linen,*
> *Saltless cabbage,*
> *Stony bedding,*
> *This filthy stable!*
> *Lord, have mercy . . .*

Discipline in the order of St Benedict in the diocese of Norwich meant standing a long while waiting in draughty corridors, knotting your legs when you wanted a piss, and being beaten with the osier rods, and having your hair plucked out by ecclesiastical fingers. One thing, the monks were fastidious – they never struck us with their fists or with the flat of their hands, or even with their feet.

85

Oblates were taught cleanliness too – that is, we were advised to wipe our hands in different parts of the one disgusting towel.

Sometimes, in the middle of the night, half-mad with lack of sleep, some of the youngest boys found the singing of Nocturns hard. Then Br Mikal would give them a heavy missal to hold. The weight kept your arm awake, and the pins and needles inspired in it helped the rest of your person to pay attention.

It was a well-ordered monastery, as monasteries go, and most of the monks were kind enough, devoted to simple pleasures – prayer, pigeons, the poor. Not that I have ever found prayer easy, except when it has been wrung out of me by misfortune.

Abbot Geffrey used to speak of the whole world, I recall, as a place of exile. In his reckoning we have to regard this life as a pilgrimage to God. Travellers on that pilgrimage need places where they can stay and refresh their spirits. That was what a monastery was, he said – a spiritual inn for the pilgrim soul. I liked the metaphor better than the actual inn-keeping and what went with it. Besides, the Boar's Head was more my style.

My friend Duncan had been brought up by his mother in a convent, his father having been a victim of the plague. When he was five Duncan was removed from his mother, and taken to Hulme, it not being thought decent that a lad of his age should continue to spend his time among the opposite sex. On the way to Hulme, the monk accompanying him – the dirty whoreson old devil! – asked Duncan what the women had been like.

'What women?' said Duncan.

'The women you've been living with,' said the monk.

'I've never seen any women,' Duncan said.

He had called the nuns *sisters*, you see, and they had called each other *sister*, so he thought that this was their name, and he did not realise that they might also be called *women* – if you wanted to call them that.

The monk must have thought to himself that he had a proper idiot here. 'Would you like to see what *women* are?' he asked.

'I think I would,' said Duncan.

They were passing a field full of goats, so the monk pointed to the goats. 'Look,' he said. 'Women.'

Duncan believed it. When he told the other oblates that he had seen women grazing in the field and running about butting each other with their horns, he swore to me that some of them thought there was nothing remarkable about this. They had been

86

educated by the same monk. This was one of the things that was wrong with the system of oblates. If boys could grow up shut away from the world and confusing goats and women, just think of the complications.

I was wearing all this while the habit of a novice, though I can tell you that I had no intention of staying in the abbey one monastic Hour later than the morning of my 16th birthday. Yet in those winter months I got to know the inside of a chapel pretty well, and the rhythms and cadences of the psalms were beaten into my bloodstream by Br Mikal.

Psalmus 150
Laudate Dominum in sanctis ejus: laudate eum in firmamento virtutis ejus.
Laudate eum in virtutibus ejus: laudate eum secundum multitudinem magnitudinis ejus.
Laudate eum in sono tubae: laudate eum in psalterio, et cithara.
Laudate eum in tympano, et choro: laudate eum in chordis, et organo.
Laudate eum in cymbalis benesonantibus: laudate eum in cymbalis jubilationis: omnis spiritus laudet Dominum.

Praise him, yes.
And if you didn't get all that Latin right, little Cyclops, it'll be the worse for your posterior understanding.

Madam, my lady Reader, you might be thinking that this matter of bodily penance and discipline did not displease me, and certainly I was the better able to bear it than poor Duncan, who was forever weeping and blubbering under the osier rod, which of course made Br Mikal whip him the more. All the same, to tell you the truth, I had less interest in the power of the birch in that year than in any other year of my existence. Perhaps it was too much a part of the dank and draughty air of the abbey, so that there was no comparison or contrast of pleasure with which to salve its sting? A man has most benefit from the rod when his belly is full and his stomach well-drenched with wine.

There was one story which I heard in the monastery – it was Duncan's story – which has stuck in my head as a single patch or image of colour from those dark days. I will never forget the boy's face as he told it to me: white in the dormitory candleflame. His story concerned King Arthur. I always loved to hear tell of King Arthur. Perhaps that is why I have remembered the story all these years.

DUNCAN'S TALE

There was once a Bishop of Winchester who was mad about hunting. He went hunting before breakfast and by moonlight. He went hunting even when he should have been saying Mass. One day, in the Forest of Arden, his beaters dispersed, the Bishop found himself riding down a long sunlit glade towards a house that he had not seen before, a house that was all shining. As he drew near, marvelling at its fineness, he was met by servants in clothes of gold, with green silk cloaks. 'Come, my lord,' they invited. 'Come without delay and eat meat at the banquet of our King.' The Bishop excused himself. He protested that he had no garment with him in which a bishop could sit down to dine. The servants turned aside. Beneath an oak there was a wicker basket. They opened the basket and immediately produced the correct mantle and smoothed it about the Bishop's shoulders and brought him to the house and into the King's presence. The Bishop sat down at the King's right hand. The banquet began. The Bishop had never tasted food more delicate or drink more delightful. When the meal was done, he asked his host where he was.

'I am Arthur,' said the King, 'the King who was and is to come.'

The Bishop rubbed his hands for joy. 'Then is this Paradise?' he said.

'It is not,' Arthur said. 'It is only Camelot, my house, where I await God's mercy. But before that day, there will be another, when England will need me, and when I shall return to her.'

Now this was all very pretty and impressive and patriotic, but the Bishop – after the way of bishops – began to wonder who would believe him when he went back to Winchester and reported that he had seen and spoken with King Arthur. He started muttering about his anxieties.

Arthur cut him short. 'Close your hand!' he said.

The Bishop closed his hand.

'Open it!' said Arthur.

The Bishop opened his hand. Out flew a butterfly.

Then Arthur said: 'All your life you shall have this memorial of me. At any season of the year, when you tell men how you met me, you have only to close your hand and open it again and one of these creatures will fly out as a token.'

And this came true just as King Arthur promised. The Bishop of Winchester's butterflies became so notorious that in time men begged him for a butterfly for a benediction, and he was known as the Bishop of the Butterfly.

'What does it mean?' cried Duncan. He would clench his fist and stare at it. His eyes burned for a butterfly. The butterfly never came.

Worcester, can you guess what Arthur was trying to teach by this sign? No. Firk me, then, I'll tell you what I was bloody taught by it. It was that in the darkest days of my caterpillarhood, as a reluctant novice, an oblate desiring nothing *less* than to continue as a monk for the rest of his life, I still had hopes of a wider wilder world of colour and sun and creatures as gay and meaningless and wonderful as butterflies, those same butterflies which once I had attached with threads to my fingers and run through the Caister corn with them streaming behind me like a plume above my shoulder. In the middle of the night, singing Nocturns half-asleep in the abbey chapel, the candles flickering on the faces of the monks and my young companions, I would clench my fist in the shadow of my robe – and imagine that if I opened it at the sign of the cross a butterfly would fly out. . . .

If it had, Br Mikal would only have smashed it with his osier rod.

No butterflies came. My clenched fist was full of sweat. I lost my voice with halloing and singing of anthems. Abbot Geffrey agreed on the morning of my 16th birthday that there could be no future for a crack-voiced Br John, who claimed that only sack could mend his throat.

At the age of sixteen, then, I emerged from Hulme abbey, my possessions in a tight pack on my back, the whole world like a football at my feet. Never was air so clear and good as the air I breathed as I came over the hill and away from Hulme.

'Remember this world is a place of pilgrimage, a place of exile. Your true home is elsewhere,' said Abbot Geffrey.

'Remember me,' said Duncan, my brother oblate, on the night that he lay dying. The monks had given him a regular robe to lie in, and promised him that when he was dead they would bury him in it, as a special favour. But Duncan did not want to die a monk. When the brothers found him in the morning he had struggled out of the robe. He was lying cold and stiff and naked among the candles.

I was my own butterfly. *Benedicite*. I flew.

XVIII

About Badby & the barrel

The day before yesterday's talk of cooking the cook and yesterday's talk of monks has reminded me of a monk I once saw roasted on a spit. The behaviour of flesh in fire is unpredictable. This man was lean and dim and covered with a mildew of religiousness. I swear his flesh part *melted* from him in the flames, leaving the white skeleton exposed for a moment to the air. He looked then like a fish or a fine coral. That appearance lasted a bare minute. Once the flames got to work on his bones they blackened and cracked and before long there was only ashes. But the moment when his skeleton stood clean and clear like a white cage dragged up through blue fathoms to the sun comes back and flashes on my mind's eye now. Also the moment when his skin melted, dripping and splashing down on the ground. This was in France.

The smell of burning flesh is much the same anywhere.

I have seen burnings in England too.

Badby and the barrel – the story will be lost if I don't tell it. It is a story that tells you all or most of Harry Monmouth, whatever way you look at it.

There was a heretic that was called John Badby, who did not believe in the sacrament of the altar, and he was brought to Smithfield to be burned according to the statute *De heretico comburendo*. He was put in a barrel.

And Harry, Prince of Wales, Duke of Cornwall, Earl of Chester, was standing there in Smithfield, and in gold shoes he counselled this Badby to hold the right belief of Holy Church.

Badby would have none of it. He was a Lollard, found guilty of heresy in the Bishop's court at Worcester, his sentence confirmed by London convocation. Archbishop Arundel had required him to recant. But Badby, who was a tailor by trade, stood by his false opinion – the bread, he said, was merely an emblem or token of Christ's body. He dared not believe, he said, that 20,000 Christs were made in England every morning. (He meant by priests saying Mass.) Arundel handed him over to the secular arm.

There he was in the barrel. Hal stepped forward to offer him a last chance of life.

'I've nothing to retract,' said the tailor.

The faggots were lit. The flames fastened on him.

'*Mercy!*' cried the tailor.

Instantly, Hal ordered the executioner to pull Badby out of the barrel and rescue him. The rakes were put in. The fire was dragged aside. They brought out Badby, half-burned, from the barrel.

'Very sensible,' said our prince. 'In the circumstances, Mr Badby, I feel that I can offer you a pension in return for your decision to recant.'

But Badby had cried out for mercy, not bargains.

'No, my lord,' he said, with his black tongue and charred lips. 'I am sorry, my lord. I can never recant.'

'Rekindle the fire then,' said Prince Henry.

Badby was put back in his barrel and burned to death.

Worcester, I say that a better prince would not have bargained with a man half-dead. By stopping the fire, he made a double agony.

Martyrs I do not like – an extravagant unnecessary bloody breed, with stiff necks and hard hearts. But this John Badby made no fuss. Was he hardened beyond redemption by the Devil? I doubt it. I remember him lying there unconscious and half-burned, his face black patches and purple, and the Prince in his gold shoes. And, when Badby came to himself, the Prince leaning over and touching him with his stick.

Threepence a day: that would have been his pension.

Mr Badby sat up very politely and refused the prince's bargain. He apologised. Said he was *sorry*. Hal did not even blink.

O England. O bugger.

John Badby did not ask for mercy twice.

The smell of roasting human flesh in Smithfield was what put me off meat dishes. Wine is clean.

The chancellor of Oxford, Mr Cortenay, he was there, standing by the barrel in his hood, to instruct the little tailor in the faith of Holy Church.

The Prior of St Bartholomew's brought the Blessed Sacrament with 13 torches and held it before the Lollard's eyes.

3d a day.

XIX

About the death of Sir John Fastolf's father

18 April

To get back to the subject. What subject? How many subjects are there, when you come down to it? One. Life is the subject. When I am dead there will be no subject. The object is not dying. Not to die. I shall not die for a long while yet. I shall live to be a hundred. Meanwhile, I have a hundred days in which to tell my story. The story of my days. Although I may most be telling that story when I seem to wander away from it. You do not always take a castle by advancing in a straight line.

But to resume these chronicles. Where was I? Just out of the monastery, God be praised. Fresh from a surfeit of prayer, my voice not improved by anthems, nor my bum by Br Mikal's osier rod. That's right, I was on my way home, on the road back to Caister, to see my mother and my father once again.

Mowbray's remark about my father agreeing that I should be made an oblate had stuck in my head, and festered. It rankled all the time I was in Hulme abbey. I wanted to find out for myself if my father really had such a low opinion of me that he considered monkhood all I was fit for.

When I reached Caister, the grass was long in the paddocks. I met my uncle Hugh on the arm of a new mistress.

'Look at this,' he said. *This* was an emerald bottle with what looked like a few drops of candlegrease in it.

'What is it?' I said.

'The sweat of St Michael the Archangel,' explained my uncle Hugh. 'Shed when he fought with Satan, you know. Priceless.'

I did not care to ask him how much priceless had been, in the case of such a relic.

'Where is my father?' I said.

'Look in this box,' said my uncle Hugh.

93

I looked. The box contained a dry black broken stalk or two, set out on purple velvet.

'Hay,' said my uncle Hugh.

'I can believe it,' I said. 'My father –'

'Not just any old hay,' explained my uncle Hugh. 'Hay from the manger in which our Lord was laid.'

'Really,' I said.

'Don't darken your mind with doubt,' said my uncle Hugh. 'It cost me a small fortune, that holy hay. Now shade your eyes and take a peek at what's hanging round Cleopatra's neck!'

I looked. The woman simpered. It seemed to be some sort of star.

'Not the one which guided the Wise Men?' I said.

My uncle Hugh pressed his finger to his lips and winked. 'I admit that may not be genuine,' he said. 'There's another in Edinburgh just like it.'

'And my father?' I said.

'My prize,' said uncle Hugh. 'The best yet. My most miraculous.' He took a pouch from his waist. He handed me a sort of sausage, all wrapped in wool and wadding. 'You'll never guess.'

I did not want to.

'The finger of St Thomas Didymus!' cried my uncle Hugh in triumph. 'Just think, boy, that finger touched the wound in our Saviour's side.'

I handed him the pouch again. 'Where is my father?' I said wearily. But I knew the answer.

'Dead,' said my uncle. 'Your father's dead.'

I sat down on the steps of the house. I wept. The tears trickled down my fingers and fell through my hands and drowned a spider. It was one of my mother's speckled spiders. They had been busy breeding ever since the bad days of the plague. Spiders thrived on the Black Death.

Seeing the spider made me dry my eyes and go and look for my mother. She had quit the family house and married a man called Farewell. One thing about my mother, even when she set fire to the arras or gave birth to puppy dogs on the hall floor – she always kept her sense of humour.

I found Mrs Farewell in good health. She assured me that the house at Caister would be mine when I came of age. It was my father's bequest. No, my father had not wanted me to be a monk. My mother indeed was horrified when she heard where I had been. She had imagined that I was still in Mowbray's retinue as a squire. That nice twat had reported merely that I was 'away on business' when she made enquiries after me.

Not, it must be admitted, that she had made so many enquiries. Her new husband occupied her days and nights very thoroughly. I gathered that they were generally to be found in bed together, going at it hammer-and-tongs.

I had an unsatisfactory interview with my mother, during which she offered most of her answers from beneath the bed-clothes while my stepfather Farewell said nothing but professed many a grunt and grumble of achievement as she kept up a running flow of chatter directed towards me.

Of this interview, I remember only one thing. I had asked my mother what my father died of.

'Laughing,' she said.

'Laughing at what?' I said.

'Nothing in particular,' she said.

I liked this.

Placut dropped down dead when he had to pay a bill.

Saufeius choked to death on an under-boiled egg.

Aeschylus met his end when an eagle flying overhead dropped a tortoise it was carrying and the tortoise fell on Aeschylus's bald head and broke his skull.

Titus Haterius died bending to kiss the hand of his wife.

The soothsayer Chalchas died of laughter at the thought that he had just outlived the hour he had predicted for his own death.

But my father died of laughing at nothing in particular.

XX

How Sir John Fastolf undressed himself of his suit of virgin white

Venus and death go hand in hand. There is always a lot of fucking after a flood or a fire, or in time of war. Pistol roaring drunk down a Paris street, doublet undone, no need of a sword, his prick sticking out as big and red as Bardolph's nose. In France, I can tell you, men ran wild for women after Agincourt and Verneuil and the other great battles. Perhaps it was the relief of finding yourself still alive. It made you want to celebrate that life. But I suspect a deeper cause. What does a child do when he is frightened? He runs to his mother, and hides his face in her lap. When the child is disguised as a man he runs to any woman *not* his mother. Death makes a man a child again.

In no other way, by no further preliminary, can I explain the swift loss of my virginity upon my learning of my father's death. You may say, when you have heard the tale of its losing, that the matter hung upon opportunity. That is always true. But there had been opportunity before. If I had been too young to do much to the maidservant Katharina, who had felt some of the potential of my cock when I was whipped by my tutor Ravenstone, then I had not been too young to mount one of my Lady Elizabeth's maids of the bedchamber when I was forced by them into my sweet bondage as a woman, and shared a bed with them, and witnessed them in all kinds of inspiring attitudes. Several of those maids would have been glad of my services. They used to touch me and tickle me, finger me amorously in their sleep (when they were not fingering themselves), caress me and rub their naked bodies up against me when they thought that *I* was asleep. The Duchess of Norfolk herself might have opened her legs for me, if I had insisted upon the identity of my burgeoning manhood

96

despite those female trappings. . ; .

The fact is that on none of these occasions did I part company with my suit of virgin white. But soon after my knowledge of my father's death, I did.

It happened like this. My stepfather Farewell had a daughter by a previous marriage of his own. This daughter was now sixteen, the same age as I was. Her name was Ophelia.

She was tall and fair, Ophelia, with hair that fell to the middle of her back. I could see the outline of eager breasts beneath her bodice, and her little bottom made a shape like two plums rubbing tight together as she walked. She had this habit of staring. Her eyes were big blue pools. She would sit and look at me – unflinching, curious, steady – until I felt uncomfortable. When she saw that I was disturbed, by some movement of my hands perhaps, or an involuntary stirring of my cloak, then she would smile a slow smile – her lips were very thin and very red – and shrug her delicate shoulders under the wispy stuff of her dress, and get up and leave the room.

I suppose that technically she was my step-sister, but this did not cross my mind at the time I am telling of. Later, in any case, when it did – and it was Ophelia herself who pointed out the forbidden nature of the relationship to me, in her usual innocent and wondering and highly provocative way – it only lent a spice to our erotic dallyings. The feeling between us was entirely a question of Eros. Just after my return to Caister, it posed a very large question.

Ophelia's appetites had been whetted by what she had to witness in her father's new married bed. For over a year this impressionable young girl had been dancing attendance on Farewell and my mother, and most of that time – from what I could work out – the couple had spent voluptuously between the sheets. When they felt hungry or thirsty, my stepfather would pull a bellrope and Ophelia had to tiptoe in with a tray for them to take refreshment. She told me that sometimes they were eating each other again before she could retire from the room. As I say, she was a curious sweet kitten, Ophelia, with those big blue eyes that didn't miss a thing. In the circumstances she was not over anxious to leave the room anyway.

By the time that I came back to Caister she was palpably itching for a man. As for me, my spell in the monastery, following my exploits in the wars with Mowbray and my previous adven-

97

tures in his wife's bedchamber, had left me in a state of readiness for anything. Thus, at sixteen, and without benefit of figs – I needed none! – I was ready for Ophelia.

The first night she came to my room, late, when I thought the house was all asleep. It was raining. I could hear the river. A fire burned in the grate.

Ophelia was wearing a blue silk nightgown, her hair braided up, and had come fresh from her bath.

'Jack,' she said.

'Yes?' I said.

'I think I have a speck in my eye,' she said. 'Will you look?'

She sat down on the edge of the bed and presented her face close to mine.

'It's in the left eye,' she said. 'Please, Jack, be careful. I know you'll be careful. You have such careful hands.'

I looked at her. I could see nothing unusual in her eye. Only myself reflected.

Ophelia sat and stared at the fire. Infrequently, she blinked. A tear touched my fingers where they touched her cheek.

'What's the matter?' I said. 'Am I hurting you?'

'No,' she said. 'Good night.'

That was that. The next night Ophelia came again. Her bare feet made a sucking sound against the floorboards as she crossed the room.

'Jack,' she said.

'Yes?' I said.

'I can't get to sleep,' she said. 'I think I have palpitations.'

'Palpitations?' I repeated stupidly.

'My heart,' she said. 'Feel.'

I had never felt a young girl's heart before. Worcester, in case you don't know, I had better explain that it is firm and white and has a pink nipple on the end of it. I could observe the virgin texture of Ophelia's nipple through the blue silk of her nightgown. My fingers felt its pricking excitement.

'Oh,' she said. Then, as though surprised to hear herself saying such things, she whispered: 'Rub it ever so softly.'

'Like this?' I said.

'That's nice,' she said. 'Good night.'

When the third night came, I was determined on action. I was tired of her 'Good-nights' when things were just starting to get interesting for me and the bed clothes were beginning to perk up. The fire flickered in the grate. The wind sighed in the arras.

Ophelia did not complain of anything in particular in any part of her person. She just sat primly on the bottom of my bed, her hand to her braided hair, and stared at me with those large liquid eyes that were like drops of sky.

'Jack,' she said at last.

'Yes,' I said.

Ophelia's fingers played with an errant wisp. 'What do you think it is,' she said, 'that keeps my father in bed all the time with your mother?'

'*What?*' I said.

'It can't be sleep,' Ophelia said. She was licking her thin red lips. Now she half-shut those bright eyes under lids of dreamy speculation. 'I've listened to them at the keyhole,' she said. 'They make all kinds of noises that people wouldn't make if they were asleep.'

Then I realised the splendour of it. This beautiful girl – far from trying to seduce me – was not conversant with the commerce of lithe limbs at all. Her own untutored instincts had been indubitably tickled and aroused by her father's goings on in the big bed with my mother, but she had no idea what amorousness was actually about. In that moment, observing her tender breasts quickly rising and falling with ignorant wishfulness under the blue silk nightgown, I determined to take Ophelia's education in hand.

I leapt from the bed.

'Ophelia,' I said, my hands covering my member.

'Jack!' she cried doubtfully.

I removed my hands.

'What do you think this is?' I said.

Ophelia's eyes had been big before. Now I swear that they were hot blue whirlpools – Hellesponts of astonishment. Her mouth opened also, hungrily. 'It's a prick,' she said, her lips pouting on the *p* and her teeth sounding the *ck* very precisely as her tongue mowed against them.

'Oho,' I said, moving towards her, 'then you're not so innocent, after all, my dear. . . .'

'Don't be silly,' she said, dodging. 'Father has one like that. Only bigger.'

This infuriated me. 'Bigger?' I cried. 'Bigger than mine? Bigger than *this*? You just come here and we'll see who's got *anything* bigger than Fastolf's fellow. It'll be big enough for you, my kitten – that I promise.'

99

Ophelia looked at me over her shoulder. Her hay-gold hair fell sideways, half-masking her flushed face. 'For *me?*' she said. 'Why should I want it? What could I do with it? Don't be silly, Jack. I know it's just what you men piss with.'

I leaned against the wall and laughed, and laughed. Ophelia turned to face me. My member shook with the force of my laughter. The blue gaze of my step-sister never left it for a second. She was fascinated by the open display of an organ she had no doubt spent most of her girlhood imagining.

I decided on mischief as the best policy. 'But naturally,' I said, folding my robe about me. 'You're not interested in *that* old hobby horse. You'll have your own to play with.'

Ophelia pouted. 'Girls don't have them, don't you know?' she said.

I forced my face to express disbelief. 'Everyone has them,' I said.

'No, no,' cried Ophelia, 'not at all. *Look!*'

And, so saying, my sweet step-sister of sixteen did what I had hoped she would do – fell back prettily across my bed and drew up her nightgown to show me the loveliest little grotto sacred to the goddess Venus which (up to that early age) it had ever been my privilege to see, or to imagine in my hardest dreams.

I knelt between her legs and kissed her there.

'Greetings,' I said. I kissed some more. 'Is that nice?'

Ophelia's fingers plunged into my hair. My tongue probed her tight slit, licking and sucking. The little knob at the top inside was like a rose-bud. I nibbled at it. She was thrusting from side to side. Her bottom thumped the bed. 'It's delicious,' she giggled. 'Oh, oh –' Then she pushed my head away from her thighs and suddenly sat bolt upright, her cheeks burning, her blue eyes ablaze.

'Listen, Jack! I've got it!' she cried. 'Why do you think you –?'

She never had to complete the question. Throwing open my robe I offered her another view of the answer. Ophelia's legs opened avidly to admit me. I pushed the head of my virgin rod into the entrance of her no less virgin cunt.

Gentleness is no great kindness when taking a maidenhead. Ophelia's cunt was deliciously tight and small. Well lodged in its satiny threshold, I thrust away like mad. Tears started to her eyes.

'Courage,' I said. I let my engine throb inside her for a

moment, while she got her breath back. Then I started in for the final assault. Ophelia screamed at first, but not too much. She bit the pillows, tossing her head this way and that in ecstasy. I was halfway in. I was there!

'Oh oh oh oh!' cried Ophelia. 'What's happened? What's happening? What have you done?'

'You little darling,' I whispered in her ear, as my hot seed gushed inside her, and her cunt tightened to drink it all down, 'it's called fucking, and we've *both* done it!'

I pronged Ophelia well, and clipped and kissed her. I slipped both hands in under her bottom, and pulled her up and down on my thick sword. She wept. Her cunt wept. I wept. My prick wept. Then we all started laughing.

I think I must have come inside her seven long times that night. Once having tasted it, Ophelia behaved like a naughty little bear that was fallen into a tub of honey and has no intention of ever getting out again. She would not leave my bed. 'Do that thing again, Jack!' was all she kept saying. 'Fuck me some more!' – murmuring the words in her sleep, even when I had worn us both out with my love-making.

After that, hey diddle dan, she came to my room every night that I remained at Caister.

My mother and my stepfather Farewell never realised what was going on. I'm sure of that. They were too busy themselves, paying similar heavy dues to the great goddess of Love. No doubt their service was more intricate than ours – it was only later that I began to learn the more sophisticated ways in which a man can please a woman, and vice versa. But I swear that no other lovers, however experienced, could have gone to it more sweetly and generously and faithfully and tenderly and eagerly than I and my Ophelia. Her wide-eyed wonder extended to other parts of her body, you see. Sometimes I felt that her pretty little cunt itself was staring at me, staring at me, with a marvellous concentration, draining me dry of all that I could offer it. She was a dear, insatiable, and simple soul. She never complained of pain, not even that first time, and she never spurned or rejected me – even if I turned to her suddenly, in the woods, say, and pushed her down on her back in a pile of autumn leaves, and thrust away so that we ended up covered with leaf-mould.

Once given a sight of my tool, and a feel of his force, Ophelia doted on it. She made me fuck her all one afternoon, in a swing which we had built together in an apple tree. There was a long trailing canopy, scarlet ribbons fluttering in the breeze. I remember the smell of honeysuckle and the light shining on fallen apples and Ophelia's sharp foxy tongue, which somehow got inserted in my nose at the moment of extremest pleasure. I remember the creak-creak-creaking of the swing, and the way the sky swayed outside as we lay afterwards, close-clasped in each other's arms. The swing began to slow, dreamily to cease, to stop. . . .

'Jack!' Ophelia whispered, her eyes sparkling with desire. 'Fuck me again! Fuck me, fuck me, fuck me again, Jack! When I was a little girl I always liked a good swing on an autumn afternoon. And now I'm a big girl – well, there's nothing like it in the world!'

I obliged. I could always oblige that warm little open-eyed grotto which made me welcome in such a wonderful wondering way.

And so I was undressed of my suit of virgin white.

And so I came to undress and understand myself for the first time.

And Ophelia, sweet Ophelia, too.

XXI

*How Sir John Fastolf came to London, &
his praise of London Bridge*

20 April

The day dawned when I began to weary of Caister and even – for
a while at least – of my adorable Ophelia. I was now sixteen,
remember, and determined as only a boy can be to make my fame
and fortune. My dead father had left me a little money and
property. But this would not be mine until I came of age. Meanwhile, like many a young man before, London called me. I
wanted to make my own way in the world. I put on my shoes
which were so long and pointed that they needed jewelled chains
to hold their toes fastened curled up to my knees, and thus
fashionably equipped I set out for what I took to be the heart of
the world.

The day I went walking to London was a day when the hedgerows were brimming with berries and blossom, and the sky was
alive with birds. The good earth smacked of pumperknickel
bread. The air was like wine. Every door I passed seemed to give
off a smell of cooking, as though you'd lifted the lid on a meat
pie. Dogs barked. Larks danced. Bells rang. Lambs with knees
dipped in coaldust skipped on the little hills. The rivers flashed.
The trees were leaved with light. Windmills wove the wind.

I walked with pilgrims and minstrels. Ladies in panelled carriages passed me on the roads, with knights accompanying them
on horseback. There were jokers on stilts and men who hopped
along to win a wager. Merchants and wandering friars. A party
from the holy land of Walsingham. Musicians mendicant with
their instruments, playing as they walked – rottes and gitterns
and citòles, lutes and mandores, the psaltery, a damsel with a
dulcimer, rebecs, humstrums with just the one string, pipes,
shawns, and boys with bumbards and buzines and bugles. I

always liked music, and counted it great good fortune to make my way to London in company with my own orchestra. A lad with a hare-lip taught me to play a kind of organ as we marched along – it hung about my neck, and I had to pump it with one hand and play it with the other. Up hill and down dale we came, tootling, thrumming, singing, and with a little dog that followed us everywhere.

And when we came at last to London the streets, if not paved with gold, seemed to me all strewn with sunlight and black-patched with shadow in a way that I had never seen before. And the light on the underside of the bridges was a miracle.

Ha! Ho! it seemed to my young eyes a magic city. Perhaps this was because I had delayed my journey to London, and had therefore the more starved an imagination to meet its sights and sounds. Perhaps it was because I made my pilgrimage on foot, walking the ways and roads from Norfolk, in my company of players and minstrels and friars and tinkers, and had the keener sense of occasion and achievement when I passed over the final hill and saw the place for the first time.

For whatever reason, it was a homecoming to me. A homecoming to a place I had never before seen in my life.

The streets were full of folk, full of bustle and noise, and colours. Apprentices ran everywhere –

'Come buy! Come buy!'

'Brooms!'

'Hot pies!'

'New shoes!'

– it didn't really matter what they were selling, it was all advertised as though it was at one and the same time a joke and a sacrament, a nonsense and the best piece of poetry in the world. Jugglers walked on their hands in the same streets where some mayor's man strutted in his robes of scarlet, tipped with fur. There were plays in the churchyards. The day I arrived I saw a guild of fishmongers do Jonah and the whale! I stood and drank ale in the dusty street and laughed and clapped till the tears came to my eyes. O *Gemini*, London was my home. And its streets to me were poetry . . . its streets and markets and churches and palaces and inns. . . . This was my litany now: London Bridge and Billingsgate, Tower Hill, St Saviour's Southwark, Thames Street and the Temple Church, Charing Cross, St Clement Danes, Temple Bar, Holborn, Tyburn, and Lincoln's Inn Fields,

Smithfield and Clerkenwell, Aldersgate and Cripplegate, St Botolph's and Bishopsgate, Fetter Lane, Shoe Lane, West Cheap, St Paul's, Watling Street, Canwicke Street, Lombard Street and Cornhill, Guildhall and White Cross Street, Houndsditch, Westminster. My music.

Not that I should make it sound too glorious. The roads round London at that time were so badly kept that there was a tax on all carts and horses bringing merchandise into the city. I saw a carrier with so much tax to pay that he just handed over horse and cart to the tax collector, and went back to the country. The rates were a penny a cart and a farthing per horse, each way, coming or going; for a cart bringing sand, or gravel, or clay, it was threepence a week. Exception was made only for carriages and horses employed in the transport of food for the great. The great! More of those buggers later.

If you ask me now what it was that *most* impressed me about London – what object it is that flashes upon my mind's eye *meaning* London, I should have one answer and one answer only: London Bridge. I had never seen anything like it.

Here was the river Thames, 900 feet wide, a vein in the heart of the greatest city in the world, and spanning it this marvellous construction, this noblest of bridges, 18 solid stone piers, varying from 25 feet to 34 feet in thickness, confining the flow of the river to less than half its natural channel.

Bad bloody engineering?

Maybe. But it allowed for grandeur. It allowed for huge blocks of building on the Bridge itself, from one end to the other. Houses four stories in height, spanning across the passageway for traffic, which was as dark as a tunnel. Shops. And about the middle, on the largest pier of all, a chapel – 60 feet by 20 – built in the 12th century, on two floors, and dedicated to St Thomas of Canterbury, called St Peter's of the Bridge.

A chapel on a bridge. I like the notion.

Some say that without the presence of the Blessed Sacrament in St Peter's, London Bridge would never have survived the dreadful fire on it in (I believe) 1212.

The passage for traffic was like a tunnel, as I told you, but there was one clear space kept. And this was big enough to be a proper place for joustings and tournaments. Fighting, as well as trade and religion.

Just a month or two after my coming to London, a Scot, Sir

David Lindsay, Earl of Crawford, fell out with John de Wells, English ambassador at the Scottish Court, and challenged him to a duel, choosing London Bridge as the place of combat. Wells had been boasting of the superiority of the English. Lindsay offered to put all questions on that point to trial. With a retinue of 24 persons, he crossed the length of the kingdom, furnished with a safe-conduct from King Richard the 2nd, and the duel was fought in front of an immense crowd. I was there.

The trumpet being blown and a handkerchief dropped, they charged at each other like demons, tearing their barbed horses with their spurs. Neither party was dislodged by the first breaking of spears. Yes, that first shock was so violent that their lances were splintered to bits – but the Scotsman stuck like porridge in his saddle. I remember the people in the houses crying out. 'He's tied to his horse,' this grocer shouted. 'That's against the rules!' Lindsay heard him. He leapt to the ground – he wore no heavy armour, just a quilted tunic – and then with one bound back up into the saddle without any assistance. The grocer was silent. Then he clapped. Lindsay charged at his opponent again. Again both spears were broken, but neither man fell. A third time – but this time the English knight was knocked to the ground. 'He's killed him!' cried the grocer. But then Lindsay did an extraordinarily fine thing. Leaping to the ground, he went to his enemy, and cradled Wells' head in his arms, until the surgeon came. The Scot remained in England for three months at the express desire of the King, and there was not one person of nobility who was not well disposed towards him. And myself and the grocer too.

London Bridge will not fall down. That I know. That I am sure of. The world is mutable, but London Bridge will last as long as the world, even though the face of London Bridge may change with the changing world.

Let me describe it again for you as it first met my eye when I was sixteen years of age and had just walked up from Norfolk.

The first thing you noticed was the houses. Houses on a bridge. A street of houses. A bridge made of houses. They were four stories high, as I've said, and they had cellars in the thickness of the piers. When the people needed water they just lowered their buckets by ropes out of the windows and had it of the Thames. If a boat ran into a pier in the dark, and you were lucky, someone might throw out a rope and help you up. More often they'd just watch you drown. O citizens of London. And the Bridge people had the hardest hearts of all.

The arches were narrow and hard to navigate. Flinty if you hit them. Massy. Any boat striking one of them, or one of the piers, was bound to be dashed to pieces, and collisions were not uncommon because of the sudden currents of the river. The Thames is full of whims.

The Bridge had its own ways too. The houses were always half of them tumbledown, ruinous. Once I saw a whole block shift, hang forward drunkenly, and topple into the river. A man's hat and a child's hobby horse swept away towards the Pool.

One of the arches of the Bridge – the 13th from the City side – was the drawbridge which let the big ships pass. The tolls were collected there. This drawbridge was also lowered and snapped shut in times of danger, to close the approach to the City. The gate at the end nearest the City was on the tower which wore the heads of executed traitors.

The Jew's eddy. When Edward the 1st drove the Jewish out of England, in the year of the Truth 1290 – better look that up later, little Cyclops, I mean we've got to get *some* of our dates right – whenever that black year was, then, a party of the richest of them were making their way down Thames in a tall ship, when the master-mariner thought of a trick which would give him possession of all their valuables. Casting anchor, he rode in one spot until, by one of the river's ebbings, his ship was on dry sand. Then he enticed the Jews to walk out with him on the sand, to stretch their legs before the long haul to foreign parts. But he led them more than a mile along the sandbank, and then nipped back to his vessel smartly when he saw the tide about to rise. The Jews lingered, unaware of the great danger. When they saw what was happening, and how they could not get back to their ship, they shouted out to the captain to save them. 'Shout for Moses!' says the captain. 'He's the only one who can help you now.' They were all drowned, and the master-mariner returned with his ship, and the King was very pleased with him. You can still see what they call the Jew's eddy – the disturbance in the river first caused at that fatal spot where the Jews were drowned – on the ebb-tide by the third pillar of London Bridge.

I thought in those days that there was nothing as beautiful as London Bridge, nothing as wonderful, nothing as strange. Every arch was stone squared, and every one of them three score feet in height. It seemed to me – and still does – one of the wonders of the world. To walk on that street, beside those painted turrets, the silver Thames beneath your feet, the sails of the ships straining up river to the Pool, the flags streaming in the wind, the Jew's eddy curling, the heads of the criminal dead dripping blood down in warning when you looked up against the sun – that was glory, that was power, that was a taste of dominion to come.

Here I was at last in my natural habitat!

XXII

The art of farting: an aside of Sir John Fastolf's

21 April

To London then I came. Farting. Farting. Who's farting? Who farted?

Ah. Ho! Bussard. What! Hullo, Pigbum. I recognise that fart. I can anatomise it. My man John Bussard fathered that fart. There is a certain yellowness to that fart – a treacle-pudding ease – which I would know in a crowd of vapours. Not a spinsterish fart. A round fart, an amiable fart, a well-meant and fraternal fart, a fart of philanthropy. Smell that unselfishness! God's teeth, a fart like that is practically an act of kindness. The good Samaritan gave off comparable fartings, who can doubt it?

My man John Bussard is a master of farts, a bachelor of farts, a farter of the first odour. Few like him in Norfolk. In the world.

Set it down, Mr Mandrake, certainly. Don't be modest. Worcester's lovely hand no doubt would not write it, could not bring its pale self to chronicle such greasy particulars; but if a man cannot take pleasure in his servants' farts at the end of a long and busy life what is there left for him to speak of on a day when memory is burdensome?

I have been myself, in my time, a considerable farter of farts. I remember the great unequivocating fart which came from me, or which I addressed to the unworthy and no doubt ungrateful population of London, one morning early in my first sojourn in the city. It was on London Bridge. At dawn. Morning came sailing up the Thames like a great white-throated or white-chested galleon to the Pool. Morning was a sweet armada. As a matter of fact, there were ships that day, and it *was* a kind of minor armada. It was Joanna, the Queen of Navarre and her little fleet, coming up to London from Brittany. I saw the flags in the dim distance, and the sun spilled on the Thames like sperm as they drew nearer.

Lord God! What a morning, what a day. I stood, my feet apart, on London Bridge. I took a deep breath, great glorious mouthfuls of the honey air. And the Queen of Navarre flowed through my legs, passed through my loins, streaming, where I stood. And as she went, as her armada left me for the Pool, I farted. Such a fart. A gull fell dead. It was an invocation. It must have been the nappy ale, and the oysters. I recall that fart had somewhat of an air of oysters, a brief reminisce of oyster-eating, about him. Once, I farted. Then twice. Then three times. Like a bugle. Like a trump. Like a clarion to welcome the Queen of Navarre to London. There was some little lady's milliner on the bridge that morning, standing near me, rearwards of me, to windward. He took five paces backwards in the wake of my blast – and dived into the Thames for fear. Sir, I had a fart like Lucifer's best cannon in those days. I could turn and fart an enemy into king-dom-come.

You know, my name is a kind of fart:

FAAAAAAAASTOLFFFFFF.

Bussard – who farted a moment ago and writes these words now at my dictation – is what you'd call a loyal student of the art. The art, I mean, of farting. He eats the right wrong foods, drinks the right wrong drinks, for the proper and manly production of blasts and breezes from the antipodean vent. That is to say, he eats peas and lentils and cucumbers with plenty of sunlight in them, and he drinks barley beer and pomegranate wine when he can get it. Turnips and crayfish help too. Also anchovies.

None of your nice nellies here. If John Bussard feels like a fart, he farts. He doesn't cross his knees or sit on it. I saw a priest attendant on Harry 6 do that once. Sit on a fart. The air came out with such a sweet unwholesome rush, despite him, that he took off three inches and hovered above the bench before plopping down again in pink confusion. A lot of levitation could be caused by farting. Do saints fart though? Yes, praise be, with an odour of violets, Madam.

Another I knew, a lady of the royal chamber, used to carry a little cork with her, which she would insert in her bum-hole when she felt the exhalations coming on. Bending once to retrieve the Queen's thimble, she fired a nearly fatal shot at Archbishop Arundel, hitting him on the mitre where he blessed the King.

Better to let Dame Nature have her way. She'll have it anyhow. To contain or restrain a necessary fart does no good to the bowels, or to the innards, or to the breech. Of course there are occasions when a fart simply will not do. Sir Thomas Erpingham farted at the coronation of King Henry the 4th. 'God save the King!' cried the Archbishop of Canterbury. And before the assembled lords of England could reiterate and augment the sentiment, Erpingham farts like a pea in a drum. There was full three seconds of astonishment while that fart lasted. It was what you might call a stained-glass fart. I mean: not uproarious, but deep and rich and altering the colour of the light. It earned Erpingham a banishment. Bolingbroke was heard to say that that fart interpreted meant Erpingham's support of King Richard. I suppose it represented Richard's imprisonment in the Tower. If Erpingham had kept it in, Richard might have been allowed to stay there. But he let it out.

Fancy rupturing your bum-gut to keep a lady's favour! That's what King James the 1st of Scotland did on his wedding night. Like a fool, he ate a ton of haggis at the wedding feast. Now your haggis, like hedgehogs, is a mighty inspiriter of ventral storms. All night long, at work like a Turk on his bride Jane Beaufort, our Jamie wanted to fart. But he thought that if he did it would lessen his bride's opinion of him, based on that poem of his *The Kingis Quair*, which he had written for her while in prison. So he had to keep his nether peace all night, to pass it in the privacy of the jakes.

Stupid. A really fruity fart would have done no harm. I have known gentle ladies of high degree who loved to hear it. I have been called in to fart farts for a college of them. Once I farted a spectral fart for the Countess of Salisbury which made a jelly change colour and a candle catch fire. She found that arousing in several ways.

These chronicles. My memorials. What are they? *Farts of the mind.*

I heard of a man once who was on a desert island, shipwrecked, without even a glass to remind him that he was himself. He fell back on farting to assure himself of his existence. I fart, therefore I am. His farts were his friends. There's nothing like the sound of another human voice.

Then there's the smell, of course. Armies fart like fury in the field. Agincourt was all farts. Not just the men farted, but the horses and the hounds and the regimental goats farted too. Our archers volleyed farts. The ground farted. The sun — it came up with a fart on St Crispin's Day. And it certainly went down with a belch of satisfaction.

Most of your famous battles can be recalled by true veterans in terms of the specific juicy farts their nostrils noticed. A conqueror farts different to a victim.

The dead don't fart.

The Dolphin of France, Lewis, the son of Charles the 6th of France, he had the stupidest, squeakiest, silliest, most apologetic namby-pamby piss-down-the-back-of-my-breeches fart you ever did hear. And it smelt like a pickled pansy.

Hal, in his prime, on the other hand, had a fart like a pack of elephants. He was an emperor of farts.

Objections to my story of my life are just a fart-long.

My secretaries can be defined in terms of their farting. Bussard farts best. His is a hard and manly fart, short, squat, but equable. It is the fart of a reliable fellow. I say so.

Worcester scarcely farts at all. He smiles and his nostrils quiver delicately and his left eyebrow goes up and a melancholy wist-fulness comes into his eye. You know he wants to fart, but he won't. He would despise himself if a snort escaped him. He has an arse like two priest's fingers pressed prim together. It's a wonder he doesn't shit little silver rings, when you come to think of it. He has too much sensibility for farting, my over-educated secretary William Worcester.

My stepson Stephen Scrope is a mean little farter. He'll go and stick his bum in the arras and let it off there. Oval farts. Mere scrupulous fetterings of wind. Posterior comments. Like talking behind your hand. As though that made him a gentleman. If he could get interest on them, no doubt he would save his farts in a bag and deposit them in a fart-bank.

Hanson and Nanton fart in duet. They're a pretty pair, those two shit-the-bed scoundrels, and many an amusing tune and descant they provide us. They had this competition once to see who could fart the highest. Nanton won. Though some of Hanson's farts were like birdcalls. There was one in particular. I can hear and smell it still. Like a nightingale with the toothache.

I had a man in France, Peter Basset, who could put the fear of God in the enemy just by turning and giving them a flash of his mighty arse. He had a fart like a roar of cannons. Once, on the wall above Orleans, he repulsed a party of Joan the Puzzle's commandoes by letting down his trousers and giving them a percussion of fartings as they ascended. French soldiers always run away well – but I've never seen any run faster than that lot. They thought it was a new secret weapon, or the voice of the Devil. Basset killed a man in single combat once, in sight of both armies. He didn't do it absolutely by farting at him, but I promise you that the peculiar and pervasive stink of attack which he did preserve from start to finish helped his victory no end.

Friar Brackley farts in the confessional. 'Bless me, father,' you say – and he farts once through the grille. 'For I have sinned,' you add, following the usual formula. He farts again. A highly disapproving and ecclesiastical fart. A lenten offering. There are certain sins, too, I have noticed, which bring him out in little farts and belches. Whether this is a sign of his anguish in the face of human nature revealed, I could not say. It is not exactly pleasant, sharing the smell of your sins with the smell of your confessor's farting as he listens. There is altogether too much human nature involved in that, you might think. Though for myself, as a principle, I could never get enough of human nature.

Bussard writes this. Bussard has stopped farting now. Good boy, Bussard. You thing!

Of all my secretaries, this John Bussard is the one to whom I can say things which otherwise I would reserve for my own hand's writing. He never blushes, my clerk Bussard, and he never turns pale. For this his reward in heaven will be a suit with flies.

Is there farting in heaven? Since heaven is our earthly bliss prolonged, but even more so, then I think there must be. For farting can be bliss. Heaven may be one long perfect fart stretched out to meet eternity. Angels may fart. (I hope that's not heretical.)

On earth, anyway, John Bussard's reward is to hear my more *peculiar* adventures direct. I can dictate *anything* to him and he writes it down. He is a bloody fool. There, I told you, he wrote that without batting an eyelid, and without asking me if he *was* to set it down, – which is Wm Worcester's doubtful trick, he's forever wanting to know shouldn't he leave that out or modify or censor this.

God looks after those who fart well. God stands up for honest farters. Bussard is my secretary and a man after my own fart.

Bless you. Bum. Balls. *Petrum! Partrum!* There he goes again.

Quick, catch it. Draw it. Write it down. Describe it. Analyse and transpose and explicate and evaluate it. It started high and finished low. Like this:

Now, if Worcester farted, it would be more like this:

Very neat and erudite, translated from the Latin don't you know. Holy Mary, Worcester farts in Latin and his breeches have to English it for our understanding.

Then Scrope, my stepson, thus:

ᵛ ᵛ ᵛ ∧ ∧ ∧ ᵛ ᵛ ᵛ

(He'd be trying to save them to sell later, the mean little bleeder.)

Hanson and Nanton would fart extra-special emasculated nightingale duets, as I've said already. That would look like this maybe:

And Friar Brackley, so:

As for John Fastolf, his fart, I will make the mark myself. Thus and thus, at a modest estimate:

That's enough for today, and enough for now on the art of farting. It is a subject to which I shall return, for my knowledge of it, and my management of the niceties of theory and performance, play no small part in the story of my success.

XXIII

*About King Brokenanus & his 24 sainted
sons & daughters*

I am criticised. I am attacked. I am told that the tone and tenour
and general temperature of these memorials is too low. I am
advised that a man of my age should set his mind on higher
things. In other words, Mr Secretary Worcester doesn't like his
master's truth-telling about fucks and farts and what we had for
dinner. For the benefit of the same Worcester, then – a moral
tale.

There was once upon a time in the darkest part of Wales a man
who was a petty king in rank. (In those days, in those regions,
they were two a penny.) His name was Brokenanus – from which
we have the Welsh province called Breakneck, there to this day.

Now this Brokenanus was married to a lady called Goneril, or
as some say it, Gladys. Queen Goneril was a reluctant bride. On
the first night of their married life, she denied her husband access
to the marriage bed.

'Sorry, dear,' she said. 'I have my period.'

The second night, the worthy Brokenanus looms up bedwards
with hope in his heart, but Queen Goneril says:

'Sorry, dear. I seem to be suffering from piles.'

On the third night, a similar sad encounter:

'My darling monarch, pray forgive me. I can't stop pissing.'

Wait. Wait, Worcester. The best is yet to be. On the fourth
and final night, yes, our King presented himself to his lady wearing woolly Welsh skins, gallygaskins, and big sewer boots, and
bearing in his fist a flaming torch.

Says his Welsh majesty: 'Mud or blood, shit or flood,
Brokenanus rides tonight!'

Wait. Wait, Worcester. The truth. The moral tale. I'm coming to it. Part of the point is how high we can rise from such low beginnings. Dung and angels are not so far apart. Only the indefinite article separates the BEAST from the BEST. It's *your* philosophy that's at fault, my friend. Hang on. Don't chew your pen. Unknot your eyebrows. Morality. I mean it. You earnest bloody bugger. Listen.

From such inauspicious nuptials she grew into a lively piece, Queen Goneril, not at all reluctant, you'll be sad to know, and our moral monarch feared that getting embedded in carnal attentions to her would deflect or distract him from that proper service which a man should give solely unto the Lord his God. So what did pious anxious Brokenanus of the Sewer Boots do? He did what many a sensible sinner's done before and since. He buggered off to Ireland.

King Brokenanus stayed in Ireland for 24 years. He was extraordinarily busy in good works. He planted lots of Irish apricots and avoided druids. He did not drink or laugh. He spent all his spare time studying the three tragic stories of the Irish – that is, the death of the children of Touran, the death of the children of Lir, and the death of the children of Usnach. As for the Blarney Stone, he never even took off his hat in the vicinity of it.

At the end of the 24 years, Brokenanus felt a wish to return to Wales (what a country! leeks and rain and wizards! God knows why); so, anyway, back he travels and finds his wife still alive, and eager to start kicking.

Brokenanus found, in other words, Worcester, that Goneril was as lively as ever, if not livelier, and that he didn't need to worry about his boots. In fact, so full of life was Goneril, that they set to and before he could come up for air King Brokenanus had fathered 24 children on her, pop pop pop moral married respectable monagamous pop. The names of these 24 sons and daughters of King Brokenanus and Queen Goneril were as follows:

Nectar	Yes
John	Morwenna
Suddenly	Wineup
Manfred	Whenhead
Delight	Cider
Teddy	Kerry
Maybe	Jonah

Whensew	Hellyou
Whensent	Lanark
Marwenna	Colander
Cenna	Adventhell
Juliana	Tantalise

All these same sons and daughters were afterwards and eventually saints and martyrs or confessors, leading the life of hermits in Devon or Cornwall, for some reason I have never heard explained. The blessed Nectar was the firstborn, and so was greater than all the rest in the honour of his life, and showed himself more outstanding in the brilliance and ingenuity and extent of his miracles. Of him for instance I can tell you for a fact that he once turned a white loaf black by mildly excommunicating it, and then by absolution he turned it white again. Bully heigh ho and moral hurrah for Nectar. *Benedicite!* Set it down big, pig. Don't miss a word, turd.

When Queen Goneril of Wales had given birth to the two dozen saints, martyrs and confessors (though they attained this status only in Cornwall, note, where it hardly counts, for temptations there are few), then our wise Brokenanus speechified and said:

'Lo, now I see the power of God which no man may resist. Lo, now I know predestination's true – that act of foreordaining by which from eternity God decrees whatever he will do in time. For, behold, he has punished me with offspring to the very tune of my dancing against him. Yea, he has punished in me what I in vain disposed against the intention of his will. For I buggered off unlawfully from my wife to Ireland for 24 years, lest I should have issue, and now he has given me for every year of that unlawful continence a child. And not just a child. O the laughter of God is endless. A saint. Every one a bloody saint. O bugger bugger bugger bugger.'

And I believe he actually said bugger 24 times if you want to know, according to the historian Nennius and my tutor Ravenstone.

Worcester, sir secretary, I tell you this story to show there is no escape from the pattern which God makes for us. More particularly, no escape from the pattern which is made for *you*. If God had meant you to have more money he would have made you a priest. I rather wish you were a priest. You would be no less use to me, and I could put some benefits your way. But no matter. Be content.

Shut your mouth, ape. Set down this:

The firstborn, the venerable Nectar, seeking through certain forest wastes appertaining to the land of his fathers –

Certain Welsh waste lands, I say, desert places, Celtic bogs, fairy lands, was attacked by robbers in the spot which to the present day is called New Town, where a church is built in his honour, Nectar's, and there on the 17th day of June anno Domini something or other, St Alban's feast day if you say so, his blessed holy half-wit head was cut off, Worcester, and taking his head, this intellectual item, in his own hands, the same Nectar steadily carried it for the space of half a furlong to a well by which he stopped, and there he set it, rimmed round with bloody sweat, on a stone.

Pay attention. You moral bugger, Worcester, you, I tell you there are permanent traces yet. Indelible traces of blood from this death and miracle remain on the stone to our day, now. Nectar's signature.

You believe me?

You don't believe me!

Right, Mr Morality. Away, Mr Earnestness. To New Town. On this day, 22nd April, the year of the Word made Flesh 1459, Sir John Fastolf, militis, directs his secretary William Worcester, alias Botoner, to journey to New Town, in darkest fairy Wales, to see for himself the truth of the signature of St Nectar's blood in the stone of the holy well there.

Why? *Why?* You fausty infidel. You scrupulous figgy sceptic. Doubting Botoner. To teach you God's disposition! What else? To advise you, like King Brokenanus, that *there is no escape from the mind of your creator.* I create you. You are my man. Go. I write you out of my book. You're gone. You're nothing. Tomorrow I may say that you never were. Tomorrow I may say, 'Worcester – who's he? Never heard of him.'

Have a nice wild goose chase, Conscience.

Goodbye, Morality.

XXIV

About St George's Day & flagellants & the earthly paradise

I want to make it quite clear why I have packed off my secretary William Worcester to Wales to see for himself the truth of St Nectar's bloody head.

I sent him about that stupid itinerary to witness not just to Nectar's head, but to mine. Fastolf's brain and being. Fastolf's will. The reader has seen and heard him go. By his absence we are true, being diminished. Nothing proves a thing better than less of it. Now we are six of us here in Caister Castle – my stepson Scrope, Hanson, Nanton, farter Bussard, and Fr Brackley. Not forgetting their author and yours: myself. In a minute – I mean, tomorrow – I shall resume these *Acta* of my days. By sending Worcester as it were out of the room, and by allowing the reader to see him go, I have imparted to my deliberations that air of reality, of precise and immediate verisimilitude, so necessary to belief.

Reader, my Guest, if you did not notice this at the time, I shall take your word for it that you do now.

Stephen Scrope has not written here yet, my stepson. Scrope is an oaf with a well-knit brow and hanging ears. He has a chip on his shoulder because I sold him once. He has translated for me two volumes – the *Dictes and Sayings of the Philosophers* and the works of the delicious Christine of Pisan. As a translator he is no traitor. None of your Gowers in my employ, N. B. Scrope is a most reluctant amanuensis, all the same. I promise you him tomorrow or the next day. I compel these scribes to my service. I am the voice, the tongue, they the hands that take down the waggings. Today I have Hanson at my disposal, assisted by Nanton. I swear that those two boys could not write a sentence without each other. (Madam, they're just good friends.) Two secretaries for the one job. Such extravagance. Let it be said that I am a provincial Maecenas. I am a provincial Maecenas.

Hey didle diddle and hey diddle dan, can it be that we have only inhabited this castle for five years? But then it was a long while in the making, and cost a pretty packet to get right. All the same, here we are, Fastolf and Co., with my tapestries and my books, my rent-rolls and my diamonds, my ruby worth more than any jewel outside King Harry's crown (which doesn't fit his pea-sized head), my cellars full of sack, and my boxes full of paper. Paper, paper, reams and quires and whazereys of it, lovely paper. One thing I will say for W. Worcester now he isn't here: he writes a fair hand. And no shit on the page where he's had to take his finger out. Not like some. Nanton, control yourself.

Today, lewd readers, is St George's Day. The 23rd April, the day of St George, our English patron, who slew the lurid dragon.

Well, fig it, perhaps not.

About St George.

Enemies of England tell his story this way. Hanson, the Cappadocian version.

George was born in a fuller's shop in Epiphania, in Sicily. He wangled this contract for supplying the Army with bacon and made a mint of money slicing rashers down the middle to double his profits. Of course the day came when he had to fly the country. He graduated in exile, from pork-butchery to Arianism, and in this new vocation so excelled his competitors that Constantius sent him to take over from Athanasius as Archbishop of Alexandria. (Athanasius himself was far too orthodox for the Church of that time, and holy too – they say that as a boy he used to baptise his playmates.) As an Archbishop, our George proved a marvellous tax-collector and a keen plunderer of pagan temples. Some of the Alexandrines complained, but George had the Army on his side. His downfall came with the accession of Julian, who had no room even for halfway Christians. George was thrown into prison and kept there for 24 days – just as long as it took the local tax-payers to beat the doors down. George's throat was cut with a pair of scissors, and some wit doubled him by doing to his corpse what George used to do to the rashers in his grocer days. All the remains were then thrown into the sea. Of course, these events made George a martyr in the eyes of the Arians. He was canonised by the Arian party as soon as it had the money and the ear of the Congregation of Rites. Miracles associated with his name during the Crusades must have helped his cause. He poked a Saracen or two for Godfrey of Bouillon at the Battle of Antioch. He appeared in white armour to Richard Lionheart before Acre and cheered him up with the news that the day was pre-destinatedly ours. From then on, George was an Englishman.

That is one version. The French believe it. They like to make us out a nation of grocers.

Here is the truth. Nanton!

George was born of generations of noble Christians, and not in Cappadocia at all. He enlisted in the Army and rose to a high rank. He did not kill a dragon, that I grant you, if by dragon you mean one of those monstrous snakes, *dracontes* to the Greeks, which used to lurk in the Alps and come swoughing down the sky every now and then to eat diamonds and belch fire. As I say, it depends what you mean by dragons. The Devil, St Augustine tells us, *leo et draco est; leo propter impetum, draco propter insidias.* George certainly resisted the persecution of Christians which was all the rage under the Emperor Diocletian, who invented far-things. George went so far as to resign his commission and to mention the Emperor in the same breath as a wild boar. (Dio-cletian had been elected Emperor by the troops at Chalcedon, after killing with his own hands one Harry Aper, prefect of the praetorians, and thus fulfilling a prophecy of some French witch that he would mount the throne as soon as he had slain a wild boar – *aper*. Like most superstitious successes, he didn't care to be reminded of this incident in his career.) Anyway, Diocletian cut off George's head, and George was sainted for it, by Pope Gelasius. Gregory of Tours says that the saint's relics were once in the French village of Le Maine. They're not there now. I know. I went to look. My uncle Hugh never claimed to have even a rasher of him either.

Make what you like of the stories, but I'll tell you one thing. George is as English as John Fastolf, and they don't come any more English than that. Some of your Latin and Greek churches have other saints sharing this 23rd of April with him, but in England there has never been a rival saint in sight. I have even heard that the real St George was *born* in England, and was actually the son of Lord Albert of Coventry, a lad with three strange marks on his body – a dragon on his chest, a garter round one of his legs, and a blood-red cross on his arm. I can tell you for a fact that King Arthur had St George's picture on his banners, that his day has been a holiday in England since the Council of Oxford commanded it in the year 12 something or other, and that in the year 13 something, the Feast of St George was further and very properly glorified by the creation of the Order of St George, or the Blue Garter. That day, 40 English knights met 40 knights from France and Burgundy, from Brabant, Hainault, Flanders, and Germany – and I don't need to tell you which 40 won. The first year of Hal's reign, and one of the best things he did – he made St George's Day a double feast. I used to light bonfires in France to keep it, or at the very least I'd polish Bardolph's nose in honour of the occasion.

Hal at Harfleur. Harry le Roy – which Pistol thought must be a Cornish name. '*God for Harry! England! And Saint George!*'

So much for villainous grocers.

As for dragons. St Romanus killed one at Rouen, by persuading it to chase a girl into an oven. This was the dragon Gargouille. St Martha killed a dragon by the name of Tarasque on the River Rhone. St Martial killed the dragon of the Garonne at Bordeaux. I've seen the head of St Martha's dragon – it's at Aix. I admit that the dragons at Marseilles and Lyons are stuffed alligators. But the dragon of Rhodes is not. That was killed by Dieudonne, of Gozo, less than a hundred years ago. Some say its head reminds them of a hippopotamus. It reminds me of a dragon.

I too, Johannes Fastolf, have been something of a slayer of dragons in my time. This will come out. Truth does.

What I am bringing to your notice by this celebration of the date is the passage of days since the start of our chronicles. We began on New Year's Day, which is to say the 25th March. Since then I have devoted part of every one of 23 days to memory, to recollection, to exemption from oblivion, commemoration, history, revisitings of my life and other hazards.

But wait, cries the mathematical reader. 23 days commencing on the 25 March does not bring us to the 23rd day of April. The fat knight lies. St George is not yet on us. The dragon goes unslain. His calendar is drunk.

Not at all, little counters of numbers. This is my Hundred Days War, yes, but in setting forth to wage it I never gave you any undertaking that I would fight every day and the days one after another, did I? I undertook only to tell my life and the truth for 100 days. That I am doing. But the most religious and foolhardy champion has to rest from his glories now and then. There

were dog days – look back or think back and you will find them –
it is easy enough – when I was busy with my niece Miranda, or
with Desdemona my rat, or with brandy, or canaries, or other
marvellous searching wines or affairs of state, and had no time for
literary labours.

So then, we are arrived, by happy chance, for our 24th Day, on
the 23rd day of April, St George's very own, and mine, and
England's – for no man lives more English than myself. St
George's Day is not a day for skipping about in the Inns of Court
some sixty dusty years ago. That can keep. Set down Sir John
Fastolf's spending of St George's Day 1459. *Now*, today, this
minute.

I woke and played with my rodent, Desdemona. First I
stripped off the bedclothes. Then I shaved. Then I rubbed some
particles of parmisan cheese between my toes. It is my pet's
delight to take her breakfast daintily from between them, and her
side-bites and nibbles save me valuable time that would otherwise
be wasted in cutting my toenails. O Desdemona, Desdemona. She
runs down my right flank and up my left. I have trained her
thoroughly. She has a remarkably witty whippy tail and eyes like
intelligent bonfires.

The long rat's friskings put me in a good mood for my breakfast. I took Palm sack for it. There's nothing like Palm sack for
putting marrow in a man's bones, and bone in his marrow.

I put on my blue coat which I always wear on this day, once a
year.

After breakfast, I took my exercise – which is to say I worked
for an hour and a half with Nanton here on my great Bill of
Claims against the Government. We have computed that King
Harry the holy 6 owes me just over £10,000 (ten thousand
pounds). When by certain extra remembrances of fact and injec-
tions of honest imagination we get it up to eleven thousand
round, I will despatch this bill to London, putting a fair copy of it
in these annals for safe-keeping. My Bill of Claims is nothing less
than a full and true account of all regal robberies done against my
person and from my estate in France, in the late lamented wars. I
will forgive the robbings of the present King's father, when he
was my son. More of that another day.

Having taken my exercise and warmed my wits a while with
Madeira sack, I grew peckish. I ate a titbit of herrings from
Macbeth the cook. They were not well smoked. I suspect his

motives with my herrings. I gave Macbeth a bollocking. This lent me more hunger, so I munched the froth off a flagon of stout before dinner.

For that meal I had burnt brandy and Friar Brackley instructing me anew in the mysteries of the sect of the Flagellants. I have heard this stuff before, but it's good stirring stuff, and doesn't stale with the repeating, or give you hiccups, and today of all days I wanted him to tell me it again.

This sect first sprang up in Italy about 200 years ago. Affected with the fear of God, noble and ignoble Romans, young and old alike, even children and philosophers, would go naked through the streets, walking in public, two by two, in the style of a procession. Every one of them held in his hand a sweet sharp scourge of leather thongs, a *flagellum*. With eager groans they lashed themselves, all the while weeping great gouts of tears as if spectators at the passion of our Lord, imploring the forgiveness of God and his Mother, praying that he, appeased by the repentance of so many sinners, would not disdain imperfect theirs. In the vast dead of night also, hundreds – thousands – no, ten thousands of these penitents ran, notwithstanding the gnaw of winter, and frostbite in their naked toes, about the streets, and into churches, lit wax candles in their hands, brokenly prostrating themselves before altars, and whipping each other merrily, miserably, with yelps. The original author of these solemn processions of the Flagellants was St Vincent Ferrer.

In the year of the Only Begotten 13-something – can't remember the exact year but it was about the time that spectacles came in, and that always fashionable Cardinal Ugone started wearing them – about the time when the plague was taking Germany, then, the Flagellants started up in that country too, with great success. The Germans danced in circles drawn in dust. (Germans will do *any*thing.) They stripped, the Huns, leaving on their bodies only a breech-cloth. Plenty of warm flesh free and firm for whipping. Each little whipper addressed his neighbour with a scourge, the scourge in the German case having knots and four iron points for luck, and the whole whipping being punctuated with the singing of Teuton-type psalms. At a signal, they would cease, and then lie throbbing and sobbing while their leader seminally sermonised, exhorting them to implore God's mercy on souls in purgatory, not to speak of themselves.

Whippers carried purple banners to advertise their enthusiasm.

When clothed they wore grim garments with red crosses on the breast, back, and cap. Wherever they went they were welcomed by bells. Bells meant good sport. Bells meant the whippers were coming.

They had a good run for their money, but at length Pope Clement VI issued a bull against them. The sect died out. But it started up again unlawfully some 50 years ago, led by a man called Conrad, who claimed he was really the prophet Enoch. This Conrad taught that the Flagellants being established, God had no further need of the Papacy. This Conrad taught also that there was no salvation save by means of a new baptism of blood through the instrumentality of the whip. The Inquisition took action against him. There was a grand inquiry into Mr Conrad, and 91 of his disciples were burned at Sangerhusen.

Pippin tarts and sherry sack for pudding.

In the afternoon I walked in my orchards in the April air and spoke with Friar Brackley concerning the earthly Paradise. I asked him three questions. To wit. –

1. Is there any such place?
2. If there is, where is it?
3. If there is, and where it is can be known, what's it like?

Fr Brackley answered the first question by saying that we have four witnesses that Paradise is in earth. First, stories that liken Sodom and Gomorrah, before they were overturned, to Paradise. I like the sound of these. Second, travellers who have said that they have been there. Third, those who have reported on its geography – e.g. the four rivers that run out of it. And – but I forget the fourth.

Ha, yes. Basilius, in his *Hexameron*, also Isidorus, *Eth. lib. quarto decimo*, and Josephus, in his first book, say that waters falling from the hill of Paradise constitute a great pond, and out of that pond – as from a well – the four rivers spring. . . .

No, – more brandy, Nanton, I can't think clearly – no, the fourth witness and proof that Paradise is in earth is the ancient fame of the idea of it. People have been talking about Paradise for six thousand years and more. People have been talking about Paradise since the beginning of the world. Fame that is false would not have lasted so long.

Paradise is not a long sailing-journey from earth, neither is it in the moon. If it were in the moon it would sometimes bereave the light and make an eclipse. Besides, God help us, if it were in the moon, in the sky, quite divorced from every land, how could those four rivers pass through the air and flow out in places which, however far-off, are certainly lands that men have lived in?

It being known by experience that in eclipses of the moon, the earth makes a spherical shield, then it follows that the earth, with all her parts and organs, must be round. Rather like a duck's egg. Everything comes to an end, and an egg comes to two. Or none. So wise men conclude that Paradise is at the uttermost end of the East, and that it is a great country of the earth no less than Ind or Egypt.

Those wise men must be mad.

We would live there still, if we had not sinned. (That's a different point. And I believe it.)

To my third question, my father confessor told me that Isidore has it, *libro quarto decimo, capitulo tertio*, (and thank God for Harry le Roy and plain English), – that this name Paradise turned out of Greek into Latin signifies *an orchard*. Yet Paradise in the Hebrew is called *Eden*, which word means *liking*.

So: Paradise is *an orchard of liking*.

No wonder, I reckon, for in that place is everything that says yes to life. There is health, for the air is in temper not too hot nor too cold, so that nothing that lives can die in it.

As John Damascene says, that place has mirth and fair weather, apples and laughter, for it is the fount of all fairness.

No tree there loses its leaves.

No flowers there wither, or are blasted by the sun, or soured by the moon.

Of paradisal fruit and trees it is written, says Fr B., in Genesis, *secundo capitulo*, that every one is sweet to eat and fair to see.

(Just look what one of them taught us. How to Fall.)

((And I am Fall stuff.))

Petrus assures us that the waters of the Flood were not permitted to reach Paradise.

Yes, double brackets.

And Isidore again – *libro nono, capitulo primo* – reminds us that our way to Paradise is fast stopped in this life by cause of the sin of our former father. (Yet every beat of my heart is another stride nearer.)

This evening I toy again with my ratkin, and drink burnt brandy. There is news tonight that the Yorkists have put down

Queen Margaret at Bloreheath, and the civil wars are on us again. Whether this news is true I have no way of knowing.

It's late. Hanson nods. Nanton scratches himself. The country's going to the dogs. You can't get secretaries without fleas anywhere.

St George save England!

(He'll bloody need to.)

XXV

How Sir John Fastolf broke Skogan's head

And this is where the story really begins. I'm standing on the edge of London and my life. I am an apologue, a vision, an ode, a call to devotion. I am a master of the art of fencing. I wear my codpiece open, and tied at the top with a bunch of ribbons. My sword slaps between my legs like a monkey's tail. My long-waisted doublet is unbuttoned half-way. And what do I have in my pockets? (What a man has in his pockets is always vital to history, and curiously omitted from the history-books. Julius Caesar carried a notebook reminding him of his triumphs. King Herod never went anywhere without his kissing-comfits. Archibald, fourth Earl of Douglas and first Duke of Touraine, that Scotch mercenary who fought for France or England, depending on who would pay him most, always carried his own left eye, knocked out at Homildon Hill by Harry Hotspur.) The Fastolf pockets contain the Fastolf nous. Also a few pounds given to me by my mother, and some I.O.U.'s from my stepfather Farewell, who professed himself well-pleased that I should absent myself from Caister and seek to make my own way in the world's ruin. Thus equipped, and with my hair curled at the back and cut in a fringe across my forehead, I put my young person in the way of friends in London. They were not slow in coming.

Friends are the enemies you're still just getting to know.

Shit me, and some say old age is when it takes all night to do what you used to do all night. In which case, mine is still to come. I ate four figs for Miranda last night. Only three of them worked, admittedly; but she enjoyed the fourth fig too.

One of my familiars was a young gentleman from Gloucestershire, Robert Shallow by name. This Mr Shallow had one important aspect in which he was my superior. He had more ready cash than I had. The Shallows are one of the oldest families in England. You can still turn up their representatives from under any stone. This particular Shallow specimen had, as I say, plenty of money, but no sense. From the beginning, when we met over a Michaelmas goose, I think he longed for nothing more this side of a heavenly mansion than to be my friend. As for me, I counted Farewell's I.O.U.'s, grew tired of drinking dew, and decided that Robert Shallow should indeed enjoy the privilege of my friendship – so long as he paid for it.

He did enjoy it.

He certainly paid for it.

I was as poor as Job. But not so patient.

Shallow was a law student. After a fashion, so was I. I suppose I was still technically Mowbray's squire. But Mowbray had been banished by Richard the 2nd, for quarrelling with Henry Bolingbroke, now Henry the 4th. So I was masterless, and worked independently and for myself.

Shallow, with whom I lodged, was five years my senior. Those five years had not improved him. In appearance he was spotty and failed to fill his breeches. The latter looked always unhooked and ready to drop off. He wore a great pair of spurs – for no particular reason, since he could not ride – and jingled like a Morris dancer everywhere he went. His face bore a great resemblance to a gallows. There was little more of him, mentally speaking, than what I have described. Which is to say that his brains were about the same size and shape and about as much use as his bollocks.

I patronised Shallow. And Shallow was my ape, my mate, my *toady. I swore at him. He swore by me. He never tired of quoting my sayings and boasting of my exploits. Often in the process they became his* sayings, and *his* exploits. We drank in the same taverns. He told me of the law, and I worked out ways to get round it.

Ophelia had sent me a new coat. It was very nice, with fur inside. Out walking one day with my friends, we were stopped in the street by a gang of villains with nothing better to do than hope that a scuffle might bring them a penny or two from our pockets. Now, I had no intention of spoiling my coat in such a fray. Ignoring the insults of our assailants, I walked quickly on until I reached London Bridge, where I leaned and loafed for an hour, watching the water flow, thinking to myself how an oiled feather is more use in easing open a lock than any amount of force.

Some of my friends were critical of this reaction. They thought

I should have bloodied my coat. The common opinion of a band of pages and students did not bother me much – but Shallow always went with the crowd, and I did not intend to lose my access to his purse.

It was at this point – when I was looking for a way of re-establishing my supremacy in Shallow's shallow eyes – that I met Henry Skogan.

There was a tavern near the Pool, which was called The Sleeveless Errand. (This sleeveless should really be written *sleaveless*, by the way, as it comes from *sleave*, which is a ravelled thread, or the raw edge of silk.) Sitting one night there, playing a gentle game of cards, I began to notice the poetical noises of a burly red-barbed fellow, far gone in his cups. His rigmarole was elaborate, and peppered with the names of heathen deities, but it appeared that he was challenging all of us present.

'I am a major poet,' he declared.

Nobody seemed much worried.

'Henry Skogan,' said the major poet. 'Ballads, fatras, fabliaux. You name it, I can do it.'

I was more interested in the Queen of Hearts. But I could sense that some of the other drinkers in the room were becoming irritated by the poet's bullying manner. Every word he uttered seemed to come as though he intended it to spit on us from a great height.

'Rhyme royal,' said Skogan. 'Give me a ghost of a theme and I will toss you off stanzas by the yard – every one correct, with the seven lines of iambic pentameter, rhyming ABABBCC. Where's your Troilus and Cressida now?'

Nobody offered any suggestions as to their whereabouts.

Skogan pulled a greasy scrap of paper from his wallet. 'My genius was once recognised by Chaucer,' he told us, 'who did himself the honour of honouring me. He'd just lost his job as Clerk of the King's Works, of course, and needed my influence to get him a decent pension.'

He thumbed back his red locks and started to read in a voice that sounded like a gong being struck over a sea of treacle:

> *Skogan, that kneelest at the stream's head*
> *Of grace, of all honour, and worthiness!*
> *In the end of which stream I am dull as dead,*
> *Forget –*

'Oh piss off with your poetry!' shouted some little critic.

'It's not my poetry,' hissed Skogan. 'This is Mr Chaucer's poetry.'

'I don't bleeding care if it's Mr Virgil's poetry!' said the critic. 'I came in here for a drink, not for envoys.'

Skogan folded the greasy scrap carefully and replaced it in his wallet. 'I am always glad,' he said in a mournful voice, 'to meet one sensibly tired of this mortal life.'

Then he leapt to his feet, snatched a cudgel from his belt, and threw himself in the general direction of the literary criticism. A messy fight ensued. Tables were turned over, benches smashed, flagons flung at the walls, fingers stamped upon. The critic ended up with a new parting in his hair that seemed to go some way into his skull.

> *Forget in solitary wilderness;*
> *Yet, Skogan. . . .*

The victorious poet, seated in a pool of blood and wine, had retrieved from his wallet the envoy addressed to him by Chaucer, and was obviously intent on reading the rest of it to the clients of The Sleeveless Errand. What was worse, nobody now dared to interrupt him. I could not concentrate upon my hand of cards. I slipped out of the tavern and made my way home. A pity. I'd had three queens.

That night I dreamed of a golden opportunity. In amongst his general thrasonical rantings and ravings concerning his own merits, Skogan had promised the company that tomorrow the world would know how good his verses were – when he read aloud at the court gate some poem which he had written in honour of the birthday of Thomas, Duke of Clarence. Here was my chance. A chance not to be missed. At the court gate, with the four princes of the blood royal in procession to the tilt-yard, this Skogan would make his poet's noise. All my friends would be there, as well as others with more money and influence. All London would be there.

Now, in the brawl with the critic I had noticed an abundance of defects in Henry Skogan's technique with the cudgel. He might do his ABABBCC's all right when it came to rhyme royal, but when it came to the ABC's of fighting he had not been to school to as good a master as I had. My uncle Hugh, before the passion for relics overcame him, had taught me a thing or two at the quintain. And I knew from my experience at the Battle of Slugs that when my blood was up I could fight like a demon.

I said my prayers to St Swithin and to the blessed St Boniface that night that Henry Skogan would not be too hung over to put in an appearance as he had promised.

The birthday of Thomas, Duke of Clarence, dawned fair, as a prince's birthday should. I put on my fur-lined coat and went early to the court gate. Robert Shallow was already there, simpering in company with the little gang of my erstwhile friends, now affecting to despise me because of what they were pleased to call my cowardice. Coward! Me – fisty Fastolf! I'd show them!

On the stroke of Phoebus's whatever-it-is (that poets are always on about), Skogan loomed up all red and arrogant and full of spondees. He had a wad of celebrations in his hand. He scattered rhymes and morals as he walked. Insincerity oozed from every pore. Or, rather, a most sincere devotion to his own magnificence and a deep conviction of the worthlessness of everything else except in so far as it could be translated into his verse and swallowed up to his greater glory. He gesticulated with his hands and arms and bushy eyebrows. He bullied. He poeticised. I suppose he looked a scraping cleaner in his person, but not so much that you'd really have noticed.

For a strophe or two, I let the people listen to Skogan's jabber, gabble, gibberish, and rhapsodies. Then I sauntered over to see my friends. They received me distantly. Even Shallow. Though Shallow being always an invincible yes-man I should not say 'even'. He dared not stand apart from a majority.

'Gentlemen,' I said, playing with the hilt of my sword in the approved manner, 'you will all be acquainted with the story of the blacksmith who, very near to death, confessed his sins to a priest, and added that he did not wish to forgive his enemies. The priest said to him, "If you don't do that, you'll go to hell for certain." "Is that so?" said the blacksmith. "Well, in that case you can cut out the Extreme Unction – I'd prefer it if the Devil ate me up raw, as I am, without any oil or salt." '

Shallow smirked. The others shifted their feet uneasily.

I went on: 'You see before you one equally impenitent. I have not the slightest intention of forgiving any of you for the doubts you have entertained concerning my courage. And as for being eaten raw by the Devil – I'm about to risk that, and make liars of the lot of you, by picking a fight with this Skogan.'

'He'll anagrammatise you!' gasped Shallow, prompted of course to the witticism by someone right behind him, whose muttered remark he managed to overhear and then blurt out in that bleating voice of his, like a sheep with the colic.

I waved my hand, stroking the feather that trailed from my hat like a fox's brush. 'If one of you could be obsequious enough to ask him to read his verses,' I invited, 'I will pick holes in them.'

They grinned, and bit their lips, and shuffled. One of them – it was, I remember, Mr John Doit, another low law student, out of Staffordshire, where the cups come from – took three hesitating steps forward, and in a cringing fashion begged the poet the favour of reciting his poem for us as a kind of rehearsal.

Such as Henry Skogan don't need asking twice. He poked his fingers in his fiery hair, tugged it out in a couple of points like a bull's horns, and commenced –

Caesarian Clarence, son of Henry 4. . . .

'Poeticule,' I said.

'What!' roared Skogan, looking round.

'Tell me, little poeticule,' I said, 'what it signifies, this hard word you have there, *Caesarian*. Do you mean to imply that our fine Prince, Thomas, Duke of Clarence, has some of the attributes of Caesar?'

Skogan's eyes rolled furiously, but there came a growl of what I took to be assent.

'Well,' I said, 'your lack of a classical education is showing. The word you have there, *Caesarian*, from the Latin, *caeso*, to cut from the womb, must mean some libel such as your thinking that the Duke of Clarence was extracted prematurely from the womb of Mary de Bohun in something other than the normal manner.'

'Who is this cacodemon?' demanded Skogan, gnawing at his own poetical parchments in his fury.

'Jack Fastolf,' I said, with a little nod of the head.

'And are you a poet, Mr Fastolf?' sneered Skogan.

'Certainly not,' I said. I shuddered, remembering my mother's experience of poets in Naples. 'Poets I regard as a lowish form of human life,' I said. 'But then you, Mr Skogan, judging from that single line of yours which I have heard, can hardly be reckoned a poet at all. That is why I addressed you as a *poeticule*, didn't you notice?'

Skogan's face was now as purple as a Flagellant's banner.

'I'll Caesarian you!' he shouted.

I slipped off the precious coat that had been Ophelia's gift to me. 'In which sense?' I enquired politely. 'Yours? Or the real one?'

Cudgel in fist, Skogan flung himself towards me in just the impetuous burly manner I had seen him employ the night before in The Sleeveless Errand. I stood aside, and allowed him to knock Robert Shallow into the arms of a grateful crone. The crowd began to dare to laugh.

'Your doggerel line embodies another lie,' I said, as the poet lumbered to his feet. 'The Duke of Clarence is of course second in line to the throne.'

Skogan paused, head down, shaking it. 'I know that,' he blustered. 'What did I say that denied it?'

'Well,' I said, 'my tutor Ravenstone instructed me that Homer and Virgil and the other true poets regarded precision of language as of the essence of poem-making.'

'Clarence is second in line! I didn't question it!'

'But you said "son of Henry 4",' I said. 'And that *could* mean, fourth son of King Henry.'

'The fellow's an idiot!' thundered Skogan. 'A suicidal idiot!' And he charged again – missed again – and went head-over-heels into the now applauding crowd.

'Ladies and gentlemen,' I said to the crone, and Shallow, and Doit, and the rest of them, 'it appears that our Mr Skogan, while now seeing double, is still capable of missing any irony going.'

Then cudgel work commenced in earnest. I let him come in close, and take a whack at me. But I had learned from Uncle Hugh to dodge and weave. I had learned also an interesting technique of fighting in which you make any fight your own fight by moving *away* from your opponent all the time. You make yourself absent, truant, fugitive. You leave all the decisions – save the final decision – to your adversary. Of course, to achieve this, you need an excellently accurate cudgel with which to answer back. If you do it right, your own answers get more and more unanswerable.

I did not just fight Henry Skogan. I entered elusively into a conversation of cudgels with him.

An unmoved mover, I was going round and round and round him like a minute hand circling the dot in the middle of a clock. Each time round, at a predetermined spot, I hit him. I woke up a bruise as red as his hair, extending his foxy eyebrows. Then the bruise was all blood.

Such conversations with the cudgels must be terminated when the principal fighter decides he has heard enough. I had heard enough when I saw Skogan's blood flow. Still on the run, soliloquising a little, thinking aloud with my stick, I thought hard and fast and hit the rotten poet twice.

Skogan's skull rang like a goblet.

His cudgelling arm fell flabby at his side.

He put his left hand up to his eyebrows and brought one of them half away with it, covered in blood.

He tried a smile. It wouldn't fit. He fell on his back with a thump.

I don't mean to suggest that I am a magician – or that my uncle Hugh taught me some kind of necromancy regarding fighting in that Caister barnyard. He taught me the rudiments of an art. When it comes to cudgels, I am an artist. And like all true artists I am quite naturally inspired by my material, at one with it even while remaining cool and separate and distinct. I had watched Skogan at work in The Sleeveless Errand. I had goaded him deliberately and crudely at the court gate. I made him shout and bluster and lose his temper, and then I listened, and then I answered.

As a warrior, if I have a secret it is that I am so obliging. I give each fighter that I meet just what that fighter wants: defeat. The nature of the defeat is of course as various as there are men needing it. But the secret of my success is simple – I hand my opponents themselves on a plate. They can never resist it.

And there's another secret within the secret. I'll tell you.

It's not exactly cowardice, I think. But it is an art of something almost the opposite of the fighting which I have done so well, and all my life.

I, John Fastolf, have made an art of not liking fighting.

If Robert Shallow and John Doit and the others had been paying close attention, instead of cheering their heads off in praise of the man who a few minutes before they had considered a failure – if they had been *really looking*, I say, Sir, they might have noticed what nobody ever noticed in my long career as a warrior, save Hal, and he misunderstood it. . . .

They might have noticed a look of outright horror and distaste on my face as I had to finish that poeticule off, and break Henry Skogan's head at the court gate.

Yes, Madam. John Fastolf does not care for blood.

XXVI

A parallel adventure: Mr Robert Shallow v. Mr Sampson Stockfish

St Mark's Day

(Hemp-seed I sow,
Hemp-seed grow;
He that is my true love,
Come after me and mow.
– Miranda was in the orchard last night, St Mark's Eve, practising the usual divination according to this formula, and scattering hemp-seed over her shoulder. The figure of your future husband is supposed to appear, with a scythe, mowing behind you. She saw nothing.)

When Robert Shallow saw how I had broken Skogan's head, he wept. I will not say that he wept like Heraclitus, since Heraclitus wept because he grieved at the folly of man in general, whereas Shallow was always concerned only with his own folly in particular. (I never cared for Heraclitus anyway. Give me a laughing philosopher, not one whose tears turn into metaphysics. Up Democritus!)

Shallow wept, then, shallowly. I saw at least four tears ooze from his right eye, proving that his mother – whatever else she was – could not have been a witch. His tears were one part rapture, three parts rupture.

'O hyssop and Hyperion!' he spluttered. 'There never were such times! Prometheus had nothing on it. Cradock Briefbras was a flop compared with this. Lancelot, Orlando, Amadis de Gaule, my uncle Horsecock –'

'Your uncle Horsecock?' I said, interested. 'What did he do?'

Shallow blushed, which made his face look like a primrose. 'It wasn't so much what he *did*, as what he had. He fell to his death from the top of the Tower of London. He saw this girl adjusting her garter in the courtyard, and the sheer weight of his member unbalanced him, you know.' Shallow shook his long head sadly. 'Oh Jack, if only I could have done it!'

'Fallen off the Tower because your cock got so big?'

'No! No! Broken Skogan's head!' cried Shallow. He scrubbed his hands together, and wrung them out. 'You know,' he went on, 'I think I'd give anything in the world to have just one exploit like that to talk of. A doughty deed, a feat, an achievement, a doings, a dolorous blow, a stroke! Something to tell my children of, and my children's children, and my children's children's child –'

At this point a little man with a long brown surcoat and a face like a debauched mole appeared at Shallow's elbow. 'Your prayer has been heard in the right quarter, sir,' he said.

'Come again?' said Shallow.

'Certainly, sir,' said the mole. 'Any time you like, sir. Every time you call, sir. But now, sir, on this particular matter, a soft word in your ear, if you please . . .'

I stroked the beginnings of my beard as Shallow went aside with his new friend into Fetter Lane.

There was a flourish of randy trumpets. The princes were coming. My own admirers flocked about me, chattering, slapping me on the back, refighting my fight in their own words. Like a nest of ninnies. I was half-drowned in apologies. I was buoyed up again on extravagant congratulation. For my part, I confess I was neither gratified nor mortified. I felt as a gentleman does on such occasions. I had fought with coolness and attention – but in reality I had suffered within all the agonies and the thousand little shocks which a keen sensibility must always experience in an encounter with violence, and physical danger, and brute force, and blood, and bad verse. I would have given anything for a glass of sherry sack.

Skogan was carried off on a handcart to have his nob mended with vinegar and brown paper.

The crowd parted. Like the Red Sea at the touch of Moses' rod.

The princes came. This was the first time I had seen them.

You would have noticed Henry anywhere. He had a look like a hawk. No – like an eagle. Lord God! Eagles are a touch fanatical. Brown hair, thick and smooth. Straight nose, long oval face, bright complexion, teeth white as snow and evenly set, ears small and well-shaped, the chin with a noticeable indentation. He was taller than the common sort, with bones and sinews firmly knit together. His back was as straight as a bolt. His jaw was a hatchet. Only when you looked close-up, or when you saw further into him than his appearance, did you notice the less pleasing things. I saw on this first encounter that the heir to the throne of England had a way of pressing his lips together until all the vermilion went out of them.

The second brother, Thomas, Duke of Clarence, was equally handsome, but with not quite such an air about him. No eagle in his eyes. Tall, though, and strong, with clear-cut features. There was something more spontaneous about Thomas, but something obstinate too, as all the world was to see when he married the widow of his uncle, John Beaufort, the Earl of Somerset, and quarrelled with Henry about the money which he had hoped to get by way of a dowry. In my view, the tussles between the two of them were much what anyone expects of brothers, blown out of all proportion by opinion simply because these two brothers happened to be princes. Beaufort this and Beaufort that, one party or the other, first Hal out of favour with his Dad, then Thomas; and Thomas of course favouring an alliance with the Orleanists against the Burgundians. But when it came to the crunch, and it was England or nothing, then this same Thomas, Duke of Clarence, showed his true mettle, and his English heart, soon mopping up the Earl of Cambridge and such traitors, and fighting gloriously at Harfleur. More of that in due course. It was to fall out that my own life grew entangled with the fortunes of Thomas, almost though never quite as much as with those of his brother Henry. The difference is that he was never Tom to me, where Henry was Hal.

The third brother, John, Duke of Bedford, was a surprise. Where Henry and Thomas were plainly made from the same kingly mould, John looked quite different. They were sinewy. He was heavy. They had clear-cut features. He had tiny deep-set eyes and a great arched nose like a beak. He was, like them, a head or more above the common height. He looked as strong as an ox, but not much more resourceful than that animal either. He had what I would call a retreating forehead.

Humphrey, Duke of Gloucester, was the joker in the pack. A pack of four princes, with this youngest one for dissolution's sake. He had remained in England all through his father's banishment, and I think this left a permanent mark on his character, for he never learned to bow to any man's authority. Hal loved him dearly, though, and at Agincourt I saw him stand astride young Humphrey's prostrate body, and rescue the lad after he had been wounded and thrown to the ground by the Duke of Alencon. Later in life, crippled by debt, he married his mistress, Eleanor Cobham, who had a wart on her left buttock. Eleanor is now in prison on the Isle of Man, on account of that wart, which Harry the holy 6th interprets as an outward and visible sign of an interior and invisible necromancy. They made her walk through the streets of London, from Queen's Hive to St Michael's Cornhill, barefoot, wearing a white sheet, and with papers advertising her sins pinned on her back. I hope she sleeps soft on that hard Isle of Man. She is no witch – unless good honest loving is witchcraft, and I the most stiff-necked wizard that ever yet was since the world turned turtle. As for Humphrey, her husband, he died in custody a couple of years ago, the last of the four princes to leave this life. He's buried at St Alban's up the road. Some say he was poisoned. I say he was poisoned by what they did to his Eleanor, and by living on into an England which has no time for heroes any more. He was a great collector of books.

A word to the historian: I give these men *as they looked to me*. You may be able to see them better, I don't doubt it, with the advantage of a few centuries between your pen and their faces. Please note at the same time that I refer to them all by the titles with which they made their mark on history. It would be boring to have to keep adding notes for you to the effect that Humphrey wasn't actually created Duke of Gloucester (and Earl of Pembroke too, if you want to know) until such and such. They were Henry, Thomas, John and Humphrey to me. I throw in their other styles for your convenience. Shallow's Uncle Horsecock was really Mr Hudibras Hors de Kock, of Devonshire.

Stories of the encounter that had lately been all the rage at the court gate must have travelled quickly through the crowd to the King's sons. I was later to learn how efficient Henry's spying service in particular could be. He had minions in any gathering, who would pay heed to the smallest detail and pass it back to him. Either from this source, or through the more popular acclaim, they had heard the news of my sport with Skogan, and his lack of sport with me.

They stopped. The princes.

'King Cudgel, my lords,' cried a wit in the press.

John and Thomas and Humphrey talked among themselves about me. Henry favoured me with a searching stare.

'You put down a poet,' he said. 'Don't you like books?'

I looked at him earnestly. 'Only those that can be read with one hand,' I said.

Prince Henry threw back his head and rocked with laughter. His laugh was something else again. It undid all the fanaticism of his eyes and mouth. It pulled the tail feathers out of that eagle.

His brothers did not laugh. I could see that he would have to explain the joke to them later. Wiping tears of merriment from his eyes, he threw me a coin which I as promptly bit. Then the royal party swept on towards the tilt-yard, with a jackass bray of trumps.

I think I may say that I sensed my own destiny was now in some manner bound up with this eldest son of King Harry the 4th's, but naturally I could not know how. I was concerned to recommend myself further to him, if possible.

The coin was good enough.

When I followed in the wake of the princes, and arrived at the tilt-yard myself, I had to struggle with a great throng of men-at-arms in getting through that narrow gateway. I was swatting busybodys right and left when I felt my sleeve pulled from behind. An eager voice, like a thistle – I mean, it was keen yet shredding itself to bits in its piping over the din – cried out:

'Jack! Wait, Jack! Don't go in yet! I've done it! Look!'

I turned round. It was Shallow. He was skipping about, treading on everyone's feet – which didn't matter so much, since this was at that time when the fashion was for shoes with pointed toes as long as knives. He was almost pink in the face. Having puppies in his breeches with excitement. His nose ran. His wan eyes dripped tallow tears of purest joy.

He dragged a man behind him, by the collar. The collar of a long surcoat of shabby brown. I saw two mole eyes blink and glint, and above them a rough bandage wrapped round the man's head and soaked with blood.

'Like Ogier! Like Robin Hood!' cried Shallow. 'Fought and won, Jack, fought and won! Like Beowulf! Like King Arthur!'

'In short,' I said, 'like Fastolf.'

'Precisely!' screamed my friend.

'Well, well,' I said, looking at the mole.

140

Shallow poked me in Ophelia's coat. 'Mind you say you saw it,' he spluttered. 'Mind you remark on it now.'

'Remarkable indeed,' I said. I wiped my coat.

'Sampson Stockfish,' said Shallow.

'Bless you,' I said.

'But I didn't sneeze,' protested Shallow. 'That's his name. Sampson Stockfish. My opponent. My victim.'

I sniffed at the mole man. 'Does he?' I said. 'Stock fish, that is. His first name certainly suggests unusual strength. The heavy-weight champion of Israel indeed. But is the man a fishmonger?'

'Don't be ridiculous,' said Shallow grumpily. 'He's a fruiterer. I made him come here to show his broken head. I can tell you – I threatened him with another!'

'Does he stock heads too?' I said.

The crowd were making further conversation difficult. Not that I had any great urge to continue this one.

'Let me go, sir,' whined the bloody mole. 'Ain't you done enough damages to my person for one day?'

'Jack! Jack! You heard him?' crowed Shallow. 'You heard him confess?'

I heard him confess. Unfortunately for Robert Shallow, though – who was at that point somewhat whacked on the head by loony old John of Gaunt making his own way to the tilt-yard – I came home along Fetter Lane that afternoon, and saw him still pursued by the mole in the brown surcoat. The mole had the bandage in his pocket, where the sheep's blood on it had made a bit of a mess.

'I'll need a new coat,' I heard him say to Shallow, as I dodged into the doorway of a shop.

'One more silver mark then,' said Shallow. 'And that's your lot.'

'You can stuff your silver mark up your silver arse,' cried the well-known fruiterer. 'I want forty.'

'Forty!' shrieked Shallow.

'That's right,' said the fruiterer. 'Moses was forty days in the mountain. Elijah was forty days fed by ravens. It rained for forty days when the Flood came. And it took forty days before Noah opened the window in the ark.'

'You sound as though you were there at the time,' moaned Shallow.

'Maybe I was,' hissed the mole. 'Shall I tell you some more

forties, my friend? The law gives a man exactly forty days to pay the fine for manslaughter. And it takes no more nor less than forty days to embalm a corpse to a turn. . . .'

'Enough,' said Shallow. 'I'll pay you forty.'

'That's better,' said the mole. 'You owe me for the imagination too, you realise?'

'The imagination!'

'That it was my idea, my plan, my bargain.'

'Yes, but –'

'It's all right,' said the mole. 'There's an account we can leave for a rainy day. Or for forty rainy days. And, don't never forget, if I don't have what I ask, I'll blow the gaff.'

Shallow gave him thirty and an I.O.U.

Shallow went on boasting for years of this epic battle of his with the fearsome Sampson Stockfish. Eventually he came to believe it himself.

XXVII

About swinge-bucklers & bona-robas

26 April

My considerable knowledge of the law was not acquired exactly by reading it as a subject at Clement's Inn. I think I should admit this. My knowledge of most matters in this world has been won in the University of Experience.

All the same, I had many friends among students who *were* reading law. There was John Doit, of Staffordshire, and Black George Barnes, and Francis Pickbone, and Will Squele, a Cotswold man, who was forever belching and remembering something that he had eaten at King Harry the 4th's crowning banquet. These four were interesting swinge-bucklers.

Doit was little. He was clever too, with a fair beard and a short cloak. He liked to swagger on high days and holidays, up and down West Smithfield, swashing and swinging with his buckler, making a great show of fury, but seldom hurting even the flies that buzzed there at noon. Doit had a monkey for his pet.

Black George Barnes was a great hairy fellow. But he had this strange longing deep inside him – he wanted to know what it was like having a baby. He went for advice to Bolus, the apothecary in Duck Lane. Bolus plugged up George's arse with wads of wool, very tight and secure, and then gave him some Angel Pills. These consisted of aloes, chicory, endive, fumitory, damask roses, rhubarb, agaric and cinnamon, and George was instructed to wash them down with a quart of castor oil. He did just as he was told and was lying on his bed in agony, but enjoying every minute of it, telling himself that this was just what his mother had felt, and his mother's mother, and so forth, when Doit's little monkey leaps into bed with him, right at the moment when the wads shoot out of George's bum. George grabs the monkey and kisses it. 'That's my boy!' he says. 'Ugly and covered in shit, but mine, all mine!'

143

Come on, Nanton, don't turn up your nose at what I make you write. Go and knog your urinals! Just because it's not *your* idea of heaven. Every man to his own nonsense. I am a traveller in temperaments, an explorer of human nature. There's a lot of it about.

Bolus that apothecary was also the inventor and sole salesman of the Everlasting Pill, which according to his claims possessed the property of purging as often as it was swallowed. The Duchess of Exeter, John of Gaunt's daughter, she took it and got dreadfully alarmed when it didn't appear to have passed through her anatomy. Back she goes to Bolus. 'Madam,' says he, 'have patience. That very same pill I gave you has passed through half the aristocracy of England.'

A small globule of metallic antimony. The Everlasting Pill.

My swinge-bucklers. Francis Pickbone. Ah, now, Francis, my Frank, he had developed the most foolproof technique for obtaining fish for nothing which it has ever been my pleasure to run across. He would saunter down to Billingsgate and select a pannier of the best, saying that it was for his master, Sir John Clifton, Sir John Norbery, Sir John Oldcastle, or who you will, and that the fish-porter would be paid as usual on delivery. Frank would then accompany the fish-porter up through the city, taking care to pass St Paul's. Once in sight of the cloisters, he would step aside, excusing himself from the fish-porter for a moment, giving some religious reason for his defection. He'd then nip speedily into the nearest confessional, and explain to the priest that he had with enormous difficulty brought his nephew along with him, a miserly miserable lad, far too fond of money, and that he'd like the friar to confess and shrive the fellow with all haste. 'Praise be to God,' says the priest, more or less, and Frank then hurries out, takes the pannier of fish from the porter, and tells him that as it happens his master, Sir John Clifton, Sir John Norbery, Sir John Oldcastle, or whoever, is just inside St Paul's and wanting to settle with him. In goes the porter, out comes the priest looking for the sinning miser, and away goes Francis Pickbone with the basket of fish.

I suppose there would then be some such choice exchange:

The Porter. 'Confess? Begging your pardon, father, but I was shriven just this Easter.'

The Priest. 'What is it you want then, my son?'

The Porter. 'Money! That's what I want! I want my money!'

The Priest. 'Ah yes. I understand. Your uncle has explained this lust of yours to me. Step inside here, my son. A little less love of money, if you please, and a little more penitence and love of God.'

Frank was a fine upstanding fellow. An impassive sort of exterior, but a fiery heart. A good man to have at your side when it came to a fight. A volcano covered with snow.

Will Squele of Cotswold was different all again. Neat and plump, very small feet and hands, a full brown beard, a high and rounded forehead, a great grasper at straws, a mighty slipper through loopholes, an endless swinger on ropes hung between heaven and earth, or earth and hell, or something. His talk was mostly odoriferous. At the time I am talking of, Will was unmarried. Later, like most of us, he came to wive. When he did, he saw fit to introduce his wife to me: 'A poor thing, Jack, but mine own.' At which his wife chirped up severely, her thumb in his direction: 'A poorer thing, Jack, but mine owner.'

Poorer than poorest, my poor friend Shallow. Shallow, now, he would have *liked* to have been a swinge-buckler, or a swash-buckler, or indeed anything that buckled, or bucked, or would even have gone in buckram or a bucket – but the fact is that he was a dead loss, a nonny, a noodle, a doodle, a goose. Well, more owl than goose. And more stick than owl. He would have liked to have been a swinge-buckler, but his wit was too slow and his sap too cool. He advised us to call him Mad Shallow, and Lusty Shallow – indeed, he advised us to call him anything at all. And some obliged. But, for his part, this was the merest and most frantic and pathetic attempt at liveliness. So far as I was concerned, I liked the man, but he was Shallow through and through, to the foreseeable bottom.

I remember he played Sir Dagonet in Arthur's show at Mile End Green. He was an upstart and appalling actor. I played King Arthur himself of course in the same play, the *Mort d' Arthur*, in which Dagonet is Arthur's fool, and Arthur has to knight him. One night I knighted Sir Dagonet Shallow so hard that he saw the constellation Pleiades complete with its invisible star Electra.

Doit, Barnes, Pickbone, Squele and I all liked one another's company. And Shallow tagged along. We helped each other whenever there was a row in Turnbull Street or anywhere. Our watchword was '*Hem, boys!*' – this *Hem* meaning *h'm*, or *hm*, or even H E M, and signifying a slight half-cough, the cry of the born toper, if you don't know, when there are to be no heel taps. (If you really don't know, Sir, how have you managed to read this far? Could you have read this far without being drunk? Or without knowing what it is to be drunk? Or without needing to be drunk in order to know why you are reading me? These are great questions. Madam, you are excused. They are not questions for a lady. But I promise to come back from the tomb and haunt forever any male fool wise enough to try and answer them.

Where's Scrope? He's always got an excuse for not being here when it's story time.)

Doit and Barnes and Pickbone and Squele (yes, and Shallow) and I – we made the Strand ring with our songs as we rolled home of an evening. We heard the chimes at midnight. Ah, yes. The chimes at midnight. When the watch had locked the gates and we had to climb, or bluff, or bully, or wheedle our way into London's fastness after hours.

Hem – that's slang for *Drink up*.

We had more:

Bube – that's the pox;

Cuffin-Quire – that's a Justice of the Peace;

Chats – the gallows;

Couch a hogshead – take a nap;

Cly the jerk – to get whipped;

Clapperdogeon – a born beggar;

Deuswins – tuppence;

By the Pope's holy farts, Sir, and a whole dictionary more. A language. A vocabulary. It was London talk. It was only partly talk of my circle round and about the Inns of Court, for there it was learned from our slight contact with what I would call the Underworld Proper. I began to pick up the rudiments of the grammar from such as Squele and Pickbone. The syntax came later, with Pistol and Bardolph and the rest.

I'll give you more of the real King's English in due course, perhaps. It must also be revealed, before that, what we did when we lay all night in the windmill in St George's fields.

It was not corn grinding.

Bugger all these dialectics – I think I may say that I was the life and soul of my party. Poor Shallow was its butt. And its butt end. Alas, poor Shallow. He looked like a man made after supper of a cheese paring. When he was naked he was for all the world

146

like a forked radish, with a head fantastically carved upon it with a knife. He was so forlorn that his dimensions to any thick sight were invisible. Imperceptible. He was the very genius of famine. Some of his friends called him the mandrake. He came ever in the rearward of the fashion, Robert Shallow – wearing liripipe hats, for instance, long after everyone else had given his to his donkey.

He came also in the rearward of the fashion in another sense. (Madam, read no further. Back to your lovely Gower. The rude knight is about to perpetrate more homicide, or honeyseed, or honeysuckle. You have been warned.) This Shallow was the very first man that I ever knew who preferred to take his pleasure with women, as they say, arsey-versey, which means with his engine of pleasure in the backward quarters (or halves?) of their anatomy.

His engine – I dignify the dejected tool with such grand comparisons of metaphor. To tell you the truth, although he spoke much of his fame and prowess among the *bona-robas* – more slang, this time from the Italian for courtesan, which in turn derives from the smart robes or dresses afforded by the higher class of whores – although Shallow boasted of his success in these directions, I say, he lacked either the person or the acumen or the salt for such encounters. His prey was more often the over-scutched huswives, the threepenny whores with well-whipped backs, both from the beadle and their own hot-blooded clients.

Shallow himself did not whip girls. But he liked to watch while others did. There was never a *Hem!* or a *H'm!* to be heard from him then. You could have heard a pin drop, or his heart beat, he was so quiet.

He liked best to stand with his watery eye pressed bloodshot to the keyhole while Doit or Pickbone or myself disported ourselves with a brace of wantons up from the country and burning for a *dock* or a good *wap*. Shallow would watch and mark points. Later, if sore provoked by our sweet rutting, he would try a trick himself, coming ever in the rearward of the fashion, as I have explained. Yet for buggery itself – the act between men (oh, Gower off!) – he had neither taste nor courage. Barnes tried once to bugger him, and had to cease for Shallow's squealing. It was just like a stuck pig.

It was this Mr Shallow's habit also to whistle to his 3d whores the tunes which he had heard the carmen whistle, – and he would swear that they were his own fancies and good-nights, his personal improvisations on a theme of love.

To be fair to the poor fool fellow – for all his made-up talk of bona-robas – I must now recall the one occasion when I did succeed in bringing him face to face (well, you know by now what I mean) with a couple of high-class whores in his own chambers. Seeing that he begged me most piteously to stay and help him out, I did. I suppose it did not take a deal of begging. One of the girls was fair and buxom, reminding me a little of my nectarious Ophelia. I had not seen Ophelia for about six months at that time. I slaked my thirst well between the thighs of her counterfeit.

R. Shallow sat up in bed in a red cotton nightcap, with a floppy tassel, studying us.

'Oh Jack!' he moaned. 'Oh, Pyramus and Thisbe! Romeo and Juliet! Hero and Leander!' He applauded a specific thrust of mine. 'If only,' he sighed, 'if only I could do something like that. . . .'

Biting my tongue which was requiring to say a word about running down to the fruitshop to see if Mrs Sampson Stockfish was available, I urged my envious friend to concentrate as hard as he could upon his own quite beddable wench. She had dark hair, soft and lustrous, fine bubbies, and a round white belly, the bottom part of it covered with a thicket of jet-black curls. From where I lay on my own wanton, I could see the dear delicious slit on this, her friend. The dark girl had evidently been aroused by the sight of her companion's pleasuring. Two plump and rosy lips gaped slightly open – I'm talking about her cunny, Hanson – as though the sweet little aperture wanted itself to express surprise, and declare what it desired done to it.

The dark girl made a grab for Shallow's apology. She seized that flaccid organ in her hands, and began to rub it for him with a deal of alacrity, as if she wished to start a fire from the results.

Poor Shallow's prick stayed desolate.

I whispered in the ear of my own whore. She smiled obligingly, rolled her eyes, and turned her head to take Shallow's flimsy weapon in her mouth. She sucked. She sucked hard. She licked and nibbled and gnawed and sought to swallow the damned thing.

Shallow went a shade pink in the chops, and his nose ran, but nothing else.

'This is about as exciting as taking the ferry to the Isle of Dogs,' complained the blonde bona-roba, removing her sucky lips

148

from Shallow's effort, and wiping her mouth with the back of her hand. She looked up at me shrewdly, 'Is it boys your friend wants?'

'Oh no,' moaned Shallow, closing his eyes, and clenching his teeth. His face was flattened in like a thing of one dimension. 'I could never abide boy flesh,' he whined. 'Boy flesh is like cold pork. Never abide it.'

I stretched out my arm and stroked his whore's white belly tenderly. Her cunt had a pretty mouth, with the longest clitoris I had ever seen. It was like a catkin. I put my finger on it, and tickled her a bit. She wriggled. I squeezed. It seemed such a waste, to me, but for friendship's sake, for Shallow's sake, I said –

'Turn over!'

'You mean he –?'

'That's right,' I advised her briefly. 'Mr Shallow likes to plough the netherlands.'

The little dark beauty raised her eyes long-sufferingly to heaven (or, more exactly, to the beams of our chambers in the Inns of Court), but then she rolled over on her belly as I had bade her, offering my friend the freedom of her buttocks. She had a fine bottom. Hardly a virgin fortress, I suspect, but not over-visited.

'Now then, Shallow old shakes,' said I, 'you can do your worst there. Spear up, man!'

Shallow still hesitated.

'They're the *best* bona-robas, Jack? I've your word for it?'

'The finest in Cheapside, tell your pocky friend,' said my blonde in my ear, as she tempted me on again, with ankles crossed behind my back and fingers contriving to frig us both at the same time. Such sweet impossibility! 'Which is the best outside the Palace of Westminster,' she added in a provocative whisper, winking her eye as if to tell me that she had heard from higher companions in the trade that the four princes were skilled in other sorts of tilting than the sort that went on in public.

For some reason, I found that last piece of information infinitely delectable. I gave myself wholly to her. Hard. The bed cracked under our thumping.

Shallow meanwhile moved tentatively upon his wanton's bottom. I could see him out of the corner of my eye. Like a swan looking for somewhere to land.

'Barlaam and Josaphat and Jormungander!' cried the girl, who had evidently had religious clients in her time. 'It tickles! It's like being stung by butterflies! It's like sitting on a pin covered with angels!'

'Silence!' shrieked Shallow. 'Oh do tell her to be quiet, Jack,' he implored me, 'or I shan't ever be able to manage, and then there'll be – – nothing – – – nothing to look back upon – – in my old – – – in my old age. . . .'

He was doing his best. Indicate that by dashes, if you please.

I was completing my third stanza of rhyme royal with the blonde.

'You shut up, Miss Metaphysics,' I grunted to her companion, where she lay beside us, face down on the one green pillow, 'or I'll do both ends of you when my friend has finished!'

I did anyway.

I had to – since Shallow couldn't.

I worked like a Turk, while my poor friend stood and watched, his miserable spindly carrot in his fist.

The blonde bona-roba stretched out her fingers – out of sheer goodness of heart, in that mood of overflowing generosity which can sometimes possess a woman well-satisfied – she stretched out her skilful fingers to take his twitching member and assist him.

'*Hands off!*' squealed Shallow, slapping her away. 'I'm being Jack! I'm doing what he's doing!'

His trouble was he couldn't. Though he tried.

I never needed to knock at the back door, either – although if one of the girls wanted it, and I was weary of the other, I had no aversion to giving it to them there as well. Witness Mrs Ford, and friend.

Mr Shallow, poor Shallow, on the occasion I am speaking of, he succeeded in capering about with his tiny trout in one hand and a lawyer's ruler in the other. With the ruler he gave the bona-robas a few stings. The blonde got angry with him, because he hit too hard, when she had expected playfulness, or that his ruler would be as ineffective as his cock. She leaped from the bed and chased him round the room. She caught him one almighty thwack which had all her fleshy arm behind it.

'O times! O morals!' cried poor Shallow, and ejaculated in the chamberpot.

XXVIII

About some more figs

I have been told that figs won't grow in England.
   They will for me!
   Dionysus planted a fig tree at the gates of Hell.
   Zaccheus climbed up a fig tree to see our Lord.
   Judas hanged himself on one.
   If you don't believe me, if you can't accept the word of an English knight – *go, and see for yourself!*
   Besides, that giant faces south.

XXIX

About great events in the wide world

And at this time, when I was whooping it up in my mad days in the city of London, with little Doit and big Black Barnes and all the rest, what was happening in the wide world, you say? What were the great men doing?

Reader, they were doing what I was doing. Only on a larger scale.

The bloody Mongols were defeating the bloody Lithuanians at the River Vorskla.

The singing masons were building a hammerbeam roof on Westminster Palace.

Henry the 4th took to addressing Parliament in English for the first time. He was short of money.

Timur the Lame carried off all the craftsmen from Damascus, and shut down the steel factories there.

A very rich Welshman called Owen Glendower had a quarrel with his neighbour, Reggie, Lord Grey of Ruthin, over a field which both of them wanted. For whatever it's worth, I think Glendower had the better claim. But the point was that when he presented his case before the King, Henry went and muttered something about *barefooted scrubs*, – and then the Welsh fat was really in the fire. Glendower went home a nationalist. There followed a sort of uproar for about six years, until Hal put an end to it, with help from me. More of that in due course.

There was the usual war between England and Scotland.

There were Lollards.

Poland got married to Lithuania.

The Spaniards starting building a cathedral in Seville – which is still not half-way finished at the date of this writing.

Timur the Lame defeated and captured Bajazet at Ankara.

Valais joined the Swiss League.

Baghdad was being rebuilt – following Timur the Lame's visit, of course.

There was some sort of nasty alliance between Manuel the 2nd and Suleiman, the Emir of Turkey.

The Scots, etc, etc.

The Welsh, etc, etc, etc.

And the Irish. Always, of course, the Irish. Etc, etc, and *ad infinitum, ad libitum, ad unum omnes, ad Graecas Calendas.* I have the inside story on the Irish Question. I was there. I was the man. Wait for it.

History!

History (have you noticed, Madam?) is so much piss and wind.

Clio is the Muse of History. And who was Clio's mother?

Mnemosyne.

Mrs Memory.

That's who.

And who was Clio's father?

Your author.

XXX

Sir John Fastolf's humble address to his readers

29 April

Your HOLINESS, my Lord Archbishop, your Beatitude, your Excellencies, your Graces, Right Reverend Monsignors, dear Provosts, my Lords, Ladies and Gentlemen, Men and Women, Children, Embryos, and Spermatozoa – *was that last chapter boring enough?*

I rather fear it wasn't. And all on account of that Timur the Lame.

To put matters right with you, and more especially with my critics, the Historians – that girl Clio sleeps with anyone these days – I issue now a solemn warning and promise that my next chapter, tomorrow's Day, will prove VERY BORING INDEED. In fact, I think I may claim even in advance of the event that it is more boring that Gower's *Confessio Amantis* laid end to end with his *Vox Clamantis* (and both poems refusing, of course, to give us a bit of the old 69).

In other words, a piece of history. Of the 'great' sort. Not cribbed from Higden either. None of your *Polychronicon* staining these pages, thank you. Nor your *De proprietatibus rerum.* I use that stuff of Glanville's to light the fire.

No, my dear Readers, what I have in hand, by Clio's clitoris, no less, is a *unique document.* Here is history before it is writ.

Remember Reggie? Lord Grey of Ruthin. That toady who started Glendower off on his nationalism. Reginald Ruthin. Lord, Lord, I could tell you a thing or two about *him.* Did you know that aftery Henry the 4th's coronation banquet he pinched all the tablecloths, and sold them for fat fees as souvenirs? But never mind that. It's History with a capital H you're after. And a dose of that I can now provide. In the shape of a letter. An authentic letter. A letter as real as my boots.

How do I come to have it, since it was written by Reggie

Ruthin to the Prince of Wales? Never mind that. You'll soon be learning how close was the company I kept with Hal. If he lived in my pockets, I sometimes lived in his. Take it that my old mistress Ursula – I mean Mrs Helen Quickly – discovered it among my effects after that grand impersonation of a death which I had once to do at the Boar's Head tavern. Less of a death than an exercise in debt, if you must know. And by the time I got to France I had other things on my mind than Reggie Ruthin's creeping letter, wanting Hal to come and sort out his Welsh problems for him with an expense of English blood.

This letter came to light again when I bought the Boar's Head, later.

Enough preamble. Prepare for serious reading.

(Scrope must be got for copying out this crap. Only his mean little hand, just the right size for a column of figures all adding up neatly, can possibly do justice to its slavishness.)

The next chapter should really be called *The Art of Royal Arse-licking.*

Verb. sap.: it's very average balls.

You can skip it if you're young, and female, and like tomatoes.

That is my private dispensation. John Fastolf, his decree.

Meanwhile, prostrate at the feet of your HOLINESS, I have the honour to profess myself with the most profound respect, your HOLINESS's most obedient and humble servant, your Eminence's earwig, your Beatitude's own bastard, and so on and so forth.

Reader, I'm off.

XXXI

Lord Grey of Ruthin to the Prince of Wales

[*Mischief Night*]

Right high and mighty PRINCE, my good and gracious LORD, I recommend me to you as lowly as I can or may with all my poor heart, desiring to hear good and gracious tidings of your worshipful estate and welfare, which I pray to ALMIGHTY GOD as good might they be as ye in your gracious heart can best devise unto the pleasance of GOD and of you. And, gracious LORD, pleaseth it unto your high estate to wit that I have received our LIEGE LORD his privy seal with your own worshipful letters to me sent, commanding me to see, and to appease the misgovernance and the riot which ye hear that is begun here in the marches of *North Wales*. Pleaseth unto your gracious LORD-SHIP to writ that I have done my power, and will do from day to day by our LIEGE LORD his commandment and by yours; but, my gracious LORD, please it you to wit that ye with advice of our LIEGE LORD his council must give me a more plainer commission than I have got, to take them in the KING's ground, other in the Earl's ground of the *March*, other in the Earl's of *Arundel*, or in any lord's ground of *North Wales*; and by the faith that I owe unto my allegiance I shall truly do my power to do our LIEGE LORD the King's commandment and yours: but, worshipful and gracious LORD, you must command the KING's officers in every county to do the same. Also, my gracious LORD, there be many officers, some of our LIEGE LORD the KING his land, some of the Earl of the *March* his land, some of the Earl his land of *Arundel*, some of the *Powys* land, some of my land, some of other lord's land here about, that be kin unto this meinie that be risen. And till ye put those officers in better governance, this country of *North Wales* shall never have peace. And if ye had those officers under your governance, they could

156

ordain remedy, where through they should be taken. And, gracious LORD, please it you to wit that the day that the KING's messenger came with the KING's letters and with yours to me, the strongest thief of *Wales* sent me a letter, which letter I send to you, that ye may know his good will and governance, with a copy of another letter that I have sent to him again of an answer. And also, gracious LORD, I beseech you lowly that ye would vouch-safe to give faith and credence to a poor squire of mine, Richard Donn, of that he shall inform you by mouth touching tidings of this country, and that ye would take to you our LIEGE LORD's council and ordain other remedy for them than we be of power for to do, otherwise truly it will be an unruly Country within short time. My gracious LORD, I can no more write at this time, but GOD that is our elder sovereign give you long life and well enduring. Written at Ruthin this xxiii day of June, 1400.

REGINALD DE GREY,
S. de Ruthyn

XXXII

*Sir John Fastolf's commentary on this
exercise in the art of royal arse-licking*

Deo gratias. Ha! ha! Hey diddle diddle! And thank God that's
over, as the Abbess said to the eel.

I think I'd have died of yawns if I'd had to copy that stuff out.
Two grounds for rejoicing then:

1. I didn't have to;
2. Scrope did. (Without apparent death though, more's the pity.)

This stepson of mine has proved curiously reluctant to enter
into my book at all. Excuses, misuses, abuses. Always some
reason why he wasn't available. But yesterday I got him where he
could not refuse. His crabbed hand copied out that spiel of
Reggie Ruthin's. He said he felt able to do that because it was a
matter of *fact*, if you please, so he could assist me without
prejudice to his immortal soul. All the same, when I reminded
him that the same act of copying is an integral part of my *Acta*,
constituting the contribution of the 31st Day, and that therefore I
required the chapter dated at the top, as is my habit, and the date
was 30 April, May-Day Eve, or Mischief Night, as we call it in
these parts, – oh, then, stepson Scrope comes out again with a
bad attack of the scruples, and insists on putting square brackets
round my superscription! Those bloody prissy brackets are
Scrope's mark. The mark of the scrupulous beast. Don't ask me,
Madam, why I don't get Hanson and Nanton to go back with
their mutual rubber and rub the brackets from my text. [Mischief
Night] is [Mischief Night]. I am a great believer in the way
things turn out. I'm superstitious about these things. If a fly
should drown in the ink, I'd write it in. I don't blot a line, you
know. It stands as I say it. No heel taps. No changes.

Scrope is now part of my pattern. Maybe that's the main thing.

This is not just a book. It's a conspiracy.

I am your author. Agreed. But I am also *their* author: Worcester (written out for the time being), Hanson, Nanton, Bussard who has contrived a punctuation out of farts, Friar Brackley, and now my stepson Stephen Scrope. *Do you know for certain that any one of them exists?* (Wipe your nose.) Do you know for certain that *I* exist? That *I* don't have an author? There was a Chinese Emperor I heard of once. He fell asleep and he dreamed that he was a butterfly. It was all green fields and flirting sunlight, and trees as delicate and soft as little wet pointed paint-brushes, and his wings beat sweetly together over his thoughts as he moved from stone to flower. And when he woke up, and saw the usual Chinese world about him, the Emperor said: *Am I an Emperor who has just dreamed that he was a butterfly, or am I a butterfly which is now dreaming that it is an Emperor?*

That's enough metaphysics for now. For ever. The good doctor Paracelsus told my uncle Hugh that the best thing metaphysics could do was suck its own prick.

The *book* – these *texts* – the *Acta* – that is certainly real. You hold it in your hands, don't you? I offer up a prayer to St George, patron saint of English warriors such as myself, that one day you will find it difficult to put down. You hold a man's life in your hands, Sir. You hold England.

Robin the Bobbin, the big-bellied Ben.

John Bull, John Smith, John Fastolf.

Yes, Madam, John Thomas too.

Two swifts in my tower at Caister here today, May Day, and swifts mate on the wing, tumbling and turning, locked as they fall together through fathoms of air, breaking apart when the deed is done. Free spirits! Paradise!

Scrope nettles me with his talk of 'fact'. I have heard the chimes at midnight, and my belly is my fact. There is no better fact than that in England. I am England's heart. And her undone womb. And her testicles. *Her* testicles? Sir, England is a Mystery.

Fact? My belly gives me licence to give imaginative body to what is essentially sparse, even skeletal material: memories, biographies, jokes, histories, conversations, letters, images, fragments. I make patterns of my fragments. This book is the pattern I am making. But I give you also the fragments in giving you this book, my pattern – I give you the fragments to a great degree untrammelled by *my* pattern – so that you, the reader, are free to

159

put upon them *your* pattern; or simply to find within them or beyond them another pattern, other patterns, an infinite series of possibilities. This must be so with any man's life half-honestly recorded. And in my case bear in mind that we may not always be dealing with anything as relatively straightforward as honesty!

Scrope can put his facts where he puts his forefinger.

The freedom I allow myself – those bright swifts mating! – I extend it to you, and you, and you, my readers. Ideally, my *listeners*. The fantastic developments of my narratives are offered undogmatically, as a personal selection from an infinite number of alternatives.

I don't draw breath. That's the general idea.

And that's enough aesthetics too, I think.

Today, which is May Day, and of all days in the calendar one of those nearest and dearest to my heart and kidneys, I find myself having to provide some commentary upon that execrable exercise in the art of arse-licking which was Ruthin's letter to get Hal on his side. Did you read it carefully? I bet all Lombard Street to a China Orange that you didn't. And I don't blame you.

I'll make my commentary brief. Like all such letters, what is most interesting is what it does not say. Reggie, Lord Grey, was out to diddle Glendower. He had seized upon some part of Glendower's estate. Now he throws up all this obfuscation in the form of land belonging to *March*, land belonging to *Arundel*, land of *Powys*, and all the riddling rest of it, and the one thing missing from his letter to Prince Henry is any mention whatsoever of Mr Owen Glendower.

The 'meinie that be risen' is our Reggie's sly way of getting in a dig at Glendower's supporters. (*Meinie* in this context being an old word for *crew*, or *set*, or generally unsavoury *party*.)

The 'strongest thief in Wales' was not Glendower, but something even more Welsh, one of his chief bullyboys, a Mr Griffith ap David Griffith. This Mr double Griffith had already promised Reggie

> *A rope, a ladder, and a ring –*
> *High on the gallows for to hang!*

But that letter served its trick. Prince Henry's arse was as susceptible as the next man's to an oily and a servile tongue. We all ended up in *North Wales*, doing our duty, doing our bit. And all on account of a seller of tablecloths who wanted to pinch fields from his neighbours too.

They were filthy fields at that. The usual Welsh variety. More stones than blades of grass.

Don't misunderstand me. Glendower went too far. He threatened the unity of the Kingdom, and England had to put him down. But the man was undoubtedly wronged in the first place by this robber Ruthin. I throw in this letter to show the cunning of our so-called masters of that time, and the deadly crawling BOREDOM of their ways. All those CAPITAL LET-TERS and *italics*, incidentally, are just as scrupulous Scrope insisted on copying them from the original. He revels in that typography. He's more than a bit of an S. de Ruthyn himself, when it comes to it, though a decent enough translator from the Greek.

Mischief Night. On the last night of April, when I was a boy, we used to throw bricks down chimneys, and pull gates off their hinges, – and later, in London, about the time I've reached in my wandering chronicles, little Doit and I once filled a barrel with stones, and sent it rolling down Gracechurch Street to London Bridge, making such a rackiling racket as it went that the people thought Glendower had arrived in person, complete with horns. The only protection an honest citizen could attempt on such occasions was to hang a brush or a broom or a shovel outside his house. If he took thought to do that, when we mischief makers let him be. It probably signified that his wife would give him hell if the gate was stolen.

Mischief Night was last night, when we were entertained (if that's the word) by Reggie pulling off Glendower's gates, and then *imploring* the GRACIOUS and WORSHIPFUL Hal to come and chuck bricks down Glendower's chimney for him. Apt, I suppose.

But having to comment upon it, and offer that defence of my book against my stepson's vulgar attacks (I'll give him facts! I'll *fact* him!) – that's left me too tired tonight to do justice to the theme of May Day. I'll write about May Day tomorrow. Which I daresay, metaphysically and aesthetically speaking, you know, will also be apt to the zig-zag progress and process of my Days.

And after that, I promise you, LIEGE LORD my GRACIOUS READER, you who have even survived the sheer torture of my Chapter XXXI, after we have celebrated May Day with proper Englishness – which is to say, not heroically or imposingly, but with a real love for what is blunt and comic and familiar – after that I shall *get back to the story*.

XXXIII

Sir John Fastolf's praise of May Day

If you're expecting me to do Morris dances for you, with bells on my balls, you've got another think coming.

All the same, I grant you, praise be – May Day.

That's a good day, that's a happy day, that's a hey-go-mad carnival festival bloody day that I happen to like. I speak holiday. I smell May. If maypoles and May carols and May bonfires and May Molloch and Maybe and the Queen of the May ever should pass quite out of fashion, then it will be bad cess for England.

May carols I love best of all:

> *I been a rambling all this night,*
> *And almost all this day.*
> *And now I'm back to you again*
> *And I bring you a branch of the May.*
> *A branch of May I've brought for you –*

and so on, no great shakes as poems go, I know that, Piggybum, but there's a something dark and bright in it that stirs the blood, and makes the prickly hairs on the back of my neck tingle, especially when you hear it as I did yesterday morning, sung by the girls as they danced from house to house, hand in hand, in and out, close chaplets on their heads, and with a doll all dressed in white in front of them, to stand for our Lady.

May Molloch is *The Maid of the Hairy Arms*. She taught me how to cheat at dominoes.

Masks of flowers and hawthorn branches mostly, brought home at sunrise, with horn and tabor playing. No fitter matter. That's *bringing home the May*.

In your teeth, hypocrite! Just *stow your whids*, or I'll commit some more honeyseed!

Listen. If I dared to lie, I would plead guilty. As it is – how lush and lusty the grass looks! How green! And the loveliest girl in Caister crowned with flowers, the *Queen of the May*. Why, once upon a time, and a very good time it was too, it was nothing for kings and queens themselves to go a-Maying. (Fat chance of seeing the pious Harry 6th at such a caper!) Chaucer, though, who was something like a real poet – especially in those *Canterbury Tales* – if we're going to allow poets, which I think Plato said we should not – but then if it's a toss up between Messrs Chaucer and Plato I'll take this:

Forth goeth all the court, both most and least, to fetch the flowers fresh.

That's the Clerk of Works. Nice. That's May Day as it should be.

May Day: a milkmaid going through the young corn with her gown drawn through the pocket-hole of her petticoat. To keep it from the foggy foggy dew. That same dew ... like round and orient pearls.

May Day: Aphrodite born from a foam of may. Foxgloves on her fingers and bluebells on her toes. Attended by rainbows and foals and daisies (that are day's eyes). Those emerald meadows trembling behind her.

May Be: *the key*, Bussard, *to our English genius.*

Oh ho, and the same milkmaid, Aphrodite, Queen of the May, my own Miranda, wading through shallow estuaries of hay. Red Admiral butterflies, soft-shipwrecked on bistort, turned pirate to plunder the argosies of her lips. Take treasure. Leave them more rich for what they yielded.

Boys looking for birds' nests. Especially the eggs of the yellow-hammer. The yellowhammer drinks one hot drop of the Devil's blood each May morning. Is that why he sings so sweet? No song so true but a touch of the old Adam can't improve it.

Rooks, bells, ringdoves, moon and stars, curds and whey, cheesecakes and custards, cream so thick you could cut it with a knife, strawberries, bees, mint, columbine, streaked gillyflowers (long before July, I promise you), lavender, marjoram, the darling buds of May.

I begin to sound like something made up by a poet. Better shut up. That's what your May Day does to a man of the most solid (I will not say *sober*) kidney.

The darling nuts of May.

England, little pigsney, was called the Land of Honey by her first discoverers. Imagine. There must have been times — centuries since — when the whole of this island was thick with forests, and those forests thick themselves with the eternal buzzing of bees. The amaranthine murmur of honey-makers. Culling from every flower the virtuous sweets.

I think that there is nothing more lovely in this world than the long leagues of our English hedgerows white with May blossoms.

Nothing that brings tears to the eyes more quickly and sweetly than the smell of May buds after a sudden shower of rain.

(Except six pickles on top of cider.)

O my Miranda. O rose of May! My more-than-May. Suppose the birds musicians. In a swashbuckling breeze, look, there, the grass is scabbards. It keeps my swords of green fire at your service. Miranda, May Queen, dance! And then become your dance, and go. When you do dance, I wish you a wave of the sea.

All right. She's somewhat deflowered for a rose. But the fairer for it. The sky changes.

> *A branch of May I've brought for you,*
> *And at your door I stand. . . .*

Tin trumpets welcoming back home from the woods those who have gone a-Maying. Such thin throats. I've known them step through drifts of snow to get drifts of flowers for their garlands, which they'd twist into a round, like hoops, with haw-thorn as I say, and sycamore, and any bits of green things, prim-roses, Mary blobs, eglantine, sops-in-wine. And the girls all washing their faces in the dew, in pursuit of beauty. And marsh marigolds on the doorposts. More matter for a May morning. And branches of silver birch, hung with cowslip balls. And I, so bedazzled with the sun, that everything I look on seems green. Green. The colour of lovers. The fields are fragrant and the woods are green. And grief is green. And memory is green. And I am a great green boy again.

See! All the shining horses in the fields, with ribbons on their bridles and in their manes. To horse, you gallant princes! Straight to horse! Bardolph, look to our horses.

But the maypole. That's your man. Pine. Larch. Ash. It doesn't matter which. So long as he's long, and strong, and fine upstanding. The rod of peace.

Which brings me to Jane Nightwork.

XXXIV

About Mrs Nightwork & the night at the windmill

There was the night I lay all night in the windmill in St George's fields.

That windmill was a brothel then. (In these emasculated days, I believe that it has been converted into a department of the Civil Service.) The brothel madam's name was Nightwork. Mrs Jane Nightwork. No doubt that was not her real name. Doit said she was of noble birth, from the wrong side of John of Gaunt's cracked blanket, and that she had turned whore only out of love of what it is that women lack. Her pander was her husband, old Nightwork, also known as Willy Wee, on account of his unusually short weapon. Doit said that Jane had once appealed to the Star Chamber to have her marriage annulled, on account of her husband's shortcomings, and that this was where her parentage had been betrayed at least to the members of that secret enclave. Old Nightwork, you see, protested a great deal when the Star Chamber demanded that it should be allowed to pass judgement on his prick, and it was finally agreed that he might be permitted to conceal himself behind a screen, with a hole cut in it, through which he was to poke his peter for the benefit of the court. Now, according to Doit, old Nightwork was no fool, and he went straight to Jane's father, John of Gaunt, and told him what was being proposed. John of Gaunt was very worried. For a lunatic. Getting rid of an illegitimate daughter is no joke, and if the Star Chamber annulled Jane's marriage then she would be back on his hands. Gaunt agreed, therefore, to stand in behind the screen for old Nightwork. Gaunt had a prick like a sceptre and when he stuck it through the hole there was absolute silence. Save from Jane herself. Who whispered, 'Daddy!' And fainted.

Doit's story. I don't believe it. I knew Kate Swynford, who was John of Gaunt's mistress for thirty years, and his wife for two, and she told me that his equipage, while adequate, was nothing out of the ordinary.

Whether by old Nightwork or not, Jane had one son, a namby creature called Robin, that used to suck its thumb all day counting his mother's earnings. One for the rook, one for the crow, one to die, and one to grow. Jane was the only member of the family who worked, by night or by day. In the case of my slack friend Shallow it was overtime all the time.

Yet she could not get rid of him. Jane Nightwork could not abide him, but she could not get rid of him. He got her into towering fits of rage – or, at least, she had to pretend to be angry with him, chasing him round the rafters of the windmill with a whip made of bramble.

Poor floppy Shallow. He yelped and ran, ran and yelped, his shirt flapping over his silly shanks, his tail between his legs. That was the trouble. His tail would not, *did* not, COULD not stand up – and a dangling lamb's tail was no sight to show Jane Nightwork, who must have had the quickest rump in christendom and thighs as accommodating as the whale's maw. I believe she was *really* furious with him in the end. Her arm ached, she told me, from hitting him and hitting him and hitting him until he spilled his seed. And then it was just a miser's drop or two, and on the mill floor, where it did her no good, and displeased the woodworms.

On the night I'm telling you about, there were three of us went out to the mill, to visit Mrs Nightwork. Myself, friend Shallow, and Frank Pickbone.

Our genial hotess gave us plenty of sack to drink, and there were little custard cakes besides. I had imported a bushel of my wonder-working figs from Dorset, from my ghostly father the giant of Cerne Abbas. We all munched handfuls of these to supply and refresh our champions for their task in the tourney ahead.

Jane Nightwork was some 30 years old then, no more, a sweet white English rose – even if already well-sniffed. Her body was delicious in every part. Her hair was dark, her eyes grey, her arms long, her legs well-fleshed and shapely. She had a most sensual and determined chin. She sang to us with a guitar. She chose that oldest of whore's madrigals, the acrostic which Eve first sang to

Adam, when she twigged he would be more fun than bananas:

> C *ome live and love with me*
> U *nder the greenwood tree!*
> N *onny nonny nonny no!*
> T *arradiddle me below!*

The evening passed very merrily. When Pickbone lay down with the lady under the starry coverlet on the great bed, there was a sort of spice of amiability and friendliness in the night air. The stars smiled down on us. The moon beamed, despite the fact that she was out of reach of the windmill's arms. I remember this vividly. The night's warmth. Diana's blessing light.

I was all for dicing with Shallow while Pickbone had his time. Then we could take it in turns with Jane, who was always willing. Indeed who was always hungry for what she called a good rummage. Meaning several men at once, in separate orifices of course.

But Shallow tossed the dice down a rat-hole in his excitement.

The great bed squeaked under Mrs Nightwork under Frank.

Shallow tiptoed to the door.

'I want to watch,' he said.

They let him.

For myself, I observed the placid disposition of the constellations above St George's fields. There was Orion. There Aquarius. I remember now. This encounter took place on the very day the tailor Badby was burned in his barrel at Smithfield. Looking at Hercules in the night sky, I had that image in my head. Hal lurked there too, or strutted (rather) in his studded shoes. His lips like a lady's purse. Flesh burnt into ashes. Threepence a day.

'NOW!'

It was Robert Shallow. Pickbone and Jane had arrived at their conclusion, and the lady amiably made room for the newcomer in her bed. Shallow rushed in, where Fastolf (knowing Frank Pickbone's notions of cleanliness) would have feared to tread.

But whatever it was he did, it did not please Mrs Nightwork.

There was a scream.

There was a smack.

There was a spindly thump as Shallow fell out of the bed. He was clutching his middle.

Jane stood over him, stark naked, a stick in her fist. It was Pickbone's stick, snatched up from the mill floor. Her eyes flashed. She was furious.

'Jack! Frank! What's he got there? Examine him!'

I stepped forward light-heartedly, still suspecting and supposing some kind of joke. But then I saw Shallow hurriedly trying to hide something out of reach of the light of the lantern. I grabbed him by the waist and turned him upside down.

Pickbone punched him.

Pickbone tickled him.

Something clouted out of Shallow's grasp and clattered to the floor.

'There!' cried Jane triumphantly. 'What is it?'

I held *it* up.

'A cucumber?' I suggested.

'A puppet?' said Frank.

'A cudgel?' I said doubtfully, fingering the thing.

Jane shrieked three times. Her grey eyes were on fire with indignation.

She started belabouring Shallow's upside-down bottom with her very capable hands. Then with Pickbone's stick.

'*That's* for trying to get it up me!' – *Thwack!*

'*That's* for tricks that could've killed me!' – THWACK!

'*That's* for practically ruining my trade for life!' – *THWACK!*

Now, damn me black, but the boulevard or thoroughfare which Mrs Nightwork referred to as her 'trade' was in fact so broad and easy and well-worn by travellers that I think a cart and horses could have been driven up inside it, turned round, and brought out again without touching the sides. Men had been known to get lost in those regions for days on end, and emerge at last laden with treasure left by previous explorers and marauders.

All the same, poor Shallow's artificial assistant did look singularly terrible and spiky.

'But – it's – Italian!' I heard him gasp, between blows on his bum.

'I'll Italian you!' cried Mrs Nightwork. 'I'll give you Italian dildoes! What you mean by your Romish tricks with an honest English whore!'

We were then treated, Frank Pickbone and I, to the spectacle of the same honest English whore heartily flagellating the exposed posteriors of Mr R. Shallow the law-student with the aforesaid foreign dildoe as her weapon.

I have to say that it did more for him than it ever did for her.

In the end, she shoved it right up his end.

This whole exercise left poor Shallow pleased enough, if somewhat dazed, and quite unable to sit down. He succeeded finally in lying on his belly and cooling his arse with cabbage leaves soaked in sack. Thus, the idiot fell asleep and was soon snoring his head off.

It takes all sorts to make an orgy.

Luckily for us, the beating had given our lusty Jane an appetite for more practical amours. We absorbed the remainder of the sack, and sweated it out again with a will. My will mostly. Jane mounted me the way a cow on heat goes to it with a bull.

That was the night we counted our way round the constellation of the Bear, or Charles's Wain. For each star up there we had to give Mrs Nightwork a shooting star down here, Pickbone or myself. And although I have no need to boast of it now, I record the plain truth that the crowning and best-shot last-shot star was mine, not Frank's. He dropped out, spent, half way up the left flank of the constellation. Jane at that point got her second wind. As for me, with my balls and my belly full of Mr Wiclif's lovely lollardy figs, I stayed the course all night, without dissent or schism, and with no need of assistance or inspiration from poor Robert Shallow's Italian ambassador.

XXXV

About correspondences

It is said (by Scrope, that miser's git, who else?) that I ought not
to have devoted such a day as Holy Cross Day to telling you
about Shallow's Italian dildoe.

I say: I am building a house, and I know my trade.

I say: John Fastolf is a master mason, and each stone has its
place in my design, and I know where I am putting them. I have
to quarry. I have to axe. I have to chisel. I have my hammers
(Scrope will be one of them too, before these Days are out, you
bloody wait and see!). I have my mallets and my saws, my chisels
and my bevels and my compasses. By God, I have my nippers
and my scissors too, and I know how to use them! Do I bother
you with scaffolding, or talk of my considerable hoisting ap-
pliances, which are necessary since *the weight of my life is not to be
measured in tons?* There is so much of it. I assure you, Reader, that
the inductive process of my *Acta* allows for no accidents or blas-
phemies. Take that greatest of houses – I mean, the Cathedral
which was built 200 years ago at Chartres, to house the Blessed
Sacrament and a portion of our Lady's dress. There is a very
great mystery in that building, which your eye may miss. It is
this: that the windows with their pictures which you see from
inside when the light falls through them match in no obvious way
the statues which you see about and over and around the doors in
corresponding places from *outside*. It is not a case of stone and
stained glass being the same, or telling similar tales. Not at all.
The correspondences go deeper. The whole place – as I understand it – was built to reveal the truth of the revealed religion
which is our Christian faith. And as that religion has two parts –
has come to us in two halves – in the Old Testament and in the
New – so you will find at Chartres, if your eye and mind go deep

enough, that what on the *inside* is some dark allegory from the Old, on the *outside* is blazed forth publicly with all the risen and illuminated truth of the New. St Augustine said that the Old Testament was just the New Testament covered with a veil. Such a house as Chartres is designed to show you how that veil was lifted by our Lord.

Does this old reprobate seek to justify his obscenities by comparing them to Chartres Cathedral? I hope that he does not. I hope you do not think I do. I mean only to suggest that there are truths and parallels and correspondences in the world, which the masons who made Chartres knew about, for the place is a book for those with eyes to read. And that there are other truths and parallels and correspondences in a man's life, which the man himself may know about, and which I trust to place before you in *this* book.

I juxtapose fact and fiction.

I make a cosmos of my days in my Days.

The *vox mundi* speaks here, as well as the *vox humana*.

SO – when you allow me my mortar and bonding, my corbels and capping stones, my gablets and jambs and quoins and plinths, and all the scontion and spalls, the templates and voussoirs and tympanum of my book, *will you permit me also my most necessary gargoyles?* Only inferior masons suppose your gargoyle to be a detail. Sometimes the gargoyle is the point.

But all this talk is so much tooth-chisel work. . . .

To answer Scrope:

Holy Cross Day commemorates that 3rd of May when St Helena – or, more precisely, her agents – found the True Cross on which our Lord was crucified. Enemies of the faith say that because the Church calls this day the Day of the Invention of the Holy Cross, it implies that St Helena's agents must have duped her, or that it was some other cross, or that they did indeed 'invent' it, – make it up. My tutor Ravenstone could have improved their understanding. *Invention* of the Holy Cross is from the Latin, *invenire*, to find or discover. And I take it that I shan't need to remind posterity that St Helena was as real as you or I, the mother of the Emperor Constantine.

Talking of Constantine, there is also the matter of Constantine's Cross. That is a different story – though, again, it depends what you mean by difference. I am concerned to show you likenesses where you see opposites. On his march to Rome, then, Constantine saw a burning cross in the sky. It looked like this:

vincēs in hoc

Since today we have the services of Fr Brackley, you can take that shape as infallibly accurate. The Latin means, of course, *By this conquer.*

Then, the night before the battle of Saxa Rubra, Constantine dreamed a dream and saw a vision in his dream and was commanded to inscribe that cross above and the selfsame motto on the shields and purple banners of his soldiers.

He did.

They won.

The monogram, now Fr Brackley reminds me, is

XPιϛτος (Christ).

Thank you, father.

May none of your sins be little ones.

What balls! What bluster! What cock! What blasphemous obfuscation and braggadocio! – Yes, I can hear you. Reader, I read your mind. But now let me add my one little stone to the pattern, to the tracery, to the architecture, so that the arch of the story of our night at the windmill in St George's fields is quite complete.

On Holy Cross Day, so I have heard, in the churches of the Byzantine rite, and most especially in the church of the Holy Sepulchre at Jerusalem, there is a great feast celebrated, which feast is called the Exaltation of the Cross. Round here, in Caister, all through Norfolk, throughout England, we order it otherwise. The children go running through the streets, carrying stinging-nettles, and they flog each other with them.

Holy Cross Day is Sting-nettle Day, Madam.

Vinces in hoc.

XXXVI

About the best meal which Sir John Fastolf
never ate

5 May

Sad tripes from the cook Macbeth. So bad I fed them to a dog, and the dog died. A plague of tripes. My mother's spiders would have spurned these particular tripes. Turned up their noses. Do spiders have noses? How else would they breathe? Or sneeze? Or express contempt? Female spiders sniff. Your male spider has to be damned quick. The female likes to eat him after copulation. No time for a bit of sadness after coitus in the spider world.

What a pity Worcester is away in Wales looking for St Nectar's bloodprints. Our William likes his tripes. He could have eaten all those fetid offerings of Macbeth's, and thereby passed to his second course and just desserts in the world to come.

Spiders spin only on dark days.

Bad food brings good food back to mind. The best meal I never ate was the meal served at the coronation banquet of King Harry the 4th, alias Henry Duke of Bedford, alias Duke of Lancaster, alias Earl of Derby, alias Bolingbroke. (He had that last name from the castle he was born in, at Bolingbroke, in Lincolnshire.) Not to be confused with the astonomer Bolingbroke, who is supposed to have made wax necromantic dolls for Eleanor Cobham, Duchess of Gloucester, and who was hung, drawn, and rather unnecessarily quartered at Tyburn.

King Bolingbroke was crowned in the Abbey Church of Westminster on a Monday – the 13th day of October, in the year of the King of Glory 1399. Hal walked in front of him, bearing the *Curtana*, that naked pointless sword which is carried before all the kings of England at their coronation, signifying the execution of justice without rancour. (It's also called the sword of Edward the Confessor, since he started such executions.) The coronation Mass was said and sung by Thomas fitzAlan, Archbishop of Canterbury. The sacred oil used for the anointing is said to have been given by our Lady to St Thomas Becket, when he was in exile at Chartres.

I say *is said to have been given* because I have my doubts about the provenance of that particular oil. I know for a fact that Bolingbroke's head became infested with lice immediately after fitzAlan had poured the holy oil upon it.

Bolingbroke had a thick red matted beard. He looked a bit like a fox. Compact. Bad conscience made him something of an insomniac towards the end of his life, and his struggles to get to sleep weren't much assisted by his habit of wearing his crown in bed. The best thing I can think of saying about him is that he did increase Mr Chaucer's pension. The worst thing I can think of saying about him I shall not say, but the second worst thing is that he patronised Mr Gower.

The coronation over, lice and all, the new-born King Henry the 4th gave the customary banquet. Except that having come to the throne by unusual routes, he had obviously decided to make the customary banquet uncustomarily magnificent.

I regret to report that I was not invited. This was hardly an oversight on Bolingbroke's part. By Monday the 13th of October, in the year of the King of Glory 1399, I had not yet even made my mark on history by marking Skogan's head. Nor had I met Prince Hal, and the other princes.

No – thank God – at the time of that banquet I had other things on my mind and in my hands. If you want to know, I was in a hayloft out the back here, keeping company with my sweet Ophelia. That was the day she discovered the delights of having my penis in her mouth and masturbating herself at the same time. She came when I came, and she swallowed the semen. Afterwards, she tempted me to tickle her anus with some straws –

But my friend Will Squele was there. At Bolingbroke's banquet, I mean. Will had employment as a servitor before he wangled his way into the Inns of Court with some financial assistance from an indulgent (and widowed) aunt.

So, Will was there. And the scope and substance and variety of that feast was an endless item of remembrance for him. He must have gone on burping about it for years. And I must have chewed over and nibbled and gnawed and munched and masticated that meal a dozen times, dining on the smells and crusts of his description.

This was the menu:

First course: Brawn; a boar's head served whole with all kinds of trimmings; cygnets from Richmond; capon; pheasant; heron. With a subtlety in sugar, paste, marzipan and jelly depicting the capture of Richard the 2nd at Flint Castle, and his journey to Chester on a donkey.

Second course: Venison; calves' foot jelly; peacocks from Windsor; cranes; bittern; eels from the Tiber, said to have been carted across half Europe by Henry's bastard half-brother, the Marquis of Dorset; tarts. A subtlety of Bolingbroke crowned, sans a single louse.

Third course: Quinces; egrets; curlew; partridges; quails from Wales; snipe; rabbits; fritters; iced eggs. A subtlety of the King's sons – Hal, Thomas, John, Humphrey.

What a spread, even in imagination! I swear if I belch I can taste those iced eggs.

The feast took place in Westminster Hall. It was Richard the 2nd who rebuilt and redecorated that hall. Now Richard was a prisoner in the Tower and the guests sat down to dine to his damnation.

'At the high table, set on a dais,' Will told me, 'the King was enthroned to eat alone. Just below him, the two archbishops, and 17 other bishops. The Earl of Westmoreland at the bottom of that table, with the royal sceptre in his hand, a great bludgeon of authority.'

Did he carve his meat with it? Will never let on.

Five other tables – one for the Lord Mayor of London, and the Aldermen of the City, sheriffs, masters of the liveried companies, that shower.

The Earl of Arundel played butler.

King Bolingbroke knighted 46 squires in honour of his crowning on that day. These new knights had another table, all to themselves. Each wore a lace on his left shoulder – a white silk cord doubled over – which was a kind of badge which he had to bear until some perceptible honour achieved allowed a lady to cut it off for him. The fledgelings looked fine in their trailing grass-green coats, Will said. Fur-lined sleeves too. Gifts from the King.

Seven minstrels played non-stop in the long gallery. Pipes and flutes and drums and cymbals. And jugglers juggled and acrobats tumbled.

The banquet lasted for five hours.

I remember also – I remember that golden straw in Ophelia's golden tangle of – but I remember also (Will Squele told me) that when the feasting was at its height, a knight by the name of Dymmok – it would be Sir Thomas Dymmok, who had this service as royal champion by reason of his mother's right to the manor of Scrivelsby in Lincolnshire – came riding into the hall on a war-horse, fully armed, girt with a sword with a golden hilt, and his steed barbed with crimson housings. In front of Dymmok came two squires – both bearing lances. Then a herald stepped forward and marched round the tables announcing, in the usual style of heralds (which is to say, offensively) that

'if any man should say that his LIEGE LORD here present and KING OF ENGLAND was not the *right* crowned KING OF ENGLAND, he – (that is, Tommy Dymmok) – was ready to prove the contrary with his body, then, and there, or when and wheresoever it might please THE KING.'

'So help me God if it wasn't fun,' said Will Squele. 'And Dymmok's horse tried to eat fitzAlan's fritters.'

But Bolingbroke, having got his compact bum on the throne of England, was nothing if not determined to keep it there.

He wiped his foxy beard, so Will Squele told me, and then he said in a voice not at all blunted by quinces or capons or even the deposition of King Richard, his cousin:

'If need be, Sir Thomas, I will in my own person ease you of this office!'

General cheering. More to eat and drink. Exit Dymmok on his naughty steed.

Ophelia bit my cock.

XXXVII

About 4 princes & 24 islands

*The Feast of St John
before the Latin Gate*

Bolingbroke had Queen Dick moved to Pontefract, where his
keeper was Sir Thomas Swynford, son of the same Kate kept as a
mistress by John of Gaunt for thirty years. O stars. O destinies.
I've heard various stories of how the ex-King met his death.
Some say Swynford starved him. Others that Richard pined
away all of his own accord, gazing in a looking-glass and wondering where his majesty had gone. The truth is that Bolingbroke
put it into Pierce Exton's head that he needed Richard out of the
way.

'Have I no faithful friend?' he said one night at table. 'Have I
no faithful friend which will deliver me of him whose life will be
my death, and whose death will be the preservation of my life?'

A very fancy way of inducing a man to commit murder. Exton
didn't need any more encouragement. He roared north with seven
accomplices. They entered Richard's cell at Pontefract all armed
with axes. Queen Dick fought bravely enough in his last minutes.
He got an axe away from one of them, and swinging it round
and round his head, like a madman, he managed to get rid of four
of his murderers, before finally being smashed down by two
slashing blows in the middle from Exton himself.

All sorts of stories were flying about London as to what had
happened, and there were those who refused to credit that
Richard could be dead at all. That was the reason why
Bolingbroke had the body brought to London – in order that the
people might have certain knowledge of his cousin's death.

The body lay in solemn state for one day and night in St
Paul's. Every outward mark of respect was paid to it. At the
Requiem, Bolingbroke insisted upon personally carrying the pall.

The body was then handed over to Dominican Friars to be buried in their church at Chiltern Langley. The Bishop of Chester was at that burying, and the Abbot of St Alban's, and the Abbot of Waltham, and a few others from these parts.

I was one of those who filed past the catafalque in St Paul's. Black pall. Six candles burning round it. I noticed that the trunk and limbs of the corpse were sealed in lead, leaving only the face uncovered from the brow to the throat.

This was to hide the terrible wounds inflicted by Pierce Exton.

I was never a great admirer of Queen Dick. He was altogether too beautiful to be a man, and too abrupt and unfortunate to be a king. Also, he was addicted to schemes of revenge which did the Kingdom no good at all. But, standing that day by his catafalque in Paul's, and knowing that he had gone before a better Judge than any of us deserve, it came to me to think that the man was in his way as well endowed as Solomon, as fair as Absalom, as glorious as Ahasuerus. Such are the benefits and charities of a classical education. Poor Richard. In the end, he was like Chosroes, King of Persia, who was delivered into the hands of Heraclius. With all those talents, and with that appalling luck, he wasn't suitable to be a king. That's certain. I remember the yellow hair falling in broad rivers on either side of the waxen face in the candlelight, and the tiny soft moustaches which sprang from the corners of his girlish mouth.

Requiescat in pace.

Bolingbroke forked out £16. 13s. 4d for the saying of a thousand Masses, to give that prayer a decent start.

Richard's murderer Exton thought he was a horse. I don't mean that he had any aspirations to race round that saucer of a racecourse at Chester every Easter, winning prizes. But he thought he was a horse, and no mistake. His idea of fun was to strip himself naked, fit a bit between his teeth and reins around his neck, then go down on all fours with his mistress on his back, complete with saddle and crop of course. Exton then would trot and canter round the room, while the lady gave him a good few cuts across the flanks with her riding whip, and meanwhile frigged him with her busy toes. He'd whinney like Spumador when he came.

(Spumador was King Arthur's horse. The name means *foaming one*.)

Whether Exton died of a surfeit of hay I do not know. I do

know that this particular equine fancy of his is not as unique as you might think. I've seen a woodcut of the philosopher Aristotle being ridden in just the selfsame manner by a courtesan of Athens.

Whoa there, Bussard. God damn! Your pen, please, not your penis.

My narrative is circumstantial enough.

To the soul of Monsieur Arnauld de Villeneuve, of Languedoc, greetings! O great interrogator of nature. O good investigator more particularly of the mysteries of chemical science as they bear upon medicine. O glorious discoverer of sulphuric, nitric, and muriatic acid. O wise and venerable doctor, first of all alchemists to make alcohol and spirits of wine.

Burnt brandy is a food.

This won't do. Let me attempt a more philosophico-political style. The warlike Harry. This grace of kings. There, that's got it going. That most renowned Prince, King Henry the 5th, late King of England, during the life of his father was noted to be fierce and of wanton courage. All in a fury, all chafed, the royal creature, a very amiable monster, a splendid pageant, his glistening eyes, his velvet paws, like something in the zoo at the Tower of London. . . .

Bugger that. Bugger the immediate heir of England stuff.

I'll go back to my own point in Hal's story. In the year after that little literary punch-up at the court gate.

Mr Poeticule Skogan continued to lurk in London with his verses. That broken head did nothing to mend his rhymes or quicken his rhythms. He was as ambitious as ever, too. Hell hath no fury like a poet reviewed in public with a cudgel. Skogan professed himself to be working on an epic which would be 50 thousand lines long but which would dispense entirely with the services of the letter E. This was supposed by the critics to be wonderfully modern. Nothing of the sort. Tryphiodorus, as a matter of fact, composed an epic poem on the adventures of Ulysses, 24 books long, the first book doing without the letter Alpha, the second without Beta, and so on. The Empress Eudoxia wrote a life of our Lord in lines taken entirely from Homer. There's nothing new under the moon. Myself, I've no time for these wretched modernists. I remember Ravenstone taught me that the ultimate in modernism was achieved in the sixth century. I refer, of course, to the critical commentaries of the grammarian

Vergilius Maro, who wrote a series of 15 epitomae on the more unusual literary experiments of his contemporaries. Number 13 is the best. *Ars Scissendi.* 'The Art of Cutting Up.' According to Vergilius Maro, the prime produce here was delivered by one Galbungus, who chopped up a sentence until it began:

PPPP. PPP. RRR. RRR. LM. SSS.

No doubt there was nothing quite as astonishing as that in the ballad read by Henry Skogan to the four brother princes – Hal, Thomas, John, and Humphrey – on the occasion of their dining with Sir John Lewis, Master of the Vintners' Company, at his house in the Vintry that night in June, the Eve of St John the Baptist, when the trouble occurred.

In vino veritas. Or should it be (rejoice!) *in risu*?

That was the night of the great stew in Eastcheap anyhow. I know. I was there. The scene at first was the Boar's Head tavern. The King's sons, all four of them, went on from the vintner's table and Skogan's poisonous poetry to take their pleasure of drink in a private room at the inn. The business I'm telling you about must have started just after the watch was broken up – between two and three o'clock in the morning.

Thomas and John got drunk in their different ways – Thomas doggedly, with a refractory fixed grin, John with the sheer thirst of an ox – and then the two of them fell into an extraordinary argument with Hal and Humphrey, who were also well on in their cups though not intoxicated. (I don't think Hal ever allowed his body the pleasure of complete divorce from his head. He was not designed for that kind of holiday. As for Humphrey – he took his cue from his eldest brother in all things. If Hal had said, 'We must get pissed!' then Good Duke Humphrey would have got pissed with the best of them. As it was, I have seen Hal weaving about mightily among kegs and barrels in capacious cellars, but I never once saw him flat on his back and dead drunk. There was always a something canny in him that called him back from going too far into the wood in the direction of Dionysus. That same something, at work in his youngest brother, who lived so much longer, may account both for his great devotion to the Church in his latter days, and for the hospitality which ruined him.)

The two middle brothers got drunk, as I say, and fell into a crazy debate with Henry and Humphrey.

This debate was on the subject of *islands off Africa*.

The drunker that Thomas and John became, and the more

shrewdly sober that Henry and Humphrey remained, the wilder this debate. It started in the tavern, but it ended in the streets. It must have gone on, in all, for over an hour. I never had a good head for geography. So I kept on the sidelines of it. But the princes had come to the Boar's Head with the usual hangers-on, the bowers and the scrapers and the little trouble-makers. These fellows by their presence threatened to turn a slanging match into an outright regal brawl.

A viol played slowly in the smoky light. Its chords were iron-cruel, prolonged. Two lank greyhounds were curled at Henry's feet. Humphrey sucked at an orange. Thomas and John drank from painted cups, and wiped their mouths on satin scraps. We were all seated about the enormous fireplace in which heavy logs crackled and glowed. Blue smoke. The smell of resin. Nimble shadows.

Hal began it, with a proclamation:

'There are 40 islands in the Greek Sea,' he said.

'Liar,' said Thomas amiably.

'40 is right,' said Humphrey.

'Barbarian,' said John.

Hal's fists stiffened on his knees. He leaned forwards with a dogmatic grunt. 'Part of the 80 islands called the Isles of the Cyclades,' he said. 'Lying between Venice and Rhodes towards Jerusalem.'

A string broke on the viol.

'Another drink,' said John, yawning, showing his sewer of a throat. The potboy hurried forward.

Thomas was making a prodigious effort to concentrate. 'King Phenius of Arcadia,' he began.

'Whose philosophy was mere antics,' snapped Hal.

'King Phenius of Arcadia,' went on Thomas, 'that King Phenius, in the verses of Virgil which begin – which commence –'

' "Bugger off to Italy",' said Humphrey, winking at Hal.

' "Bugger off to Italy",' said Thomas obstinately. 'King Phenius –'

Hal slapped his thighs. 'Put away your Phenius,' he advised his younger brother. 'I will name you the names of these 40 islands.'

'He will,' said Humphrey. 'He will name you their names.'

I chuckled in the chimney corner. Humphrey clapped his hands and glared in my direction.

'I am laughing at my rheumatism,' I explained.

Hal had not even noticed the interruption. 'There is Madeira,' he declared, 'and the isle of Porto, which is 20 miles from Madeira, and the isle of St Mary which is a day and a half's sailing from Madeira, and another day and a half's sailing from St Mary island to the north there are two islands –'

John, always a hefty sniffer at offences, said: 'The whole world, the whole dumb sky, must be a day and a half away in the cosmology of my brother the Prince of Wales.'

'A Welsh cosmology,' said Thomas.

But Hal continued, unabashed: 'One called Pico, one called the Isle of Hawks, where in still green water –'

'What about the Azores?' demanded Thomas.

'That is the Azores,' said Hal.

'What is?'

'The Isle of Hawks and Pico.'

Thomas rubbed his thick neck with his thumb. His brows came together like two claws over eyes that ached with alcohol and fraternal rivalry. 'There is no hawks in the Azores,' he protested. 'No hawks and no Pico.'

Hal smiled at him. 'There are hawks, there are hang-nails, and there are angels and lemon-bushes and the mewing of cats in Pico,' he said softly. 'There is also the Grace of God, and a few jackdaws.'

There was a pause. Thomas was trying hard to concentrate his mind upon these possibilities.

'The Trinity of the Africans,' he said slowly, his jaw barely supplying the needs of his vocal chords, 'is such that angels and other ministers have no more chance of survival there than a snowball in hell.'

'Don't spoil your immortal soul for the sake of a feeble witticism,' Hal instructed him.

Humphrey nodded approval. Tears filled his eyes.

'Hog! Nightingale!' cried John. 'Give us the truth!' His head slumped. 'God will pardon Thomas,' he mumbled. 'But whether he will pardon Mr Skogan is another matter.'

'Let's have another drink,' suggested Thomas. And the potboy was at his elbow immediately.

I was beginning to see eight princes. Their faces all screwed to the size of a single fist.

Hal resumed his litany, unoiled by any further wine:

'Verde island, St Jorge island, the isle of Teneriffe, the Grand

Canary island –'

Thomas sighed. He closed his eyes.

'A grocer's list,' he said. 'The childish recitation of an old nurse woman. The beating of an empty drum.' He put down his bowl with much deliberation and gave his elder brother a look that was like the flick of a lash. 'The Azores,' he said, 'are simply those islands in the south of the world – no Christian soul disputes it – in the land or province of the kingdom of Guinea in West Africa – as one goes eastward or as one goes southward – with St Miguel island, which is north of the island of Jesus Cristo –'

(Humphrey crossed himself.)

'– and Santa Maria island,' went on Thomas, 'which is to the east of St Miguel – and I swear I never heard any argument so glib or so thin-lipped in my life!' he added, with an inconclusive leer of aggression.

Hal's nostrils shivered. 'I never said they weren't,' he said.

'He never did,' said Humphrey. 'It is the truth.'

'He never said they were not what?' said John.

'Azores,' said Hal.

'He never denied for a second that they were Azores,' suggested Humphrey.

One of the greyhounds yawned.

The viol screamed.

I mashed my tongue.

The princes drank in silence for a while. John scrubbed at his stubby tower of a neck. Thomas examined the contents of his bowl with vague disgust. Humphrey proposed a game of chess, but this was ignored. Hal's eyes were more like weasels now than hawks.

'The island of Graciosa,' he said at last, in a very loud voice, 'is the most westerly of the Azores.'

'Northerly,' said Thomas.

'And St Jorge island is more to the south than Graciosa,' Hal continued, 'with the island of Pico, again to the south, and opposite the same Graciosa.'

'But you said before –' began John, then stopped. He could not remember what it was that his brother had said before.

'Then the island of Jesus Christo –'

(✠ by Humphrey)

183

'is directly opposite Graciosa,' said Henry, 'but more to the east.'

'By God, it's moving!' roared Thomas. 'My brother the Prince of Wales has invented an island that travels!'

'Shut up!' warned Henry – and sitting in the shadows I would have advised his brothers to heed him. But Thomas and John were too deep in their cups to care. Mr Poeticule Skogan's bad verses no doubt. A man can be driven to drink by exposure to bad verses. I have often observed it.

When the princes came out into the street – the stars dipping long fingers into the Thames – Prince Hal began chanting the names of his precious islands in a very irritable and irritating psalm.

'The island of Sal, the island of Boa Vista, the island of Maio, the island of Sao Tiago –'

'Stuff your islands!' shouted Thomas.

'Santa Luzia,' chanted Henry. 'St Vicente, which lies due east. Ilheu Branco. Sao Nicolau. Brava. . . .'

'Brava basta!' cried Thomas, and hit him.

'Fogo!' cried Henry. And hit him back.

They had played the fox. They had played the goat. And now the four princes were determined to play the lion and the tiger too. A sprawling brawl soon occupied the street. Hal and Humphrey were easily getting the better of Thomas and John. The offspring of King Henry the 4th were beating each other with pieces of rolled up parchment and bags of beans. I lurked in the doorway of the Boar's Head, out of the starlight, out of the moonlight, and completed some of my education in the ways of the world of power.

And all the while the four of them hurled these names of their stupid islands back and forth like bad fruit. Like exotic insults.

'Ufantanta!'

'Bulama!'

'Buavo!'

'Iwonchi!'

'SALVA!'

'SPOSA!'

'BAUCHI!!'

The brawl spilled all through Eastcheap. Windows were broken. Carts overturned.

At last, some frightened citizens, roused from their beds by the racket, called for the Mayor and the sheriffs to save them from what was supposed to be Mr Glendower at least and the End of the World more likely. It was not so much the princes. But their followers were breaking bones in earnest. I think some of the thicker hangers-on imagined the names of those islands were new-fangled abuse in Italian. I did my best to save Hal from disgrace, tugging at his sleeve and warning him the Mayor had been sent for. All I received for my trouble was a black eye. But he was to recall the attempt at rescue with more kindness and gratitude later.

So much for England, Harry, and St George. Four princes of the Blood Royal were arrested, and spent the night in jail.

Bolingbroke had the news next morning. He sent for the Mayor and the Aldermen and the sheriffs. Nobody quite anticipated what the King would do. It was guessed that Hal would have complained to him. And it was assumed that Humphrey would follow him in every suit. I know that William Gascoigne, the Chief Justice, made a good show of brow-beating the Mayor at first, demanding to know what the city of London had been thinking of.

'The law of England,' said the Mayor. 'And the keeping of the King's peace.'

Bolingbroke must have liked this answer. Perhaps he was already being troubled with bad dreams, and the notion of his peace being defended and upheld by his loyal citizens of London was more powerful at that moment in his mind than the affront which his sons had brought upon themselves and him by riotous behaviour.

Hal was in a fury. But there was nothing he could do about it. If anything, I think this single event inspired some of his attitude towards the sober citizenry of London in the years to come, for he resented their criticism, and their abrogating to themselves the right to interfere in his quarrel with his brothers. He remembered also the fat man in the streets of Eastcheap who had tried to warn him of the Mayor's approach.

For myself: I observed that the highest men in the land were prepared to fall out over the lowest and smallest things. If princes fight over the names of islands they have never seen, and which they will never even visit in all likelihood, how can the King have a peace to keep?

Late. I began this late, and I finish it as the chimes again remind me it is midnight. Chimes at midnight in a different context now.

One word more. This is – this was – the Feast of St John of the Latin Gate. Because such dates may one day pass from the minds of men – who knows how the world might change, with England the way it is going? – I set it down briefly that the feast we celebrated today remembers the dedication of the basilica by the Porta Latina in Rome, where the blessed St John was hurled into a vat of boiling oil by order of the Emperor Domitian. And jumped out again unharmed, uncooked, unworried. St John, indeed, was the only one of the 12 apostles who was not called to martyrdom. He died at Ephesus at a great age. About the year 100.

XXXVIII

Sir John Fastolf's farewell

8 May

Hanson and Nanton take this down. The heavenly twins. Castor and Pollux. Caster oil and bollocks. My pet Dioscuri. And Hanson in his day has been something of a horse-tamer. And Nanton was a boxer. My morning and my evening stars. My Gemini of baboons. God's farts, Sir, an inseparable case of coxcombs.

Speaking of baboons – Nanton's face is not unlike the face of the great baboon you can see in the show at Southwark. I suppose it was the boxing did it. Put the finishing touches to what his mother and his father first began. As for Hanson, he is more delicate. He *walks* like the baboon.

My brace, my composite crystal, my pair of twingle-twangles. They took the same girl to Chester Races once. The girl grew excited watching the stallions parade, so Hanson slipped his hand in under her dress, and was soon playing with her there in the middle of the crowd. Such a press, such excitement, nobody noticed. But Hanson sneezed, and snatched his hand away an instant. When he put it back up under the girl's dress, in search of the wet playing-place, he found another hand already there, busy at work doing what he had been doing. It was Nanton, of course. They stood side by side, with the girl just in front, leaning herself against the fence, and they finished her off between them. The horse lost.

There. Did you write all that, Hanson? More bloody fool you. But faithful. They're faithful dogs, these henchmen.

I make my men write lies about themselves. I tell the truth about me, but I tell lies about them. For the pleasure of having them write it down. Yet, having said that I tell lies about them, I have told the truth about me. Thus the reader will learn the scope and power of my honesty. It is unparalleled, like my girth.

I skipped a day yesterday.

It's a piss-pot of a day today, and again to tell you the truth I've no stomach for much memory.

I spent yesterday afternoon with Miranda in the garden. Ineffably sweet air. Dark boughs and our pale blue Norfolk sky. Flowers starting to sprout, and shrubs to do the things shrubs are supposed to do at this time of the year. (I never took much interest in the under earth. That can wait until I get there.) My skin felt as dry as a snake's. Yet the air was exquisite. We watched the scarlet and black carp twist in and out of the iris roots in my pool. Miranda spoke for an hour of the terrible punishments we are promised for a little pleasant sin. I took her hand in a manner so quiet that she felt no wish to withdraw it from my grasp. Her voice trailed off and her eyes filled up with burning tears.

I said: 'We owe a debt of punishment, yes, my dear. That we must pay in Purgatory, helped by the prayers of our friends who remain behind. But even in Purgatory there will be more joy than there is on earth. As for sins, and the forgiveness of sins – I believe in them both. I'd be a fool if I didn't believe in the former, and I'd be a damned fool if I didn't believe in the latter.' I stroked her hair as we stood by a pointed lily, an arm's length in height, with a great shining pod as tongue, fleshy in substance, of the darkest crimson, black veiled with red. I said: 'Do you think that I could bear for an instant the thought of the great moral eye of God fixed upon me, if it were not for our Lord Jesus Christ?'

'What do you mean?' said Miranda. Her hair was plaited and braided with pearls. She wore a broad silk girdle tied about her waist.

'I mean,' I said, 'what the Church means – or so I trust, and Friar Brackley puts me right when I stray into opinions that are just motions of my own mind. The mind of the Church is clear enough, as it seems to me. We sin. We are born into sin. We sin and we sin again and again, despite all our penance and good intentions and all the wishing that it could be otherwise. We can't change human nature. But Christ translates it. The grace of our Lord's sacrifice is the complete removal of all that guilt and stain of our poor sins. I could come before God with sorrow – but that would not be enough. It is our Lord that is enough.'

'You do not often talk like this,' said Miranda.

'I am hardly a holy man,' I pointed out, 'but since you brought up the subject, I'm making my own position clear.'

'Which is that of a sinner,' said Miranda.

'A sinner,' I said.

Miranda touched the lily's tongue. 'A boy told me once that really bad sins committed after baptism could *not* be forgiven,' she murmured.

'Ask Friar Brackley,' I told her. 'But I know what he will tell you. Deny the Church her power to forgive sins, and you deny Christ. The Montanists did that, any many other sorts of heretics.' I caught her hand again. 'Oh it is hard enough to believe any of it,' I cried. 'God is a tall story. The crucifixion and the resurrection – both tall stories. But don't you see, that might well be because they are *true*? If they were lies or fables they would look more plausible, they would suit us better. As it is, they suit us only in the sense that *we* are a tall story too. The world – the nature of man – our natural, actual, formal, and habitual sins. All tall stories.'

Miranda snatched her hand away. 'And you believe them?'

I laughed. 'Yes.'

'But when why do you laugh?'

'Because it is all so simple and all so complicated,' I said.

'I love our Lady and I like very much the going to Mass, and hearing it well sung,' said Miranda childishly. 'But I'll admit to you now – where no one can hear us or heed us – that it does sometimes seem to me pretty far-fetched. Heaven and Hell. The whole thing.'

'*Certum est, quia impossibile,*' I said. 'That is Tertullian. He saw it could well be true *because* it was so unlikely.'

Miranda's pretty face was now so puzzled that I had to laugh again – for sympathy's sake.

But she misinterpreted the laugh, and stamped her foot. 'I wish you wouldn't laugh so much,' she said.

'I like laughter,' I explained. 'I have this passion for clowns and fools, for the wisdom of foolishness, for those who dare to stand established order on its head so that its disestablishments show. Forgive me, dear niece. Down and out is my proper linear direction. I dare to go further. I am a down and downer, an out and outer.'

'And a great big baby,' said Miranda, pouting, toying with the hilt of my sword.

'A monster,' I agreed. 'An abstruse infant playing with his own ego.'

Then I kissed her. 'I will tell you an old man's secret,' I

whispered in her sweet little whirlpool of an ear. 'It is this. *Water will taste like wine if you use your tongue well.*'

'Now you've lost me again,' complained Miranda.

'Then it is time to find you properly,' I said.

I chased her down a steep path under the flowering trees. Bearing in mind my years, no doubt, and my great rotundity – not to speak of her real desire to be caught – Miranda did not run so very fast. She let me take off her scarlet dress in the vegetable patch, and despite a sudden May shower of warm rain we had quick sport and business in the buttercups.

In the evening we went together down to the shore and watched a fine storm. The lightning shivered the masts on one of my ships. Sirius baring his fang. Not that I care for storms or weather much. But the sight put Miranda in a high mood and a passion. The night has left me knackered and I confess it.

How are we for figs from Cerne Abbas?

Memo. Put down an order for Macbeth to send.

The usual.

No. Double it. *Benedicite!*

I reflect and deliberate this morning on the curious task I have set myself in undertaking these annals. Here am I, a captain of men and a knight of the realm of England, four score years beneath my belt, in my prime, worth my weight in silver if not gold, a most respected (if not respectable) and amazing (if rarely amazed) citizen, a denizen you might say of the wide world which I have made my home – here I am, an old man in a dry month, having fought in the warm rain with Miranda yesterday, and at the hot gates of Harfleur and Hell with Harry Monmouth and the pride of England, heaving a cutlass, all that – here I am, employing my days in this making of Days, in this long act of recall of my youth and other follies.

It is no occupation for a gentleman.

If I were not driven by the demon *Truth*, I should not undertake it.

Truth. What is it? Pilate's question. And he had the answer under his nose.

Ravenstone taught me that Plato's opinion was that a man would know the truth if he could sublimate his mind to its original purity. Greek nonsense. I do not believe my mind ever had any original purity. It was always as filthy as it is now, only less full of stuff when I was a child, since then I knew less of the ways of the world.

Ravenstone taught me also that Arcesilaos said that man's understanding is not capable of knowing what truth is. That may be so. But a man may also have been to bed with a woman, and known her carnally, without knowing her name – and then she was gone in the morning. How can I be sure I have not slept with Truth? Of course, if I were to accept the opinion of Carneades also – which is that not only is our understanding not capable of comprehending Truth, but that our senses are wholly inadequate to help us in the investigation – well, then I'd be well and truly sunk.

Well. And *truly* sunk.

I like the philosophy of Democritus best of all. That laughing doctor, that dear droll of Abdera, he taught that Truth lies at the bottom of a well. A well of what? Of memory perhaps. Not just *my* memory, mark you, or *your* memory. A common memory of more-than-us. A river might make a better image than a well. And truth there, in the river's flowing. Never to be had, quite, because the moment you step into the river it is a different river.

Up Democritus, in any case! That laughing philosopher is my friend and mentor. He taught that the *summum bonum* is the maximum of pleasure with the minimum of pain, but did not make the vulgar mistake of supposing all pain antithetical to pleasure, or all pleasure identical with mere sensual enjoyment. Laughter has its principle in the soul.

The soul laughs. Being the root of all forms of vital activity. A soul that could not laugh would be a dead soul, a stick, a devil.

Besides, by Clio's tits, Madam, there is this ambition on a lower plane: to formulate some kind of truth from my experience. Not imposing a set pattern upon the reality of it. The form of what I write here is shaped by the tale and the telling itself.

These Days – this process – my acts of attention to my life. My acts of attention form my *Acta*.

Also, to tell you the plain truth, it passes the time. Which otherwise passes slowly, plain truth to tell.

Now if only Eve had liked bananas better. We'd all still be in Paradise. And no need then for this fine fiddle about the individual consciousness or conscience. And sins. And forgiveness. And figs.

I have done more work of a substantial character on my great Bill of Claims against the Crown. In due course it shall appear here, before going off to London by special delivery.

Another reason for making these memorials – apart, that is, from the doubtful pleasure of remembering days now slipped for ever from my fingers – is in *annoying my secretaries*. I do not underestimate this motive. Here they sit, O Reader between the lines, singly or together, thin men all, skeletal things, thimbles, thieves of my adventures, and I make them dance like puppets to go about fetching boxes of pens and haystacks of paper to write down every word I care to say. I confess that it crosses my mind that it might be as good as mustard to compel a celibate priest to take down details of my little tricks with my niece Miranda. Just as it was sweet to watch Worcester wax hot and hotter at having to consider my memories of that tugging on the pink wet nipple of my young nurse Jaquenetta. Or pigsbum Bussard with his eyes popping out of his codpiece at the news of what poor Shallow failed to do to Mrs Nightwork in the mill in St George's fields. Not that I *have* yet employed Fr Brackley in any such part. I keep him for my more sacramental confessions, do you see. In the tribunal of my penance. But you catch the piquancy? Thin men having to set down fat meals. Men whose only pleasure in women has come in the impotent extravagance of imagination being compelled to record the sober details of my many and most intricate amours. In the pages to follow, cowards will have to tell the tale of my heroic deeds in the battlefield.

Hanson and Nanton, heavenly twins, I ask myself the question which your own eyes formulate: Is it a something cruel and vengeful in my nature that spurs me to such pleasure in this?

Perhaps. I am large. I have room for some cruelty amidst what I take to be an over-abundant supply of the milk (and fat) of human kindness.

But I prefer to see it all as a desire for *the round*. Circles and spheres are my idea of geometry. Breasts are spherical, and bums – and the rounder parts of females are altogether the best, not forgetting the womb and its sweet oval entrance.

Square pegs in round holes. That's one way to get at the truth.

King Arthur had a Round Table. And Lancelot had a lance, and King Arthur's wife.

God damn it all, and Democritus lived to be exactly 100 years old. I know Diodorus Siculus said it was only 90. But Diodorus Siculus was a liar.

Since I'm feeling especially truthful today, what with that pointed lily yesterday afternoon and the rain pissing down right now as it has since sunrise, I put it on record as well that I'm telling my life to my secretaries because it is *easier* than labouring away to scribble it all down myself.

But I'm telling it also in this particular dictatorial way – *to shock and to educate these thin fellows.*

NB: When I began, some Robin Goodfellow of false modesty made me confine my secret adventures – I mean, of the bedchamber and environs, and of Miranda, and Ophelia, and the whip, and suchlike – to the mute witness of my own hand, on days when my secretaries were away on business or otherwise engaged. Not any more. Hanson takes this down, while I kick Nanton round about the room to help the twin cause of inspiration and digestion. Each of this pretty pair lusts after my Miranda. Did you think I didn't know it? Did you imagine that I didn't see your eyes undress her as she passed you in the gallery that day? And who has a scarf of hers concealed in a chest beneath his bed?

Reader, the rogues are red. Truth makes men change colours. Hanson's had to drop the pen. Never mind, Hanson. Come here and I will kick *you*, for a change, while friend Nanton takes over the scribbling.

Now, my blue baboon face, go, go, and take down this:

Last night Sir John Fastolf, K.G., and his sweet niece, made the beast with two backs seven times. Which is 14 backs. Like the Cichivache, that French monster, the sorry cow that lives only on the flesh of good women, and is consequently all skin and bone, because its food is so extremely scarce these days. Or like the Bicorn, our English bull, as fat as the other is lean, but again with 14 backs, feeding on good and enduring husbands, under petticoat rule, and with two horns – always plenty of that sort of diet.

To the particular meat of *our* 14-backed beast.

First, Sir John Fastolf's niece Miranda disposed her limbs below. She put one of her legs between his legs and wrapped the other round his back. Her cunny gobbled up his cock. Then Sir John Fastolf and his young mistress performed the same act again, this time with her thighs bent back until her knees were touching her tits. The storm had aroused the rare Miranda. She was *hot*. After a few deep thrusts from Sir John's weapon in this position, the weight of the knight's belly and the length and strength of the same weapon became too much for his niece to bear. Knight and lady then changed roles. Sir John Fastolf observed the supine part, with the Lady Miranda on top. She brought up her legs carefully, until she was in a sitting position with his penis right up inside her. Sir John Fastolf then held his sweet Miranda by the hips and bounced her up and down on the carnal maypole.

These basic themes, with a few variations, being played – the tender Miranda lay upon Sir John Fastolf's chest, with one hand in his beard, and the other in his bush. She took her usual pleasure in arousing the might of his member even when that loyal warrior looked spent. It was her joy to tie ribbons about it, taking them from her hair, and then to dance her fingers round and round his towering pillar of flesh like maids about the maypole. It was with the ribbons still attached to his organ that he futtered her thoroughly upon the windowseat in the upper chamber.

Set down also that the dowager Margaret Paston, together with her husband John Paston, Sir John Fastolf's friend and neighbour, of the manor of Gresham, visited Sir John Fastolf this evening, and that these boring Pastons were still making their elaborate departure when the master retired with his love to the same room upstairs. Miranda had been touching her uncle's foot with hers beneath the table, nibbling at his ankles with her toes, and making all manner of big eyes and little kisses as she took her supper, by these tokens reminding him of yesterday's enjoyments. Once inside the upper room, another event took place such as Mr Nanton has described – with such wobbly fingers! – above. It was then, pressed hard into Miranda upon the windowseat, that the said Sir John Fastolf, K.G., observed his guests departing in the courtyard below. He took thought to draw his niece's attention to the departure of the Pastons, and at the same moment the dowager Margaret chanced herself to look up.

Being ever the perfect host, and considerate lest his guest should think he was slighting her by looking down from the window with his head in such an odd position, Sir John Fastolf took care to draw his niece Miranda to her feet, holding her body in front of his own naked body, she being naked only from the waist down, and then to bend her forwards out of the window so that she might wave good-bye to Mrs Paston and her husband. Sir John Fastolf called out cheerfully over Miranda's shoulder to his departing guests, remarking on the sweetness of the night air now that the storm of yesterday night had cleared it, and the day's rain momentarily had ceased. And all the while he futtered Miranda's anal canal from behind, and frigged her clitoris.

'How lovely the moon is too!' he whispered in his dear companion's ear. And, indeed, one of the advantages of the position for erotic intercourse just described is that it affords each partner an opportunity of observing sunrise or sunset, or the moon, or stars, or a circus, or any other entertainment which requires them both to be looking in the same direction.

'Bid goodnight to Margaret Paston too, my darling,' he told Miranda.

However, the busy Miranda was finding herself somewhat overwhelmed at that moment, and the effort of speaking proved beyond her. She managed, however, a squeak.

Sir John Fastolf has determined to practise this farewell on other guests to his Caister Castle.

The Lady Miranda found it so agreeable and amusing that she is writing some invitations right now.

XXXIX

Sir John Fastolf's permission for his translation

Hum, ha! Hang you, you mechanical salt-butter rogues. Faust me and foin me and fig me and firk me, but the Devil can have one of you, and his dam the other. I see that Luke Nanton, that little humorist, in setting down the last morsel of yesterday's pages, grew so excited or distempered with what I had to say that by the end of the session he had me translated into the Third Person Singular.

Sir John Fastolf, he says. . . . He, he says. . . .

I, I, I, myself sometimes. Myselves very often. The most First Person Plural Man in the world. We, figging Fastolf. Us, fausty Jack.

But I'm not surprised. We are not surprised. He is not surprised. That windowseat. That windowsill. O, and when we turned round again and into the room, my Miranda so coursed over my exteriors – with such a greedy intention! And at dinner with Margaret and John Paston: the appetite of Miranda's eye scorching me up like a burning-glass! O powerful love! It makes a beast a man. And a man a beast. By cock we are to blame!

But this Third Person very Singular. Looking it over this morning I am not altogether displeased with the effect. Indeed, the Third Person Singular has a certain *roundness* to it that fits me. On occasion, therefore, speaking to my twins, I shall let them employ it. It seems to me that a person as rich and omnipotent and multifarious as myself(selves) may only be understood by approaches from different directions.

Let these annals contain Fastolf in the First Person Singular therefore – and as Singular as is true!

Let them also embrace Fastolf in the First Person Plural – the royal Fastolf. Us, Jove. When we are a bull for our niece Europa. And so forth.

Each First Person, that is, being Fastolf talking, in propria persona, himself, ourselves, my words set down faithfully every one by my scribbling scribes and scratching secretaries here at Caister Castle.

But let these *Acta* contain also some little geography couched in the Third Person Singular – in which the doings and sayings of the same Sir John, me, the fattest stag in the forest, are chronicled with what will therefore appear to be a greater historicity.

That's a good word. I like that word. *Historicity*. It has a smell like a princess's garters.

In any case, dictating to Hanson and Nanton on the subject of my rut-times with my saucy niece Miranda obviously wrings the poor wet rags so tight with distress and desire and distraction that they have to cross their legs as they write the words that enflame them. Yesterday afternoon Hanson in particular got so worked up it was a wonder he didn't swallow his pen and disappear up his own arse in pursuit of his prick.

Follow me into the pit.

Luke Nanton takes today's instalment down. It's no especial day. No saints looming. Fr Brackley mutters about St Hermas and St Gregory Nazianzen – but I'm leaving them. All that theology and the lily's tongue with Miranda the other day. I think I'll just leave the fear of God on my left hand for a little.

Scrope would be ideal for amorous chapters. Nothing excites my stepson. Except, perhaps, a rise in his allowance?

Ah, by God, the fishy eye looked up. A tear gleamed in it, Reader. That moist hand, yellow from years of envy, trembled.

I'll have that Stephen Scrope to author yet.

Pathetic buggers. Every one of them. All the same, lads, I shall see to it that you are suitably rewarded when the heroic tale of Sir John Fastolf is done, and his Hundred Days War has been won.

> *Where are those Spani-ards*
> *That make so great a boast O –*
> *They shall eat the Grey Goose Feather*
> *And we will eat the Roast O!*

I will give you battles and sieges and arblasters.

I will provide you with swords and sabres. Comfort you with scimitars. Stay you with rapiers.

O times, O manners, O armaments.

Set down the trumpets and the fighting and the marching and

the spoils. The pages mounting in that corner are the bounty. A King's ransom of paper. My lovely whazerys. Yet there will be better bounty and richer reward for you all. A whazery of immortality. Wait and see.

In pursuit of this rotund *Third Person*, this mountain that I am – ah, ah, hey diddle diddle, the very tag brings back to me the swigh-sigh-swish of my tutor Ravenstone, with his Latin verbs and nouns and all those dark declensions – with regard to writing *Sir J.F.*, I say, rather than 'I' at every turn, – when we come to my time in France I intend to give you all a holiday from hanging on my every word as I pace up and down my library here in Caister. Soldiers are not the best of authors, and I admit it. Here is none of your literature, but a plain man's life. Still, a holiday, my spaniels! A dogs' holiday indeed. There already exists, do you see, a full record and complement of my adventures in France, in Normandy and Anjou, in Pacy and Coursay, up at Basle and down at Arras. The jolly story of my principal manoeuvres in the One Hundred Years War, no less, and of my extensive and still imperfectly renumerated service to the Crown. This was compiled at my direction many years ago by my man in France, Peter Basset. Now my man Basset was a soldier and he wrote a good hand, and his record is terse and complete. I see no point in concocting new versions when the truth has already been established.

However, little geese – here's the bad news.

Basset wrote in Latin.

I am going to require Basset's version of my *Acta* in France to be translated into good round sloping English by you, Nanton, and by friend Hanson, and by the Friar (if he can get his finger out of that freckled boatboy), and by Stephen Scrope my ignoble stepson. You will find the matter peculiar enough to warm your organs in the pursuit, I promise. Fastolf's war was not exactly a crusade.

This won't be for some Days yet. Weeks of our Days, in fact. First, there is all my experience in Ireland to be gone into. And then my adventures in London and everywhere with Prince Hal.

Enough of *historicity* for today. O History, History, your face is your arse in profile.

I feel suddenly fartuous. I'm dying for a shit. Fry me some cow-parsley fritters.

XL

About Sir John Fastolf's prick

I have reached my 40th Day without having once described my mainspring. This sin of omission must be immediately repaired.

It is fourteen and a half inches long, my tool, with a girth of six inches, and in appearance rather like a well-baked Norfolk loaf. It achieved these dimensions quite naturally. Not like Hal's efforts – always pulling at his princely cock to make it longer. Not like Pistol's pistol either. When Pistol was a boy he worked on his thing with a suction cup, and then with a stone with a hole through it. He hung the stone on a string which he tied round his member. Result: he had a long thin pizzle like a runner bean. But no girth, no thickness, no staying power at all.

Ophelia liked to call my prick by different names.

Swinging with her in the swing all the afternoon, rubbing our bacon together –

'Get out your pillicock, Jack!' *or*

'Let's have a game with your pike!' *or*

'I can feel your poperin pear in your pocket!' *or*

'Come on! Where's that potato-finger of yours?'

Miranda has a whole set of different nicknames, as well as these ones.

My bugle.

My lance.

My sword.

My standard.

My hook.

My horn.

My instrument.

My stump.

My root.

My dart of love.
My poll-axe.
My potent regiment.
My carrot.
My tail.
My holy thistle.
My thorn.
My bauble.
My lag end.
My distaff.
My needle.
My pin.
My pipe.
My organ.
My pen.
My yard.
My roger.
And so on. But mostly she likes to call a prick a prick, and my prick especially.

Paradisi. . . . Temporie. . . .

My mother Mary Fastolf never favoured the cruel habit of the ancient Jews, which was to cut away the foreskin from this most sensitive and ticklish and alarmed and alarming of wild beasts. My man comes therefore in his natural hood. He looks like a Franciscan. The foreskin is indeed wonderfully pliable, stretchy, and agreeable, and moves backwards and forwards upon the head of my fellow with a hot gulping rapidity and smoothness which ladies without number have told me is much to their pleasuring.

I have the usual amount of baggage.

When I was a young man this prick of mine was somewhat of an upstart. He was forever discharging himself. He existed in a near-permanent state of standing to attention, like something in the company of a Queen. The merest glimpse of a girl, the slightest rustling wisp of an underskirt as a lady brushed past his master in the street, and up he would pop, my fool, like a genie in one of the tales of the Arabian desert. Once up, also, nothing could persuade the cocky villain to lower his head again but to have himself dipped and immersed in one or another of the more satisfactory grottoes of the feminine anatomy.

He was not religious about the central one. O, he hymned hymens when in the mood, and he sifted and stroked the velvet leaves, and he certainly got stuck into that dearest bodily part a woman has. But he loved any den, any lap, any hole, any scut, any nest of spicery. He would come off in Venus' glove as soon as in her mound. He would beggar himself of my marrow as quickly in a warm mouth, a tight little brown bum-hole, a chaste arm-pit, a fleshy elbow, or even an intricate ear.

There was a time, in my early days in London, in company with the same riggish Mrs Nightwork whom I have already spoken of, when my young cock favoured the ear quite acutely. I cannot say why. Jane Nightwork had a most delectable and definitive and musical ear. It was like a little filigree, a whirlpool, a veritable shell. It was her delight to run her tongue up and down my chap until he began to drool at the tip. I would lie on my back with my thighs apart and my legs drawn up to afford her utter access to what she wanted. She used to hold my damsons gently in her hand and tug with her nibbly lips at my long foreskin. She liked to kiss me up and down the cock as he swelled to her fondling. She'd dally with her fingers, and tease me with her nostrils, and cherish and tickle until she sensed the sperm begin to stir. Then Jane would pop her hot red lips about my prick, and suck me six or seven times most rigorously, until I waved my hands about, unable to speak with the sharp surfeit of it.

But that was not the end. Not by a long shot. Jane Nightwork was incredible for dalliance. 'The longer the stronger, the more the merrier,' she'd whisper as she played and stopped, dallied and teased, brought me deliberately to the boil and then as deliberately made me throb and suffer as she smacked down my near-to-bursting soldier.

The lovely focative sucking over, just this side of emission, she'd let my engine out of her spiced trap – (Mrs Nightwork was a great one for eating garlic and cloves.) Then she's press my prick to her cheek, which was usually cool as cream. She had a trick of fluttering her eyelashes upon the delicate skin just below the head, where the foreskin puckers, which I found delicious. When at last Jane could see and feel by the uncontrollable spasms that I was past the point of return, irretrievably advanced by all these gorgeous attentions, then she would grab me in her hands and push as much of me as would go into the complicated country of her ear.

I was smaller in the yard in those days, and she inevitably got it in far enough to satisfy her. Such charged chambers! Such cracks! Such virgin circles! Secret parts! It was like bursting into a sea where no ship had ever thrust. It was like entering an Oriental palace. There were whirls and galleries to that ear, whorls and twirls, windings and turnings, tight spirals, scallops such as I cannot describe. It was like fucking a little labyrinth.

My thrust and paddle there brought both of us to discharge. I'd have my whole fist stuck between her pumping legs. My thumb up her cunt. She'd shake her head marvellously, as though the hot seed I shot into her ear was like good news from another world.

This was a curious voluptuousness, and I mention it since it is a facet of human nature to wish to know the most bizarre before encountering the orthodox. I cannot say that I preferred Jane's ear to her cunt. But it made a change. And for her part, she professed herself weary of men forever grinding away between her thighs, and could not get enough of the Fastolf horn in her ear. She said that it beat listening in shells for the sound of the sea any day. The sound of John Fastolf's coming must always have been mightier than any ocean – and to hear him coming right in your ear is a treat which has been reserved for some few extremely blessed and well-chosen ladies.

Ears, though, are the merest prologue to love's comedy. The rose, the ring, the rudder, the ruff – O, in a word, the *cunt*. Ah, hey now, there's the rub! There's your true comfort, entertainment, pranks and provocation. It makes my tail wag just to think of it. *Benedicite!*

And the names that have gone with it. The ladies I have fucked. O Imogen, whose bedchamber I had to enter in a trunk, and who fought like a cat until she found she liked what I wanted to do to her, and ended up fitting a bracelet on my cock to try and keep him in a condition of uprightness all night! O Juliet, whose green young boyfriend Romeo was as ignorant of what to do as you were, until I pushed him off your virgin belly and showed him how to do it! O Perdita, who liked to lie and have the lambkins nibble at your naked crack, until I came and made it wider! O strange Titania, who demanded the use of a donkey's thing as well as my own! O Beatrice, who liked to whip and be whipped, with the tongue and other instruments of pleasure!

Life is a shuttle. Follow me. I'll tell you strange things. Follow. Strange things in hand, dear reader. Follow.

In my middle life, now, when I was a man you could call a man, this same sword of flesh of mine was a terror to the enemy. In Vaudemont once, bargaining with some dishonest reeve, his daughter chanced to wander through the chamber. A little creature, features like a fairy queen's, a nymph, with silky black hair neatly braided, a light slippered step. Something about her – something about the innocence and longing mingled in those eyes – something about the incipient swell of her breasts under a piece of Breton lace – something or other, or all of it, so stirred and stung and struck me in the groin that – still arguing with the little lying Frenchman – I loosened my apparel in my chair and let my prick out for a peek at her.

The girl was startled. A dainty doe. But she was a true daughter of her country. She did not run away from the English milord's great red throbbing eye cocked out to inspect her charms.

She came closer, as a matter of fact, fidgetting with withered roses in a bowl, pretending to look elsewhere while watching all the while my erect and attent admirer of her beauty.

Her father, however, obsequious but shocked, noting the size and usefulness of my tool – for I swear it grew half an inch with every tripping tiptoe step the daughter took towards me, this being an occasion when what with pressure of battles and the other affairs of Mars I had not offered a drop to Venus for two weeks – the miserable father began to jabber away in French at a rascal rate, and grabbed his daughter, and thrust her from the room. Adieu, French velvet!

I had to spin off my stuff, and conjure my cock down quickly. Drop by drop. The marrow liquored my boots. When the Frenchman came back my codpiece was as crestfallen as a dried pear.

I learnt later from Basset – who had been an amused witness of the scene – that the upshot of the reeve's complaint and fear was that the gross enormity and gianthood of the Englishman's John Thomas would do some murderous injury to his child. These superstitions are of course nonsense – as any decent whore will tell you. (If you don't have a whore, ask your wife.) For though a man's member may be as long and as thick and as hard as a truncheon, it always contrives to slide happily into any hole well-oiled, and then to grow again when it has entered and made itself at home. This gift of swelling, shrinking, and then swelling again is one of the grand mysteries by which Dame Nature looks after her own. It is a trick that I have perfected – either by concentration, or by passion, or by Cerne Abbas figs. Or by a mixture or addition of all three. It has stood me in erectile stead on many occasions, when delicacy was required.

With virgins, though, a different technique is needed. It is no kindness to be slow or gentle with the cracking of a virgin glass. Put a hard pillow under the girl's buttocks. Get her hot with your tongue and fingers. Suck her nipples. Tickle her button. Then push your lance in an inch – and *charge*! (It may be as well to give her something to bite on. A diamond necklace works wonders, distracting the mind from the initial inevitable pain. Then, when she begins to enjoy things, the membrane broken, you can always retrieve the diamonds for someone else.)

With matrons – something else again. Most of them think they know everything. You must presume that their husbands have tried to satisfy them in every way their own imaginations could cook up, after all. So let it be your ambition to bring your older mistress to some cliff-edge of passion which she had not known was there to fall over. Take her upon your knee, and treat her like a naughty little girl. It is quite wonderful, what the simple command –

'*Bend over!*'

will do to stimulate the well-worn wife. Slap her bum with the flat of your hand. Hands never really hurt anyone, and she will soon be begging you, 'Harder! Harder!' until her posteriors tingle. A useful trick then is to push up your fingers and make them converse with her bum. I did this once with my Mrs Ford of Windsor. She got so excited she tried to trap my hand there for ever. So I slipped two fingers into her back passage, and pulling them in and out soon had her in ecstasies. Naturally, she told her friend Mrs Page. And naturally then *she* required some of the same treatment. Ever resourceful, I dreamt up a new refinement. After a similar spanking, I inserted my tongue.

French matrons, in my experience, are not so likely to find these games so novel. But then, half expecting them, they are also more given to washing that particular seat of love, and even to sprinkling some scent up it.

My prick is a good prick. The times when it has served me a fault I can count on the fingers of one hand. I have noted, by the way, that the more exercise I give it, the more energy it appears to possess in itself. I mean, in these latter years. (For in my young age it was not a question of energy but of trying to find a way to quieten the animal down from his state of perpetual rage! In a London street, or in the environs of the court, he had overweening ambitions then to get up every woman I could see.)

Hence I abjure those false moralists who say that in old age a man should not indulge in the appetites of the flesh. Dame Milicent, my late wife, caught me one day in the cellar with a servant girl. We were doing it with me leaning back against a wine-cask, and Ursula, that's the servant girl, held an inch off the ground on the end of my prong. Next day, Milicent was surprised when Ursula came to her and said that she felt so ashamed she would have to leave. 'My lady,' she said, 'after what you saw in the cellar. . . .' 'Don't be absurd,' snapped my darling wife. 'Do you think I mind? It all helps. It all helps. What with you in the cellar, and me in the bedroom, perhaps we can keep the old devil at home between the two of us!'

Compare what Mrs Quickly said of me at an earlier date:

'In good faith, he cares not what mischief he does, if his weapon be out! He will foin like any devil! He will spare neither man, woman, nor child!'

(Not strictly speaking true. I can think of men and children I *have* spared.)

The world's my oyster. With this sword I still open it.

Up, rogue! Stand upon your honour! Lust and luxury. Sinful fire. I am in haste. With a Goliath like this between my legs, who am I to bewail that the pricking capacity of my prong has been blunted or otherwise reduced by the passage of years? *The boy is still growing!* He has a hunger now for Miranda which if I do not feed it will cause him to batter down the door and spend his honeyseed on the three serving wenches who are about to bring me my mid-day flagons. It is my pleasure, incidentally, to have these girls attend me with their lower portions bare save for a thin silk about the posteriors. In this garb, I can correct them quickly if they err in their manners. It is a refinement I acquired from my classical education. You may recall my tutor Ravenstone and his tales of Trimalchio's banquet. He told me also of a Roman Empress who kept her slave girls undressed in this way so that there was *no impediment to an instant whipping*.

I have done many things with my Jack-a-Dandy. I have lit fires, and put them out. I have made cuckoos, and charmed the birds from the trees. I have tickled little trout and groped for them in a peculiar river. I have found out countries with it. I have picked locks. I have taken treasure. I have pissed tallow and mandrake. I have ploughed. I have plucked. I have possessed. I have procured. I have put down, put in, put to, and put to sea. (Above deck, and under hatches.) I have cracked bonds of chastity. I have fed in dales and mountains. I have lived in ladies' hearts, died in their laps, and been buried in their eyes. I have discharged upon my hostess of the Boar's Head tavern. I have dribbled darts of love. I have ferred, and firked, and ferreted, and functioned. I have been cruel with maids, and cut off their heads. I have ridden hobby-horses. I have lusted. I have loved.

He is a fearless friend and formidable foe. Ladies have been known to faint at the sight of him, but to come round with one eye open and very bright. Thomas, eighth baron Clifford of Clifford, standing beside me once to piss against a wall in Calais, spying my creature out of the corner of his eye, remarked: 'So *that's* how we won at Agincourt!'

Reader, my friend, my brother, I lay no claim to the possession of a secret weapon. On the contrary, I have opened my heart and my codpiece to you. My pubic matter is now public knowledge.

Of the particular amorous adventures of my fellow I shall have more to record in the course of these memorials. The purpose of this disquisition of a prick is not to recount adventures, but to offer a simple inventory of my closest friend and most significant part.

I tell him that it's rude to point. But he won't listen. He is a deaf brute, and a hard man. There it is.

It occurs to me that if I didn't have secretaries and couldn't write with my own hand, here is the ideal instrument with which to tell my story. Take it that this penal gentleman is writing. *He* is certainly the one who is talking. From the first of my Hundred Days he has been talking his head off.

The pen is mightier than the sword. The penis is mightier than the pen.

No doubt this is the first record of a man's life ever to tell some of the true aspects of it which I am telling.

Vile worm.

But this is the short and the long of it.

The bawdy hand of the dial is now upon the prick of noon.

Up, gentlemen. You shall see sport anon. Follow me, gentle-men. (And ladies too – I promise you some penetrating prose!)

May I never spit white again if this isn't the first record of a man's life to be written by his prick.

XLI

How Sir John Fastolf fell in love with a lady of London

Love. Love is a villain. You love sack, and so do I; would you desire better sympathy? *Is* there better sympathy? Fr Brackley tells me so. In love the heavens themselves do guide the state. Angels must be made of love. The seraphim and cherubim, and thrones, in the first circle; the dominions and virtues and powers, in the second circle; the principalities and archangels, and then the ordinary common or guardian angels, in the third circle. Abdiel, Gabriel, Michael, Raguel, Raphael, Simiel, Uriel. The seven holy angels. Love, all made of love. Of course, there are knotty points about angels. But then there are tangles in love down here. *Utrum Angelus moveatur de loco ad locum transeundo per medium?* God knows. Or maybe St Thomas Aquinas, who was a doctor of angels.

Love. I do not underestimate it, Madam. Nothing else is, in the last analysis. That great member of mine which occupied the last chapter – nothing, nothing at all, merest nothing, without love. Just a muscle, Sir.

Henry the 6th may owe me ten thousand pounds. His father owed me a million. I do not exaggerate. Hal owed me his love. His love was worth a million.

As for my foining aforementioned. I am not such a gross of hypocrites as to claim that it was all for love. But that part of it which was, was surely justified? Love is too young to know what conscience is. Eros is a great little god, and Venus my lovely gossip.

In the early days of my first time in London – not long after I came to the city – it was my foul good fortune to fall in love. The depth of this love into which I fell was deep, though not as bad as

Leander's. I mean, I did not drown in it. But it was deep enough, and bad enough, and good enough, and true enough, and while the ferocious sweet fever lasted I believed it to be at once the best and the worst thing in the world, now spinning me up to the stars, now dragging me down to the gutters. And once I was out of it I resolved never again to venture into such regions.

But we have no choice in the matter. Love and death are strange sisters, and *they choose us*. Barbarous sisters, sisters from a foreign country, a land that has never yet nor ever will be discovered perhaps. O enigmatic sisters, spare me. It crosses my mind that all my desire is desire for death. Death is that lost continuity which I – I, I, I, myself sometimes, shuffling, hedging, lurching, discontinuous – long for. I am a man. Define me by my mortality. By the incompleteness implicit in my passions. It would be an irrelevance to imagine existence without these passions. Celibates dwell as much upon them as do whores and strumpets. Celibates probably *think* more lust than wantons do. At the same time, don't I modify my mortality by this need for the infinite, by my nostalgia for death? How can I feel nostalgia for what I have never known? I don't know; but I do. And then I find it most convenient and easy to celebrate death in voluptuousness, in acts and actures, in the amorous rite. I exorcise myself in my beloved. And in that deed of darkness I have often found that I am gaining more than I am losing – that lechery is only a foretaste of ecstasy. O unreasoning fury – and here I am trying to reason with you! At the root of love I discover a lust for disorder, violence, and indignity. Is my thirst for the grave? Woman is death, or the way to die, then. She is certainly the only cure for life.

I revisit my confusions of that state, I see.

Truth to tell, I can mention the matter now with scarcely a twinge of pain in the right kneecap – but it still remains my task to set this down among less honourable pursuits. (Honour! But I'll come to honour.)

I have recorded, when all is said and done, my first adventures of the flesh with my stepsister Ophelia, and my later encounters with those flashy creatures poor Mr Shallow insisted upon knowing (to the best of his limited ability) as bona-robas. It is only fair, then, to confess that on just one occasion in my youth I fell so low as to love where I would lust.

The curious thing I have to tell you is that I never knew the lady's name. I saw her three times. Three apparitions. In St Botolph's, Shoreditch, just beyond the Bishop's Gate in London Wall.

The first time I saw her I had entered the church by mistake, taking a wrong turn when pursued by the watch, and stopping a moment in that painted peace when I realised the place was empty save for myself and one other. St Botolph's was a lovely church. A picture-book of the Faith. Windows, paintings, gilded statues. All telling the one story.

The other person in the church was a lady all in blue, who knelt before a statue of the Virgin, and did not look up as the door slammed shut behind me, or show by the slightest movement of her head that she heard my footsteps as I walked slowly through the candled gloom.

My idea had been to leave St Botolph's by a side-door, thus making doubly sure that the watch did not get scent of me again. But something in this lady kneeling made me stop. I slipped behind a pillar and waited patiently for her to finish her prayers, hoping that when she had done so she might pass by me on her way to the great door.

Deo gratias, she did.

I think I never saw a face so beautiful. There was a light about it. A radiance. A glory. Her cheek-bones were high and her brow as white as snow. Her eyes were blue and bright. Her face a perfect oval. She looked straight ahead as she walked and gave no gesture which would betray that she had the slightest suspicion I might be behind the pillar. She had this *straight shy look* which I find difficult to describe.

I cleared my throat. I wanted to speak to her. To exchange a greeting. To make some comment on the beauty and the peace of that hallowed ground. Something. Anything. But my tongue would not move.

I made to hurry after her, thinking that in the street it might be easier to attract her attention to me, since in the church there was plainly such an air of *concentration* about her.

But my feet were as though they were nailed to the stone floor. I could not budge.

The great door swung behind her. Then it swung again, and a spotted priest entered. He stared at me suspiciously where I stood like an idiot, my back to the high altar, gazing at him. The sight of his spots cured the paralysis or whatever it was that was affecting my limbs, anyway. I crossed myself and inclined my head pleasantly enough to the cleric, so that he would believe I had no intention of dipping my fingers in his Poor Box.

Then I went to kneel where the lady had knelt. On a little rush-mat before the fine statue of the Blessed Virgin. No doubt the spotty priest thought I had my eyes on the gold candlesticks. I wanted only to bless my knees by having them where that blessed creature had lately been.

I said three Paternosters and seven Hail Marys.

I believe I never in my life prayed so fervently, before or since. When I was about to go out, I was moved also to open a psalter – watched closely still by the red-eyed priest. I knew that it would speak to me in some way. Sure enough, my eyes fell instantly on the verse in the psalms: *I have loved, because the Lord will hear the voice of my prayer*. (I translate it for you. So great is my benevolence even at the memory!)

I closed the book.

'God knows my heart's desire!' I murmured to the priest as I passed him on the way out. He did not look convinced. When I glanced back from the door, he was busy checking that the jewels were still in the statues.

The next day and the next I haunted that church. And was myself haunted by the priest with the spots and the red eyes, obviously unable to believe in this sudden access of holiness in one who already had something of a small reputation as a sinner.

The lady did not come.

I lurked also in the churchyard, at night. I slept out of sight of the watch, wrapping myself in my great cloak and keeping as warm as a man can with only a tombstone for a sheet and himself not quite yet clay. It was as though I felt compelled not to stray far from what was now to me very holy ground indeed. Holy because it was a church. Holy because *she* had been there.

There was a nightingale in that churchyard, and this being about the month of May it sang its nocturns there in an apple tree which was just in flower. Soft flower, sweet bird, such painful song. Under this tree I lay – yes, even I, Sir John Fastolf, K.G., though not then *that* of course, but see the depths of my melancholy degradation in this extraordinary sickness, Love, dear reader, and *be warned!* – (this is a moral tale) – under that tree I lay, as pale as the apple blossom, eating out my heart with the nightingale.

Tiouou tiouou tiouou tiouou! Lu, lu, lu, ly, ly, ly, li li, li, li!

That is what the nightingale sang. And so mad are men in love that I thought it must *mean* something.

Laugh at me if you like.

I can laugh at most of the things I have done in my life, and at most of the things which I am. But I have never yet learned the art of laughing at this.

So there I was – covered in apple blossom and bird shit – wrapped in my melancholy cloak and praying to God that he might have it planned to grant me my heart's desire.

And sometimes I added a P.S.:

That he would then restore me to my right mind again!

Tiouou tiouou tiouou was the only answer I heard.

On the third day, half-blind, half-deaf, what with love and nightingales, I had given up hope.

Picture my unspeakable joy when at noon all birdsong ceased and the bell rang for Mass and the object of my devotion passed before me through the churchyard, bound for St Botolph's. I hurried after her. She knelt in the Lady Chapel and I slipped into a seat in the choir, where I could spy her, myself unseen, through a little knocked-out knot-hole.

Her face was more beautiful than I had perceived it to be at our first encounter. She wore a veil that crossed it just down the left cheek – but even so I could make out high cheekbones, that smooth brow, a delicately curved mouth.

I attended on my beloved all through that Mass. My heart was beating as though it wanted to jump out. No one ever heard the *Missa est* with more reluctance than I did that day. Because, yes, her devotions ended, the lovely lady melted away again into the mid-day throng of people that used St Botolph's, and search as I did through all Shoreditch, and the other way, right as far as Moorgate, I could not find her.

Now I started asking questions of the spotty priest with red eyes, and all the other clerics of St Botolph's, and the grave-diggers, and people who lived in houses and shops round and about the church. Who was the lady in the blue dress? But I got the same unbelievable reply from all of them. They did not know. They had never noticed her. What lady in the blue dress? The spotty priest thought I was mad, or possessed by devils, and recommended exorcism.

I hung about for a week – two weeks – three. . . . Not a sign of her. I began to doubt the whole thing myself. I started to wonder if she was a fantasy, some ethereal ideal, a beautiful shadow strangely cast out of my own brain. I was worn away (believe it or not!) to little or nothing. I was being consumed by my own sighs. The torments and abominations of love had me by the throat and were choking me to death. My legs had grown scraggy. My stockings flapped at my knees. My shoes were all down at heel in that strange despondency of shoes which afflicts unrequited lovers – ask any cobbler! (It will be providing half his business.) As for my voice: it was quite scratched to bits with so much praying. I was at those altars, or before the statue of our Lady, night and day, and the priests had grown bored with hearing my confession.

Then, once more at noon, as the Mass bell sounded, I saw her again!

This time it happened that I was standing just inside St Botolph's, but to the side, when the great door swung open and she came in. Sun streamed, half-rose, half-purple, through the stained-glass windows, warming the stones. But she was brighter than the sun. Her face dazzled me. My eyes filled with tears.

She stood a moment in the portal, her eyes downcast. Then she looked up. She looked up and gazed directly at me!

At her entrance – so glad, so mad with joy at realising she was *not* a phantom after all – I had rushed forward into the aisle, not caring what anyone thought of me, just so long as my beloved should see me and acknowledge my existence also in this wretched (but because of her, wonderful) world. Now, she looked for a moment full upon my face with those shy clear blue eyes under the long eyelashes, and *she smiled....*

Such a smile!

I think I must have stammered something. I cannot remember what it could have been.

But, anyway, the lady answered not a word. She smiled and smiled, and then with a faint whisper of her blue dress she passed by me and on, on down the church to her place.

I hurried after.

The priest was leading in the antiphon:

Asperges me, Domine....

I came into the choir again, and fell to heartily –

hyssopo et mundabor!

O and I felt sprinkled with hyssop, Lord, just by her look, just by her blessed smile, just by the fact that those eyes had seen me. *Gloria Patri!*

I swear that I roared the whole versicle as it had never been sung before in that great minster.

My love did not sing. My love knelt with her sweet head bowed towards the white chapel of her praying hands.

The priest passed out of the choir. A villain trotted after him with the holy water. The priest sprinkled and sprinkled with the hyssop, casting the salt water, as best he could, direct upon the head of my beloved. For her part, she looked up – O shining gaze! O blue eyes burning in that holy gloom! – and parted her hair beneath its soft coif, smoothing her hair with her pearlpale hand, parted it meekly and gently in the middle, the better to receive that benison.

Her skin was white and tender. The sun, spilling suddenly into the church where a side-door swung, did her much courtesy – lighting straight upon her where she knelt, bathing her in his golden rays like Danae under the loving care of Jove. When I saw this, my heart leapt for joy. I swear it. My heart laughed and leapt for joy. And the meanwhile my lips chanted forth the *Signum salutis.* . . .

Tall yellow candles on the altar. The clink of censers.

And O my love! my love! With her high white forehead which had in the gold shade of that church the exquisite look of tinted alabaster.

I noticed then the spotty priest, the same little red-eyed clerk who had followed me so miserably with his suspicions wherever I wandered in the church in the first days of my love. He was gliding down the aisle in the wake of the celebrating priest. And he bore in his hand a breviary.

Immediately, I knew what I must do.

How? By inspiration, that's how!

Stepping out of the choir, I moved directly into the path of the little priest as he came towards me.

I bowed. He stopped, surprised. But returned my bow.

I held out my hands for the breviary.

His mouth fell open. But, astonished, as if in a trance, or not knowing why he was doing what he was doing, he handed it to me. Perhaps I appeared to him then – with the stained-glass sun at my elbow – like an angel or some other authority! (Laugh, reader, if you can.) Possibly he mistook me for one of his confreres.

Anyway, for whatever reason, or none, or all, and because it was God's will, he handed me the book. . . .

I bowed again to him, in thanks, and then turned to the place where my lady knelt.

Now, the pax was applied to this book. I mean – the celebrating priest had kissed it and passed it to the little clerk and now it was with me and it was my chance to pass it to my love. The kiss of peace was made by applying the lips to the same holy object one after another. Usually it was an engraved tablet or a crucifix – but in this church and on this day it was the breviary. This little volume of psalms, hymns, gospels, prayers, responses, versicles and lessons was about to receive the benefit of those adorable lips.

As she kissed it, I saw her mouth pressed close with love. I never saw or knew such a kiss in all my life. Her lips kissed only a book, but her soul spoke in that kiss.

She moved then herself as if in a dream, to return the breviary to the little clerk –

He hesitated –

He was lost –

I seized my chance.

I reached out my hand –

She handed *me* the book again!

Ah God, what bliss! I fell into such prayer over that breviary that not a hundred red-eyed priests all covered in spots from top to toe could have torn it from me. I bent low and kissed the book more than a hundred times. I wet the pages with my tears. The whole world seemed mine, and heaven too.

The little priest tugged at my sleeve, but I ignored him. Meanwhile, the canon proper of the Mass had begun, and our red-eyed friend was needed to assist back at the high altar. Dillying and dallying, shillying and shallying, at length he returned to his duties there, thinking no doubt to grab hold of me after and have the book back without fail.

I cannot remember the next quarter hour. Mass was said, and sung. And I was only technically in this world at all.

Ite, Missa est. . . .

Deo gratias!

O thanks thanks thanks be to God.

I looked up.

She was gone.

I knew she would be gone.

She was gone. And left me here alone.

I ran from the church. Still clutching the little breviary. The red-eyed priest ran after me, tripping in his chasuble. No doubt he thought it had all been an elaborate plot for the stealing of a not *very* valuable book.

I shook him off in Houndsditch.

She was gone. And left me here alone. All alone, as unknown.

And I have been alone in this world ever since, for I never saw her again from that day to this.

But I shall see her again. In Heaven. Of that I am certain. Beauty like hers – chance-seen and evanishing – is the surest proof of Heaven we are given. It is a fall of snow from the moon itself. And when I do see her again, in Heaven, I shall return to her that kiss of peace which she gave this breviary.

Yes. This is it. The very book. Father, my friend, there is no need to bless it. That book blesses your fingers which touch it. Those sweet pages were once hallowed by the sweetest lips I never kissed. That breviary has been with me in battle, in siege, in plague, in fire, in flood – in Ireland and in France – in courts and dungeons – in all kinds of places, high and low – in all manner of fortune and misfortune.

It has gone with me next to my heart.

It *is* my heart.

When I die, I say you are to bury it with me.

XLII

How Sir John Fastolf went to Ireland
in company with Prince Thomas

12 May

Remember Skogan? That abortion of the Muse. Sweet Clio's bastard. He died of trying to find a rhyme for SCARCE. My exploit in ventilating his wits at the court gate, my refusal to take sides in that quarrel in Eastcheap about bloody silly African islands, and no doubt some good noise of my reputation in London generally – all this recommended me to the party of the King's sons. From now on I was in and out of their company, passed from hand to hand as often as a dildoe in a nunnery. Hal I found as extraordinary as ever, a true prince, a dove when not provoked, a lion when stirred to anger. John was still the ox in the regal zoo, the taciturn one. Humphrey was just Hal's shadow, but a nice boy. Curiously, and for what reason I cannot say, it was in the eyes of Bolingbroke's second son, Thomas, Duke of Clarence, that I made most ascendancy at first. I say curiously because looking back on it now, over the long interval of years, and with both of them dead, I think I can perceive in this another small item in the rivalry that there always was between Hal and this brother who was just one year his junior. It is my belief that Thomas sensed already the bond that was to exist between myself and Hal. He perceived it almost before it was apparent to Hal or to me. And he was jealous. And he wanted his part of the action. And he always desired to do his brother down a little, if he could. So, in stepped Thomas, and for a while at least I was supposed to be his man. As for Hal himself – he was biding his time, in this as in several other Dionysian matters. There was a great wildness in the lad, a delight in disorder, a longing to see the world turned upside-down. And all these things conspired to make John Fastolf a kind of magnet for him. Why? Because he sensed in me

King Riot. An English Bacchus. The mischief, the pressure, the fire were all there in Harry Monmouth's eyes, and gathering force. Showing in a smoky glaze at times. But as yet he held back a little. He hesitated. Unwilling to consecrate himself entirely a priest of Bacchus, or to encourage me in giving reign and rein to a whole Bacchanalia. He waited for the right moment, having meanwhile to do some of his father's business, dealing with History in the shape of tablecloth-stealers like Reggie Ruthin, for instance. Hm, and the Welsh were singing their song about independence. Glendower sent Hal something like a challenge. So Hal went off to Taffy's house (at Glendourdy) but Taffy Glendower wasn't home. So Hal burnt Taffy's house down and then went for a march round Merionethshire and Powysland, having to pawn his jewels to pay his men. He was spoiling for a fight, but the Welsh nationalists had this quality of invisibility. Hal came back to London looking for me and some fun. But I had gone to Ireland.

Ireland. The Land of Ire. Erin isle. Where men are men and sheep are scared to death.

This was Prince Thomas's doing. It was – I should think – the year of the Hypostatic Union 1401. That's right. The very year that bugger Timur the Lame was sodding up the steelworks in Damascus. (Bad news travels fast, especially in the steel industry.) The year after Exton carved a peephole in Queen Dick. The same year of that monstrous statute of *Heretico Comburendo*, under which poor Badby was burned in his barrel.

I went to Ireland in company with Prince Thomas, who had been appointed the King's deputy in that place.

Ireland I did not care for.

The chief cause of my dislike was the Irish. I have found that a good Irishman is as rare as a good unicorn. Perhaps it's just bad luck, but all the unicorns I've known have been feckless devils with the one horn sawn off.

I don't say the Irish are a wicked race, mind you. Some of my best friends have been Irish. But there *is* a certain – shall we say *Irishness?* – about them. . . . There's the story of the Irish plough-boy, for instance, who was troubled by his little shillelagh turning into a big shillelagh every time he saw his master's wife. He took his problem to his master.

'Mick,' said the master (whose name was Paddy). 'Mick, me bhoy, me budding genius, I've a powerful deal of sympathy for you in your deformed predicament. And, because you're like a son to me, I'll tell you what to do about it.'

'Oh, sir,' says Mick, 'Oh thank you, sir.'

(Always polite, the Irish. Especially when they're murdering you.)

'Yes,' says Mick's master Paddy. 'Now, when you feel this terrible hardness coming into your shamrock, Mick, you go straight into the barn that's behind the cowshed, and you slap two handfuls of cow dung on your fellow. That'll do the trick. That's the secret. It's St Patrick's answer, Mick. St Patrick himself.'

So Mick the ploughboy did as his master told him. Every time he got an erection he ran straight for the cow dung and pelted his prick with the stuff. Until one fine morning, caught in the act by the farmer's wife – the original cause of the trouble, you'll recall – it is suggested to him by this kind lady that there might be *a better cure* for his affliction.

'Oh madam,' says Mick. 'Oh thank you, madam.' A pause. 'What is it?' he asks.

Whereupon the Irish farm-wife takes the young ploughboy by the prick and leads him up to the hayloft. She takes off her dress. She slips down her undergarments. She lies down on her back in the sweet-smelling hay, and she opens wide her lovely legs.

'Now,' she pants. 'Now put it in!'

'*You mean the whole two handfuls?*' says our Mick.

The price for catching old moles in Ireland at that time was two shillings a hundred. Young moles were 1s 3d a hundred. Rats were a farthing each. Not that I saw any rats you could call a rat in Desdemona's hearing. But then the Irish poets practise their poems on the rats in the fields, and rhyme most of them to death.

At that time, when I was in the country in the retinue of Prince Thomas, Ireland was in an even more unsettled condition than usual. There was rioting and murder and cannibalism and pedophilia and a superabundance of fleas. Finding themselves in such difficulties in a singularly unpleasant island, the Irish had turned patriots. This is always a consequence of ill fortune, and only to be expected I daresay, but emblems and flowers tell all and where England has a rose and Wales a leek, what does Ireland have?

A *sham* rock, –

i.e. a *shillelagh*.

The King's forces were often hard put to it to keep a semblance of order and control. I have always believed in law and order, but the Irish are notoriously indifferent to those virtues.

XLIII

How Sir John Fastolf conducted the militia at the siege of Kildare

13 May

Not long after our arrival in Ireland, we found ourselves in Kildare. We were quite without funds, cut off, and beleaguered by a gaggle or bubble or squeak of bog Irish of various species. The town itself had a cathedral which these brigands were forever burning down or building up again. I gathered that this burning and building of the cathedral of Kildare had been the local sport for centuries. In Ireland, a little arson goes a long way. But a great deal of arson is considered holier. There is some tutelary local deity or patroness called the Fair Maid of Ireland, or *Ignis fatuus*. I confess I have never quite grasped the mystery of her worship. This Agnes Fatuus must be some kind of fatuous fire. I saw her running once up Gadshill in the night to catch my horse. The Boglanders themselves appear to set fire to each other in her honour.

Kildare is from the Irish *Kill dara*, which for a change is not at all violent in implication, meaning simply 'church of the oaks'. This church, the cathedral, was St Bridget's Fane, founded by her in the fifth century. You might have thought the Irish would have liked it better than they did. There was this fire, sacred to the memory of the saint, inextinguishable, because the nuns never let it go out, and because every twentieth night St Bridget herself would pop in with some coals or a few slices of peat to make sure it was still on the go. It was kept burning in a small chapel called the Fire House.

I remember standing by that flame on a winter morning in the first December of my tour of Ireland, and cursing my luck in being sent to this sainted yet God-forsaken dump. There were some hundred of us stationed in the castle hard by. When the local rebels attacked, we withdrew into the castle. Leaning from the battlements, I passed down a discreet enquiry as to what our assailants were after.

'Devolution!' came the answer.

I had never heard this word before, nor have I heard it since. I take it to be some Irishism to do with a rolling motion in a bog, from the Latin *devolutionem*, to descend or fall like a ball. Seeing that at Gadshill the *Ignis fatuus* rolled distinctly uphill in pursuit of my horse, perhaps this *Devolution* may be a fatuous fire that rolls downhill in pursuit of a jakes. But I leave this to later students of etymology and the Home Rule question.

In the siege that followed I displayed for the second time my genius for military affairs.

It was customary, as everyone will know, to cast down upon invading troops all manner of unpleasant material, chiefly hot and wet, or lumps of iron. (Some martial manuals still recommend this tactic, despite what I might call Fastolf's Principle, now to be revealed to you in practice.)

This traditional behaviour of besieged persons struck me at the time, and still does, as a singularly crude and wasteful exercise. A dropped bar of iron, or a poured out vat of boiling oil, will certainly kill or maim or deter a man or two – possibly six, if they happen to be standing close enough together and disposing themselves conveniently to await your ammunition's most lethal arrival.

But in a flash I was tapped on the shoulder by St George with the notion that true-born thirsty Irishmen would be far better deterred by potations.

For *potations* read

POTATOES and POTEEN.

POTATOES.

POTEEN.

In other words, I saw to it that we cast down from the battlements of Kildare Castle great heads and hogskins of poteen and other inflammatory liquid of an interior character.

And potatoes too. O how I made it rain potatoes.

Your Irish peasant is a great eater of potatoes. He will always lay down his sword and his banshee to pick one up.

In this manner, assailed and assoiled by alcohol and vegetables, the insurgent besiegers soon lost heart. They set to in the ditch and enjoyed some kind of wake or bounty, or as they called it, a kaley, at the foot of the castle walls. There were fiddlers and jugglers and Hibernian acrobats. There were toasts –

'To St Patrick!'

'To the snakes driven out by St Patrick!'

'To the drum beaten by St Patrick in driving out the snakes!'

'To the hole knocked in the drum by St Patrick in his fury at the snakes!'

'To the angel that appeared to St Patrick and mended St Patrick's drum!'

'To the patch which the angel patched on that holy drum!'

And so on.

One or two weedy stalwarts attempted another assault, when fully flushed with the drink, but we deterred them easily enough with sausages. I recall one fellow in particular, a young man rather like a question-mark in shape, whose battle-cry was something about History being a nightmare from which he was trying to awake. An Irish proverb, no doubt.

At last, when the greater number of these Boglanders lay drunk and fast asleep, we fell upon them from our great height and killed them off with very little fuss. I made myself responsible only for collecting the unconsumed bait.

This second taste of the ardours and pleasures and enterprise of soldiering taught me that it was to my kidney. Those who have never been to war may find it difficult to understand – but those who *have* enjoyed that privilege will recognise that there was nothing small or ignoble in the skirmish or siege I have just described. War is a chance business, and a chancy occupation, and a battle takes whatever course a captain's imagination can provide it with. I fancy the writing of verses is much the same, only easier. You think of a rhyme and then find words to fit the rhythm in between. In a battle, you conceive a stratagem which will achieve your object, and then find an advance or retreat which will lead you to it.

The secret is not to choose an impossible object.

Like a rhyme for SCARCE.

In this siege of Kildare I was hardly a captain – yet I can claim that the notion of the poteen and the potatoes was my idea (with a little help from St George), and it brought me immediate fame with my master, Prince Thomas. It was clear that I was marked out for some great role in the fields of Mars.

XLIV

About leprechauns & St Boniface

I stayed on in Ireland for some little while after the siege of Kildare, and to tell you the truth that period remains in my memory as a very fair image of eternity. I do not say a *good* eternity, or a *bad* eternity. Just bloody eternity.

Whenever any metaphysician asks me how to picture or conceive of the idea of our eternal existence, our life in the world next door, where some will enjoy the beatific vision in Heaven and some will have to put up with less than that in Hell, I summon up remembrance of time past in Ireland in the first decade of this fifteenth century. To be sure, the fields were green, and I have always had a fondness for green fields. To be sure, the sky was blue, when you could see it, which was not often, on account of the rain, which is a good deal wetter and more opaque than English rain. I remember Ireland as sitting waiting for the rain to stop and the Irish to stop burning the cathedral in Kildare, or alternatively to stop trying to rebuild it. If I had had my way, I would have let them play whatever wildfire games they liked with their unfortunate cathedral, and amused myself kindling the local girls more kindly. Colleens, they called them. Not to be confused with collywobbles.

There were enough of these colleens to pass the time between sieges, though hardly enough to satisfy the requirements of a man in his prime.

No – my prime came later. At primero. Until I foreswore myself, and never prospered after. But here was my preparatory prime – and I could have done with a few score more women.

Instead of a women, God blast it, there was rain, and sieges, and then the leprechauns.

There was also, some say, an earthquake – but it can have

been no great shakes, since I slept through it.

On this question of leprechauns, I have a word to say. I have met men who profess not to believe in them. These were not wise men, or men with any roundness to them, let alone bottom. In my view, no man has a right to say that leprechauns do not exist until he has *seen* them not existing. Which is a very different thing from not seeing them existing.

I have myself seen seven leprechauns, but not one of them had a single word of any interest to say. The word *leprechaun*, by the way, is the Irish for a cobbler who makes only one shoe. That is what these leprechauns do. They sit about idly making odd shoes, never completing a pair. They dine on toadstools, which is again a damn fool thing to do.

Still, I would rather meet a leprechaun any day than an Irishman. Let the leprechauns inherit Ireland, I suggest, and that unhappy saint-soaked island will be at last a place of peace and plenty. And odd shoes.

Today is St Boniface Day. St Boniface is one of my favourite saints. I pray to him to help save England in her present mess. Because Boniface is one of our most *English* saints.

He was born at Crediton, in Devon. When he was seven he went to school in the monastery at Exeter. As soon as he became a priest he made it his task to convert the heathen Germans. He had the help of Pope Gregory II. One of his problems was that many of the German tribes considered themselves already Christians – but the job of their conversion had been done by Irish monks, some of them more Irish than orthodox, and Boniface had to teach them their catechisms all over again, which is harder than starting from scratch. Of the out-and-out pagans left, the chief sects were the Hessians and the Thuringians. The Hessians worshipped an enormous oak tree, which stood in the forest at Geismar, near Fritzlar. A trial of strength was proposed and accepted. Boniface said he would cut down the tree. The Hessians said that their gods would never permit it. A great crowd gathered. Boniface took up his axe, licked his finger, held his finger up to the wind, and then brought the axe down with crashing blows in the direction in which the wind was blowing. The oak tree fell. It was smashed into seven pieces. Woden was conquered. The Hessians all got baptised.

It is that licking the finger and holding it up to the wind which is so English. Your English saints believe in miracles, but they like to help them along.

Fr Brackley tells me that only one Englishman has ever been Pope, and that his name was Nicholas Brakespear.

All the same, there was a Pope Boniface who did something else very English – and if he was not the same Boniface the woodcutter then I'll try intercoursing with leprechauns again! For this dear Pope Boniface instituted a special indulgence to those who drink his good health after grace, or the health of any Pope. St Boniface's cup, they call it.

Father, if you please, how many Popes have we had since St Peter?

XLV

About Sir John Fastolf's nose & other noses

How many Popes since St Peter?

It is more than a month since I gave those words to Hanson – or was it Nanton? I can't remember and it doesn't matter. What counts is that the conduct of my 100 Days' War, the cut and thrust and cannonade, the onslaught, the bombardment, the storming energy of my attack on the citadel of my life, has been interrupted.

By what? Better go the whole hog. Better confess it. By INDULGENCES then, in the first place. I vowed to take advantage of the mighty spiritual benefits offered to such drinking-men as myself by the blessed Pope Boniface. (Oh, Mother Church takes care of all her sons, including hogs and cormorants!) Seeing that some time off in Purgatory was promised for each toast drunk to the Pope, living or dead, I had Fr Brackley draw up a list for me, and Macbeth and his minions running up and down the steps from the cellar with gallons and gallipots and general gallimaufries of sack, and burnt brandy, and double beer, and wine, and cider, and hydromel, and alcohol of all sorts, little merry bottles full of foretastes of eternity, stirrup cups of paradise, drink in such abundance that you could paddle where my waiters walked, deep potations, caldrons, casks, O noggins and firkins and pipkins and jugs, jorums and pitchers and saucepans and BUCKETS of the stuff – and then I, I, I, John Fastolf, myself sometimes, sat down and set to and started to drink my great sequence of Toasts to the Bishops of Rome, Supreme Pontiffs of the Universal Church.

Ladies and gentleman, I give you, the POPE!

St Peter –
St Linus –

St Cletus – (some say *Anacletus*, so here's to him as well) –
St Clement I –
St Evaristus –
St Alexander I –
St Sixtus I –
St Telesphorus –
St Hyginus –
St Pius I –
St Anicetus –
St Soter –
St Eleutherius –
St Victor I –
St Zephyrinus –
St Calixtus I –
St Urban I –
St Pontian –
St Antherus –
St Fabian –
St Cornelius –
St Lucius I –
St Stephen I –
St Sixtus II –
St Dionysius – (two for him!)
St Felix I –
St Eutychian –
St Caius –
St Marcellinus –
St Marcellus I –
St Eusebius –
St Miltiades –
St Silvester I –
St Mark –
St Julius I –
Liberius – – – – –

I drew the line at Liberius. For a while. Here, after all, was the
first Pope left in an uncanonised condition by his children. I felt
sorry for Liberius. Not being a saint. Amongst all those other
Popes in Heaven. And him being the only one the angels called
Your Holiness. Instead of Your Saintliness. I got curious about
this unworthy-of-sainthood Liberius. I asked Fr Brackley about
him, and was told that he was the bugger who approved of the

condemnation of St Athanasius, and went hand-in-glove with the Emperor Constantius, and was himself a sort of semi-Arian. But then, Providence is a wonderful thing, and you have to have some bounders at the top, otherwise certain other histories wouldn't follow, and in the case of Liberius maybe St George wouldn't have made it as Archbishop of Alexandria –

But then I remembered that was the *wrong* George. The Cappadocian article.

I totted up this little lot, anyway, and realised that it came to 36. 38, if you count Cletus being Anacletus as well, and let me have two toasts for Dionysius.

38 Indulgences, according to the *Ebrietatis Encomium*.

After *that*, I was interrupted by May. May, you understand, the month. May is Mary's month, and the Spring's beginning, even at Caister Castle, even here where you can sometimes hardly tell the difference between the sea and the sky.

By May and sap rising and Miranda my niece.

By the affairs of a busy lord of the manor, with estates to manage, deeds to sign, suits to fight, rents to collect, food to eat, coins to count, ships to despatch, visits to make, guests to receive, clauses to revoke, items to include in his household inventory, wounds to lick, time to kill, and all the rest of it, all the weary wearying rest of it.

It was the pressure of time to kill that surprised me most. In my days, in my own Spring, in my prime, before that unfortunate incident at primero – (it is a game of cards, Madam) – I have not been one of those sly discontented fellows mooning about in cloaks, with boils on their arses, ever rich-picking at their beadle noses with complaints that time has to be *killed*. Not a bit of it. I am none of your murderers of the clock. My life has raced, has galloped, has gone a great rate always. Yet here – in this month that is now dead and as though it had never been, May, Mary's month, now gone and green – I never returned to these pages, these wazerys, this making of the substance of my life, these words, these works, this testament and testimonial, my redemption, my justification, my confession, my truth.

And because I have not written, *I might as well have been dead*. What a curious discovery. At my age, at my stage, to learn that there could be such power in language, such mortal magic in words. Faced with the discovery, you might have thought I would have returned to the assault like a shot. Like one of the arrows at Agincourt – ah, wait till I come to Agincourt, that

Crispin Crispian glory! You might have thought I would have rushed back to my telling of my life, but I did not. Why not?

Not altogether because of Miranda's *et cetera*, though that is very nice. The day after the dictating of my opinions about the leprechauns and the beastly Irish rain – which is for ever falling on the beastly Irish, softly, falling, ever, and on the Irish sea, so that you'd think the Irish sea fell upwards and then down again upon the island, softly of course, softly falling – the day after that my saucy young niece invented a new game for me. Such sport. Tossing her on the bed and spanking her in mid-air as she bounced. Then stripping dress and under-garments from her as she kicked her legs and tickled my now very eager fellow with her pretty little toes. Twice I came between her big toe and the busy little ones a-rubbing and a -mousing at me. *This little pig went to market – this little pig stayed at home – this little piggy had roast beef–*

'Ooh, Uncle, now you've gone and come! The hot cream's all over my ankles, look!'

Amusing. A few hours of that kind of pastime and a man loses enthusiasm for his own biography. Especially when that biography has reached a stage and a place – pre-Hal, Ireland – that no longer interests him. Enough of it then, I thought. And to hell with the probability of leprechauns and the holding actions of Prince Thomas, when there is the warmer nearer probability of your niece in your bed and *her* holding actions to contend with in your 81st year.

But then there is the matter of my feeling there was time to kill. . . . That came later. Later, that is, than the seven days I spent in bed with Miranda. I sent the servants packing and I fucked her for a week. There is no need for modesty here. These memoirs are from a point beyond modesty. There is a style that is no style. A style beyond styles. Clean, stripped-down, plain. The style of truth. That's the only style I'm after. Madam, you say I am obsessed with sex? I admit it. I am impenitent about the obsession, though not about the acts. Did you not realise that all the great autobiographies are obsessed with sex? Did you never read a fellow called Augustine?

We angled then together, my niece and I. And *after* that, Miranda having gone off to her parents at Norwich well-satisfied (though I say it myself) and with cheeks like roses, glowing all over under her bodice too, I knew, in that way a well-fucked woman does and nothing else does (with the possible exception of a fine horse that has just galloped seven furlongs well within himself on a sunny morning just before the dew has risen) – Miranda being gone, I returned to my labours, and for the first time they *were* labours. I hawked. I stopped. I was constipated with the matter of my life. Kicking Hanson and Nanton together did not help, nor chasing my idle stepson Scrope, nor lighting candles from John Bussard's purple farting. Nothing helped. I had not a word to say to any of them on the subject of my life and valiant deeds. Nor had I a word to write when I dismissed the lot of them, and Friar Brackley, and tried to write myself.

SO – the reason now becomes apparent!

Worcester. William Botoner Worcester.

Worcester is back.

Worcester writes these words about himself at my dictation – his hand not hesitating, his eye no longer flickering from the page as the eyes of the others do when it is themselves or the present moment I make them write of.

Worcester is a professional.

Worcester is a writer.

He is my man, and in his absence I could go on no further with these annals. There – I concede and confess it. This book, which when it is finished with will encompass in its entirety all my deeds and days, and the English wars in France, and the affairs of state and my own affairs (so far as those two conditions are not one, which is a variable far) – this book, the *Acta domini Johannis Fastolfe*, is *his* book. The writing of it is his. I am the author, but Wm Worcester is my hand. Without that hand, I have been at a loss this month of wasted writing days, no work of words done, and I freely now admit it.

Today's chapter was to be on the not unimportant subject of my nose. I have a note for it, squeezed out of the time when I could not compose a thing. DAY XLV: *About Sir JF's nose & other noses*. I will come to it. It's Midsummer Eve too, and they're lighting the bonfire on the hill and no doubt Stephen Scrope will be up there leaping through the flames to change what he thinks is his bad luck. But, first, a word for Worcester.

A WORD FOR WORCESTER. (There, let's have it in capitals.)

He was born in the year of Agincourt, this man of mine, this son to me. Ha! I will say it, Worcester. I have no son save one, the bastard, now in the monastery in damned Ireland, which is to

229

say in Purgatory or worse – for how a man could be more damn-
ably damned than to be

1) a bastard
2) a monk
3) in Ireland

is beyond me. Apart from that whore's abortion, then, I have no
offspring, no scatterings in the shape of men, so my man Worcester
will stand me for one. He has a son's loyalty and a son's courage. Who
else would set off to see the bloody traces of St Whoever-it-was just
because I told him to? I am especially moved that he returned to me
without once washing his right hand, so that I could see and smell for
myself the saintly sanctified piss-awful blood which attaches to it. A
joke, Worcester. In God's earnest then, in the bowels of our Lord, I
am grateful for this dog's loyalty, who tramped out that long
itinerary into Wales, and came back home again to Caister, and
entered the hall with the one laconic greeting:
'*They seem to have cleaned it up!*'
Good for you, Worcester. Very English. I approve a man like
that. That was the return of a man after my own heart. Such a
return Ulysses made, when he came back to his wife Penelope
after his wanderings and all Troy, and greeted her with the muttered, '*What's for supper?*'
There is a poetry in such forms of speech on such occasions. A
poet of the kind who makes them is born not made. Worcester,
then, is my son, my poet, my annalist, and I am glad to have him
back. Having him back, I find the story of my days again tripping,
again flowing along as sweetly as the Queen of Navarre's barges
when she came up to the Pool that morning, sailing between the
legs of your author while he stood and farted that noble and
majestic and long-winded fart which I can remember now as if I
could still smell it. Ah, the farts of youth. They have a careless
rapture beyond the farts of age. They are many-coloured farts,
and there is no recapturing them in a colander.
My nose – the subject of my nose –
Worcester was born in Bristol, where the milk comes from. His
mother's name was Elizabeth Botoner. His father's name. . . . His
mother could never remember it. A joke, Worcester, a joke. In
truth, the fellow is bred well enough, of the best blood in
England, like myself, which is to say of yeoman stock, uncor-
rupted by your Norman pimps and bullies, a freeholder, a wine-
drinker, a beaf-eater, a true Englishman. There are not many of us

230

left. One day no doubt there will be none, and England will sink under the weight of French and Irish and other dealers in horses.

Reader, we English have to stick together.

This same itchy irascible scribe Worcester, librarian, Mr Bookworm Esquire, proceeded to Oxford at my expense. (Write down you are grateful, Worcester.) At Oxford, there, he studied astronomy with Friar John Hobby. Soon after that he entered my household as my secretary, my general factotum and scrubber of scrotum. I am his patron. He is my man. He writes a neat hand and he has a good eye. I say eye singular, since he lost the other in a small accident. I hit him with an inkpot that had sack in it. My little Cyclops. But his one eye is as big as the full moon. And here he sits doing truly Cyclopean work for me, making my book like the Gallery of Tiryns, the Gate of Lyons, the Treasury of Athens, and the Tombs of Phoroneus and Danaos. Cyclopean masonry: huge blocks fitted together without mortar, but as nice as you please. A living cyclopaedia too. I am your Vulcan, eh, Worcester? And you forge iron for me in these Days.

His complexion is swarthy. His cheeks are dun. As to his character, it is that of an English scholar. He is as pleased to buy a new book as I am to buy a new manor or a fat parcel of land.

This Subject of my nose –

To hell with my nose, if not the rest of me! We will kill the fatted calf, since Wm Worcester is back from Wales with the good news that St Someone's head has stopped bleeding at last, and with other items culled from a stupid itinerary. In truth, he enjoys these journeys, and since we came down here to Caister when the building of my life's Castle was finally completed in the year of the Incarnation 1454, he has been off seven times on similar fool's errands. So we will eat and we will drink, as my son is home and restored to me.

As to *noses*: I knew a man once, called Bardolph, that was hanged in the end for looting French churches. He had a nose like that St John's Eve bonfire you can see out there on the hill. You could have found your way safe by it on a dark night. I warmed my poor turnip fingers on it once in winter. That was a sun among noses, a terrible comet, a blazing torch with snot dropping out of it and the snot sizzling where it fell. More of him anon.

XLVI

About Sir John Fastolf's soul

I come to the problem of my soul. Do I have one? you say.
Madam, of course I have one. I may even have two. I am
large enough to have the use or rent of two souls. Every
created person has a soul, as sure as eggs have meat, and men
have shadows. The soul is the shadow cast by the flesh – or,
more likely, the other way round. The flesh is the shadow cast
by the soul. Yes. I approve that definition. *Ergo*, the mortal
flesh being the shadow cast by the immortal part, the body being
the mere extension or reflection of the soul, it follows that I have
a possibly worthy, probably glorious, and certainly substantial
soul, since I have something in the way of a mountain for a
body.

I should say that my soul was about the size of Spain, though
in a better spiritual condition.

Aristotle recognised several different kinds of soul, some of
which were used by the Greek warriors for padding their helmets.
My corpuscular soul is too much for that. Not even Achilles
could have crammed it into his helmet, thank you very much.
It might have served Agamemnon as a shield or buckler, my
companionable soul, my consubstantial bronze immortal part.

Even Moslems admit the existence of the soul. When he's
strangling you to death, your devout Moslem always slackens the
rope just a bit before you croak it – to let your soul escape.

Some say the soul is the wit's principle – that by which we feel
and know and will, and by which the body is animated. In that
case my soul is a vast and complicated engine of war. It has in its
charge and command, this captain soul of mine, great territories
of flesh and terrible cohorts of blood. It controls a continent. It
rules over and administrates an empire of sense. It is the emperor

of my senses, and some of those fellows are arch rebels I can tell you. Hence, I daresay, my sins.

But one of the thieves was saved. Remember that. St Luke tells the story. The first thief mocked and blasphemed, but the other thief said only:

'Jesus, Lord, remember me when thou comest into thy kingdom.'

And Jesus said unto him, *'Verily I say unto thee, To day shalt thou be with me in paradise.'*

Friar Brackley, pressed for a definition, informs me that in his opinion the soul is a substance or being which exists per se, which is to say for and in itself, – and he adds also that it is simple or unextended, which is to say not composed of separate principles of any kind, and he concludes furthermore that it is spiritual in the essence of its existence, so that to some degree its operations are independent of matter.

I can't understand any of that.

But I can understand the Thief.

He is in paradise.

There were all these gnostics and people who taught that salvation was difficult, or only for the fit and few, the initiates. The gnostics got it wrong. That Thief was no initiate. Neither was the blessed St Mary Magdalen.

(I have seen the Magdalen's skull. It is at La Sainte Baume, in Provence. They keep it in a jewelled casket with a wig of gold hair about it.)

Mary Magdalen is in paradise too.

The soul cannot be killed.

My soul is my immortal organ. The others will perish. Though one day they shall be re-animated, on the Last Day, when time glories to a stop. I will be Christian dust until that Day. Until I hear *the final chimes at midnight*.

In the meantime. . . .

In the meantime, bruising my brains even on this definition of Fr Brackley's, concerning the soul's operations being in a degree independent of matter – while I can nod my head and say I think I like it well enough as a sort of diagram of how these things will fall out after my death, I don't think I'm half as well pleased with it as a sufficient picture of how it is just now (three o'clock) between my soul and me.

My soul is as close to my flesh as a smile is to my face, or as laughter to my lungs and throat. In other words, as you cannot have laughter without lungs, so I doubt the necessity of souls without bodies at least while we are alive.

(But I leave these matters finally to the doctors of the Church, as I do all things concerning the ultimate meaning and purpose of life.)

Jesus, Lord, remember me. . . .

I read somewhere that there are in fact three kinds of soul.

First, your vegetative soul – which is the root of vital activity in plants. The fire in the rose.

Second, your sensitive soul – which is the root of vital activity in animals. The fire in the lion.

Third, your intellectual soul – which is the root of vital activity in man. The fire in Jack Fastolf.

And yet –

And yet it seems to me that the soul of Jack Fastolf is a triple or *triune* creature, and that he has his vegetable and sensitive ways as well as his allowable intellectual ones. Does this make me a cabbage or an onion? Or a dog or a fish? I think not.

I am a man made of stars and mud, like the rest of us.

Like *you*, reader? Do *I* read *you*?

I met a philosopher once in Damascus who spoke much of the transmigation of souls. He went in fear all the time down the street in case he should tread on a beetle who might have been his grandmother in a previous incarnation. I have never hesitated in the path of beetles. My grandmother is with God, and not a beetle. If my soul is an intellectual soul then it contains the sensitive and vetetative elements also. These vegetables and sensitives are just unfinished versions of a man. They are incapable of existing apart from matter after death. There will be no onions in heaven.

XLVII

About a base attack upon Sir John Fastolf

Once, though, in Ireland, on a lavatory –

Start again. A little vellum here, Worcester, if you please.

I, I, I, Sir John Fastolf, quarterly *or* and *az.* on a bend *gul.* three croslets trefflé *arg.* –

I, Knight in the train of King Henry the 5th on his first expedition across the channel, which expedition was known among the common soldiery as the Fucking Expedition, on account of the great amount of Guess What that was forbidden on it –

I, distinguished for my courage and resourcefulness in the plashy field at Agincourt, and in the affrays and affairs at Rouen and Caen and Falaise and Seez, capturer of innumerable castles and fortresses in that duchy –

I, Lieutenant of Harfleur and Grand Butler of Normandy –

I, victor over John the 2nd, Duke of Alençon, which little frog I caught with my own bare hands at the Battle of Verneuil, sending him back here in a box (with holes in it) to keep at Caister until his ransom money was paid (which money was then unlawfully retained by the Crown and Lord Willoughby, so that the sum of £2666. 13s. 5d is owing to me to this very day) –

I, Baron of Gingingle in France and Knight of the Garter in England –

I, Ambassador Extraordinary to the Council at Basle –

once –

was violated, *raped*, privily invaded –

in the lavatory above the moat of the castle at Kildare!

Botoner, stop laughing. Worcester, you Botoner buttoner, stop laughing, or I'll have your other eye on toast for breakfast. Poached eye on holy ghost. One day I swear you'll meet your

Ulysses. Listen, and we'll get this over. I promise it will make an end of Ireland, that ignominious interval, although to be sure I'll have to return there for the affair of my matrimony. . . .

It was in Kildare Castle. The boggers were busy at their burning and building. (Old Irish proverb number seven: *Rome wasn't burnt in a day*. Thank God and St Columba, I've forgotten the other six.) The rain fell from the sky which was as grey and as desolate as an old widow's arse.

There was in the castle this lavatory, this garderobe, this jakes, this suitable hole for pissing and shitting, which careful providence in the form of an architect with more practical wit than appreciation of draughts upon the tender fundament of the bumgut, had caused to be built in the tower. You ascended a stone spiral stairway, and there was the garderobe, with the lavatory, in the tower, a cavity, some four feet wide from side to side, in a hole in the wall.

It was, as I say, above the moat.

Now, God help us, there was in the county of Kildare a tailor, a poxed-out weasel by the name of O'Tallow – O' being an Irish patronymic, and this specimen being indefatigably descended from generations of candlegrease. O'Tallow danced adipose attendance upon me from moon to moon in earnest of some trifling payment of a couple of crowns for a cloak lined with ermine which I had ordered him to run up for me as a little comfort against the Irish cold. The man was a pain in the neck. I used his bills for a nether purpose.

I tell you – it was my pleasure of a Spring evening to sit upon this lavatory and to meditate. Opposite there was a long narrow perpendicular slit cut in the castle wall, affording as fair a prospect of green fields as any you are likely to see in a day's march in Hibernia, if ever the rain lifts a soggy inch or two and the good Lord preserves you for five minutes from a shillelagh on the back of the head or a colleen with her clog in your crutch.

There I would sit. Thus I would shit. King of the castle, lord of the lavatory, gentleman of the garderobe, as like as not still sporting my beastly ermine robe, wrapped well about me, for even in Spring the draught that blew up that funnel from the moat was no one's bloody business and bleak critical inspiration to the bowels I can tell you.

I report this tragedy, Worcester, as a warning against too great a trust. When a man is private, when a man is seated thus about some of his most intimate, necessary, and useless business, doing no harm to anyone, cogitating and reflecting upon nothing in particular, turning over in his rectum the price of a leg of mutton or a joke to tell his master Prince Thomas at supper – well, then he might suppose that he is *safe*. But not a bit of it, as you shall hear. Life is short and mortality is at us always, avid to strike and penetrate and pit us against eternity. In the midst of life, even on a lavatory, we are in death.

This is a moral story. All my stories are moral stories. Aesop was very deformed and a slave, but his fables are true. I am myself the grossest moralist that ever lived, and here's the proof of it.

This jealous tailor, this O'Tallow, having taken it into his epileptic head to pay me back for what in his eyes was my defection in the matter of his vastly exaggerated bill, had evidently consulted with the master of the drains at Kildare Castle, or some other equally elevated and well-informed student of the building's architecture and engines. By hook or by crook, by bidding farewell to his tranquil mind and swimming the moat or following some conduit, O'Tallow had succeeded in introducing himself to a platform some 20 feet down the shaft, just where the droppings from the lavatory achieved the absolution of the moat. There he was crouched, in the dark, below, though all unbeknown to innocent me, at ease, bowels generous and open, above. . . .

He had, the knave, a spear of fir –

Worcester! *Write!*

The recollection offends me yet. It gives me fundamental pain to think of it. Ravished! Defiled! Deflowered! It was a sore affront. A base attack. Such insult! Such surprise!

One minute, an English soldier is sitting shitting, minding his own business, his concentration all upon the relaxed enjoyment of the ripple of his wind, the movement of his bowels – the next he is three feet in the air, shrieking, yelling, with a horrible spike of fir jabbing and stabbing most horribly at his largest orifice.

Ransacked, Worcester! That's the only bloody word for it. I was ransacked in the Netherlands!

It was a trenchant experience, my son, and an undermining one too. It epitomised Ireland and the Irish for me. Never forget. Your Irishman is a fellow who can swim a turd-filled moat with a spike between his teeth, worm his way along a conduit, and then most subtly and perpendicularly prong you up the arse with a

237

spear of fir while you, his master, sit in state upon the jakes above.

O drains. O bum.

I daresay, if my reflexes had not been good, and my constitution resilient in all essentials, that experience would have spoiled me for life. As it was, it taught me this lesson: Never relax too far. Never think the enemy has lost interest. The Devil is most likely to strike when you have your trousers down.

That is the reason why, when I go into a new room, I stand always with my back to the wall. And if they move the wall, I move with it. And before standing there at all, I inspect the wall for holes.

XLVIII

About honour & onions

26 June

With her usual flair for the dramatic, my mother chose Ash Wednesday for her day to die on. Just as the priest was applying the ashes in the sign of the cross to her forehead, murmuring *'Memento, homo, quia pulvis es et in pulverem revertis'* ('Remember, man, that thou art dust and unto dust thou shalt return'), Mother remembered, fell sideways, and started that return.

Madam, my mother, forgive your son.

I remember you once displayed your collected evening shoes in a glass case.

Two years before my mother's death, while I was still in Ireland, she had given Caister to me. As well as the next-door manor of Repps. I have in front of me her deed granting these. It includes also the freehold of Caister Hall – which is now transformed into this Castle. And the advowson of the chapel of St John with the Caister manor. All these houses and property to hold to John Fastolf and his heirs for ever, it says, and dated the first day of October, in the sixth year of the reign of Harry the 4th, and the 1405th of our Redemption. Her seal is attached. Lady Mortimer, her seal. She was the daughter, as I may have told you, of Nicholas Park, Esquire, and the widow of Sir Richard Mortimer (among others), of Attleburgh, in Norfolk.

My mother's gifts did not make me a man of substance. In point of finance, my resource was not materially increased until the time of my marriage. However, for the present, in that first decade of this fifteenth century, here I am with two fair manors and the advowson of a chapel to my name – albeit in enforced military residence in the country called Juverna by Juvenal no doubt because he found it juvenile, and still running all riot of risks

239

from long spears, cathedral burning, and Irishmen.

The prospect of my property was a comfort to me in exile. I am an Englishman and I love our country. My idea of riches is a handful of English earth. It was for that which men fought and died in the wars in France. I fought for other reasons besides, as you shall shortly hear, and the same no doubt is true of any other professional soldier since the time of Hannibal and Achilles. I fought when I had to, and there was no getting out of it. All the same, I fought then not only to save my own skin, but to save that inch of England's skin which is my Caister even – for that bleak and barren coast beyond the windows out there, the low shifting sandbanks, the few trees with their backs turned towards the east. This is a flat county. There is nothing in it to attract or distract attention from the soft line where land and sea meet sky – save this my Castle, my great tower.

I am in Ireland. I am at Kildare. Prince Thomas is with me, hot arrived from England, and critical of my conduct of another siege. Yet it had gone well enough. Seven Irish bodies swung on gibbets outside.

Inside, we talked of honour. (The Duke of Clarence disapproved of fighting with potatoes and poteen.)

'Honour,' he said, fixing me with a stern look that was meant to emulate Hal. 'Honour is the emblem of chivalry. Honour is what chivalry *does*. Honour is gallantry in battle. To do chivalry is to act the knight.'

The Irish bayed across the moat. Those seven were acting as martyrs, not deterrents. You could hear the cathedral crackling.

'Honour pricks me on too,' I said. 'But how if honour pricks me off when I come on? How then?'

Thomas did not like the way I had associated his grand theme of honour with talk of pricks and comings. His worried expression gave him a canine look. He sat and stared at the matted rushes on the floor. He was his own worst enemy. I heard the soft thud of the hanged men against the castellated wall. When an Irishman flatters you he always calls you *Your honour*. . . .

'Can honour set to a leg?' I said. 'No. Or an arm? No. Or take away the grief of a wound? No. What is honour? A word. What is that word honour? What is that honour? Air.'

'You owe God a death,' Thomas reminded me.

'Which I pray is not due yet!'

'Yes, but honour –'

240

'Who has it, this honour of yours?' I demanded. 'He that died on Wednesday. And does he feel it? No. Does he hear it? No.' I jerked my thumb. 'Those seven outside. That's honour.'

Prince Thomas kicked a log further into the fire with his pointed boot. 'Honour is an insensible quality,' he said.

'Yes,' I said, 'that's why it suits the dead.'

He shrugged. 'You will never make a knight,' he muttered.

'Knighthood,' I said, 'is more than mere scutcheons. Honour is your scutcheon. Just a cheap piece of heraldry to grace a funeral.'

'You owe God a death,' Thomas said again, with a flash of the usual obstinacy.

'So do we all,' I said. 'And I'll pay my debt when it falls due.'

There was a silence as the wind stirred in the tapestries. The gibbets creaked. 'And so ends my catechism,' I said quietly. Adding, after another lengthy pause, 'My lord.'

This answer of mine concerning the particularities of *Honour* did not please Prince Thomas and I knew it. It marked the beginning of a certain intellectual disagreement – a divorce of minds – between myself and him, which persisted until the end of his life. He preferred to talk of Amadis de Gaule, while I ate onions.

Onions, now. That was the year of the onions in Kildare. I never knew a fruit more succulent than the onions were that autumn. Amused with wine, as the night wore on, while my royal master talked endlessly, repeating and reciting very boring tales of chivalry and knights errant designed to controvert my view of honour – tales which I shall certainly not bore you with, dear reader, for you can find them to hand in any tavern where old dilettantes gather who never saw cold steel in their prissy lives, although I'll bet you'll rarely see a true soldier look up from his game of cards to enter in – while Thomas, Duke of Clarence, spoke of HONOUR, it diverted me in my cups to substitute for his word HONOUR the richer and lovelier word ONION.

'Your ONION, now, is the emblem of chivalry – ONIONS are what chivalry achieves. . . . The ancient Romans knew all there is to know about ONIONS. . . . Jealous in ONIONS, sudden and quick in quarrel. . . . ONION, high ONION, and renown. . . . Have you not set my ONION at the stake?. . . . Save him from danger, do him love and ONIONS. . . . My ONION is my life; both grow in one; take ONIONS from me, and my life is done. . . . There is my ONION's pawn. . . . The fewer men, the greater share of ONIONS. . . . All men's ONIONS lie like one lump before him. . . . The gods assist you! And keep your ONIONS safe!. . . . Set ONIONS in one eye and death in the other, and I will look on both indifferently, for let the gods so speed me as I love the name of ONIONS more than I fear death. . . . Knighthoods and ONIONS!. . . . If you were born to ONIONS, show it now. . . .'

And so on. This substitution of the word ONION for the word HONOUR seemed to be giving me some clue as to the relationship between Thomas and Hal. And the fact that my sackbefuddled (or be-sharpened) wits kept making the substitution was telling me something about what Hal required of me. Because all the four princes were to some extent mirrors of each other, and what you learnt of one you applied to the others. And particularly to Hal, who was the mirror of them all, and the frame also.

As a matter of fact, I had it of an old yeoman of Repps that your onion came into Britain before the Romans (and thereby, perhaps, before your HONOUR) – indeed, it came from the deeps and caverns of the world, and entered our soil from the bottom up, so to speak, and not in the pocket or pouch of any mere invader. You will find onions embossed and carved on the monuments of Egypt. Some of the lords of Egypt used to worship the onion. Its very name, so my man Worcester tells me this minute, from the French *oignon*, which is derived from the Latin *unio*, implies such liberal unity and oneness as I approve in and from the depths of my onion-growing heart. There is not a world of difference between a pearl and an onion.

Pickles, though, like honour, are another story.

HONOUR and ONIONS, and my mother dead.

What's for supper?

Tomorrow I promise you matter of greater swiftness and import. To wit, how Francis Pickbone and Black George Barnes, with my sweet step-sister, brought me back from Ireland to London, where I again fell in with that reprobate Prince Hal.

XLIX

How Sir John Fastolf came back to London

27 June

Up early in kill-me-by-inches Kildare, to memories of Caister –
that bleak, that barren bitter coast I like so well, mackerel and
herring taken from the sea in season, in winter the skiffs drawn
up in a smoke of rain and spray on the long grey shore. The cry
of curlews. Your footprints filling up with water the moment you
make them.

I walked by the flame in the cathedral of St Bridget. It gave no
warmth to my hands. The three miles of country between Caister
and Yarmouth were in my mind's eye wherever I turned my gaze
on Irish stone or Irish grass or Irish sky. That stretch of England
presents as level and unbroken an aspect as the opposing coast of
Holland, or as the melancholy ocean in between. It is a long green
expanse, covered on the side nearest the sea with little blowing
bushes of furze, bright and sweet in summer with gold flowers.
To the west, inland, the same stretch offers only a pancake of
marshes, in winter always overflowed, but dotted and diversified
at other times of the year with the brown-and-white and black-
and-white of grazing cattle. In my skull I saw this, at a remove in
Ireland. In my skull also, having just inherited Caister from my
mother, I was beginning to dream of the Castle I would one day
build here. My Castle would be the answer to that place Elsinore
I once saw in Zealand. My tower would be the Pharos of the
marshes.

It is a curious phenomenon which I have observed of myself –
when I am *in* a place I do not dwell much upon its physical
character (having so much of my own to contend with?); but
when I am *out* of the same scene I see it well and vividly, and
reflect a lot upon its contours. This is not just a matter of
homesickness. I daresay that now, writing in Caister, I could if I

243

so wished recall each wretched blade of grass on which I wiped my arse in Ireland. But I do not so wish.

Upon the morning I am telling you about – returned from St Bridget's flickering forked flame to my quarters in the garrison, I found horses in the courtyard. Nothing remarkable in that. But one of the horses was a giant. And, even so, this Bucephalos or Brigliadoro of a horse had a kind of dip or dent in his back where his rider had been seated in the ride across country. Discounting the possibility that Orlando or Alexander the Great had come to visit me, I realised in a flash that there was only one man I knew who would make a mark in a huge horse like that –

Black George Barnes!

I went up the stairs like a bouncing salmon – for in these years in Ireland, what with poteen and potatoes, my own dimensions had improved to the point where I was now about two yards round the waist. This was the first thing Ophelia noticed – yes, she was there too, my sweet stepsister, warming her pretty little bottom before the fire and turning a rose in her hands. George Barnes and Frank Pickbone were with her in the upper room.

'Jack! You've got fat!'

She caught my hands and kissed me, standing on tip-toes. 'Something has come between us,' she said, rubbing my belly. 'What do you feed it on?'

'Roses,' I said.

I took her on my lap and she touched the red rose to my cheek. 'Hullo, mountain,' she said. 'My own dear darling whale.'

Pickbone cleared his throat and shifted quickly away from the fire where it was burning his jambarts. 'Good to see you, Fastolf,' he grunted.

'Good to see *more* of you,' added Black George, with a chuckle. 'How's life in Ultima Thule?'

We exchanged the usual gruff jokes and greetings, the courtesies of Englishmen, the marvellous irrelevancies. My visitors had not been impressed by their journey across Ireland. One thing stuck in Pickbone's head. They'd been riding through a village, he said, when they saw a clothes-line hanging across the main street with a pair of cat's tails dangling from it, bleeding, but no sign of any cats. 'We asked what had happened there,' he said, 'and they told us that two cats had been fighting and had eaten every bit of each other except the tails!'

'Poor pussy,' Ophelia whispered in my ear, playing cat's cradle with my codpiece. 'It does seem a terribly *fierce* country, Jack.'

I laughed. 'The villagers saw you coming,' I told Pickbone. 'It's just a local sport. They tie the cats together by their tails and throw them up over the line and then lay bets on which one will scratch the other's eyes out first. If they're interrupted all bets are void, and someone cuts the cats down with his sword.'

Ophelia shivered, plucking one petal from the rose.

'And thereby hangs a tail,' I said. And kissed her.

George Barnes was at his pacing, up and down, hands behind his back, black buggerly beard thrust forward like a trident. 'Well, Fastolf,' he said, 'as you can guess, we've not come all this way to talk about cruelty to animals.'

I wasn't paying much attention to him. 'I'd hate to lose *my* tail,' I whispered in Ophelia's ear. 'But I wouldn't mind losing my tongue. In *your* tail!'

She giggled, and wriggled on my lap, and I was glad to see that she could still blush. Her cheeks approached the colour of the rose as I shifted some of my bulk beneath her.

'We have come,' barked Barnes, 'to fetch you back home!'

I almost dropped Ophelia when *that* sank in.

'To Caister?' I said.

'No,' said Barnes. 'To London. To your friends.'

I frowned. 'Nothing I'd like better,' I said. 'But my friends aren't England, and England is having to do without me, since England wants me here in Bogland with the Duke of Clarence. You know that. You know Jack Fastolf can't come back to Cheapside just because his good friends miss his company.'

Pickbone was pouring jugs of sack for all of us. He gave me mine into my hands with a significant small smile, then said: 'One of your friends *is* England, Jack. Or one day will be. You know what I mean. You were fetched out here to Ireland by Prince Thomas because of some jealousy between him and his brother that no one needs to understand, and which they probably don't yet admit to in themselves.'

I twined arms with Ophelia, and we drank from each others' jugs. 'Go on,' I said. 'I'm beginning to get the hang of it.'

'As well that you do,' sniffed Pickbone, 'since if you don't, we're instructed to fetch you back to England – to the Tower! And people have a way of getting the hang of things damned fast in there.'

'The Tower,' I said smoothly, leading him on, 'might be interesting. I could keep company with the Royal Mint.'

Barnes slapped his side with his broad black hat. 'Henry the 3rd kept an elephant there,' he said. 'You're growing mighty like an elephant yourself, and I can tell you that a certain person will have Henry the 4th keep Fastolf for *his* elephant in the Tower if you don't come back with us.'

I put down my jug. I put down Ophelia's jug.

'A *certain person?*' I pressed. 'Let me guess. Is it our friend Mr Shallow who has abrogated to himself such authority? Has he now graduated? Is he to be Lord Chief Justice of England?'

Ophelia poked her tongue in my ear and rubbed her breasts against me. She had breasts like tennis balls. Then she whisked her tongue out again, jumped off my lap, and said: 'You know what they are driving at, you rascal. You have friends in high places, Jack. You have one friend, as Pickbone says, who *will* one day be England. It's Harry Monmouth. It's Prince Hal. He wants you back. He's the *certain person* who has sent us.'

And so it was.

We drank a lot more sack to my good fortune in that upper room before we made our way to the Duke of Clarence. Then a letter with a great heavy seal on it was passed from Pickbone's hands into the Duke's. The letter was read at a glance – I'll say this for Prince Thomas, he was always a quick reader. Then torn up. Then thrust into a candleflame. Shoulders were shrugged, and a door slammed. Our party were left grinning at each other.

I was given a Spanish horse.

And I set forth for England again, for London, my heart high, my head singing, in company with my two friends and my dear Ophelia.

Along the way, about half way across St George's Channel, I learned the sad glad news that Ophelia was to marry. That is to say: I was happy for her, for she married a man of substance, although their union was not blessed with children, and she died some seven years after, of a fever in what would have been her first childbed had she and the infant survived. Ophelia had come to bring me back to begin one of the greatest and happiest periods of my life, a time of pure high carnival, and the most full of events and wisdoms. She had come to do this out of the sheer goodness of her heart, and from the love she bore me, for she knew of my misery in Ireland and that a sight of her dear face and the knowledge coming from her sweet lips that I was summoned by Prince Henry back to England, would be the greatest pleasure to me and the best inducement. Not that I needed inducing. Or seducing. I was curious as to why the Prince required me back at this particular time, but not surprised. There was some spark between us, some St Elmo's Fire such as you see blaze up and down the masts of ships before a storm, and I guessed that Hal had known and felt this as acutely as I had on the occasion of that first encounter when Skogan's head was cleft at the court gate. The ships were about to engage. The storm was about to break.

As we rode up from Holyhead, I heard from Barnes and Pickbone that the Prince had been mixing anonymously, and not so anonymously, in the merry crowd that had been my crew, my gang, my company when I was camped in London. It was from the way the name Jack Fastolf cropped up in every tavern in Eastcheap whenever cakes and ale were mentioned, that he had conceived for himself this desire to have me at hand to help him consume them. 'He's fallen in love with Dame Mischief, and wants you to marry him to the heifer,' was how Black George put it.

'I've no doubts concerning the validity of my unholy orders,' I said piously.

'He's hell-bent on setting up court among thieves, and he needs a court jester,' said Pickbone.

'You mean,' I said proudly, 'a king.'

L

About heroes

28 June

Having more flesh than most men, I beg to be excused for displaying a greater amount of that frailty to which flesh is heir.

Pass the figs.

What is a hero?

Having dealt with that important question – *What is honour?* – it is time to address ourselves to its brother.

Achilles, you say.

Caesar, you say.

Alexander, you say.

Reader, I did not say WHO. I said WHAT. I wanted a definition of this word *hero*. But, since you've brought these fellows up, Sir, let's take a look at their credentials.

Achilles certainly rushed about a good deal at Troy Town, after his boyfriend Patroclus was killed. But some of that was hysteria, and the rest dysentery. Besides, Achilles had a supernatural mamma, and you can bet she Pulled Strings for him. Demi-gods don't count. Even demi-gods with weak ankles. I dismiss Achilles.

Caesar is a marginally more interesting case. Certainly he won 320 triumphs, but I wouldn't want to go too deeply into his triumphs with Nicomedes of Bithynia (known as Knickers Bitters to his friends). Besides, Caesar had unlimited credit and didn't make much of a job of invading Britain – high water at Dover on the 27th of August, in the 55th year before God's Death, being at 7.31 a.m., by which miscalculation Caesar landed 8000 men in 80 galleys bang in the middle of Romney Marsh. Hail, Pheezar. You won't do.

But Alexander, you insist, – I must allow Alexander to be what the world means by a hero. Sir, I concede only that he was a pretty good master of war. But he aimed at conquering the whole world (which I regard as childish), and he demanded to be worshipped as a god (which is worse). I can't take Alexander very seriously.

There does remain KING ARTHUR.

And there you have me. I will never say a word against King Arthur, or King Arthur's sword, or King Arthur's spear, or King Arthur's shield, or King Arthur's dog. (His dog was named Cavall.) You will never hear a word from these lips in criticism of the great Round Table of that English King.

Has Bussard gone to Yarmouth for those hog's lice? There's a stone in my bum-gut. As a matter of fact, there's a Stonehenge in my bum-gut. We'll need 20 drops of tincture of salt tartar as well.

A hero is a knight errant with knobs on.

How's that?

We are a dying breed, Madam. Like unicorns.

O once and future King. O Camelot. O my piles.

Think of the Round Table.

I AM THE ROUND TABLE.

LI

About Prince Hal

He was in the days of his youth a diligent follower of idle practices, much given to instruments of music, and one who, loosing the reins of modesty, though zealously serving Mars, yet fired with the torches of Venus herself, and, in the intervals of his brave deeds as a soldier, wont to occupy himself with the other extravagances that attend the days of undisciplined youth.

Worcester's translated that for me. It's from the *Gesta Henrici Quinti*.

And, allowing for monkish reserve, it gets Hal about right.

I mean: I recognise in that description the lad who was twice sick in my hat.

Some think the *Gesta* was written by Jean de Bordin, but it wasn't. I can tell you the author. It was Thomas Elmham, sometime a Benedictine monk at Canterbury, then a Cluniac, and prior of Lenton Abbey, near Nottingham. He died in the year of Man's Redemption 1420, or thereabouts, anyway I had pimples on my bum that year, owing me £4. 5s. 11d and a shirt, but I forgive him his debts as I trust that he will forgive me mine. This Elmham was the King's chaplain in France. He was at Agincourt. He knew him well.

I throw in this bit of authentic History from a disinterested but well-instructed source, just to prepare you for the high jinks which must follow. Without it, you might not believe me.

I put it in also to introduce HAL in the days when he *was* HAL.

My diligent follower of idle practices.

My undisciplined youth.

My mad lad, sweet lag, most comparative, rascalliest, sweet young prince, mad wag, the young prince that misled me.

King Hal! My royal Hal!

I was the fellow with the great belly. And he my dog.

LII

About some other villains

Other principal villains in the chapters that now follow.

BARDOLPH, *Esquire*. Bardolph was the most esquired esquire I ever knew. His chances of knighthood were always nil. He lacked the necessary gentle blood. Bardolph's blood was the opposite of gentle. Coax it and reason with it and dilute it as he would, it persisted in inhabiting his nose. My knight of the burning lamp. His face was his misfortune. It was full of meteors. It was covered with bubukles, and whelks, and knobs, and flames of fire. He assisted in the development of my soul. Whenever I looked at him I thought upon hell-fire.

PISTOL, *Ancient*. My ensign. An old soldier. A swaggerer. Known as *Peesel* to Mrs Quickly, who must have known, because he married her. I mean to say: this less-than-affectionate nickname can only have derived from Pistol's failure to discharge upon her.

PETO. An inefficient thief and tell-tale-tit.

GADSHILL. Not to be confused with Gadshill. But see the next few chapters.

NYM, *Corporal*. A humorous bloody villain. Betrothed at one time to Mrs Quickly – weren't we all? – but was lucky enough to lose her to Pistol. Served in France, as did Bardolph, and was hanged with him for looting churches. To nim is to steal. Corporals generally have a stripe or two. Nym was distinguished by a lot.

POINS, *Mr Edward*. A friend of Prince Hal's. A practical joker. A scoffer. A shit. Fortunately disappears without explanation in chapter LXXI.

LIII

About the preparations for the Battle of Gadshill

London was in a turmoil when I returned. This new word *Devolution* danced on every tongue. It seemed to mean something to do with deflowering the kingdom. Bolingbroke pronounced it *Devil-lotion* and proposed taking an English army on a new crusade to cure it. But Bolingbroke had put on centuries of guilt in putting on the crown, and besides that he was suffering from leprosy and syphilis and a gangrene. When you add to these complaints the fact that Wales was in revolt and doing rather well at it – Mr Glendower had just defeated Lord Mortimer in the Welsh Marches – and that the Scots were knocking holes in what was left of Hadrian's Wall, you see why Henry the 4th was not a happy man. Even the good news turned bad in his head. Hotspur, scourge of the Scots, managed to dispatch ten thousand of them to a warmer climate at the Battle of Holmedon. But he took some valuable prisoners too, and he wanted to keep these for himself for the ransom money. Bolingbroke was furious. Scotch earls were worth a lot. He summoned Hotspur to London to settle up.

Meanwhile – in another part of the Palace of Westminster, in a private apartment of the Prince of Wales' – other affairs of war were being planned. From the moment when I set foot again in London, Hal and I had been inseparable. We stuck together like Hercules and Iolaos, like Amys and Amylion, like Alpha and Omega. Or like flies and a jampot, if you want to know. He was the flies.

I do believe our bantering never ceased.

'What's the time?' I'd say – I mean, something as simple and civil as that, but he'd turn a decent question on its head and make a sod of it. . . .

'You! What the devil have you to do with the time of day? Hours would only interest you if they were cups of sack. Minutes if they were capons. Clocks if they were bawds' tongues. Dials if they hung them up outside the brothels to advertise the shape of what they were selling. The sun itself wouldn't interest you unless it turned into a hot girl in flame-coloured taffeta. Don't be superfluous!'

I undid a league of buttons, and grinned. 'You have me there,' I admitted. 'But then the time of *day* has nothing to do with me. I'm a night-worker.'

Hal grimaced. We were alone. He rolled down his boots and planted one foot on the table. Then he poured three drinks with a lazy but careful hand, using his elbow as a kind of pivot, watching his own wrist with the fascinated attention that always comes into a man's eyes when he is half-drunk and his wits are more or less *following* his body's actions. One of the drinks was for him.

'When you are King,' I said, taking the other two, 'will you hang thieves?'

'No,' said Hal.

I drank to the abolition of the death penalty.

'I shan't hang thieves,' said Hal, observing me narrowly, that hint of the eagle hovering in his hooded eyes. '*You* will!'

I drank to myself from the other cup. 'Shall I?' I said. 'That's nice. Well, I'll make a good judge.'

'You're a lousy judge already,' said Hal. 'I didn't mean I'd make you a judge. I'd make you my hangman!'

I drank to him from both cups at once.

'Where did you learn that trick?' he demanded, for I prided myself on the fact that hardly a dribble of wine ran down my shirt front during the exercise.

'In the service of a great Prince,' I said. 'Only a great Prince *deserves* such double toasting,' I added, between gulps. I smacked the empty cups down on the table. 'Before I knew you,' I concluded, wiping my beard meticulously with the back of my hand, 'I knew nothing.'

'And now?'

'Now I am little better than one of the wicked,' I said. I sighed. Across my mind's eye for a moment flashed an image of my friend Duncan, my brother oblate, laying cold and stiff among the candles in that monastery where the walls were always wet. 'I must give over this life,' I muttered. 'I must. And I will.' I

253

belched. 'By the Lord,' I said, 'if I don't, I'm a villain.' Buttons on my belly were now undoing of themselves. I watched one of them pop off, and Hal flick out his hand to catch it like a cat a mouse. So he was not *that* drunk, I thought. It was usually this way. He liked to get me seven times as drunk as he was. He always liked to revel in my revels.

I said (and I think I meant it): 'I don't intend to be damned for any King's son in Christendom.'

Hal sipped his sack. He flipped the little button up and down in the palm of his free hand. Then he leaned forwards suddenly, spilling his drink on my sleeve. *'Where shall we take a purse tomorrow, Jack?'*

His excitement was infectious. So was his malice. And his comedy. 'Wherever you like, lad!' I cried. 'Wherever you like!'

'Hm!' the Prince teased me. 'I see you are suddenly reformed. But from praying to purse-taking!'

He flicked the button in my face.

I laughed. 'It's my vocation,' I said solemnly. 'It's no sin for a man to labour in his vocation.'

Upon this particular morning, or afternoon, or evening – it was always twilight in the corridors of power at Westminster, and especially behind locked doors in the Prince of Wales' private apartments, and besides Hal never did answer that perfectly reasonable question I had asked him – upon this *occasion* then, while poor old Bolingbroke was holding council in another part of the palace, and feeling torn to pieces what with the Welsh and the Scots and his erysipelas, not to speak of Hotspur hanging on to those rich prisoners, *we* were waiting for the arrival (by a side-door) of a squire of Prince Hal's, a greasy little prick called Poins.

I never liked Ned Poins. He didn't like me either. He had nicknames for me: *Monsieur Remorse, Sir John Sack, Sugar Jack.* Nothing to write home to the Devil about. Talking of the Devil, this Poins fancied also to insinuate that I had sold my soul to that roaring lion, *and on a Good Friday too!* His libel was that I had struck this terrible bargain in return for a cup of Madeira and a cold capon's leg. Now, I ask you, would I have done such a stupid thing on the strictest of fast days?

Poins was a poof. I refrain from telling you the worst thing about him, but the second worst thing I heard from Nell Quickly. Poins had spent the night with her, just to win a bet with another masculine whore. It was a night full of 'tirrits and frights' (Nell's own words), Poins being scared out of his wits by the sight of her bird's nest and shitting the bed when (to quote Nell again) she 'tried to make his pulsidge beat'. Then, in the morning, standing in front of the looking-glass at the Boar's Head, she just lifted her arms to pin up her hair, and –

'St Sebastian save me!' screams Poins. 'Two more!'

And he jumped in the buck-basket to hide from the terrors of female anatomy!

'My harm pits, O Jesu!' Nell told me. 'The bastardly rogue thought that harm pits were for canvass too!'

Ah well. Buzz, *benedicite*, buzz. Every man to his own. These male milliners like to shave every part of their bodies. They emulate eggs. Not that Edward Poins ever had to lather or scrape at an inch of his perfectly hairless person, if you ask me. Though I am glad to say this is opinion, not observation.

Poins was a toady and an eaves-dropper, as well as a refugee from ladies' armpits. He was addicted to practical jokes, which I regard as quite the lowest form of wit. Stupid too. He thought Aquinas was a mineral water.

But enough about the Prince of Wales' male varlet. Sufficient to say that it will give me great pleasure to write him right out of my book when we reach Chapter LXXI. No, I shan't kill him off, Sir. Because I *didn't*, Madam, that's why, and I'm not going to start telling lies at my time of life. Allow me to indulge myself in one of the little incidental pleasures of authorship. Namely, *forgetting* a character.

Poins brought us news that a plan of mine for a little work in Kent was coming along splendidly. This concerned a crossroads at Gadshill, just outside Rochester, about 27 miles from London. The beauty of this place was that it saw a lot of two-way traffic. On the one side, you had pilgrims going to Canterbury with rich offerings for the shrine of St Thomas Becket. On the other side, you had travellers returned from abroad and riding up to London with fat purses. It was an ideal spot for some robbery, and robbery was the Prince's present sport.

I did not begin these *Acta* with the intention of devoting a large part of them to an analysis of the character of Harry Monmouth, and I am not going to change my mind now and fall into that trap. All the same, while I cannot explain Hal, or any man, and while he has now passed before the one Judge who knows all the secrets of a man's heart, so that any further sen-

255

tence of mine is uncalled-for, I have to say that at this stage in his life the Prince was playing the part of the Prodigal Son with more resource and enthusiasm than I have ever seen it played before or since. It was a complicated Prodigality. He was capable of striking Gascoigne, the Chief Justice, just for the hell of it, and using as excuse the fact that Gascoigne had been obliged to imprison my man Bardolph on account of a rape. On the other hand, in the opposite mood, this young weathercock of a Prince was capable of coming before his father, in Westminster Hall, penitent, dressed in his old student's gown, with the needle and thread still stuck in its collar, and kneeling before the King and offering his own dagger from its sheath and held pointed towards his own heart, begging Bolingbroke to plunge it in immediately if he thought that there could be any feelings but those of love and loyalty in the same organ. Then again, a few nights later, he would be back with me in Eastcheap, weaving about among wine-butts in the cellars of the Boar's Head, roaring drunk at that carnival court where I was King Riot for him, plotting with me and urging me on to do robberies in which nothing delighted him more than to take cash from his own tax-collectors. 'It's the King's coin,' he said. 'But let some of it be the Prince's!' I confess I never worked out the extent to which these vagaries and varieties and wildnesses and intricate wildernesses in Harry Monmouth's character could be attributed to

1) the fact that his father was dying by degrees, and horribly, so that the responsibilities of kingship would be soon thrust upon him;

2) the fact that I, John Fastolf, was in some way his own father's *opposite*, the father he might have liked to have, representative of a freedom he could never now enjoy, since Bolingbroke had tangled him up in the crown; I should add, in this matter of fatherhood, that it pleased Hal always to regard me as much older than I was – his *Latter Spring*, his *Allhallown summer* – whereas while I *was* his senior of course, this came out most truly in my superior wisdom and experience;

3) the fact that at least one of his brothers – I mean Thomas, Duke of Clarence, my ex-employer in Ireland – was a jealous and obstinate soul, with his own followers, who sometimes didn't bother to disguise their opinion that *their* man would make a better King;

4) the fact that the duties and formalities of power already

oppressed and obsessed him – that he could already feel the Crown of England tightening round his head – and there, for the moment, was I, John Fastolf, a man of the moment, a free spirit, his tutor in another kind of Englishness.

His tutor in another kind of Englishness.

I've written that out again since I suspect it is the key to the contradictions. Whatever Harry Monmouth learned from me was not ill-used at Agincourt.

For *Englishness*, Madam, – if you happen to be an Ethiopian – read *Human Nature*. It is our English pride or penitence (notice I do not say prejudice) to imagine that we have as much of this commodity as any tribe now going.

Well, there was Hal, busy at his Prodigal Sonship, and making a surrogate father of one of the pigs, you may say.

I don't mind you saying it. I like pigs. Give me a pig any day, in front of a prig. Jupiter was suckled by a sow. Watch your pigs closely. They will teach you to turn up the earth.

To return to our strategy for the Battle of Gadshill, however. . . . I hope I have made it clear to the unbiassed reader, and to Clio, that for my part this expedition was undertaken in jest, and to please my Prince. You can imagine my surprise, then, when the same Prince turned abrupt about-face as soon as the plan was seriously mooted, and I began to draw lines of battle in the spilt wine on the tabletop.

'Hal,' I said, 'you will be *here*' – stabbing with my finger at my wine-map – 'We can wear masks, or better still, friars' hoods –'

The royal boots swung off the scribbled table. 'I rob?' said the Prince. 'I a thief? Not I.'

'Manhood,' I muttered.

That got him, or so at first it seemed. 'Well then,' he said grudgingly, 'once in my days I'll be a madcap.'

'Well said!'

But the Prince was about his own sly tricks with me again, for no sooner had I praised him, even ironically (*once in my days* indeed!), than he stood up to dismiss me with an airy wave of his goblet. 'Come what will,' he said, 'I'm staying at home.'

I perceived in this shuttlecock that he was playing with me as he played with his father the King. Here was a situation in which I had taken the trouble to draw up perfectly good plans for a robbery as safe as you please, purely for his entertainment, and now he was dismissing all my effort, giving me the back of his hand, and declaring he'd take no part.

'By the Lord, then,' I grunted, 'I'll be a traitor when you are King.' (For *this* was a kind of treason he offered to me.)

'Who cares?' said Hal.

He was flinging my plans back at me like a child with a lot of toy bricks. I turned aside. Poins caught at my sleeve with a perfumed hand. 'Fastolf,' he whispered, winking, 'leave the Prince and me alone. I'll see that he comes to Gadshill tomorrow.'

'By four o'clock,' I said, not caring for his wink.

'Of course.'

'In the morning,' I said, removing his hand from my sleeve.

'Trust me.'

Like a snake. But I left them to it.

LIV

How the Battle of Gadshill was won: 1st version

2 July

Moonlight. Thin trees. Gadshill.

Four o'clock in the morning.

I had at my command a company of three – Bardolph, Peto, and Gadshill. (*Mr* Gadshill, that is, and not to be confused with our battleground. You may call him Cuthbert Cutter, if you wish.)

We were masked.

The enemy were carrying £200 (Two Hundred Pounds) in gold. One of them was an official of the Exchequer. They had breakfasted on eggs and butter at Rochester.

Prince Hal and Mr Poins were performing an extra-military exercise called *walking lower*. That is, they had run away, and left the work to us.

We confronted the enemy in a narrow lane. There were 8 or 10 of them.

'Stand!' I cried. 'Stand!' cried Bardolph. 'Stand!' cried Peto. 'Stand!' cried Mr Gadshill and/or Cuthbert Cutter.

'Jesus bless us!' cried the enemy 8 or 10 times.

'Strike!' I cried.

'Down with them!' cried Bardolph.

'Cut the villains' throats!' cried Peto.

'Ah whoreson caterpillars!' cried Mr Gadshill, who in his Cuthbert Cutter moods possessed quite a poetical turn. 'Bacon-fed knaves!' he added. (There *was* a smell of grocers' shops about them.)

'We are undone,' cried the enemy.

'They hate us youth!' I noticed.

'Down with them!' cried Bardolph, who was always repeating himself.

'Fleece them!' suggested Peto.

'O,' cried the enemy.

'Young men must live,' I remarked.

We tied them up and took their money.

No sooner had we done so, than our gallant band was set upon by a hundred men.

'Your money!' they shouted. And, 'Villains!' they shouted.

It was altogether a most unpleasant experience. I fought with a dozen of them for two hours. I escaped by a miracle, eight times thrust through the doublet, four times through the hose, my buckler bent through and through, my sword hacked like a hand-saw. Two men – in buckram suits – I killed. But it was to no avail. We were hopelessly outnumbered. We retreated in good order.

LV

How the Battle of Gadshill was won: 2nd version

3 July

Moonlight. Thin trees. Gadshill.

Four o'clock in the morning.

I had at my command a company of three – Bardolph, Peto, and Gadshill. (*Alias* Cuthbert Cutter.)

We were masked.

The enemy were carrying £1000 (One Thousand Pounds) in gold. One of them was a freeholder from Kent. They had breakfasted at an inn in Rochester on eggs and butter.

Prince Hal and Mr Poins had run away like cowards. At this critical juncture in the history of England, Mr Poins had also seen fit to remove my horse. He had tied that noble beast I know not where. I do not bitch, but I believe King Arthur and St George and even Timur the Lame were not required to cope with horse-thieves in their own party.

We accosted the enemy in the narrow lane. There were 12 or 16 of them.

'Stand!' we cried. Four times.

'Jesus bless us!' cried the enemy. 12 or 16 times.

'Strike!' I cried. 'Down with them!' cried Bardolph. 'Cut the villains' throats!' cried Peto. And so on.

'We are undone,' cried the enemy.

'They hate us youth!' I noticed. 'Young men must live!' I remarked.

We tied up every man of them. Peto avers that four of us could not have tied up 16 men, but I am as expert in knots as Alexander, and I am a Jew if they weren't *all* tied up.

Then, as we were sharing the money, some 6 or 7 fresh men set upon us, and unbound the 16, and came at us with the 100.

I fought with 50 of them. Or I am a bunch of radish.

I never fought better in my life.

If I didn't fight with 53 of them then I'm no two-legged creature.

I peppered two of them.

I put paid to two of them – *two rogues in buckram suits.*

But to no avail. All would not do.

If I tell you a lie, spit in my face!

LVI

How the Battle of Gadshill was won: 3rd version

4 July

Here I stood, and thus I held my sword. Four rogues in buckram
suits let drive at me –
    No, reader, I did not tell you two. I said 4, all abreast.
    I took their 7 points on my shield.
    Seven? you say, Sir. But there were only 4 just now. . . .
    In buckram. 7, or I'm a villain.
    You think I will have more in this story in a minute?
    These nine *in buckram* that I told you of –
    So, you say, two more already –
    Wait, just wait, Madam, all will be clear as the moon over
Gadshill in a moment. . . . These 9, giving me ground, coming in
foot and hand – I put paid to 7 out of the 11 of them!
    Right, Worcester! I heard that! But you mutter no more than
the Common Reader might. . . .
    Eleven buckram men grown out of two!
    Notice all this
    BUCKRAM.
    Then, as the Devil would have it, three misbegotten knaves in
Kendal green came at my back and let drive at me – *for it was so
dark that you could not see your hand!*
    BUCK BUCK BUCK!
    You get my drift now, Worcester my son?
    2, 4, 7, 9, 11.
    And the 3 in Kendal green.
    But *essentially* this BUCKRAM.
    No?
    Never mind. I will analyse and explicate tomorrow. I will
demonstrate also why for these three days I have spoken of the
winning of the Battle of Gadshill. This engagement constitutes (in

fact) one of the subtlest (if misunderstood) manoeuvres of my military career – and I shall be glad to explain it for the benefit of those who have discovered in it nothing but defeat and chaos and confusion.

But not right now. I've wearied myself in fighting those BUCKRAM MEN again, all over and over.

It's just my wound talking now.

LVII

*Sir John Fastolf's review of the action, strategy,
& tactics of the Battle of Gadshill*

5 July

Reader, truth is various. And there is nothing more various than the truth about a battle. Men coming and going in the dark, fighting and falling, your foe turning into your friend, your friends running away. . . . Only historians say otherwise. Never believe historians. Historians say what they are paid to say, or what they pay themselves to believe, which amounts to the same economy of lies. If you want to come at the truth of a single event you had better allow for at least three stabs at it, and then allow for the fact that you may still have missed the heart in some way. That is why I have given you *three* versions of how the Battle of Gadshill was won. I do not claim that any single one of them is true. But I do claim that if you add the three together, and look at them closely, you will see what I have been driving at all along, and why I speak of this engagement as *a victory*.

To dispense first with the inessentials. What does it matter whether the enemy carried £200 (Two Hundred Pounds) or £1000 (One Thousand Pounds)? Booty is booty. And, besides, *all this booty ended up where I intended it to end up*. It is not for me to say how much it amounted to when *he* came to count it. . . .

Were there 8, 10, 12, or 16 in the original enemy force? It was four o'clock in the morning. The encounter was in a narrow lane of thin trees on a hillside. You could not see so well as you might at noon from the spire of St Paul's. Some of the travellers might have been trees. There *were* travellers. One of them *was* an official of the Exchequer, and another was certainly a freeholder from Kent. Mr Gadshill had established this (and precisely what they had eaten for breakfast) by a spot of judicious spy-work in their inn at Rochester. As for the other details, I suggest that they matter as little as whether you choose to think of Mr Gadshill in that personality or as Cuthbert Cutter. It might be better, on the whole, if you fix it firmly in your head that he figured as Cuthbert Cutter (just to avoid confusion with the battleground). It would be as well if you would allow that we overpowered those travellers easily enough – Bardolph and Peto and Cutter and I – though without doing them any of the unnecessary violence (throat-cutting, hair-cutting etc) recommended by Peto, whose mouth was always bigger than his brain.

Well then, now then, hey diddle dan, we come to the military crunch.

The second engagement.

The attack on my gallant band by the *two men in buckram suits*, with masked faces.

Worcester, my writer, and you, my reader, how long is it since you wore buckram? Buckram is not cheap. Buckram makes expensive suits. Did you suppose for one minute that I did not immediately guess the identity of those *two men in buckram suits*?

By the Lord, I swear it, and by the Pope's belly, I recognised Hal and Poins from the very start! They had gone slinking off like cowards to do their *walking lower*. I smelt a rat. The rat was Poins. How else had he persuaded Hal to come to the robbery at Gadshill than by promising him some practical joke at Jack Fastolf's expense? To tell you the truth, I had been anticipating some such turn-about all night long. And when Poins disappeared with my horse, and the Prince made excuses for joining him, it was in the back of my head all through the fight with the travellers that there was some nonsense to come.

It came. It came in buckram suits.

BUCKRAM!

Worcester, I have pondered this for years. It is my conclusion that this wearing of *buckram* must have been Poins' idea. In the first place, *buckram* is kinky, and your queer boys love it. In the second place, *buckram* is uncommon, and would give me some warning that inhabitants of suits fashioned out of it might be no ordinary offal for my sword. In the third place, which is the sum of the first two places, they were somewhat banking, the Prince and his mannikin, on the fact that their Fastolf was not a fool, and that he would

a) recognise them;
b) refrain from killing them;
c) leave them the loot, and retreat in good order.

And all these things came to pass.

Madam, I heard your mind. That was unworthy of your face,

266

dear. Do not think of 'lies' (even with commas round them) or 'subterfuges' (ditto). Look again at my 3rd version of the glorious Battle of Gadshill. (Glorious, Sir, on account of its subtlety, which was extreme as anything in Pythagoras, and makes Timur the Lame look like a butterfingers.) Notice how in that 3rd version, while conveying *deliberate doubt* as to how many men there were attacking us in buckram suits, I mention also cheap thieves in Kendal *green* –and then in the same breath I tell you that *it was so dark at that point you could not see your own hand!*

Worcester is smiling. His one eye lights up. He has it!

You too, Sir? I congratulate you. You would make a diplomat, if never a general.

Madam, don't throw my book down in disgust at your own lack of understanding. These are men's matters. I will spell them out for your benefit.

It was my object all along to make the Prince of Wales believe himself to be a much finer fellow than he was. I flattered him by turning him into 4, 7, 9, 11 men in buckram suits. (Or $3\frac{1}{2}$, $6\frac{1}{2}$, $8\frac{1}{2}$, $10\frac{1}{2}$, if we allow Edward Poins to count as half a man, which in our magnanimity we might.) But, then, in conversation with the Prince himself, I had eventually not only to flatter him with the success of his expedition against me but *to put an end to the joke without him losing face.* Hence, the green I claimed to observe in pitch darkness. In other words, madam, by this signal to my Prince, *I deliberately lied.*

Fr Brackley has heard the tale a hundred times, and has come to the conclusion that my sin was venial. I committed it for Harry Monmouth's benefit, and for England's. *If Hal had been defeated at the Battle of Gadshill, what would have happened at Agincourt?*

Was it for me to kill the heir-apparent?

Was it for me to destroy the lad's confidence?

Of course not. And I ran the faster away (in good order) the better not to kill him, or to tamper with his confidence. For, as you know, Madam, I am a man of instinct, and here I was, a lion, in the presence of a true prince. Pliny used to teach that the lion, being the king of beasts, will not touch a true prince, respecting this other kingship. Edward the 3rd dared Philip of Valois to go into a lions' den to prove his kingliness.

The greatest glory of Gadshill, then, was that it proved Prince Hal a true prince to himself, and that it taught him a thing or two about lions and Jack Fastolf.

I could have killed that Poins, though.

LVIII

About a play at the Boar's Head tavern

6 July

Truth, as I told you yesterday, is various. But all the same, in its infinite variety, the truth *is* the truth, and men don't like it. The night after the Battle of Gadshill, gathered in our usual court at the Boar's Head tavern, in Eastcheap, with Hal and Poins and Bardolph and Peto and Cuthbert Cutter – Francis the potboy ferrying sack between us when he could avoid Poins' fingers prying and pinching at his buttocks – it fell to the Prince of Wales to show another side of his character by calling me names for his own amusement, and no doubt to cover his confusion at several sharp answers which I gave him when he asked me how that battle had gone.

Woolsack, he called me. And
You whoreson round man, he called me. And
Villain, he called me. And
Gross as a mountain, he called me. And
A clay-brained guts;
A knotty-pated fool;
A whoreson, obscene, greasy tallow-catch;
A sanguine coward;
A bed-presser;
A horseback-breaker;
A huge hill of flesh –
Enough was enough. Especially when Hal and Poins sat down, one on each side of me, and started talking to me about REASON and COMPULSION. If there are two things I hate in this bad world it is REASON and COMPULSION. Reason is the rogue that will one day cut kings' heads off, and then try and stick them on again the next for another reason. As for Compulsion. When I hear the word compulsion, or feel its pre-

sence, I smell poor Badby burning in his barrel.

'Come,' minces Poins, 'your reason, Jack, your reason.'

I kicked at him under the table. 'What?' I said. 'Upon *compulsion*? Give you a reason upon compulsion? If reasons were as plentiful as blackberries, I'd give no man a reason upon compulsion.'

Hal looked uneasy. He knew I knew he knew I knew he knew. If you see what I mean. Both about Badby and buckram.

I turned on him next. 'There is something in you, Hal,' I said, 'that reminds me quite distinctly of an eel-skin. Or is it a bull's pizzle?'

Hal liked that last comparison. He had worked so hard on his prick, of course, to make it long enough to rule a kingdom with. And to have your member compared with a bull's is no disgrace. He started to laugh. So then Poins started to laugh – or, rather, giggle. And Bardolph made his noise like a kind of cannon. And Peto sniggered. And Cuthbert Cutter grinned.

I laughed myself. I, I, I, Jack Fastolf, to whom laughter is a sort of familiar spirit, never failing to come at my call. 'Shall we be merry then?' I cried. 'Shall we have a play?'

'Yes,' said the Prince. 'Let its theme be your running away!'

But I turned that aside with a splash of two fingers dipped in sack and offered to his royal highness thus:

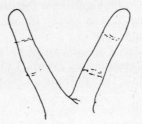

Which, being translated from Old English, Madam, means more or less:

'No more of that, Hal, if you love me.'

Mrs Quickly entered. Our hostess looked more like a good pint-pot than ever. Just now she was frothing over with fresh tidings too.

'O Jesu, my lord the prince – There's a nobleman of the court at the door – He says he comes from your father.'

'What sort of man?' I asked.

'An old man,' said Nell.

'Gravity out of his bed at midnight,' I mused. I turned to Hal: 'Shall I send him packing?'

'Please do, Jack.'

Now *that* was a more agreeable music. I went.

I found at the door an antique turd called Bracy. Sir John Bracy. Of the Bracy family seated at Madresfield, Worcestershire, from the time of King John. Seated is the word. This ancient was one of the few who had ever stirred far from the fire-side. He brought bad news now. Hal was to present himself at court in the morning. Hotspur had joined forces with his Scotch prisoners, placed himself at their head, and was marching south-westward to join up with Mr Glendower. *Devil-lotion* wasn't the word for it. This was open rebellion. They were after the English crown.

I gave the fellow sixpence, and returned with this news to the Prince.

If Hal was disturbed or distressed by the prospect of war, he did not show it. His courage rode high from his great success at Gadshill. (Clio, ask England to be one day just a little bit grateful to *me* for my part in that.)

I was inspired, though, to suggest that we should improvise a play, in which Hal could practise answers for his interview with his Dad. The Prince, with his flair for the dramatic, and his half-fear of the leper King, agreed on the instant.

The whole tavern gathered.

I was to be the King. I seated myself on a chair on top of the table. I put on a saucepan for my crown. I called for more sack – to make my eyes red, as though from weeping at the misdemeanours of my son.

'Nobility,' I said, to a somewhat surprised Poins, caught playing smell-finger with the potboy. 'Stand aside.'

Mrs Quickly was already rocking with laughter. 'O Jesu, this is excellent sport!' she cried, tears trickling down her cheeks.

I cleared my throat, and spoke like Bolingbroke: 'Weep not, sweet queen, for trickling tears are vain.'

'The spit and image,' shrieked Nell.

'For God's sake, lords,' I said – to Bardolph and Peto and Cuthbert Cutter – '*convey* my tristful queen. . . . For tears do stop the flood-gates of her eyes.'

'Eh?' said Bardolph.

'Shut her up!' I hissed.

'He's just as good as any of those bloody actors!' screamed Nell, roaring with laughter, before Peto got his hairy fist over her maw.

Hal bowed. He knelt before me on a cushion.

'Harry,' I said, 'you seem to be my son. I have partly your mother's word for it, partly my own opinion, but chiefly that villainous look that sometimes comes into your eye, and the way your lower lip droops when you're not busy shutting both lips tight together so that all the blood rushes to your boots. If, then, you *are* my son – and here's the point – why do you go around pinching blackberries? Worse. Why does the son of England prove a thief and steal purses?'

I fixed him with a tiger's burning eye, and adjusted my saucepan by the handle. 'There is a thing, Harry, which you have often heard of. It is known to many in our land by the name of *pitch*. This pitch defiles. My son, I have heard reports that you touch it, that you play with it, that you keep company with this pitch. Harry, it's not the drink talking. It's the tears.'

I was so carried away by my impersonation of Bolingbroke that I managed to shed a few tears at this point. The whores shrieked with laughter – Nell had all her girls in for the fun.

'And yet!' I said sternly, wiping my cheeks and beard dry. 'And yet there is also *one virtuous man* whom I have often noted in your company, though I do not know his name.'

'What manner of man,' asked Hal, 'if it please your majesty?'

'A goodly portly man,' I said, 'and a corpulent. Of a cheerful look. Of a pleasing eye. Of a most noble carriage.'

('Hear! Hear!' shouted one of the whores, my dear Doll Tearsheet.)

I beamed upon her, and then glared at Hal. 'Ah, now I remember,' I said solemnly. 'His name is Fastolf.'

Hal opened his mouth, but I was too quick for him.

'There is virtue in that Fastolf,' I said. 'Him keep with. The rest banish.'

Hal was on his feet now, grinning, but grim-eyed as ever, pulling me down from my improvised throne and quickly establishing himself in the majesty of government.

For a moment it must have crossed his mind that – in *his* case – this was not so much of a joke. 'Well,' he said, 'here I am set.' And as he said it the words hung heavily upon the air, for he knew that one day he *would* be.

He sat as though he had a ruler down his back. 'I hear,' he said gruffly, 'that there is a devil that haunts you in the likeness of an old fat man.'

I bowed my head modestly.

('Not so much of the *old*, ducky,' called my dear Doll loyally.)

'A trunk of humours,' went on Hal in his new role as my father and my judge. 'A bolting-hutch of beastliness. A swollen parcel of dropsies. A huge bombard of sack. A stuffed cloak-bag of guts. A roasted Manningtree ox with a pudding in his belly. A reverend Vice. A grey Iniquity. A Father Ruffian. Would you mind telling me what this fellow is good for, except to taste sack and drink it?'

'I would your grace would take me with you,' I murmured politely. 'Whom means your grace?'

Hal said: 'That villainous abominable misleader of youth, Fastolf, that old white-bearded Satan.'

('There ain't a white hair on him, darling,' cries my Doll, waving her bottle. 'Save one. In a place *you* won't have seen!')

I drew myself up to my full height.

'My lord,' I said, 'the man I know.'

The whores roared. Bardolph rubbed his nose with delight. Poins kissed the potboy when he thought no one was looking. Mrs Quickly and my dear Doll performed a little jig.

I held up my hand, and at a wave of it the revels ceased. I stuck my thumbs in my belt and looked Hal straight in the eye. Straight *through* the eye. Suddenly I saw Hal, and he saw me.

'The man I know,' I said. 'But to say I know more harm in him than in myself were to say more than I know.'

There was a silence. I could see that Hal was working out whether I meant that I was saying this in my role as *him*, penitent before his father, or as myself, impenitent before princes or any other sons and fathers outside Heaven.

Outside, in the street, the wind was rising. A shutter creaked. I heard a sound far off like the beating of a drum. But perhaps it was just my heart.

I said: 'If sack and sugar be a fault, God help the wicked! No, my good lord – banish Peto, banish Bardolph, banish Poins. But for sweet Jack Fastolf, kind Jack Fastolf, true Jack Fastolf, valiant Jack Fastolf – banish him not your Harry's company. Banish him not your Harry's company. Banish plump Jack, and banish all the world.'

There was a terrible knocking at the door. A whore cried out, 'The sheriff! The watch!'

More knocking and banging. General confusion. Tables turned over. People escaping through windows and hiding in cupboards and under trapdoors.

But, amidst all the uproar, there was a moment when Hal and I stayed looking at each other, kept on gazing steadily at each other, and that eagle in his eyes was suddenly as cold as death, and I was the only person in the Boar's Head tavern who heard him say, the future King of England, Henry the 5th:

'I do. I will.'

LIX

About the picking of Sir John Fastolf's pocket

I do. I will.

I do not remember much else about that evening. Those promises, those thunderbolts knocked out my wits. I remember Bardolph running here and there, looking in vain for some disguise for his nose. I am sure that Nell Quickly was crying *O Jesu, my lord, my lord!* – but then she always was, even when she was dancing with her heels. Certainly, Hal kept his head. 'The devil rides upon a fiddlestick!' he said, meaning that here was ˙nothing to make a great fuss about. He told me to hide behind the arras. The rest went upstairs. I suppose he bluffed it out with Poins for company, browbeating the sheriff.

I expect he lied on my behalf. And that I should be grateful.

I know I fell asleep behind the arras, worn out with analysis of the Battle of Gadshill, and that subsequent cross-questioning by the Prince and Poins, and then the play in which I had to be both King and Hal by turns. Not to speak of a deal of sack with too much lime in it.

And I know that my pocket was then picked, and that I was robbed of three or four bonds of £40 (Forty Pounds) apiece, and a seal-ring given to me by my uncle Hugh. I suspect that Mr Poins was the pocket-picker. I am only glad that he found nothing else there to his liking.

A deal of papers were taken from me at the same time by Prince Henry – later, he more or less confessed to it. These consisted of memorandums of bawdy-houses (I still liked to know, *pace* Mr R. Shallow, where the best bona-robas were to be found) and certain tavern reckonings.

The Prince kept one of these to mock me:

Item, A capon	2s. 2d.
Item, Sauce	4d.
Item, Sack, two gallons	5s. 8d.
Item, Anchovies and sack after supper.................	2s. 6d.
Item, Bread	ob.

(*Ob* signifying an obulus, which is to say a halfpenny.)

It was Prince Hal's delight to dangle this bill in front of my eyes when he wanted to jibe at my habits.

'Monstrous!' he'd cry. 'But one halfpennyworth of bread to this intolerable deal of sack.'

Man cannot live by bread alone. Besides, my bread-basket was full enough.

As for the sack: two gallons never drowned anyone, did it?

I'm surprised his royal highness missed the sugar-candy. More likely, Edward Poins would have had it. It is of use to fighting cocks such as myself in that it prolongs the breath. To such as Poins it had another use.

LX

*About the Hotspur & Mr Glendower, with an
interruption*

Hal patched things up with his father. Bolingbroke was mustering
an army to deal with Glendower and Harry Hotspur, and when
Hal heard his father comparing him with King Richard, Queen
Dick, *the skipping king*, and lamenting all the time that he, Hal,
Bolingbroke's own eldest son, was now his nearest and his dearest
enemy, he got the wind up.

It had been Hal's style to sneer somewhat at Hotspur.

'He that kills some six or seven dozen Scots at breakfast,' he
used to say, 'and washes his hands, and says to his wife, "Bugger
this for a quiet life! I want work."'

Harry Monmouth's own approach was always oblique, less
workmanlike. But, once roused, once touched, he could be
plumes and flags as much as any man.

'I shall redeem myself on Hotspur's head!'

That's what they say he told his Dad.

I can believe it . Hal always liked to make a quarrel personal.
He would fight his father, he would fight the Chief Justice, he
would fight me, he would fight the Dolphin of France. But the
adversary had to be an *individual*.

Perhaps Bolingbroke knew this, and practised great cunning in
holding up Hotspur in front of his son's eyes as a rival Prince. If
that is so, then Hal gulped down the bait. It was to be the gallant
Hotspur against the unthought-of Harry? Very well then. Hal had
no doubt as to which was the better man. He was brimming over
with confidence from Gadshill, remember.

Thank you, Clio. Tell England, will you?

Soon the royal drums were drumming and the first of the
King's armies marched west towards Wales – towards Glendower
and Hotspur, the Welsh magician with the eyes like leeks, and the

human volcano who was perhaps the embodiment of that *Honour* I once debated with Prince Thomas. Hotspur had honour all right. He was composed of honour from his poll to the soles of his feet. He was all impatience and cold baths. I think he had constructed a kind of theology upon courage. 'If you don't come back *with* your shield, then come back *on* it.' That was the mentality and motto of those Percies.

I did hear that when Hotspur and Glendower met at Bangor, a few sparks flew. Mr Glendower was a great one for portents and magics. Hotspur, as you might imagine, was not. 'I can call spirits from the vasty deep,' the Welshman boasted. To which, the Hotspur:

'Why so can I, or so can any man – but will they *come* when you do call for them?'

A scepticism which I liked. But the two rebels were soon hand-in-glove in their devil-lotionary ambitions. They carved up Britain on a map. This for me, that for you. Another clue to Hotspur – when it was proposed that the River Trent be used as a boundary for his share, and he disliked its inroads into fertile land, he seriously put forward the notion of *changing the course of the river*.

God save England from fanatics and magicians alike!

Hal was entrusted with a wing of the army proceeding against Hotspur. Sir Walter Blunt –

Enough. Miranda's insisting that I suckle her. She's taken my head in her arms and slipped her breast out of her dress and her nipples are as erect as my prick and –

Worcester, I give you the gist of it, of England's destiny at this point just prior to the Battle of Shrewsbury. I mean – how the Devil can a man remember dates and factions when his niece has a grip of his weapon, and is trying to make it discharge?

And when he is now in fact *in bed with her*, busy futtering, with his secretary scribbling on a parchment by the pillow while he jerks out the memories from that corner of his mind not directly engaged with the young lady's satisfaction? Damned if it isn't too much even for your author. History is being interfered with. Time is being somewhat buggered up. By these sudden inventions of my niece Miranda in singularly sportive mood.

And if Miranda becomes a character in these annals, why not? O sweet. O interruption. What author was ever more pleasantly misled by an alternate Muse?

Madam, my lord, dear readers: the final paragraphs of today's Day must constitute the first section or stitch of History ever put into a book by an English gentleman and knight when *on the job*.

LXI

Bardolph's tale

Bardolph. My man Bardolph. My friend. Hey now. His face was my *memento mori*. Every time I looked at it I thought of Dives – there he was, still in his purple robes, but burning, burning. Bardolph. If he had been in any way given to virtue, I would have sworn by his face, and my oath would have been, *By this fire, that is God's angel!* But Bardolph and virtue had long ago gone their separate ways. He was altogether given over to virtue's posteriors. He was, as a matter of fact, always excepting the light in his face, the son of utter darkness.

By the light in his face I refer, of course, to HIS NOSE.

There never was a nose that came near the nose of my man Bardolph. Not for brilliancy, refulgor, or resplendence. Not for irradiation or sheer unmatched capacity for frightening the horses in the streets.

It was not a nose, it was a phosphorus.

Bardolph, that nose made you a perpetual triumph, an everlasting bonfire.

It must have saved me £1000 (One Thousand Pounds) in torches, that nose of Bardolph's, walking with him in the night between tavern and tavern. (On the other hand, think of the cost of all the sack I bought to fuel that nose! It would amount to more than a thousand pounds' worth of torches.) Well, I maintained that salamander of Bardolph's nose for 32 years. 32 years I fed it with the necessary wildfire. God reward me for it!

Once, near Deptford, in the depths of despair, at the ends of extremity – I mean, we had no ready cash for sack or beer – it was on the Retreat from Gadshill – once, just once, I saw this same Bardolph *drink water*.

Madam, forgive me. I have to put in all the grisly details. This truth-telling is sometimes a promiscuous and obscene pursuit. I serve a stern mistress. Clio. She's none of your nice Nellies, I'm afraid.

WATER.

In Deptford.

From a horse trough.

Singular phenomena attended upon this prodigy, this violation of Nature, this riot of right dancing among the elements. As Bardolph brought his face to a level with the noxious liquid, a hissing sound was heard, and a quick cloud of steam came scorching from its surface. Also the same water, on the withdrawal of that ravishing proboscis, was discovered to be *hot*, as if a blacksmith's iron had been thrust into it.

Bardolph. The very name is like a little light pilfering of church alms-boxes.

He had a Tyburn face. His complexion was a kind of constellations. He very rarely opened his mouth, I'll say that for him, except to pour something into it. His upper lip had a permanent smile – the result of a dagger slash from the priest at St Clement Danes, where he had once sought sanctuary. He walked like a lank cat treading on eggs.

All the same, on one occasion, following a good influx of liquor, I obtained from this Bardolph *his story*.

It is my content and contention to believe that every man alive has a story, has matter enough in him for a book – and a very good place for it to stay, in most cases. When the story which sack eventually elicits from the darkest regions of the human heart is as sad and unusual as the tale which Bardolph told me, it seems worth the writing down, however, and since to my knowledge no man has ever heard Bardolph's strange story except myself, I will tell it to you now.

Today seems the right day to do it, too. There is a slight hiatus here in History – we pause on the eve (in these annals) of the Prince procuring for me a small command of infantry, and the March to Coventry, and the Battle of Shrewsbury. Besides which, William Worcester has retired to his couch quite knackered from his extra-curricular duties of last night, when you may recall that he had to follow Miranda and your author to bed – so determined I was not to lose the thread of my discourse, despite (as you might say) my intercourse.

So we have Bussard back with us. Pigbum. Which is appropriate to

BARDOLPH'S TALE

'My mother,' Bardolph said, 'was Tannakin Skinker.'

We were sprawling at our ease in the Boar's Head tavern. Just the two of us. From the state of my legs I would say that the time must have been about eleven o'clock at night.

'*The* Tannakin Skinker,' Bardolph said, as if this addition of the definite article would explain everything. It didn't. I must have looked at him with questions in my eyes, there in the light of the great logs crackling on the hearth, and his glowing nose.

'You mean to tell me,' Bardolph said, with a sniff like a fanfare of trumpets, 'that you never *heard* of Tannakin Skinker?'

I shook my head. 'Forgive me,' I said, stirring my sack with my finger, round and round, and thinking all the while how my dear darling Doll liked stirring like this, round and round in her little clack-dish. 'Forgive me, old friend, for not having heard of your mother. I've lived the quiet life of a country gentleman. In town, it is true, I've found harlots cheaper than hotels. But then,' I added hastily, 'no doubt that's why I've not met your mother.'

'Nobody met my mother,' growled Bardolph. 'That's the point,'

'Perhaps your father?' I said, sipping sack. '*Met* her, I mean.'

'Not at the time,' Bardolph grunted. 'He didn't.'

I took a deep breath. 'The age of miracles will never pass,' I said. 'I believe it. Only yesterday I heard that Timur the Lame has snuffed it, and they're going to put him in a mausoleum in the golden city of Samarcand just to make sure. But Bardolph, old bugger-in-arms that you are, if you're expecting me to credit that your entrance into this world was the result of some kind of immaculate conception, accompanied without prejudice to your mother's virginity, then –'

I left the sentence unfinished, and crossed myself.

Bardolph blew snot into the fire, pinching his nose in his fingers. The snot flared like sea coals.

'Nothing of the sort,' he said. 'Tannakin Skinker, she was. I thought the whole world knew of Tannakin Skinker. I walk about all the time, night and day, man and boy, thinking to myself that people go pointing after me in the street, whispering, "That must be Skinker's spawn!" '

He looked so sorry for himself that I handed him my handkerchief. He inspected it. Then he handed it back.

Despite this uncalled-for insult, I remarked gently:

'The world forgets.'

'Eh?'

'Whatever the sins of Tannakin Skinker, the world has forgotten them.'

'I don't think she *had* many sins,' said Bardolph. 'Sins are hard to come by in that condition.'

'For God's sake,' I said. '*What* condition?'

'It was more on account of *her* mother's sins,' said Bardolph.

A sudden shower of rain beat at the shutters. Outside, I heard the watch at their long march away down Eastcheap. Beside us, between us, candleflames nodded like monks in their thin hoods of wax. I thought of Duncan, dead. I felt suddenly like a father confessor.

'Unburden your conscience,' I said.

'Not likely,' said Bardolph. He snorted. 'Nothing so filthy,' he said. He took a long draught of sack, then smacked his lips and stretched out his boots to the roaring fire. 'I just want to tell you my story.'

'Which involves your mother.'

'Who was Tannakin Skinker.'

'Right,' I said. 'That is established. We know the worst. Fire ahead.'

Bardolph stared deep into the fire, as though past and present and his life to come all met there. Then something seemed to click – I heard it! – either in his head or his throat or (most likely) his NOSE, and he started to talk. He talked and he talked, while I listened.

'My story begins with my mother's own mother,' he said. 'She came from a place called Wirkham, a town on the River Rhine. Oh yes, I have foreign blood in me, some, and maybe worse. . . . But she was a person of consequence, my mother's mother. A lady of some kind of rank and fashion. At least among Hollanders. She would be, I should estimate, a burgheress.' He picked thoughtfully at his nose, withdrawing his finger as if it was singed. 'Well,' went on Bardolph, 'she was married, you see, she was pregnant, and one day she opened the door on an old beggar-woman, you know the type of person, and the beggar-woman asked her for sixpence, for the sake of the child which she held in her arms. She was a particularly filthy beggar-woman, and it was a particularly filthy child. What's more, it squalled and it squealed, and my grandmother was in no especially charitable mood – having just discovered my grandfather in the broom-cupboard and up the serving maid – and she told the old beggar-woman to bugger off and take her nasty pig away with her. To which, because she was – I mean, *a* witch! – the beggar-woman turns round and snaps, "When your own child comes out of your womb it'll be more like a pig than mine, you just wait and see!" And she trots off, muttering to herself the Devil's *Paternoster*. Well, Fastolf, I tell you, my grandmother didn't think too much of this, not being one of your superstitious Dutch, but when she was brought to bed, and her baby was born, oh oh oh Fastolf, oh Jack, conceive of her horror when she was safely delivered of a daughter, correct in all parts, all limbs and lineaments of the body well-featured and proportioned, save only her face – save only her NOSE. . . . *The babe had the snout of a pig!* A hog's nozzle! A swine's proboscis! An organ of smell in the shape of the neb of a sow! O horror, horror, horror!'

I could think of no words adequate to the occasion. So I belched. Not out of contumely, you understand. It was a sympathetic belch, a belch of brotherhood. Bardolph accepted it as such. He went on quickly:

'They bribed the midwife, my grandmother and my grandfather, and swore her thus to secrecy. They called the pig-child Tannakin, and never let her out of the house. They were persons of some substance, remember, and these things can be arranged, especially on the continent. They took care that whenever anyone *had* to be present in the room where Tannakin was, then the girl's face was so veiled and covered that nobody ever saw her nose. They fed her secretly. They taught her. It is all lies, incidentally, that my mother would eat swine-grub only from a silver trough, and that all she ever learned to say was some hoggish Dutch *Ough! Ough!* or French *Owee! Owee!* She could talk and eat, this Tannakin, just like an ordinary everyday person. The only difference between her and the rest of the human race was her NOSE.'

Bardolph scratched at his own inheritance reflectively.

I said nothing. I kicked a log on the fire. I poured us some more sack to drink.

'My grandparents consulted the most learned doctors in Europe,' Bardolph continued. 'Wolfram von Eschenbach, Matthew Paris, Michael Scot, Fibonacci, Snorri Sturluson, Yaqut ibn Abdallah ur-Rumi, Thomas of Cantimpre, Bartholomaeus Anglicus, Albert Magnus, Thomas Aquinas, Vincent of Beauvais, William of Saliceto, Jean de Meung, Rutebeuf, Bonaventura, Ristoro, Rufinus, Lanfranchi, even –'

'Roger Bacon,' I said.

My friend nodded glumly. 'Even Roger Bacon,' he said. He took a slow pull at his sack.

'Medical knowledge was in its infancy in those days,' I observed. 'But didn't one of these learned doctors come up with a single idea that might help?'

Bardolph gargled with his sack and spat some in the fire. '*Always* too much lime in Boar's Head sack,' he complained. But he accepted the fresh jug I poured him. 'Oh yes,' he went on. 'An idea was found. A solution. A cure. An antidote.'

'Hurrah!' I shouted, drinking to it. 'Which doctor?'

'Bacon.'

'Who else?'

'But naturally.'

We drank to the author of *De Speculis, De Mirabili Potesate Artis et Naturae, De Computo Naturali, Opus Maius, Opus Minus, Opus Tertius, Compendium Studii Philosophiae, De Retardandis Senectutis Accidentibus, Speculum Alchimiae, De Secretis Operibus Naturae, Libellus de Retardandis Senectutis Accidentibus.* And so on. A glorious bibliography of sack.

Then I said, the last toast drunk:

'And what was the cure that Roger Bacon prescribed?'

'Me,' said Bardolph.

'You?' I said.

'Me,' said Bardolph. 'I have a kind of self,' he added.

'I drink to it!' I said. 'To you and your yard and your little finger! But how could *you* be a cure for your mother's affliction when you were not even as much as a twinkle in your father's whatsit?'

'Attend,' said Bardolph.

He spilled sack from the flagon on the table, and began to draw with his finger across it.

'That learned Dr Bacon had a theory,' he explained, 'relating to natural agents and their activities. In other words, to matter and to force. In other words, to *virtus, species, imago agentis* – God's teeth, I can't remember all the fancy names he gave them. But, roughly speaking, the main idea in his philosophy was that *change*, in any of your natural phenomenon, is produced by the impression of a VIRTUS or SPECIES on *matter*.'

'Roughly speaking,' I said.

'Roughly speaking,' said Bardolph, still drawing in the sack.

'Not rough enough for my five wits,' I said. 'I can't follow a bloody word you're saying, my boy.'

'Physical action,' said Bardolph grimly, gritting his teeth, as though reciting a lesson that had been drummed into him time and again to justify or explain his own existence, or perhaps the *shape* of his own existence, 'physical action is *impression*. Transmission.'

'Transmission of what?' I said.

'Of force,' said Bardolph.

'In what?' I said.

'In lines,' said Bardolph. 'Look.'

He had finished tracing with his finger in the sack.

This is what he had drawn:

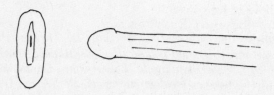

I stroked my beard. 'Bardolph,' I said, 'you are no Praxiteles. But I take it from these crude and imperfect representations that you wish to refer me to those parts of the human body, the one male, the other female, which are of use to us in copulation? I take it that you are trying to draw for me the things which prudish times disguise with fig-leaves?'

'That there's a cunt,' said Bardolph. 'And that's a prick.'

'I have your drift. Proceed.'

'Dr Bacon's diagnosis,' went on Bardolph, 'was that my mother's gross deformity could be cured only by the wrack and ruin of her maidenhead. Your prick was to be the VIRTUS, with its SPECIES, which would effect the *change*, not only upon her cunt, but upon her NOSE.'

'If you will forgive a pun,' I murmured, 'this sounds like a nostrum to me.'

'It worked,' said Bardolph simply. He scrubbed out his drawing with his sleeve, took another draught of sack, then said: 'Not wishing to cause scandal in the Rhineland, and to come where they would not be known at all, my grandparents brought my mother to England, here, to London. A little discreet advertising was done. Of course, they couldn't expect anyone to *marry* my mother with her nose like that, and of course they couldn't even guarantee to a prospective husband that her nose would improve with lechery. But a way was worked out. Remember, my grandfather was a wealthy burgher. For 25 pounds and a pony he discovered a tinker who was only too willing to project his VIRTUS through a hole in a tapestry, and so squirt his SPECIES –'

'Into your mother's *matter*,' I concluded.

'You have it,' said Bardolph.

'And she had you,' said I.

'And her nose came down to normal overnight,' said Bardolph.

I clapped my hands. 'A happy ending,' I said. 'A moral tale.'

'Not quite,' said Bardolph. 'The tinker, whose name was Skinker – he jumped in the Thames.'

'With lead in his boots?'

'No. Iron cartwheel. Round his neck.'

'But why?'

Bardolph shrugged, and picked at his carbuncles. 'Matter and force,' he said, 'matter and force. They're funny things. There's a delicate sort of balance we don't understand.'

'But with your mother's nose transformed to normal,' I mused, 'I should have thought Skinker could even have brought himself to *marry* her, seeing the wealth in the family and all that.'

'He did marry her,' said Bardolph. 'They lived down at Windsor. They were merry as cock and hen for about a year. Then, one midsummer night, poor Skinker wakes up and needs a piss. He goes to the window – they lived in this fine house, right by the river's edge – and gets out his tool, and what does he find?'

'Let me guess,' I said.

I held up my little finger.

'Right first time,' said Bardolph. 'Shrunk to the size of a pig's tail. And with a little curly twist in it besides.'

I shook my head. Outside, the chimes were sounding midnight.

'It's a wicked and wonderful world,' I said.

Bardolph grunted.

Then he looked up and grinned at me, rubbing his nose in the firelight.

'Things could be worse,' he said. '*At least I don't favour my father!*'

LXII

About the holy number 7

Desdemona, a word in your ear.

Upon upon a time there was a Roman lady, a rich widow, called Felicity. The name means happiness. No one knows much about her, except God. She was a Christian. She had 7 sons. During the reign of Antoninus Pius they were all arrested. That puts it round about the year of God's Death 140, since it was at that time that Lollius Urbicus, legate of this Emperor, built the Antonine Wall from Dunglass Castle, on the Clyde, to Castle Blackness, on the Firth of Forth, taking his cue from Hadrian's earlier job. O Picts. O devolution.

The lady Felicity and her 7 sons declined to offer sacrifices to the pagan gods. (Which gods would have included Antoninus Pius himself, and his slightly less pious wife called Faustina.) The whole family was brought before 4 different judges, and sentenced to death in 7 differing ways. The sons were killed first. Their names were Felix, Philip, Martial, Vitalis, Alexander, Silvanus, and Januarius. St Felicity was the last to be put to death. All that is mortal of them is buried on the Salarian Way.

Today is the day we remember those 7 martyrs and their mother. Pope St Symmachus added Alexander as representative of them to the canon of the Mass in the 6th century.

Seven, my sweet Desdemona. A holy number.

7 Deadly Sins.

7 Last Words of our Saviour on the Cross.

7 Joys of the Virgin.

7 Days in Creation.

7 Graces.

7 Wonders of the World.

7 Spirits of God.

7 Stations of the Cross.
7 Ages in the Life of Man.
7 Sleepers.
7 Divisions in the Lord's Prayer.
7 Churches of Asia.
7 Sages of Greece.
7 Phases of the Moon.
7 Candlesticks.
7 Stars.
7 Trumpets.
7 Eyes of the Lamb.
7 Champions of Christendom.
7 League Boots.
7 Senses.
7 Sisters.
And as for me – I never diced more than 7 times a week.

And when I die – they'll need no more than 7 coffins knocked together to house me.

And at the Resurrection – put me down for 7 seats, please, at the Lord's Round Table.

LXIII

About some things beyond numbers

Desdemona, there are numbers and numbers. There are numerals and ordinals. And there are some things beyond numbers and numbers and numerals and ordinals.

The Prince said once to me:

'Sir, do I owe you a thousand pounds?'

And I said to the Prince:

'A thousand pounds, Hal! A million. Your love is worth a million. You owe me your love.'

And you know how he replied to that?

By prattling on about my uncle Hugh's ring being copper, and about how if my girdle should break my guts would fall out round my knees.

God save your grace, King Hal! My royal Hal!

God save you, my sweet boy!

LXIV

About the march to Coventry

12 July

A charge of foot. I was entrusted with a charge of foot. That was my declension, my appointment, my custody. This charge of foot was procured for me by Prince Henry. Anarchy rode, disguised as Mr Glendower, a Welsh wizard. The revolting Hotspur, assisted by this fairy, and abetted by the Scots he had set free, all were now pitched against the English crown. There was to be a fight. And I was to command a charge of foot in that fight.

Prince Henry, alias Hal embryo imperator, was staking a lot on this stinking little shindy, I can tell you. His standing with his father was not certain. The leper King still wanted to lead his armies in a crusade – to expiate the pale ghost of Queen Dick. No doubt he hoped in some vague way to atone for his own sins and to put an end to civil war by uniting the country against a foreign enemy. Civil war is often a disorder in the body of the King. But Hotspur was not easily ignored. Disadvantaged by the non-arrival of various promised troops, with Mr Glendower in particular lost on a dim mountain, he still pranced up and down at Shrewsbury. Gunpowder Percy. Earl Honour himself. When they told him So-and-so wasn't coming to his side, or that What-do-you-call-him had decided to hang his bugle in an invisible baldric rather than come to the wars after all, he just shouted things like: 'Our powers will serve! Die all, die merrily!'

Shrewsbury. Sloppsbury. Salop. That's where the rebels and the King's force were encamped, awaiting my approach from London. Is it in order to speak of the place of battles as inevitable and pre-ordained? Fr Brackley concedes and confirms that there are more things in Heaven and earth (not to speak of Hell) than are mentioned in the Army Manual. The geography of war may be strangely spiritual. There are reflections in the stars of these our struggles. I wipe my sword on a blade of grass and a comet whizzes. Or do we reflect great cosmic wars down here?

Prince Henry, needing to win, sickened at last of his role as self-defeating madcap, picked me to help him. (When a prince hates himself, let his most loyal, taxed and thieving subjects beware his love.) Still, he came expressly into Eastcheap to summon me to his banner. 'The land is burning,' he said. 'I have procured you, Jack, a charge of foot,' he said. I saw in this some small appreciation of the tactics and strategy I had taught him – and, above all, the great confidence I had inspired in him – by my action at the Battle of Gadshill.

Better have a stab at a date – it must have been about this same day of July, a half a century ago, that I, John Fastolf, militis, marched off to gather troops on my way from the Boar's Head tavern to the field of Sloppsbury. I went via the Midlands. The sun shone on my back and the flies buzzed in my beard.

I had my own methods of recruitment.

These may be explained by a simple piece of algebra. Thus:

$$(X - Y) + Z = Z^2 + X^2$$

In this mystery,

X represents the number of selected soldiers able to buy themselves out;

Y represents the amount of ready cash it took them to buy themselves out;

Z represents the rubbish who could not afford to buy themselves out;

And, thus,

Z^2 equals my company, while

X^2 equals my profit.

Madam, I am sorry you are not in possession of a truly algebraic brain. If you will kindly cross your legs to allow me to concentrate the better on the matter in hand, I will spell the thing out in its *human detail* then.

I marched into the Midlands, with Hal's warrant in my hand, which gave me power to pick men at random for the King's wars. I chose none but men of substance – good householders, yeomen's sons, men about to be married, a whole commodity of warm slaves who no more wanted to hear a drum than to shake hands with the Devil. I chose fellows with plenty of toast-and-butter about them, and money in their pockets. I then allowed these same *gentle*men to buy themselves out of my service. They were glad to be excused from an early death. I was glad of their paying for that privilege. In exchange for their rapid release from military service, I received £300 (Three Hundred Pounds). Or so. O Mars. O conscription.

My bought-out men I replaced with such as were incapable of buying themselves out of a jelly, or indeed of fighting their way out of a paper bag. What a regiment! What an army!

Slaves as ragged as Lazarus in the painted cloth, where the glutton's dogs licked his sores.

Discarded unjust serving-men.

Revolted tapsters.

Ostlers trade-fallen.

150 men (of a sort) to fill the places of the 150 men who bought their way out.

150 tattered prodigals.

No eye ever saw such scarecrows on the march.

I met a mad boy on the road and he wanted to know if I'd been unloading all the gibbets and teaching the corpses to march.

I say *mad* because anyone in his right senses would have seen – not necessarily that this army of mine was *alive*, but that it consisted not of hanged men, but of criminals just out of prison. You could tell that from the bandy way they marched. They hadn't yet got used to not having irons on their legs.

On reflection, I decided to make a detour round Coventry.

Hal passed us on the road. Riding of course. Princes travel well.

'Jack,' he called out, 'whose fellows are these?'

'Mine, Hal, mine.'

'I never saw such pitiful rascals!' said the Prince.

'Tut, tut,' said I. 'Good enough to die, Hal. Food for powder, food for powder. What more do you want? They'll fill a pit as well as any. Mortal men, Hal, mortal men. They'll do.'

They did.

LXV

About the Battle of Shrewsbury

13 July

The wind blew all day. We had to march against Hotspur over a
field sown with peas, and that cunning bugger had been up in the
night with his men binding all these pea-shoots together and
entangling them, so that our advance was not as furious or
straightforward as it might have been. So much for chivalry.

Our side used *tactics* too. Henry the 4th directed several gentlemen of his company to wear armour bearing the royal insignia,
and to decorate their heads with helmets just like this. That ruse
bemused the Scots. They rushed about killing (as they thought)
King after King after King. Your Scotsman is never well clad,
and in some parts of his Highlands he wears nothing at all in the
natural state. So the more stupid of these victors tried on the
royal insignia for size. And then, of course, they started killing
each other.

'*Esperance!* Percy!' cried Hotspur all the time, advertising himself, as he roared up and down in search of Hal.

I had seen the Prince in his tent just before dawn, and asked
him – for friendship's sake – if he would be so kind as to bestride
and defend me, if he should see me fallen in the field.

Again, the eagle flash. 'Nothing but a colossus could do you
that friendship,' he snapped, buckling on his sword. 'Say your
prayers.'

I did not need command from any princeling to do that.

'You owe God a death,' he added, going out.

His brother had said the same. They all spoke alike, these sons
of Bolingbroke. Spoke alike and thought alike. As for their
philosophy of *honour* – my view of that had not changed since the
days in Ireland. Up your honourable arse, your honour!

Esperance! Percy! Who ever heard such rubbish?

292

Hang me, I saw plenty of honour at Shrewsbury. I give you my word for it. My word of honour. My word for honour.

My word for honour is CANT.

Not cannot, Sir. CANT.

With an A, Madam. An A for *a*live.

O honour. O cut guts hanging out.

I saw the knights lowered onto their horses by ropes chucked over the branches of trees. I saw the same knights ploughed into the ground, hacked down by axes, which made bubbling new lyric mouths from the sides of their necks to the bulb of their shoulderblades. I saw the same horses, their throat-vessels ripped, being eaten by rats before darkfall. Cages of skeletons, all so much smashed you couldn't be sure whether the bits of bones had ever belonged to a man or a horse. Patches of flesh on snapped lances. Knotted veins crammed into mud like vermeil tape. Carrion picked at by crows.

I saw honour at the Battle of Shrewsbury. His name was Sir Walter Blunt. His throat had been cut from ear to ear, and his legs chopped off.

I saw honour at the Battle of Shrewsbury. He was no longer a man. This honour, this *it*, was all that was left of one of my poor ragamuffins plucked from the hedgerows near Coventry. It had no eyes. It had both legs and one arm torn off. It had been stabbed in the groin and the blade had cut up and round as it came, so that no bone would impede its progress. It smelt like vomit. Blood and brains in a pool in the mud. The flies thought it was turds. They buzzed about it.

Three men survived of the 150 I brought to the Battle of Shrewsbury, not counting myself.

2300 men of the Rebel party were killed.

2000 of our Royalists.

There were also 3000 wounded. Most of these died later.

This battle was fought on a Saturday, the vigil of St Mary Magdalene, and those who were there say that there was never a fiercer battle. Men on both sides were still fighting when night came, although by then the victory was ours. Mingled together, weary, wounded, bleeding, I saw a Rebel and a Royalist stab each other to death in a strange embrace like love. And the crows were on their skulls and had their eyes out even before the bodies had ceased twitching.

The site of this noble engagement was a plain overlooked by

Haughmond Hill. King Henry the 4th had his post there, on top of the hill. This gave him a splendid view of the dead and the dying, and enabled his civil servants to tot up the score every now and again, to see who was winning, and then to declare that the King had eventually won.

Poor Henry 4. Poor leprous syphilitic Bolingbroke. He observed the Battle of Shrewsbury while his heart cried out to see Jerusalem. A religious bird was dining on his liver. I saw him ride by me at darkfall, a flourish of banners. His face looked like Westminster Abbey.

And I?

I was sad, Madam. I killed one or two when I had to. But it gave me no pleasure to add to such meaningless carnage. All the same, I exposed my person in the thickest of the fight. Indeed, you might even say that I *was* the thickest of the fight. I provided the enemy with something of a target for their arrows. St Mary Magdalene looks after her own. Not an arrow touched me. Hal, on the other hand, got one in the left cheek. Of his face, Sir.

I fought, as I say, when I had to. For the rest – I drank sack. I went to the Battle of Shrewsbury armed with a sword and a bottle. You will recall my original use of alcohol in my first taste of warfare, at the Sea Fight at Slugs? I have sworn by it ever since. In war, as in time of plague, my uncle Hugh's maxim has it about right:

Neither drunk, nor yet too sober
Is the way of getting over.

I drank, as I fought, like a Turk. To be precise, like Turk Gregory, that great Pope, whom some call Hildebrand, whose valour in adversity was never in question, but who never (so far as I know) prattled on about honour. Honour, now I come to think of it, is a *pagan* virtue. I mean honour of the Hotspur kind, the Harry Monmouth breed. Look at Turk Gregory. He had to struggle all his pontificate against that Emperor Henry IV who was *always* harping on the honour string. In the end, the good Pope was driven from Rome. He died in exile at Salerno. Fr Brackley tells me that his last words were: *Dilexi justitiam et odivi iniquitatem: propterea morior in exilio.* Which, being Englished, is 'I have loved righteousness and hated iniquity; that's why I die in exile'. Not a word there about HONOUR.

Don't get me wrong. I'm not going to pitch my last words as

high as that. I'd be a damned fool if I tried. I have loved cakes and ale, and I don't seem to be dying in exile. (I shall live to be 100.) But I'd rather be in exile with Turk Gregory, than at home with all that honour lying arse-upwards in the mud on Shrewsbury field.

Fr Brackley tells me that Aquinas taught that honour (like glory) is only good and to be lawfully sought *if charity is its principle* and *if the love of God or the good of one's neighbour is its object*.

You could have looked all night through scraps of bodies, ditches of blood, hacked-off heads, torn-out innards, whole hillocks of corpses slung together awaiting the cart to Dead Men's Dump, that night at Shrewsbury, the vigil of St Mary Magdalene, and if you'd found one man – or part of a man – that died or was killed for such a principle or towards such an object, then may I never spit white again.

Esperance! Percy! Honour!
Give me life!

LXVI

Who killed Hotspur?

14 July

The wind blew all day. When night came it had flecks of blood in it, like rain, and they struck you in the face and got stuck to your beard. Most of the flags had fallen, or were so besmeared with mud and blood that it was hard to tell who was who.

The battle was over. The day was ours. A solitary drum –
Well done, William Worcester!
I've been waiting for that.
I thought no one would ever get round to asking me. . . .
The vital question. The question that decided the Battle of Shrewsbury. The thing that did it.
In other words (Worcester's, just now):
Who killed Hotspur?
Reader, let me tell you a story. Once upon a time, and a pretty nasty time it was too, even by the standards of the Roman Empire, there was an unpleasant little fellow called Heliogabalus. Ate pickles. Elephant troubles. That's right. This Heliogabalus was the Emperor, remember. His two chief pleasures in life were dressing himself up as a woman – flowing toga, tiny jewels, fingers dripping with rings – and drinking hot blood out of golden goblets. I might have called him the Empress. There was a lot of doubt on the subject. He liked to declare himself Brother of the Sun and Sister of the Moon. Most of all, he liked to dance in his palace, with a wreath on his head, calling himself Terpsichore, Queen of the Dance. Well, one day, dear reader – I call you dear because I presume you are being patient with an old man whose wits you suppose to have wandered a long way away from the subject in hand, namely *Who killed Hotspur?* – one day the Emperor/Empress Heliogabalus invited all the leading citizens of Rome to a great banquet. 'It is in your *honour*,' he said. 'For you are all men, all *honourable* men.' He plied them with food and

drink, in the Roman manner, and then he pulled at a silken cord by the side of his throne, and behold, roses started raining down upon them. 'I shower you with roses,' cried Heliogabalus, clapping his smooth hands together. 'In your *honour*, gentlemen. In your *honour*.' His throne was situated on a dias some twenty feet above the main couches and tables where his guests were dining. It rained and rained roses. At first, people smiled politely. How harmlessly quaint of the soft effeminate youth! The roses reached their ankles, the floor was covered. How strange, how novel! The roses fell thicker and thicker. They filled all the air. They buried the tables. Men started to get up, but found that it was difficult now to move for roses. To wade through roses is no easy matter. And now the roses came faster and faster out of the dozens of canopies which the Emperor Heliogabalus had ordered his slaves to supply in the roof for his fun. It went on raining roses for seven hours. It went on raining roses and roses and roses and roses and roses and roses and roses until the petals finally reached the feet of the Emperor's throne, and every single one of his honoured guests had been buried and smothered beneath them. Then Heliogabalus stood up, yawned, scratched himself, remarked on how boring even this little Roman Imperial treat had turned out to be, and had himself crushed to death by his favourite eunuch.

Or, at least, that's one version.

Another has Heliogabalus drown in the roses himself.

And another has Heliogabalus die of pure pleasure.

Which do *you* prefer?

Worcester, my one-eyed son, I'm inclined to agree with you. *I couldn't care less. So long as the little shit bought it.*

And, thus, to your question:

The Hotspur. Who killed him?

First, the facts.

I faced the Earl of Douglas in single combat. You will recall that he lost an eye at the Battle of Holmedon. We met. We fought. He did not see me clearly. He gave me one thwack with the flat of his sword – which would no doubt have been to the point if he had enjoyed the benefit of two eyes. I fell. I lay. I was wounded.

Dry your nose, Madam. Not dangerously wounded. Not severely even. Not so much as scratched in any useful part.

But wounded.

And winded.

And rather confused and concussed.

What with such a God Almighty fall coming on top of so much sack.

Now, while I was fighting with Douglas, I had spied Hal – oh yes, I have eyes in my arse, Sir, like your dog Argus – and he was going at it hammer-and-tongs with the Hotspur.

As a matter of figgy fact, I remember distinctly trying to encourage the young prince – with some such remark as 'Go to it, Hal!' or 'Give it to him, Hal!' – just before Douglas knocked me down, and then ran off.

What happened next I simply do not know. And nor does any of Clio's minions. And the girl keeps her lips as tight shut as her pussy. Tighter.

What I *do* know is that as I began to come round from my concussion, I heard a voice like Harry Monmouth's – but it seemed a million miles away – saying something about *embowelling me*. I suppose now, having thought it all out, that he took me for dead, and was looking forward in that grimly efficient Plantagenet way of his to the process of seeing the magnanimous belly of your author laid open to the public view for purpose of embalming.

But by the time I got up on one elbow to make some joke to the effect that if he had me embowelled today, I'd give him permission to steep me in brine and eat me like venison tomorrow – he was gone.

And that left me.

And the Hotspur.

Reader, I was dazed.

Reader, I was as a man returned from the dead.

Reader, for one moment I thought I was a ghost, a counterfeit. This flesh! I even touched my parts.

No. Not dead. All present and correct. I embraced my belly like a bride.

To die, I decided, *that* was to be made a counterfeit. No doubt I had saved my life by *seeming* to be dead in the one eye of hasty Douglas. Was it my fault he wore no monocle?

I had seemed to be dead, but that was not a counterfeit, for here I was now, alive. Such a counterfeit may be considered the true and perfect image of life.

The better part of valour is discretion.

In which better part I had saved my life.

But. . . .

that still left. . . .

HOTSPUR!!!

There he was. There he lay. He might be dead. He might not be dead. I might have been dead. I had not been dead. I had risen from the dead. *What about if he now did the same?*

I drank some sack and thought this problem out very very carefully I can tell you. Then I drank some more sack. And some more. I consulted the 3 Fates, the 3 Graces, the 3 Harpies, the 3 Sheets in the Wind, and the Muses that are 3 times 3. My problem was thus gradually reduced by itself to these 3 heads:

1) Was Hotspur dead?
2) If Hotspur was dead, who killed him?
3) If Hotspur was not dead, who was going to kill him?

I realised in a blinding flash of sack that by answering the third and final question, I could settle the other two.

So, Sir – (and, Madam, please skip this bit) – I drew my sword and stabbed him in the thigh!

Yes – as quick as it would take you to piss, Sir.

Then I drank some more sack three or three times and reconsidered the situation, going over my accounts as you might say:

1) Hotspur was now *definitely* dead.
2) If he had not been dead before I killed him, then I had killed Hotspur.
3) There was no further point in anyone else killing Hotspur.

These matters clear, I took it upon myself to take upon my back this mighty Honour. I mean, Worcester, I picked him up and carried him round my shoulders like a dead deer.

And this is where the story gets confused. (Before, remember, only *I* was confused.) For in striding from the field with Hotspur across my shoulders I met the Prince of Wales, and he immediately launches into some complicated rigmarole about *me* being dead, and *him* having killed Hotspur.

'Lord, Lord,' I said, in the heat of the moment, 'how this world is given to lying!'

I regretted the words the moment I had said them. They were words for which Harry Monmouth never forgave me. They were also unfair words.

Hal *may* have killed the Hotspur.

He *thought* he had. He apparently left him for dead.

But then he apparently left me for dead too. And if he was wrong about me, how can anyone be sure he was right about Hotspur?

But he never forgave me for what he considered a lie.

And he never forgave me for the implication that *his* claim to Hotspur's killing might be a lie.

I appeal to you, Clio. And to our posterity.

Gentle Reader, in whatever age you live. . . . Turn to your wives and your servants. Ask them to fetch you a volume of the history of this century in which I have lived. Turn to the Battle of Shrewsbury and see for yourself if any dispassionate hack has come up with a definite answer to that puzzle: *Who killed Hotspur?*

I lay you 100 to 7 that History will say it is an Open Question.

More curiously and subtly – though it is a thing I cannot prove – I estimate the odds in reverse, at about 100 to 7 *on*, that Prince Hal bore me a grudge to his dying day, either because I sowed seeds of doubt in his mind and his courage, by making him think that perhaps it was *not* his own blow that had killed Hotspur, but mine after all; or because he just crudely resented the fact that anyone, and maybe especially me, should have even put forward his name as alternative hero.

Hal had his heart set on high heroism now. His Dad had watched him from the hilltop. He had won his spurs. More, he had won Hotspur's spurs. Or had he?

He never forgave me for being the one gentleman in England who provided the living excuse for those three little words: *Or had he?*

If you think I belabour the point, be assured that I do so for the sake of making clear something which is still to come. Namely, the base ingratitude of this same Prince Hal. He had no motive for his later treatment of me. Only this one. This matter of *Who killed Hotspur?*

Worcester, I confess I erred. In the heat of battle. At the end of that long day at Shrewsbury plain, when the wind would not stop blowing. Oh I can still hear it howling in the sedge, and the screams of the horses, the groans of the dying, the endless drum that beat and beat all night. And, search as they might, no one could find out the drummer.

I should have allowed that Hotspur was killed by a man in a buckram suit.

Heliogabalus, Madam?

Heliogabalus was Hotspur turned inside out.

Heliogabalus was Hal turned upside down.

To hell with Heliogabalus.

LXVII

About St Swithin, Mrs Quickly, & the Lord Chief Justice

It's raining, of course. Out there, and in here.

Hanson and Nanton, my two pretty boys.

One writes one sentence for me.

And the other the next.

Well, it makes a change. And it keeps their fingers out of the treasury of my Miranda.

You know the reason for St Swithin's Day? He was Bishop of Winchester, and when he died (in the year of our At-one-ment 862), he wanted to be buried in the churchyard of the minster, for he loved the sweet rain, like St Francis, the rain was his sister, hey ho, the gentle rain. But when he was canonised the monks thought it was not right that a saint should be left in the common earth, under the open sky. So they translated Swithin's body into the choir, and they fixed this day, 15 July, for his feast day. But Swithin was not comfortable in the cathedral choir. He wanted the stars and the moon and the sun and the green green grass, and above all he wanted the rain which is sometimes like grace itself falling from heaven. So he had a word or two with whatever Weather Angel orders these things, and from that 15 July of his removal into the choir at Winchester it rained day after day for 40 days, until even the monks got the point and moved his bones back.

I think of him as christening the apples.

St Swithin is also the patron saint of drunkards.

Blessed Swithin, pray for me.

The rebellion was put down. The King was sick. I met the Lord Chief Justice in the street, and while conceding that my day's work in the field at Shrewsbury had proved more to his liking and his understanding than my night's exploit on Gadshill, he saw fit to remark:

'God send the Prince a better companion!'

But I knew that the wind that had started blowing at dawn on that Shrewsbury field had not finished blowing yet, and blowing no good for me.

'God send the companion a better Prince!' I answered.

Things seemed to go from bad to worse. Mrs Quickly, my good mistress Ursula, my nice Dame Partlet the hen, in one of her sillier moods, engaged a couple of sheriff's officers, Fang and Snare, to arrest me for debt and breach of promise. We met in Lombard Street. Bardolph was all for cutting off Fang's head, and throwing Nell Quickly in the Thames. Some choice abuse –

'You scullion!'

'You rampallian!'

'You fustilarian!'

'I'll tickle your catastrophe!'

– was interrupted only by the arrival of the Lord Chief Justice again, who was taking his duties quite seriously at this time, and patrolling the streets with his men on the look-out for any disturbance of the King's peace.

'I am a poor widow of Eastcheap,' Nell cried dramatically, 'and he is arrested at my suit.'

'For what sum?'

'For all I have,' said Nell. 'He has eaten me out of house and home.'

Tear-jerking stuff, I agree. There was sadder to come.

'What is the gross sum that I owe you?' I asked quietly.

And off she went. . . .

If I were an honest man, she declared, I owed her myself and my money as well. She claimed that I had sworn to marry her (hadn't we all?). But she remembered the occasion so vividly that I came to quite hazily remember it too. At a round table. By a sea-coal fire. In the Dolphin chamber at the Boar's Head tavern. A Wednesday in Whitsun week. When Hal had hit me on the head for saying that his father was like the lowest form of human life, your choirboy. And when she, Nell, had been washing my wound. Oh, there was a good deal else of circumstantial evidence – we had been offered, at the time, a dish of prawns by a butcher's wife called Keech, and Nell had prevented me from eating them, on the grounds that they would aggravate my wound. And

I had kissed her. And then borrowed 30 shillings.

The same old story.

I was very fond of Nell. She was very fond of me. We had these little differences of *interpretation*. They were no business of the Lord Chief Justice.

I sighed, and smiled, and took her on one side.

Within a minute I had persuaded her to dry her tears and pawn her plate and her tapestries. I was suffering from a consumption of the purse.

'We owe God a death,' I whispered in her ear.

'Oh Jack! Don't speak of it! No more of that!'

I kissed her.

'Well, we owe him a life as well,' I said, laughing. 'And *that* is a debt I will willingly pay with you, lovingly pay with you, pay with you better than any man living.'

Nell's eyes were meteors now.

'Come to supper,' she said.

'I will,' I said.

'Doll Tearsheet?' she said.

I touched my finger to her lips. 'No more words,' I said. 'Let's have her.'

Needless to say, the Lord Chief Justice didn't know what to make of it. Lord Chief Justices don't.

LXVIII

About Doll Tearsheet & a night at the Boar's Head

16 July

Figs are figs and apple-johns are apple-johns. That was the first blot on a merry evening later marred by certain droppings from the eaves in the Boar's Head. I noticed the drawers withdrawing with a dish of apple-johns. I was once in company with Hal and five of these dry little, round little, withered old fruits. He took off his hat and said good night to the six of us. I can't endure the sight of apple-johns. Your apple-john stands in for impotence.

My adorable Doll had drunk a good deal of canary.

'Drink canaries, dance canaries,' Nell Quickly was half-prattling, half-chanting, as I rolled into the Dolphin Chamber. 'Canary wine/ is very fine/ a drink to make you dance!'

'Bloody piss,' said Doll. 'From the Isle of Dogs.'

'Explain her, Jack,' Nell begged me, trying to get Doll to lie down on a carved couch by the fire. 'Explain her that your canaries is not from the Isle of Dogs.'

Insula graunt Caneree. But that was a far cry from the mucky spot where King Edward the 3rd had kept his greyhounds. *Canerees veluti insula de graunt Caneree.* And your word *canary*, Ravenstone saying, as in *Canaria insula* (Isle of Dogs) certainly coming from Pliny's *canarius,* formed on *canis,* your dog. AND the 4 Princes arguing that night in this same tavern (how many snows ago, now?) on the subject of islands off Africa. Which certainly included your Grand Canary. Lord, Lord, the amount of intolerable information a man is enabled by kind Providence to forget until a lady asks him a question!

Neither of the same ladies looking at this moment very capable of imbibing etymologies, I sang them instead my song of King Arthur. *One* of my songs of King Arthur:

> *When good King Arthur ruled this land,*
> *He was a goodly king;*
> *He stole three pecks of barley-meal*
> *To make a bag-pudding.*

'That's true poetry,' said Mrs Quickly. 'I always liked a bit of true poetry. Beauty is truth, truth beauty. I mean to say – it's an escape from your personalities, isn't it?' She belched. 'How do you feel now, Doll?' she asked tenderly, looking in her handbag for sal volatile, and emptying out carraways, cummin seed, two green cheeses, a stick of liquorice, a tiny pepper-quern, a rosary, a carrot, and a volley of prunes and raisons. Also a bottle of aqua vitae.

'Better,' said Doll, 'than I was.' She settled for the aqua vitae, sitting down finally by the fire, and shaking off her slippers to warm her pretty little toes.

> *A bag-pudding the king did make,*
> *And stuffed it well with plums;*
> *And in it put great lumps of fat,*
> *As big as my two thumbs.*

'Sweetheart,' said Mrs Quickly, combing Doll's hair – (Doll's hair was the colour of golden bread) – 'Sweetheart, your cheeks are red as roses now, and that's the truth. But, no more the same of that, you have drunk too much canaries, and that's a marvellous searching wine, and it perfumes the blood before you can say, "What's this?" '

'*Hem!*' said Doll. By which she meant to cough and hiccough and drink a new toast in her awua vitae – all in the one three-letter word. And succeeded. Such power in wine! New thresholds, new anatomies! The singing canary had flown round the whole aviary of her being.

> *The king and queen did eat thereof,*
> *And noblemen beside;*
> *And what they could not eat that night,*
> *The queen next morning fried.*

They laughed and clapped, they clapped and laughed, Doll and Nell, the two of them, my sweet ladies, my dear companions.

I held my nose. 'Empty the jordan,' I said. 'It smells like one of the fleshpots of Egypt.'

'Did you say fleshprosts of Eastchept?' demanded Mrs Quickly.

'I did not,' I said. 'That was a man in another song and dance. An Irishman.'

We started to quarrel and chaff, my Doll and I.

'O Jesu, just like old times,' Nell murmured contentedly. 'You two never meet but you have to fall out before you fall in. You rub each other up like two bits of dry toast.' She pranced about the chamber, looking for all the world like a sacred cow, since she was wearing one of those monstrous head-dresses the ladies liked just then, with a great horn curving upwards at each ear.

Doll, my Doll, sweeter and simpler in her thin blue petticoat, poked me in the belly with the aqua vitae bottle. 'Nevermind dry. There's a whole cargo of Bordeaux wine in there!' she laughed. 'I've not seen a hulk better stuffed to the hold!'

'Talking of stuffing –'

'Now, Jack!'

'And holding –'

Doll slapped playfully at my codpiece with her slipper. 'Don't worry,' she said. 'I'll be friends with you, Jack.'

We played hunt the slipper down her petticoat. I rubbed her titties. I stripped down her clothes to her waist, and bounced her plump breasts in the palms of my hands. Doll had tits like cannon balls. The fire sparkled. The wine sparkled. I sparkled. Doll sparkled. Mrs Quickly seemed to be having a sparkling good time too, just watching us, and sparkling herself.

All this brilliance was interrupted by a sudden eruption in the room downstairs. I heard a noise like a cross between a bull-calf and a volcano, and someone stamping up and down. That could only mean one thing.

Pistol.

Now, my man Pistol was a decent sort of rogue, as I've explained. He was a swaggerer, that is true. He was a roaring boy. Or, rather, a roaring old boy. Or bore. Always going on about his battles and his bastinadoes and what have you. But he was my Ancient, and my ensign, and as a matter of fact this is the place to celebrate him as the *one* – out of the whole lot of us who promised to, at some time or another – *who actually went and married Mrs Quickly*. Whether that was valour or discretion or sheer bloody stupidity, I refrain from guessing.

Anyhow, Pistol wanted to join us now. Pistol sniffed action and wanted a piece of it. Doll was all for hanging him. But I was all for getting him bolstered up in a focative sense with Mrs Quickly.

That would give Doll and me a little peace for some pranks. Or some paddling. Or whatever you care to call it, Madam.

'One drink will do no harm to an old soldier,' I said, winking at Nell. She shrugged. She stroked her horns. So I called him up.

This entertainment did not work out well. Doll was further on in her cups than I had gauged. She also regretted rather bitterly the intermission which Pistol's arrival occasioned in my fondling of her titties. Pistol, for his part, the silly old fool, started making dirty jokes and puns which nobody could have followed without footnotes. This was a fault of his. He was a kind of failed actor.

Doll replied to the complicated insinuations with straightforward names –

> *Filthy bung!*
> *Fustian!*
> *Mouldy rogue!*

and worse. She also accused him of living on stewed prunes and dried cakes. Which seemed a bit much. On his salary.

Pistol started off on some extraordinary rigmarole about packhorses and hollow pampered jades of Asia, apparently only capable of travelling at thirty miles a day, which he was inviting us to compare with (I think it was) Caesars and cannibals and Trojan Greeks.

That was enough for me.

'Pistol,' I said, 'I want to be quiet.'

That started him off into a kind of Italian, and stuff about those three old spinsters, Clotho, Lachesis, and Atropos. Atropos, the Fate who did the cutting, especially excited him.

'My rapier,' I said.

And kicked him down the stairs.

Doll was enchanted by this small display of gallantry on her behalf. 'You valiant little villain you!' she cried. 'Come here! Come here! I want to feel your rapier!'

Nell threw a whole shovelfull of sea-coals on the fire, and went on in a kind of ecstasy about *naked weapons*. She grew even more ecstatic when the possibility occurred to her that I might have been hurt in the groin in the tussle with Pistol. She wanted to examine me.

I wanted to be rid of her. I pretended to be worried about Pistol.

'The man's a villain,' said Nell.

307

'I know that,' I said. 'But he *is* my friend. Besides, he was drunk. And he thinks you are Helen of Troy.'

'Go on!' said Nell.

'My fair Calipolis,' I said. 'His very words. He thinks you have a face capable of launching a thousand ships and burning the topless towers of Ilium.'

'I'll go and see if the gentleman's got no confirmities,' said Nell immediately. And left us.

We were alone. The fire blazed bright.

'Jack, you sweet little rogue, you!' cried Doll. She trickled her fingers through my beard. 'I love you,' she said. 'You're as valorous as Hector of Troy. Worth five of Agamemnon. Ten times better than the Nine Worthies.'

'That Pistol!' I growled. 'I'd like to toss him up in a blanket!'

'That Fastolf!' purred Doll. 'I'd like to toss him off between sheets!'

She sat on my lap. We kissed and played. There were musicians in the chamber next to ours, and the music was both sweet and sad. It had an edge to it. As though the strings could scarcely bear the beauty of what they had to sing.

All at once Doll said – and I swear in that moment, inspired no doubt by the sweet sadness of the lutes, she had a look in her eyes such as I have seen lately again in the eyes of my niece Miranda:

'Jack, when will you leave off fighting by day and fucking by night, and begin to patch up your body for heaven?'

I kissed her mouth. 'Peace,' I said.

Our tongues played together.

'Don't speak like a death's head,' I muttered, when that was done. I stroked her cheeks and her chin. 'Don't ask me to remember my end.'

Doll nibbled at my ear. She was off already on another tack.

'What's that Prince Hal like, *really*?' she said.

I watched the armies fighting in the fire. The sparks in the chimneyback. I selected my words quite carefully. 'Good,' I said. 'Shallow,' I said. 'Young,' I said. I could see Badby in that fire. And Hotspur too. And the eyes that flashed like eagles and the mouth that always drank the one cup to my two. And the Mock King in that room downstairs in this very tavern, addressing me as his Mock Son, and promising with no mockery – suddenly Hal himself again – that at the end of time he'd have no time for Fastolf. Banish plump Jack? *I do. I will.*

I sighed. I smiled. 'A good shallow young fellow,' I said.

Doll started rubbing at my codpiece. 'They say that Mr Poins has a good wit,' she remarked provocatively, putting an emphasis on the word *wit* which I can only describe as voluptuous.

'Wit!' I said. 'Is that what you'd call it? His wit is about as thick as Tewkesbury mustard.' I roared with laughter. 'Little Miss Poins!'. I said. 'You know the tale about him and Nellie's harm-pits?'

Doll nodded and giggled. She had my member out. She was playing with it, making it slap up and down against my belly. 'Then why does Prince Henry love him?' she asked.

I plunged my fingers between her legs and whispered a suggestion in her ear.

'Ugh,' she said.

'Well, no more of that,' I said. 'Kiss me, Doll!'

She did. On the tipmost top of my towering prick. She was very drunk. Yet also, I think, she was very sincere. 'I kiss you,' she said, 'with a most constant heart.'

'And a most heartstant cunt?'

'You know, you know.'

'Let's to bed!'

'One more little cup of sack before we go?' Doll whispered.

'Of course,' I said. I snapped my fingers.

Two potboys stepped forward out of the shadows to attend us.

Two sweet little potboys in leather jerkins and shiny aprons.

Two potboys.

Two spies.

Two practical jokers.

Two poppinjays.

Two prigs.

'I *love* your leather jerkins, lads,' I said. 'But buckram suits you better. Buckram becomes you. It goes with your eyes.'

LXIX

How Sir John Fastolf went to war again

17 July

His Royal Highness the Prince of Wales saw fit graciously to observe that I was a globe of sinful continents.

I put away my Africa.

'What a life you lead!' muttered Hal, striding up and down the chamber, kicking at the furniture for want of anything more sensible to do. What bit of kingship there was in him at that moment – and it always fluctuated, reader, like one of those stars that is at some times a bright glory, at others so much a speck you doubt its very existence – that bit of kingship was suddenly embarrassed by the trick he had played upon me, dressing up as a potboy at the instigation of that master-mistress archimandrite of practical jokers, Yedward Poins, and spying from the shadows on my love-making with Doll. 'What a *life!*' he shouted, booting a cushion into the fire.

I watched it burn, and I watched him watch it burn.

'A better than yours,' I said.

3d a day.

KNOCK KNOCK KNOCK.

KNOCK KNOCK KNOCK.

(You absolute idiot, Nanton. Sit down. I don't mean there's anyone *here*. I mean there was great knockings *there*, *then*. God has sent me gowks for secretaries. O nit. O wit.

Hanson has it right at least. *Deo gratias.* One quarter of something like a brain out of these two half-wits. I suppose in a world ruled by reason it's as much as a gentleman might dare expect.)

KNOCK KNOCK KNOCK.

It was Peto. My man Peto (a born knocker if ever there was one), come as it happened to put an end to this pretty scene in the Dolphin Chamber, with the news that messengers were charging

310

into London from the north with reports of a fresh insurrection. The Leper King, at Westminster, was howling for Hal. His mind was cracking, Peto said, since he kept comparing his own estate as King of England very unfavourably with the situation of a ship-boy clinging to the top of a mast in a storm-tossed ship. He seemed to think the boy up the mast would be able to *sleep* better than he could. As usual, he was bemoaning the civil wars which prevented his crusade to the Holy Land. 'He talks to himself a lot,' said Peto.

'What does he say?' Hal demanded.

'Uneasy lies the head that wears a crown,' said Peto.

Poins giggled.

But Hal already had his leather jerkin off. 'My sword and cloak!' he said. They were brought. He put them on. He stopped in the door, and turned.

'Fastolf,' he said, 'good night.'

It was the closest he ever came to an apology.

I paid the musicians. I said goodnight to Doll. She wept.

LXX

Why Sir John Fastolf went to war again

Why did I follow Hal? Why did I go to the wars again?

Two questions, Worcester. Three answers.

First, I followed Hal because I was his education.

I do not say I was his tutor. No dry nurse, I. No proctor or praelector. No abecedarian. Nor of course was I anything in the way of an example to the young Prince, a model for his imitation.

No. John Fastolf was Hal's university. I was his teaching, not his teacher. In me, with me, by me, *through* me he was prepared for the throne of England and of France. The battle of Agincourt was won on the playing fields of Gadshill.

Harry Monmouth, you see, was essentially an actor. Without a role, he was nothing. What some have since chosen to speak of as his mis-spent youth in my company was really his rehearsal in a variety of parts. I led him on. I let him play. I provided his preparation and his training ground.

Consider. A King is a man who plays a King. In the court of my company, Hal was always acting. I let him play at thieves. I let him play at putting thieves to rout. I let him play at roaring boy and whorer. I let him play at drunkard – and never let on that I noticed his weak head and iron will, the emptying of the tankards in the flower-pots when he thought no one was watching, the drinking of the one glass only to my two, or three, or four, or seven. I let him play at being his own father, admonishing me, his son, his prodigal. I let him play at potboys and Peeping Toms. *I let him play at being himself.*

(And that not just when I was cast in the role of his father.)

I come now to the hardest thing to say. It is even possible that I let him play at having feelings. God knows now what ever passed through Harry Monmouth's heart, and if there was ever in that strange cold organ a movement, a stirring of affection, a feeling of true friendship for me. If there was, then I salute you, Hal. And not as an Emperor, either. If there was not, then I salute you only as an Emperor, a King who learned to play at making friends by his play-acting friendship for his fat court fool.

I followed Hal because I was his shadow.

Shadows at sunset, Madam, as at dawn, are longer than what casts them. Only at noon is your shadow underfoot. At Agincourt was Harry's noon.

But *why did I go to the wars again?*

First, because I am an Englishman, and my country needed me.

Second, because I needed the money.

LXXI

About glory & double Gloucester cheese

Not that there was much of it. Money, I mean. There never was, for me, in England. France was where the pickings were to be picked. And the pluckings plucked. Still, in that long hot summer, following Hal north to face the rebel forces, I mislaid a map and found myself in Gloucestershire.

Gloucestershire is a state of mind I am very fond of. Apart from the double cheeses and the cider and the perry, there is the fact that the word Gloucester comes from the old British word *Glou* (meaning city) and *ceaster* (meaning camp). *Caer Glou* – the bright city. That's what they used to call the town of Gloucester in ancient times. And from CEASTER to CAISTER is just a couple of hops.

I had my eye on bright possibilities in Gloucestershire, and discovering myself there I determined on a recruiting drive. I stayed with our old friend Mr Shallow, now Justice Shallow, his majesty's judicial scourge of the Cotswolds. Shallow was in business there with his cousin, Silence. Never was jurisdiction better christened.

Shallow had assembled men for me. There was

> *Ralph Mouldy*
> *Simon Shadow*
> *Thomas Wart*
> *Francis Feeble*
> *Peter Bullcalf*

– fine old English names.

It fell to me to examine them for military service, and to assess their pecuniary status as regards buying themselves out of the Army once enrolled. The two most likely lads from the martial point of view were Mouldy and Bullcalf. But Mouldy was worried about how his old woman would get on without him, and besides could afford to pay Bardolph 40 shillings for his release. Bullcalf, for his part, coughed up another 40, so we released him also. Wart was a very ragged wart. No money to buy himself out. I took him. Shadow ditto. And Feeble, a woman's tailor.

Shallow, as bird-brained as ever, missed the whole point. He thought I should have selected Mouldy and Bullcalf, because they were young and strong. I had to *explain* to him my principles:

'Do you think I care for the mere limbs?' I said. 'It is the *spirit* that counts. And, besides, your choice of sturdy men shows how little you know of the realities of battle. Look at this Shallow. Give me a man like that any day! He's so thin he presents no target to the enemy. Their archers might just as well take aim at the edge of a penknife.'

I pointed at Francis Feeble, the woman's tailor. 'Then there is the question of retreats,' I said.

'Retreats?' said Shallow.

'Your retreat,' I explained, 'is a military manoeuvre by which many a knight has carried all before him. This Feeble here, this woman's tailor. Now there is a man built for running. A spare man.'

'A spare man,' said Shallow, ever the little Sir Echo.

'Unanimously,' I said. 'Give me the spare men, and spare me the great ones.'

My Corporal Bardolph marched the men away.

You think this episode inglorious, Sir? Ah, well, it depends what you mean by glory. I mean what the Psalmist meant, when he cried out: *Awake up my glory, awake psaltery and harp*. No doubt you mean something else. No doubt you mean the great glory which – while I was at work in Gloucestershire – attended the confrontation of the Rebels and the Royalists in the north?

Gloria virtutis umbra. The shadow of virtue there was cast by the trees in Gaultree Forest, in Yorkshire. The Rebels were gloriously persuaded to meet in the middle of the wood, with Hal and the bull-necked John, Duke of Bedford, where they were promised that all their grievances would be redressed, so long as they dismissed their men immediately.

'Let's drink to friendship here,' said Hal.

The insurgents took him at his word. They dispersed their forces. The next minute, Hal and John had the ringleaders arrested and clapped in irons. They were brought to London, and their heads were soon singing all kinds of old songs about glory from the tower on London Bridge nearest the city gate. Some wit – I should think it was Poins – persuaded the Prince of Wales to arrange the heads also so that the two principals, the Archbishop of York, and Lord Hastings, were turned to be facing each other, with their lips kissing.

Just to remind us that they had been more than good friends.

Or that they had drunk to something more than friendship in Hal's glorious Gall Tree Wood?

Dismas. That was his name. The Penitent Thief.

O glory. O piss off.

And Justice Shallow and Justice Silence talking in that summer afternoon, while the flies buzzed, and the wasps on the fallen apples:

'Jesu! Jesu! The mad days that I have spent!'

Silence.

'And to see how many of my old acquaintance are dead!'

'We shall all follow,' Silence said.

'Certain,' said Shallow. 'That's certain. That's sure. That's very sure. Death, as the Psalmist says, is certain to all. All shall die. How much for a good yoke of bullocks at Stamford Fair?'

'I wasn't there myself,' said Silence.

'Death,' said Shallow. 'Death is certain. Is old Double of your town still alive?'

'Dead, sir.'

'Jesu! Jesu! Dead!'

'Dead, sir.'

'He drew a good bow.'

'Dead.'

'How much for a score of ewes?'

'Depends. Good ones – say, ten pounds.'

Dismas. His feast is kept in some places. The Good Thief. He's named in the Martyrology on 25 March. Fr Brackley tells me that's his day. It's in the *Acta sanctorum Martii* of Bede and Florus. It's in Wandelbert and Notker and Rhabanus Maurus. It's in the *Depositio martyrum* and the *Depositio episcoporum*, which go back to the year of Our Forgiveness 354. It's in Usuard. 25 March. Dismas.

That's right, Worcester. It is the day on which we started this book.

LXXII

About the death of the Leper King

Hal now indulged his talent for play-acting to the very hilt. It was the night of his father's dying. Bolingbroke's face was hideously disfigured with disease. He looked like a toad. His nose, his fingers, and his toes were all rotted away. His body was so contracted that it was scarcely a cubit long.

The Leper King lay on a pallet of straw in front of a great fire in a room of Westminster Palace called the Jerusalem Chamber. The Crown of England was set beside his pillow on a cushion of gold cloth. Bolingbroke came by that crown by a crooked path, and since he'd had it he had hardly let the thing out of his sight.

Now Hal sat by the King beside the crown.

It was too much for him. Before the King was decently dead, his fingers reached out and touched it. Having touched it, he had to try it on. Hal was always a great one for trying things on.

With the crown on his head, he crossed the Jerusalem Chamber in search of a looking-glass. What did he see when he looked into that glass?

His father's face! Sans nose, sans teeth, the eyes bleeding, the flesh already falling from the bone. Bolingbroke was not dead yet. He had stirred, seen Harry stealing, and in the last throes of his dying agony had come up off the bed and stood behind his son.

They say that he touched the crown with the withered stumps where his hands had been, and said: 'What right have you to it, my son, seeing that I had none?'

And that Harry answered: 'Sire, as you have held and kept it by the sword, so will I hold and keep it while my life shall last.'

Maybe.

I can believe, anyway, that Hal knelt by his father as he died. For Bolingbroke was now beyond even the great trivia of kinghood. He fell back on his straw pallet and the death rattle rose in his throat as he prayed God to have mercy on his soul. In his last moments they say he realised that he was dying in a room called Jerusalem, which afforded him strange comfort.

This was St Cuthbert's Day, 20 March, in the year 1413 of our Lord, the year I caught the pox, and the 46th year of Bolingbroke's age. Hal himself was 26 at that time.

Were they reconciled at the end?

Madam, it depends what you mean by reconciliation.

Bolingbroke's last words were to beg his son to find himself a good confessor.

I can believe, as I say, that Hal knelt by his father's side, and that tears ran down his cheeks, and that he even kissed what remained of that leper mouth.

But I shouldn't imagine he thought to take the crown off.

LXXIII

How Pistol brought the good news from Jerusalem to Paradise

That night the Leper King died in Jerusalem I lay drunk in a great blazing barn in that sweet perry-apple paradise I call Gloucestershire. I mean I was lost in a bright city. In an orchard. In an arbour. Where twilight fell with snowflakes in it and cider was like a drowned December wind, shivering on the tongue.

Shallow was there. And Silence. And Shallow's man Davy, who ran his estate. And my man Bardolph, who ran a great arson of a nose. There we were. Here we were gathered. Under the trees and then in the vast cathedral of that barn. A cathedral smelling of hay and dung, running with chickens, eggs found in your cap, where a man could sprawl with his flagons in warm nests of straw, and look up at Orion through the hole that gaped in the roof.

That was a little later in the evening, though. We began in Shallow's arbour, wrapped up in rugs and skins, eating Shallow's pippins of his own grafting, and with a dish of caraways and so forth to help us break our wind.

'Why, this is the Land of Cockaigne!' I told my good host. 'Where the sun shines on both sides of the hedge, and the pigs come running all hot from the spit with knives and forks stuck in their backsides ready to eat! This is Eden, Arcadia, and Avalon.'

Poor Shallow was having trouble with his cousin, who kept falling down.

Poor Shallow was also having trouble with himself, for the same reason.

Sitting there under the apple-boughs, I instructed them in the wise dispensation of St Boniface. We drank the health of a hell of a lot of Popes that night.

319

It grew duskier. We processed into the barn. Davy lit seven great braziers of sea-coals. Bardolph lit his nose. We were snug in the barn. The whole sky over us was like an ear of whorled cloud, listening to the frozen music of the spheres and the names of the Bishops of Rome. Then Silence, doing the dirt on his own name and everything else in sight, started to sing the most drivelling ballad I ever heard in my life:

> *Do nothing but eat, and make good cheer,*
> *And praise God for the merry year;*
> *When flesh is cheap and females dear,*
> *And lusty lads roam here and there*
>   *So merrily,*
> *And ever among so merrily.*

Don't get me wrong. The sentiments were splendid. But the words, in my opinion, were trite enough for that Neapolitan lot who showered my mother with sonnets and such.

'Wait a bit!' I cried. 'Good Mr Silence, I'll give you a health for that.'

And I did. In fact I gave him 100 TOASTS.

I had grown a little tired of toasting Popes (much as they all deserve it, and I stood in need of the indulgences). So, instead, I proposed a general anthology of TOASTS TO GIANTS . . .

To *Adamastor!*	To *Brontes!*	To *Cacus!*
To *Agrios!*	To *Caligorant!*	To *Colbronde!*
To *Alcyoneus!*	To *Corflambo!*	To *Cormoran!*
To *Alifanfaron!*	To *Dondasch!*	To *Erix!*
To *Aloeos!*	To *Eurytos!*	To *Fion!*
To *Amerant!*	To *Galabra!*	To *Goliath!*
To *Angoulaffre!*	To *Galapas!*	To *Garian!*
To *Atlas!*	To *Godmer!*	To *Grim!*
To *Balan!*	To *Grumbo!*	To *Gyges!*
To *Blunderbore!*	To *Hapmouche!*	To *Irus!*
To *Juliance!*	To *Kottos!*	To *Marguttes!*
To *Maul!*	To *Ogias!*	To *Orgoglio!*
To *Otos!*	To *Pallas!*	To *Ritho!*
To *Slaygood!*	To *Tartaro!*	To *Thaon!*
To *Typhon!*	To *Widenostrils!*	To *Anak!*
To *Pot!*	To *Vust!*	To *Seriously!*
To *Downright!*	To *Muckle!*	To *Outrance!*

How many is that, Bussard?

51.

That gives the general shape and idea. A cup of sack or cider for each giant. And I wasn't too fussy about disliking some of the giants for personal reasons – e.g. *Ritho*, who wanted King Arthur's beard to line his robe.

My giants could not silence Mr Silence. He sat huddled, his rug up to his ears, his nose dribbling into his wispy grey beard.

> *Be merry, be merry, my wife has all;*
> *For women are shrews, both short and tall;*
> *'Tis merry in hall when beards wag all,*
>   *And welcome merry Shrove-tide.*
> *Be merry, be merry.*

And so on. I ran out of giants before he ran out of doggerel.

KNOCK. KNOCK. KNOCK.

(Well done, Pigbum. Caught Hanson with that the other day!)

Mr Silence was toasting *me* now:

>   *Do me right,*
>   *And dub me knight,*
>   *Samingo.*

This Sir Mingo being a loyal knight of your immortal Bacchus I preferred the ditty to the crap about beards wagging all, but at the same time –

KNOCK KNOCK KNOCK KNOCK KNOCK KNOCK KNOCK.

'I think,' said Shallow slowly, 'there is someone at the door.'

'There isn't a door.'

'I think,' said Shallow, 'that there is someone knocking at a door which is not there.'

'Ah,' I said. 'In that case, it will be Pistol.'

'It is Mr Pistol,' Shallow said to his man Davy. 'Let in Mr Pistol.'

And at this point it is my distinct recollection that Pistol arrived through the hole in the roof of the great barn, sliding down a rope of hay twisted, his moustaches waxed to fine points, a scarlet cloak about his shoulders. Nearly getting roasted on a brazier in the process.

Remember. It was late into the night. In effect, it was later. It must have been dawn. It was certainly Pistol, and he had galloped all the way from London, horses dropping dead beneath his thighs, new horses supplied, my incredible Ancient.

'What wind blows you here?' I asked.

'Not the ill wind,' roared Pistol.

Silence looked at the flamboyant intruder. 'Is this gentleman's name Puff?' he said.

'Puff!' boomed Pistol. 'I'll puff you, you silly old cunt!' He dismissed Silence with a snap of his fingers, and turned to me, cloak swirling. 'You are now one of the greatest men in the realm,' he announced.

I saw a rat leap in the corner of the barn. O Desdemona, not a patch on you!

'Could you just give me your news as if you belonged to this world?' I said.

'Fuck the world,' said Pistol.

I began to be interested. Pistol was always extravagant, but here was extravagance with knobs on. He was rolling his eyes and twirling his moustaches like a Spanish minion.

Shallow drew himself up on a bale of hay, trying to make a bearskin do service as ermine round his shoulders. He spoke with what was left of such dignity as he had ever possessed: 'Pardon me, sir. If, sir, you come with news from the court, then I take it that there's but two ways – either to tell it, or to conceal it.' He sniffed. He looked in that moment more than ever like a forked radish, or like something made after supper out of a cheese-paring. He waved his hand round the barn in general and at the seven braziers in particular as though they proved something. He said: 'I am, sir, under the King, in some authority.'

'Under which King?' demanded Pistol.

'Under King Harry.'

'Harry the fourth? Or *fifth*?'

I heard a fox bark on the hill. A shiver ran down my spine.

'Harry the fourth,' I heard poor Shallow say, and then I saw Pistol giving him the V-sign.

It was like a dream. Silence, indeed, had fallen asleep in the hay, his head in a manger. Shallow collapsed by slow degrees down the bales until he was quite bumped down and sitting in a heap of dung. He touched it wonderingly with his fingers and then smelt them. He smiled. He did not seem to care.

From a long way off, a million miles away, from among those stars dangling at Orion's belt, I heard Pistol's voice, that hoarse tiger-voice, yet it seemed to me no more than a girl's whisper: 'Harry the Fifth's the man. I speak the truth.'

I took a little sip of sack. 'What?' I said, softly. 'Is the old king dead?'

'As a doornail,' snapped Pistol.

Then I rose up out of the hay with a roar like a lion.

With a roar like three lions. The lions in the arms of England.

I flung one of my flagons to my right. It rang like a bell, smashing into a brazier, sending sea-coals flying in all directions like stars.

The other flagon I hurled UP – up – up – up – a giant throw, a throw worthy of Balan and Blunderbore and Grumbo and Outrance, clean through that hole in the roof of the barn.

I think I hit the moon, and she bled sack.

'Saddle my horse!' I shouted.

The sea-coals set fire to the hay.

'I am fortune's steward!' I shouted.

The bales blazed. The whole barn was on fire.

'Get on your boots!' I cried. 'We ride all night!'

LXXIV

About the coronation of King Henry the 5th

I meant all day.

There was not much left of the night. The sun rose up before us out of the road as we galloped on towards London. I galloped. And Shallow. And Pistol. And Bardolph. Silence we left behind in Gloucestershire, to sleep off the effect of his songs and my toasts to the Popes and the giants and the sack and the cider and the night's general merriment. Of course we dragged the old greybeard out of the burning barn and tucked him up safely in bed before we clapped spurs to our horses.

Shallow was inclined for the first few miles to keep looking back over his shoulder at that blazing barn. A perilous regret, since it involved him twice in falling off.

'My barn! My great barn!'

'Think nothing of it. Think of it as a torch lit for King Hal!'

'But there wasn't such another barn in Gloucestershire.'

'You shall have bigger barns. For me to burn. I shall be rich. You shall be rich. We are all rich already!'

On we galloped.

Snow in our teeth.

But the wind was up, and the snow did not settle, and we found roads enough, and stables enough, and fresh stallions enough, and altogether made good progress towards London.

There, on a barge, the body of Bolingbroke would have been going for its last journey in this world. The barber surgeons would have washed him and disembowelled him and embalmed him, then wrapped him in a well-waxed winding sheet. Westminster Abbey would be a twinkling forest of candles and tapers. The bells of the City were sounding the Leper King's knell.

From Gravesend, where the black barge stopped, the coffin

was taken to Canterbury on a horse-drawn bier. Hal and his brothers rode around it, their pennons cased, their shields draped with black velvet.

Bolingbroke, King Henry the 4th of England, was buried by fitzAlan the Archbishop in a grave in the chapel of St Thomas a Becket, close by the tomb of the Black Prince.

Worcester, I did not like the man, but liking is neither here nor there, and no doubt God will have more time for him. I never liked his father either, that maniac John of Gaunt. (His piss was congealed ice.) They were a tough lot. Usurpers. But then, with success, suspicion and patriotism set in, as they often do, and I daresay the King died of his conscience as much as the leprosy. I never admired that statute *De Heretico Comburendo*, which was Bolingbroke's contribution to the law of the land. You know why he brought that in, of course? *To save money*. Fig me, but they were all so *mean*, those spawn of Gaunt's! Bolingbroke was not so concerned about heresy as it endangers the safety of the soul. It was where it threatened to disrupt the safety of the Kingdom that it worried him. And by giving fitzAlan the power to hunt down heretics and burn them he saved himself a great deal of money in costly proceedings against subversives.

BUT –

The King is dead! Long live the King!

And so to Harry's Coronation. . . .

There was a decent lapse of time, naturally, between the burying and the crowning. After an hour or two of galloping at full-tilt with a stomach full of sack and a head full of stars, the certainty of this began to break in upon me. Since at about the same time one of my horses collapsed under the weight of my womb it was just as well. . . .

We proceeded towards London in a more leisurely manner thereafter, as befitted our new dignity, as was consonant with our position as men of substance under the fresh dispensation. We followed, if I recall it right, a most delicious and circuitous route, and contrived to get drunk in seven counties on the way.

The young King was crowned on 10 April, which was the Sunday before Easter, in the midst of a great snowstorm. All the bells of London rang. The royal trumpets pealed. The streets were lined with soldiers holding lances.

I was a little hurt to receive no invitation to the Abbey. But as yet I suspected no treason, Worcester. In my euphoria, in my hopefulness, I trusted my friend, the new King, where he was being crowned by the Archbishop just down the road there, in the Abbey Church.

I waited with my party in the snow, not a hundred yards from the cathedral doors.

I waited patiently. I let snow fall on my hair and in my beard. I let myself be jostled by officious soldiers. What did I care? When I saw Hal again, and he saw me, all would be well, all would be put right, and I would come into my own.

'Stand here by me, Mr Robert Shallow,' I said. 'I will see that you are brought to the King's notice.'

Pistol's red cloak was stained with mud and sack.

'Come here, Pistol,' I said. 'Stand behind me. If I'd had time, I'd have had new liveries made for all my men.'

'You could have,' piped Shallow, 'with that thousand pounds you borrowed from me –'

'Think nothing of it,' I said. 'These poor clothes show my zeal.'

'That's true,' said Shallow.

'My earnestness of affection.'

'That's true,' said Shallow.

'My devotion.'

'Yes.'

'Riding, as it were, day and night –'

'With some few stops for drinking,' growled Pistol, twirling his moustaches.

'For drinking the King's health!' I said. 'But not to deliberate. Not to remember. Not to take much thought of myself at all.'

'Or my barn,' said Shallow.

'And now to stand here,' I said, shaking my bare head so that the snow flew round about me like a plucked goose. 'To stand in the street all stained with travel, and sweating with desire to see him. Thinking of nothing else. Putting everything else into oblivion.' I stamped my feet with the cold. 'As if there was nothing else to be done but to see him.'

'Harry Monmouth,' said Shallow.

'Harry the Fifth,' said Pistol.

'The King,' said Bardolph.

There were shouts from within the Abbey. The trumpets sounded.

The tall doors swung open.

I strained to see. Those lances lining the route were a nuisance.

The snow was everywhere, whirling, falling, tossed up again in the bitter wind.

'God save the King!'

'God save the King!'

'GOD SAVE THE KING!'

And there he was, mounted now, in full panoply, riding from the Abbey steps, coming towards us, approaching *me*.

I used my belly as a battering-ram.

In a trice, I was through the line of soldiers and standing in the middle of the street.

I stood in the middle of the street, in the falling snow, in front of Harry Monmouth with the crown upon his head.

'God save your grace!' I cried. 'King Hal! My royal Hal!'

For a terrible moment, it crossed my mind that he was not even going to draw rein. He was mounted on a great black horse, which struck horribly at the rush-strewn cobbles already an inch deep in snow, and as I say it seemed for a second that he had every intention of letting that horse trot on, and buffet me, and strike me down, and ride right over me.

But no. Black gloves moved on those reins, and shortened them. He stopped.

'God save you, my sweet boy!' I cried.

King Henry the 5th did not look at me. He turned round in his saddle and addressed Gascoigne.

'My Lord Chief Justice,' he said, 'speak to that vain man.'

Gascoigne, that prick, pushed his nag forward and looked down at me. 'Are you out of your wits?' he hissed.

I wasn't going to be gascoigned.

I used my belly again. I butted his nag. The startled creature danced aside. I snatched at the King's foot.

'My King!' I cried. 'My Jove!'

The King, that Jove, quite deliberately moved his boot through the stirrup so that the spur dug into my hand.

I let my arm fall.

I looked up at him. His eyes looked over my head.

I looked down at my hand. Blood welled from the star-shaped wound in it.

I said, 'Harry.'

I said, 'I speak to you, my heart.'

King Henry the 5th lowered his gaze. He consented to look at me. He saw.

What did those cold eyes see? What did those King's eyes find before them in the London Street?

A fat man.

Standing.

Bleeding.

In the snow.

The King's lips moved. King Henry the 5th spoke:

'I know you not, old man,' he said. 'Fall to your prayers.'

My hand stung from that wound.

The King went on: 'I have long dreamed of such a man as you. But, being awake, I now despise my dream.'

Those eyes observed my belly with distaste.

'Know,' said the King, 'that the grave gapes for you, with a mouth three times wider than it gapes for other men.'

Seven, I thought. Damn it, SEVEN TIMES WIDER. I opened my mouth. King Henry the 5th cut me short:

'No fool-born jest!'

I could look at His Majesty no more. I watched the blood drip from my hand onto the ground. It stained the snow.

'Do not presume,' the King went on inexorably, 'that I am the thing I was. God knows, and soon the world shall see, that I have turned away my former self. In the same way, I turn from those who kept me company.'

He paused. Someone sniggered in the crowd. I remember Gascoigne's nag starting to piss.

'You are banished,' said King Henry the Fifth.

Steam rose from that horse-piss where it hit the snow.

'Do not come near our person by ten miles,' said King Henry the Fifth.

'Set on!' said King Henry the Fifth.

The black horse lunged at me. I fell aside.

The glorious procession passed on its way.

'Mr Shallow,' I said, 'I owe you a thousand pounds.'

Poor Shallow thought I meant him. I did not.

LXXV

Sir John Fastolf's review of his banishment

23 July

Well, things could have been worse. I could have been burnt in seven barrels.

Here I was –

Banished.

But only from the King's immediate company. Banished, as it were, to the whole world as that world held good in a ten-mile limit from the person of Harry Monmouth. And I can tell you, Worcester, that in my mood of that moment, he could have set the bounds at double his 10 and I would not have minded.

I confess I was a little stunned at first. I did not know then, you see, what Clio and Harry the Prig's own publicity have since made common knowledge. Namely, that Hal had taken the Leper King's advice most seriously to heart. The very night of his father's death, before the disembowellers had moved in, almost before a cloth of gauze had been drawn across that noseless ruined face, Harry had gone under cover of dark to a recluse of holy life at Westminster. On his kness before this hermit, in the secrecy of the Sacrament of Penance, he had unpacked his heart, poured out his sins, confessed his every wickedness and guilt.

They say that confession took him all the hours till dawn. And that then, washed in the laver of true repentance, and receiving the antidote of absolution against the poison which he had swallowed before, Hal came out a new man.

Madam, I am not laughing.

Madam, I was never further from laughter in my life. I, I, I, John Fastolf, knowing the great benefits of the Sacrament of Penance as well or better than any man now living – having stood in at least as much need of it as the Prince of Wales can ever have stood – and – well, but it would hardly do to *boast* in such a context! Suffice it then to say that I do not condemn Harry Monmouth his contrition – Nor do I doubt for a moment that he detested his past sins, and that he promised amendment of life, and that he performed his penance as a man should, and that he was released from his guilt by that Power of the Keys which our Lord gave to St Peter and his Church.

All I condemn is the priggishness.

All I dislike is the vanity which assumes that human nature (a man's whole being, Madam) is so simple that you can, as it were, walk in one door wearing a mantle of vice and come out of another decently adorned in a cloak of virtue. And, even then –

Because we are suddenly become virtuous, shall there be no more cakes and ale?

But I must bite my tongue. And leave it for the reader to decide for himself whether there was evidence of true virtue in the later career of King Henry the 5th.

Things, as I say, could have been worse. As it was, I and my company were escorted to the Fleet Prison by the Lord Chief Justice, where we underwent a little temporary detention, in the usual style, for the purpose of my giving my word that I would abide by the King's conditions regarding the banishment.

That done – the 10 miles, in other words, being agreed to – I was told by Gascoigne that I was to be allowed a small but regular competence of money by the King, to assist me, as he put it, in seeing that 'lack of means did not enforce me to evils.' I was also told, by the same Lord Chief Justice, that the King was even prepared to 'give me advancement' according to my 'strengths and qualities' if he heard that I was (as they called it) reforming myself.

No comment.

LXXVI

About the marrying of Sir John Fastolf

24 July

I celebrated my banishment by marrying. It seemed at the time a sensible thing to do. It seemed at the time the *only* thing to do. Probably I didn't *choose* to anyway. As a whore said to me once in Harfleur, while making both ends of me blush, *'Les marriages se font an ciel et se consomment sur la terre.'* Which means, more or less, that these matters are arranged in heaven, and it's just up to us to consummate them on earth. As well as we can.

I was married on the Feast of St Hilary, 13 January, which as everyone knows is always the coldest day of the year.

My wife was Milicent, daughter of Robert, third Lord Tibetot. More significantly, Milicent came to me also as the widow of Sir Stephen Scrope. This same Scrope was the right hand of Thomas, Duke of Clarence, in managing the Irish. I think I touched again on that old rivalry between Hal and his second brother, in thus betrothing myself (as it were) to the glove that had just lately been on the second brother's right hand. The Scropes were a family known for double dealing. Dead Sir Stephen had been straight enough, but his brother Richard was that queer Archbishop of York who ended up kissing Lord Hastings on London Bridge. And there was another Scrope, Henry, who took huge bribes in France and joined the conspiracy of the Earl of Cambridge to murder Hal on the eve of his embarkation. For which he had his head chopped off at Southampton.

Milicent brought with her from her marriage to the *decent* Scrope one son, Stephen, that ingrate, my stepson, who refuses all the time to write here. (But I will get him yet, one Day, you see.) This Stephen was from the start a poxy mandrake, I could tell that. He was fitter to be worn in my cap than to wait at my heels. What a pretty boy! What a pansy! Even now, when he is

331

old, he has no beard. I know that a beard will grow in the palm of my hand before he ever gets one on his face.

The hell with the family Scrope.

Milicent, though. My Milicent was another matter. She was a sweet and wealthy hag. She owned property near Doncaster, and also the estate of Castle Combe in Wiltshire. All this besides what she had gained through her first marriage.

Milicent, my shrew. (Don't be jealous, Desdemona.)

Milicent loved me well.

Milicent had a quick eye.

Milicent prayed a good deal, which is always a good sign in a woman. Dame Milicent prayed like a windmill.

Milicent had a tongue like a whetted sword.

Milicent had thighs like a triumphal arch.

Thanks to the competence settled upon me by King Henry the 5th, in return for the pleasure of avoiding his company by 10 miles, I was able to bring to Milicent a little in return for the money and estates which she brought to me.

I delay until tomorrow the account of our nuptials concocted by Mrs Quickly. As I have said, the sacrament was celebrated on the Feast of St Hilary, Hilary of Poitiers, that Athanasius of the West and great enemy of the Arians. (I once met a man in Poitiers who married a calf. The trouble there was that he'd been advised by his mother to lengthen and strengthen his penis by dipping it in milk every day and getting a calf to suck it. 'After a month of that,' he told me, 'no one in his right mind would settle for a woman.')

The fact of this winter wedding ran riot in Nell Quickly's tickle-brain fancy, and she created for my friends an amazing version of its consummation. I daresay this is no more fiction than many another account of coupling – for I have noted that there is no other subject on which men so willingly deceive themselves than in stories of their love-making. They lie when they are at it, and they lie the more when they are not.

332

LXXVII

Mrs Quickly's account of the nuptials of Sir John Fastolf

St Anne's Eve

O Jesu. O *et cetera*. This was an infinitive focative. This was an act and an acture. An angling. An amorous impleachment. This was some husbandry. Some pricking usury. O cock. O St Venus.

All dally day it had snowed, it had seminared snowflakes, and in bright afternoon light, hard time for a deed of darkness, Sir John took Dame Milicent into the garden. To fox her. To fox his dear, his doe with the black scut. The gold fish all were frozen in the ponds. Long purples. Like dead men's fingers, or priests' pricks. There were bare bushes and black statues. Those newly married, those marrow birds, the man and his mammets, stood by the fountain thick with icicles. There was a marble terrace and a quivering thigh. Dame Milicent was his demesnes now. And Sir John *dominus*. Dame Milicent in lace and russet velvet. Sir John in his round hose and with that king of codpieces.

Sir John's hands roamed under her dress, about her ruff and rudder. Sir John's great hands roamed where they liked, and that Dame Milicent she liked where they roamed. The bridal two ran hand in hand down a snowy path. Dame Milicent's slippers made marks like little bird's feet in the snow, but Sir John's boots went in deep, so vast a man he was. He comes continuantly, when he comes. O her low countries. O his privates.

Sir John and Dame Milicent fell over feasts and favours in the snow. Dame Milicent fell first and Sir John fell on her. He fell to her and she fell to him. Her hair was in his mouth. She felt his thing.

Sir John tore the dress from Dame Milicent's back, and her shift he ripped off also. Her dens and commodities lay open now to a most potent regiment. O goats and monkeys: Sir John started rubbing and scrubbing at Dame Milicent's hot breasts with fistfuls of snow. O Jesu, he fingered her, he tickled her, he paddled her, he pinched her and he fondled her, he cherished and he stirred. Dame Milicent loved it. Dame Milicent squealed as the rude snow made her nipples hard and horny. Sir John cried out because she looked so wanton sweet, so virgin patent, his wife, Dame Milicent, naked to the waist, snow trickling down to melt like milk or marrow at the kissing of her tits. Dame Milicent scooped up snow also, the moist mischief. She rubbed it in her master's eyes. And when he stumbled, her husband, Sir John, blinded, confused, and roaring like a bullcalf, Dame Milicent had his prick out in a trice. Dame Milicent's hands moved happily. They worked busily. She turned him on. She tossed him off. Love's labour's lost. But no, that clever widow, Dame Milicent, put a handful of stark snow to Sir John Fastolf's cock. Sir John chased Dame Milicent round the snow-drowned sundial. Dame Milicent tripped. Dame Milicent was down on her face. Dame Milicent's breasts bit deep into the drift. O luxury. O ruffian lust.

Now then he gave her measure for measure.

Sir John Fastolf had her sprawled in the snow, across his spermy lap, her Netherlands upmost, and he slapped and he smacked and he spanked at her bottom, Dame Milicent's, the widow of love's diets – not hard, his slapping, not at first, his smacking, but just enough to tickle those white half-moons, his spanking, those tender unplumbed buttocks.

And it was as she liked it.

It was without doubt the lusty oversight of Dame Milicent's plum growing rosy under his great hand's dominion – the contrast of the white flesh of her secret parts, the red marks made by his tasty punishings, and the shining pricky splendour of the snow – that made Sir John roar out the more with longing. Besides which, he cares not what mischief he does, if his weapon be out. (My own case is openly known to the world.)

Sir John took a handful of snow, so softly, so soft and so softly his lady Dame Milicent had no dream of the getting-up fate now in store for her. Sir John paused then a moment, to savour the sweet steam yielding from Dame Milicent's hot body there in the freezing air, gazing at those hillocks, that ravine, those forfended places he had so lately spanked and drubbed until they blushed. . . .

Then Sir John plunged with his potency of snow!

Dame Milicent bucked.

Dame Milicent kicked.

Dame Milicent wrestled.
Dame Milicent rolled in the snow like a scalded cat.
But O now Sir John, he would give her no quarter.
But O now Sir John, he would show her no mercy.
He broached that proud Dame.
Sir John impaled Dame Milicent on his great icicle.
Sir John made love to his lady like an avalanche.
He had her.
He joyed her.
He manned her.
He managed her.
He picked her lock.
He pleased her, he ploughed her, and O how he possessed her.
He rammed her.
He rode her.
He scaled her.
He served her.
He stabbed her.
He stuffed her.
He foined her.
He tupped her.
She took him upwards and downwards and sideways and
everyways.
She took him in her belly, and wagging her tail.
O Jesu, O my lord, but how he fucked her!
Fixed her and foxed her and fetched her and fexed her.
Figged her and firked her and ferred her and fired her.
Forked her, all frosty, and brought her to fruition.
Of function.
Of junction.
Of conversation, copulation, much ado, the taming of the shrew.
Of carnal stings and spendings and sweet spicery.
She was his Juliet. He her Romeo.
She was his Cressida. He her Troilus.
She was his Cleopatra. He her Antony, bestriding her
Like a Colossus.
And all was well that ended well.
And all this glory ended with an O,
Foaming.
Oes and eyes.
So deep an O.

So full an O.
So overflown, so fucked
an O. And O. And
O. An
o

LXXVIII

How Sir John Fastolf went on a pilgrimage to the Holy Land

(*1st Note by Stephen Scrope*)

Lammas

Scrope writes this.

N.B.: Not him saying 'Scrope writes this.'

He is saying something else altogether. He is boasting about some pilgrimage he claims to have made to the Holy Land with his man 'Bardolph'.

Lies!

I do not write that.

I do not write lies.

I do not write Fastolf.

These dolls, these pawns, these puppets – they do what he tells them. They write what he tells them. Worcester & Hanson & Nanton & Bussard & Even (may God forgive him) Friar John Brackley.

They write him.

I write me.

I write Scrope.

It is time for the Truth!

Scrope will tell you the Truth.

Scrope will go through his monstrous lies one by one and kill them for ever.

I cannot kill him.

(God knows I have tried. But he cannot be killed.)

His lies, though, they can be killed. His lies and his dreams and his wicked stories.

Scrope will kill them all. Every one. Wait and see.

'John Fastolf.'

Who is he?

To be the author of such a Hellish pack of lies. . . .

How old is he?
I saw with my own eyes he was already old in the days of Henry Five. . . .
I think he is that One who is always the same age.
I think he is the devil himself!
I think the others here are ghosts.
I think that this is Cobweb Castle.
And that this Fastolf is King Liar.

LXXIX

About some merry tricks of Sir John Fastolf's

It occurs to me tonight that I have now got myself married, and made my pilgrimage to the Holy Land, and consulted the three Popes, and that it will soon be time to set forth on my wars in France – and all before justice has been done to my days of knavery. Paper and inkhorn, then, must now be devoted to calling up again the memory of one or two of my more merry tricks.

Light more candles here.

Let's see if I can tell out the night.

Coherence, continuity – that's all. I'll take a team of my secretaries. Worcester starts. When his hand burns with the telling, I'll have Hanson and Nanton in. Then that lazy Scrope. And so on.

(Fr Brackley is, of course, excused. It being the Feast of the Transfiguration. And here I might take the opportunity to explain to you, reader, whoever you are, that delay there was between my 77th and my 78th Days, and then my 78th and this present writing. It is to be confessed that your author grew overexcited in reciting Mrs Quickly's account of country matters to Messrs Hanson and Nanton. Yes, I had to retire to bed. With Miranda. For a week. – Miranda is my medicine. She keeps me young. – Then, again, since Lammas, when I dictated to my stepson Stephen Scrope that report of how in Jerusalem I learned how roses first came into the world, and the age of our Lady, and the precise date of the Day of Doom, I have been resting from my *Acta* for another week. I find it harder to say why. Something in Scrope exhausted me. Though I am glad he should *at last* have consented to write here, to help me, to be one of my scribes, to join our company. – Copying Reggie Tuthin's letter didn't count. – And I enjoyed telling him of my interviews with the three Popes there were in the world at that time, as much as I trust that you, dear reader, have enjoyed hearing about them.)

Incidentally, it occurs to me tonight that this Great Schism, this superfluity of religion, or duplication of the Vicars of Christ, began, *by a curious coincidence*, in the year of my birth, namely the year of Our Forgiveness 1378. And since it is reliably reported that my coming forth into the world was an occasion for a minor earthquake which threw fishes up out of the pond of Mr Beckington, the Bishop of Wells, and onto his table where he was eating breakfast, I ask myself: Could my entrance into this little theatre of shadows have had something to do, albeit thousands of miles away from Wookey Hole, with those 15 cardinals up and declaring the election of Urban VI invalid? Could my mother's labour pains have affected Urban's retort in naming 28 new cardinals? And could the cutting of my birth-cord – which deed my father did with his bright sword – have metaphysically interfered with Christendom to such an extent that the first 15 at once proceeded to elect Cardinal Robert of Geneva as Pope Clement VII, the Pope who went to live at Avignon?

These questions are possibly due to an excess of piety, or a defect of pride, or an indigestion of lamphreys. I admit it.

Everyone knows *now* that the Popes at Rome were the true Popes, the Urbanist line. Everyone knew it *then*, too, save the French and the Neapolitans and the Scots, who supported the Clementine claimants for *political* reasons. As you will know from what I told you *via* Scrope regarding my assessment of the personalities of John XXIII, Benedict XIII, and Gregory XII, it came as no surprise to me when the Church looked back and said that Gregory had been true Pope all along.

And yet – and yet – That verdict of mine was a shallow and irrelevant one. The larger point is that the character of a man is not in question. A bad Pope may be a true Pope. The truth is in the office, not the man. Those antipopes could have been angels, but they would still have had no validity or authority.

As a matter of fact, though, I *liked* Gregory. He was such a weak and nice old man, easily influenced, with an untouchable dignity in the middle of it. He blessed this medal which hangs around my neck.

Such pleasure to have Scrope in our book at last! He writes a fair hand, Worcester says.

My eyes are going.

O the vines and demoiselles of Provence, where Bardolph and I lingered coming home. In our travels we saw many wonders. And no doubt we were wonders to other travellers, who in their travelling saw us.

Worcester, what was it I was going to do tonight?

Ah, yes. *Benedicite*. Thank you, Mr Cyclops.

My time among knaves and kings.

I was always one for fitting my suit to the scene. Among villains I determined early to play them at their own game, and to win if I could. I don't know if I succeeded in this design – or if it would have been better (I will *not* say more 'honourable') to have failed. What is certain is that no man of our time has tried harder. I had, after all, a kind of court in Cheapside. The Boar's Head tavern was my palace. There I reigned. There I ruled. A roast-beef bullcalf. The British Bacchus. England's heart. Her hero.

God's teeth, her stomach.

We laughed a lot. Yes. *In risu veritas*, as that Irishman said who spiked me up the bum.

What a comedian. O we were all comedians: Bardolph and Pistol and Doll and Nell; Peto and Shallow and Nym and Hal. Especially that Hal. A great comedian.

And I? The life and soul of the party, Madam.

Or, to put it another way: Men of all sorts take a pride to gird at me. The brain of this foolish-compounded clay, man, is not able to invent anything that tends to laughter, more than I invent or is invented on me. I am not only witty in myself, but the cause that wit is in other men.

Worcester, what did the doctor say about my water?

Tell him to piss off then.

Knaves and kings. Everyone has to start somewhere. Where did I begin?

Threadneedle Street, if you want to know. The third street from Cheapside to the thoroughfare from London Bridge to Bishop's Gate. That is, not New Fish Street, Madam. Nor, as you might have hoped, Gracious Street.

I would have been young. Of course. And new and raw to London. I would have been hungry.

It was nine o'clock at night. St Mary Woolnoth had just sounded.

I saw a confectioner's shop. There was a basket of raisins on the counter. I whipped in, snatched it up, and set off at the trot.

The confectioner came after me –

'Stop, thief!' –

such nervous originality! –

341

and so did all his neighbours. (Londoners at that time of night like nothing better than a spot of thief-bashing, if they can get it.)

These gentlemen could easily have caught me – I being handicapped with raisins.

It was a time for philosophy.

Turning the corner of Threadneedle Street, I set the basket down quick on the ground, sat on it, and wrapped my cloak about my leg. At the same moment, most dramatically, without hesitation, I started howling. 'God forgive him! God forgive him! God forgive the bloody bugger!'

Up runs the honest confectioner and his cronies. 'What's happened?'

I held my leg with both hands. I writhed like a centipede with gout.

'I have been crippled by a running thief,' I said.

'A bastard with a basket?'

'He attacked you also? The villain! Oh, my leg! He has broken my leg! Sir, have you mastered the elements of surgery?'

'Which way did he go?'

'I forgive him his gross violence,' I said. 'The Scriptures so enjoin us, and be sure I do. Oh, sirs, for the Lord's sake pity the lame!'

'Yes, yes!' cried the confectioner. 'Which way?'

'Down towards the Thames.'

And off they run, with never a Christian surgeon among them to stop and succour the broken boy by the wayside.

I went home quietly with the raisins to my lodgings in the Inns of Court. With 4lbs of prunes they made a decent supper.

Beginner's stuff.

Shallow, that second-hand man, wanted to see me in action. Of course. The usual story. Being so backward and lacking in any kind of act himself. So I invited him along to see me abstract a box of peaches. This was when I was a little more advanced in my vocation. He came, with one or two others, students of law. I was to show them how best to bend or break it.

I chose a shop not far from the previous one. (Always commit your crimes in the same place. No one will ever suspect that anyone could be so stupid. And stupidity, properly deployed, is a fine weapon in the right criminal hands.)

When Mr Shallow saw that all the boxes in this selected shop were heaped up deep inside, so that there was no easy reaching them by just leaning through the door, he concluded that my attack was impracticable, especially since the grocer, knowing what had happened to the confectioner, was on his guard. However, Jack Fastolf was always more than a match for anyone who needed to make his living by selling peaches.

My method was this – and copy it to the letter next time you are in need of peaches for your lady's tongue, to freshen that organ of sinful fantasy!

I drew my sword on the pavement.

I kicked open the door with my foot.

I ran in roaring, 'Dead, dead, dead for a ducat! Dead, sir!' – and in the same invasion made a wild thrasonical thrust in front of the shopman's eyes.

He, of course, fell flat down on the floor behind his counter. Where he squealed and shouted for help.

My weapon, meanwhile, had passed clear and clean through a nice tight box of peaches. The sound of my sword through that thin wood was excellent music.

I ran from the establishment with the dead meat on my blade. A trickle of peach juice followed me. We were all so busy laughing we could scarcely run. Those peaches were bleeding their sweet juice, a thin delicious scent on the summer twilight air.

R. Shallow of course stayed pissing himself to watch – and reported to me later that the spruce grocer had his friends strip all his clothes off him in searching for the deep imaginary wound that had felled him. When it was at length established that only a box of his peaches had been raped and rifled, the grocer's relief was such that he fell to blessing himself as if he would never stop.

I never ate anything that pleased my imagination half as much as those peaches.

I might have been eating four dozen virgins.

I was.

Such things were the merest tricks and knaveries, slight jokes, small pickings. Apprentice work. Later I graduated to the task of disarming the watch.

Now *that* was something. I had no ulterior motive. It was an exercise in the academics of deceit. It marked my transition from the status of craftsman to artist.

I chose the watch on Blackfriars Gate. Twelfth Night, it was. We'd had lamb's wool for our wassail bowl – roasted apples, sugar, nutmeg, ginger, wine. Spiced cake, as well. (Some actors once plotted to murder Bolingbroke as part of a play to be performed at court on Twelfth Night, but that's another story. The Glastonbury Thorn always blossoms on Twelfth Night too.)

That particular Twelfth Night I set forth with Mr Shallow and the usual hangers-on. I marched in front· with Bardolph. Our machination this time was that while we might have *looked* like a party of wassailers, we steadfastly did not wassail. Instead: we wailed.

Encountering the watch, I wrung my hands.

'Is it the watch? The watch that watches over us? Oh by the Arimathean Thorn, is it really you?'

'He's drunk,' said one.

'Sir, I am sober,' I said. 'A sober citizen requires an officer.'

The officer exhibited himself.

Then I kneeled down and kissed his boots and said: 'Lord officer, it is presently in your power to do the state some service, and revenge my father's ghost.'

'How's that?' asked the idiot.

'Step on one side,' I advised him, 'and I will soliloquize and tell you something very privy concerning rapers.'

He came all ears and eagerness to the wall.

'Star of the watch,' I said, 'I have ridden to London from Glastonbury, in pursuit of six of the most wicked men in Christendom. All are thieves, and two are murderers. Among them is one who poured poison in my father's ears, ravished my mother, and sodomized my brother Amleth the poet, without any provocation but to give his barbarity a trot down the alley.'

'Who are these vipers?'

'After the ravishing and the sodomy he cut their throats.'

'*Who* did?'

'And just look what his accomplices have done to my poor sister's nose!'

'Your *sister*?' said the watchman, squinting at Bardolph where he simpered with his lamp.

'O horror! Horror! Horror!' I howled. 'But now, no more of that, my master. From such atrocities and beasts who stop at *nothing*, the law alone can save us. Law and order, that's the stuff.'

'I am law and order,' said the officer.

'Thank God,' I said. 'She used to be a lovely girl, and now. . . .'

'It is monstrous,' agreed the officer, leering at poor Bardolph. 'But you must tell me more of –'

'Sssh!' I counselled. 'The man I dare not name is with those five other fiends I mentioned. They are keeping company with a French spy not a hundred yards from where we stand.'

'*French spies?*' Promotion flashed in the idiot's gaze. He had his sword out. His eyes ran up and down the street.

'In Mrs Quickly's brothel,' I informed him. 'Master, be brave. Wise King Henry will reward you well. Not to speak of my mother in heaven and my brother in purgatory.'

With fierce and moral cries, the watch, led by this beetle-brained enthusiast for justice and self-betterment, blundered up the street towards the Boar's Head.

I had to run like a greyhound to head them off, and divert the officer aside again into the shadows.

'O Sir,' I hissed, 'this whole business will be spoiled if you proceed so crudely. Put up your bright swords. The right way to do this apprehension is for you to send your men in one by one, unarmed. For that devil is above with sweet Doll Tearsheet, and he may turn desperate and harm innocent whores if he sees mighty officers coming after him with swords. It would be politic to go in on tiptoe with a pot of pepper each – my sister has them! Just throw the pepper in his eyes and cock. Do the job stealthily, like immortal Ulysses. The girls, I am sure, will know how to thank you.'

The jobbernowl approved this incredible plan. (If you want the impossible done, always suggest an improbable manner of doing it.)

He told his men to hide their swords in a heap against the wall. They did.

Then they went one by one up the stairs and into Mrs Quickly's leaping house, each getting a kiss and a pepperpot from Bardolph on the door.

My fellows then snatched up the discarded swords and made off at speed.

When the watch came out – to the laughter of the crowd that had gathered, and pursued by naked girls, so Shallow told me – that master officer was in a fine spermy rage at the trick I had played on his reputation. He was the more furious when he found his weapons gone. And when Nell Quickly emptied either a wassail bowl or a chamberpot over him from the upstairs window. (Shallow said the scene was so confused by then that he couldn't be specific as to contents. But I suggest that even if this *was* a Twelfth Night concoction it had passed through the kidneys of half the whores in Cheapside at least once.)

The officer sent out the watch to search for me.

And they found me too.

But by the time they marched into my attic, I was stretched out white and stiff upon my cot, a nightcap on my head, a candle lighted in one hand and a crucifix in the other, with Peto playing priest beside me, dribbling viaticums, and all the rest of my companions on their knees about the bed.

'It's the Glastonbury Thorn,' said Bardolph.

'The Glastonbury Thorn?'

'He pricked his hand on it and ran mad since. We have to humour him, and now he's dying. Why, would you believe it, he even thinks I'm Queen Guinever!'

'But what about our swords?'

'Oh them. . . . They're over there!'

Bardolph pointed with his nose.

There were the swords of the watch, all neatly arranged in a circle, stuck to the hilts in a vast round hairy cheese.

'He's got this thing about King Arthur, you see,' explained Bardolph. 'It goes with it. The Glastonbury Thorn!'

The officer tugged his sword out of the cheddar with a grunt.

'Mind you,' said Bardolph, moving closer to the man and polishing his whelks significantly, 'there are more things in heaven and earth than are dreamed of in your philosophy. We're all expecting Merlin any minute!'

The officer wiped his sword on his bum, ambiguously.

They didn't know what to do, or what to say.

'Pray for him,' barked Fr Peto.

(When the outrage is complete, put in requests for prayer.)

(Make them peremptory.)

LXXX

About Bartholomew Fair

Look at my shadow on the rafters there!
A fat man greeting the abyss with laughter.
A tidy little Bartholomew boar-pig.
That's me.
Father, that shadow hovers all the time on the edge of some tremendous revelation –
A revelation, maybe, of the meaning of the word *Ducdame!*
Or an initiation into what fools truly signify by all they do when called into a circle?
I am a fool.
Kings need their fools.
Because there is more instruction to be had from a fool than from a wise man.
Because *the fool dares to tell the truth.*
Sir Dagonet was Arthur's fool.
Harun al-Reshid had a fool called Bahalul.
Edmund Ironside's fool was called Hitard.
I have heard tell also of one Bertoldo, who appeared at the court of Alboin, King of the Lombards. This Bertoldo was a peasant. He was wonderfully ugly. Wonderfully truthful. And wonderfully foolish.
Philip of Macedon kept a court fool.
Philip of Macedon kept a court philosopher.
Philip of Macedon was wondrous wise.
Philip of Macedon would have been wondrous wiser to have kept one man: *a foolosopher.*
Father, I stand on my head and I turn *your* world upside-down.
Father, I live for the tragic merrymaking of a minute and

347

persuade you, against your 'better' judgement, that this is the only way to live.

Father, I am shameless. I make you ashamed of your shame.

Father, I tell you my truth as jokes. I beckon you to a black pit.

Rahere. He started Bartholomew Fair.

Rahere was court fool to King Henry the 1st.

All those jugglers and jesters and tumblers and clowns.

The charlatans and posturemasters, the gipsies and the pantaloons.

Jack Adams. Jack-a-dandy. Jack-a-dreams. Jack-a-drogues. Jack Brag. Jack Fool. Jack Sauce. Jack Pudding. Jack Straw. Jack Frost. Jack Sprat. Jack the Giant Killer. Jack-a-napes and little Jack-a-lent.

I think that England's Christian name is Jack.

I saw him all at Bartholomew Fair.

I saw him eat fern seed at Bartholomew Fair. But he did not disappear to *my* eyes. (Though some about me said he did.)

I saw him wash his hands in molten lead at Bartholomew Fair.

I saw him riding on a unicorn.

I saw him turning a parcel of rabbits loose in the crowd.

I saw him selling salamander cloth.

I saw his salamander too. He threw it in the fire. It swelled and swelled, and then spat out a great spew of thick slime, which quite extinguished all the coals. The same Jack then plunged his lizard into spirits of wine. It seemed none the worse for its burning.

Deo gratias.

Hee-haw, Hee-haw, Hee-haw.

The Bishop of Worms condemned the Feast of Fools.

Rahere saw the apostle Bartholomew in a vision, and turned monk.

But didn't we laugh because we could not understand?

And *after* the Fair, that moment, in Osier Lane, walking, our shadow long before us, didn't we have this knowledge that our laughter had been *stolen* from us? – That those fools had feasted on it for some secret of their own?

Do not suppose that the fool's folly conceals wisdom.

Ducdame!

Nothing so simple.

It *is* wisdom, if only we knew how to fathom it.

I think St Dismas is the patron saint of fools.

The other thief, called Gismas, was the reasonable man. 'Look,' he said, 'do us a favour. If you're really the Christ, save yourself and us as well.'

I once kissed a woman with 3 breasts at Bartholomew Fair.

Father, has anyone ever worked out why – of all those 100 knights who set out from King Arthur's court to seek the Holy Grail – it was that Parsifal who found it?

Parsifal.

The name means *Perfect Fool.*

LXXXI

How Sir John Fastolf went as a nun to a nunnery

(*2nd Note by Stephen Scrope*)

St Giles's Day

For instance, he died.

The King had killed his heart.

He died shouting out for drink and women in that Cheapside brothel, the Boar's Head.

I heard this from several reliable sources.

I hurried to London, rejoicing.

I met him on the road. Dead drunk, but not dead. His story was that he had staged some kind of death to escape from his creditors.

What are we to believe? All reason says the false death must be true. There he sits, I see him with my own eyes, in that gold cauldron of a tub, taking his bath, before the fire, on this St Giles's Day 1459 A.D. (and all the time telling me some gross tale of a time he took refuge in a convent disguised as a nun. Absolute nonsense. I would cut off my hand rather than let it write down a word of his filth.)

Reason says he did not die.

Yet I say reason cannot cope with this great Devil.

I say that *of course* he was not born in the way he says he was born.

I say that this is a monster. That this is like someone's dream. That he is a made-up man. That this made-up monster uses words I never heard on any living tongue. That he is a lie. That he is a lie that lies and lies and lies. About his wars and amours. About his battles and companions. About all and everything.

For instance, *figs*.

There is no fig tree on the giant of Cerne Abbas. There are no figs growing anywhere in England. I, Scrope, state this for a fact. I have not travelled as he claims to have travelled, but I have heard that the fig tree is indigenous to Asia Minor and to Syria, and to most of the countries around the Mediterranean Sea. Perhaps, *if* he travelled in those parts ever, he saw a fig tree and this was the source of his dream. (Certainly he has figs sent to him for his bowels, but these do not come from Cerne Abbas, and he gets them through the usual trade of merchants.) I trust that is enough to kill the whole lie which constitutes the first of his so-called 'Days'. The fig being untrue, you can take it from me that the rest is as false as the fig.

For instance, *potatoes*.

What are these 'potatoes'? I never heard this word. Does it represent some infernal magic? Worcester, Bussard, Hanson and Nanton, his hoggish henchmen, they write down every word he utters out of fear of him, barely daring to lift their eyes from the writing. But I refer posterity – if posterity ever sees these papers – to that absurd story in which he claimed to win a battle at Kildare by the employment of an article which does not exist. *There are no such things in this world as potatoes.*

For instance, *Slugs*.

In some other early part of this book he is pleased to call his 'Acta', he gives a ridiculous account of winning a sea fight at a place called Slugs. I never heard of this Slugs. There *was* once a sea fight at a place called Sluys, off Flanders, in which the English defeated the French. But not, of course, in the cowardly and drunken way which insults history in his version of a sea fight at 'Slugs'. And, besides, *Our Glorious Victory at Sluys was in the Year 1339*. In the time of the Black Prince. That is to say, many years before this Devil who calls himself 'Fastolf' was even born, if you are to believe his own account of how he came into the world.

I will leave on one side his base suggestion that Sir Thomas Erpingham was a traitor, and worse. (Why he should wish to imply that, I cannot imagine. Erpingham played a prominent part in the Agincourt campaign, and gave the signal for the English attack, by throwing his truncheon in the air and shouting, 'now!')

I will leave until later his disgusting fantasies about the women he has known. I shall have much to say on this subject when another opportunity occurs.

He insults my mother.

He insults me.

I am destroying his 'Acta'.

351

Worcester knows, of course, and Friar John Brackley, and I know from the eyes of the others that they know too. But they will not *dare* tell him. The knowledge that one of his precious 'Days' has not been done – that Scrope has ignored his dictation, and written down something else altogether, and that something else the Truth – that would throw him into such a rage that it would kill him. Or he would kill them.

He is going blind. He cannot see for himself what I have written.

He lives for these 'Days' of his, and they come so hard to him now that there are long lapses between one and the next.

If anything is ever to rid the world of this great Devil, it will be a realisation of how I, Stephen Scrope, am destroying his life's work!

Which might be the way to do it. . . .

He is ill.

He will *not* live to be a hundred.

Unless he is already a hundred? Or more?

He is as old as his sins.

'John Fastolf'.

He calls himself that.

But I have heard that in his days with Prince Henry they called him 'Falstaff', and that his *real* name might even be 'Oldcastle', a Lollard, a brand plucked from the burning.

And that he was a *Knight* already in those days, as well as already an old man, so that whatever he intends to say in these pages about how he eventually came by his knighthood will again be lies.

Lies about a living lie.

Fastolf.

Falstaff.

What does it matter what he calls himself.

The Devil is the Devil under any name.

LXXXII

Pistol's tale

At about the same time that red-haired Mother Superior caught me in the cellar with those seven novices, the Dolphin sent King Henry the 5th a bag of tennis-balls. Hal was not amused. No more was the Mother Superior. I was expelled from the convent. England declared war on France.

Hal was resolved to recover the inheritance of his predecessors. He wanted Normandy and Maine and Anjou for a start, plus Aquitaine and half Provence. He also wanted the arrears on the ransom of King John which, with interest, now amounted to about £1200,000 (Twelve Hundred Thousand Pounds). He also wanted the Princess Katharine of Valois, the youngest daughter of the mad French King, to marry, with a dowry of £2000,000 (Two Million Pounds) thrown in.

These tennis-balls from the Dolphin were by way of an answer. The French heir-apparent evidently thought that he still had a madcap prince to deal with. He soon learned otherwise. (The Dolphin's own name, incidentally, was Lewis. But his friends called him Monsieur Basimecu – from the French, Madam, *baise mon cul*, which is in good round English, *Kiss my arse*.)

As for me, I did not go reluctant from that nunnery. It was not so much the dispensations with Sister Emilia. It was all those penances which Sister Perdita demanded of me. Mother Suprior was just the last straw.

All that Spring the hammers rang. Ships were summoned to Southampton water. All round the port, in the countryside, horses and engines of war were massing in the fields, awaiting the order for embarkation.

I'll say this for Hal. He spared no expense in making his army an efficient machine. First, he imbued all England with his military enthusiasm. Then, he got the Privy Seal to make contracts with different lords and gentlemen, who bound themselves to serve with a certain number of men for a year from the day on which they were mustered. The pay wasn't bad. Dukes got 13s. 4d. a day. Earls got 6s. 8d. Barons and bannerets, 3s. 4d. Knights, 2s. Esquires, 1s. Archers, 6d. Better still, the pay, or a security for its amount, was delivered by the Treasury a quarter in advance – and if you hadn't received all your pay by the beginning of the 4th quarter, then you could consider the engagement at an end. As a bonus, each contractor got £100 for every 30 men-at-arms he brought with him. A duke was to have 50 horses, an earl 24, a baron or banneret 16, a knight 6, an esquire 4, an archer one. The horses had to be furnished by the contractor, but most equipment was provided by the King. Other terms in the contract were that all prisoners taken in the wars were to be regarded as the property of the captor for purposes of ransom – unless they happened to be kings, or sons of kings, or officers holding personal commissions from kings, in which cases they were to belong to the Crown, but only on payment of a reasonable recompense to the captors. All booty taken was to be divided into three parts: two parts for the men in the company; the third again divided into three parts, of which the leader of the company took two, leaving the third for the King.

Under the terms of this contract, and keeping my ten miles' distance quite religiously, acting through intermediaries, I signed on to provide myself, 10 men-at-arms, and 30 archers. My company included Pistol, Peto, Nym, and Bardolph. We rode down from Windsor to Southampton in a cloud of butterflies.

Ah, ha, Worcester, Worcester, the days of war! The dogs we were!

As we rode, I heard the tale of my ensign Pistol.

Now Pistol was a fire-eater. His scarlet cloak and his spiked moustaches made him conspicuous in any gathering. Yet he was not all turgidity. Such heart as he had was capable of something more than rant. He married Nell Quickly before setting forth for France. We'd all been *saying* we would for years – I mean, in my own case, before the knotting of my nuptials with Dame Milicent. But Pistol actually went and did it. Committed that Sacrament! Put his head in that noose of matrimony! And with what a handful of quicksilver to wife! Poor chap. His last words to her, before swinging his leg across his horse and leaving for the wars, had to be an anxious,

'*Keep close!* I command it!'

And I don't need to tell you that he wasn't referring to keeping her purse or her mouth shut.

Anyhow, as we rode down from Windsor to Southampton, we heard:

PISTOL'S TALE

'You will know that at Walsingham, not far from our Lady's shrine, there is a cave where a hermit lives in great seclusion. There is only ever one hermit living there, and he prays night and day and is usually a man of much goodness. All the same, human nature being what it is, there was once one hermit of Walsingham who did not come up to the standards set by the others. I suppose he might be forgiven if you take into account the peculiar temptations besetting a man seeking to live such a solitary life. Personally, I forgave him long ago.

This third-rate hermit was, in effect, as lecherous as an old monkey, and three times as cunning. But existing, as I say, in such isolation in his cave, he found it difficult to do much more with his desires than merely entertain them.

Then he got word – you know how some of these bad friars rub noses and wink – that down in Walsingham there was a very beautiful girl whose mother was a simple-minded widow of extremest piety. This sounded promising. The hermit equipped himself with a long hollow cane, and waited for a dark and stormy night.

In due course, about St Agnes' Eve, there came a dark and stormy night. The hermit came with it, down from his cave, bearing his long hollow cane. He made his way, under cover of the rain and the dark, to the hut where the girl and her mother lived. The walls were not thick. It was an easy job for the hermit to bore a little hole with his tool in one of these walls, not far from the bed where the simple widow lay sleeping. Then he inserted the long hollow cane into the hole, poked it through until it was close to the widow's ear, and whispered three times:

"I am an angel of the Lord!"

Silence. But he could hear from the woman's changed breathing that he had woken her.

"I am an angel of the Lord!" he whispered again, a little more urgently.

Still silence.

"Answer me softly to show that you hear!" the hermit commanded. "I am an angel of – – –"

"Amen, amen," said the widow woman. "It's just that I don't know the proper way of addressing angels."

"The form," said the hermit, "may be modified by the occasion and the degree of acquaintanceship."

"Amen," said the widow woman.

"Your Holiness," said the hermit.

"Beg pardon?"

"*Your Holiness* will do," whispered the hermit. "For you to address me with." Then he remembered the desirable daughter asleep somewhere else in this same hut, and his member grew hot and hard, and he lost all interest in correct ecclesiastical usage in modes of address for angels, and he said: "I have been sent to you by the Lord. I have a message for you. The message is this. The Lord wishes to reform his bride the Church by means of an heir of your flesh – in a word, your daughter."

"Fancy!" said the widow woman. "Your Holiness," she added.

"This is how the great deed shall be done," said the hermit down the tube. "You must take your daughter up to the cave of the holy hermit of Walsingham. Then you must tell him the message that God has given you through me. The hermit will know what to do. I tell you, O chosen one, that from their union will come a son who is destined by God to be Pope." ' –

'Wait a bit,' cried Bardolph, as I remember, at this point. 'If you're intending to tell us the tale of Nicholas Breakspear, you've got it wrong. He didn't – – –'

'This is not the tale of Nicholas Breakspear,' said Pistol grandly. 'This is MY tale. Lend me your ears! Listen!'

And he went on –

'The pious widow woman was amazed and delighted with this message. In the morning, she told her daughter the angelic good news, and asked her what she had to say about it. The girl replied:

"Thanks be to God!"

"That's my girl!" cried the mother. After all, it's not every day that a woman is presented with the prospect of being grandmother to a Supreme Pontiff. "Put on your hat," she told her daughter. "We shall go up to the cave and see the holy hermit of Walsingham, just as His Holiness the angel ordered."

The hermit saw them coming. He knelt down, so as to be found at prayer. The widow coughed. He looked up. She took him aside and told him the story. When she had finished, he said:

"God be praised! We could all do with a good Pope!"

Then he pretended to hesitate. He said:

"But, my good woman, can you be quite sure that what you heard in the night was not a dream?"

"I don't think it was a dream," said the widow woman. "It was an angel."

"And what was the angel's name?"

"He didn't say."

"Well," said the hermit, "it seems to me that we should sleep on it."

"*Sleep* on it?"

"Have I not vowed my chastity to God?" said the hermit indignantly. "This is no light or easy thing which you require of me, you and your daughter. Go home. Say your prayers. We shall see what tomorrow brings."

Bitterly disappointed, but impressed in her heart by the hermit's apparent goodness, the old woman went home to her hut with her daughter. And that night, of course, the dirty old hermit came down from his cave again and gave exactly the same message to her through the long hollow cane. Only this time, as he was finishing, the widow asked,

"What's your name, Your Holiness?"

"Malvolio," said the hermit.

Next day, up early, the woman and her daughter rush to the hermit's cave. Again she gave him a long and circumstantial account of the message which had been delivered to her by the angel. "And he said his name is Malvolio," she concluded.

"Malvolio, eh?" mused the hermit. "Well, he's certainly a top angel."

"Then what are we waiting for?" said the old woman impatiently.

"Truth comes in threes," said the hermit. "Go home. Say your prayers. If the angel speaks again to you tonight, then we will do his bidding."

That night he came creeping down once more from his cave and put his long hollow cane to her ear and told her in no uncertain terms that God was fed up with the delays and wanted action.

At dawn, therefore, the widow and her daughter presented themselves to the hermit. The mother, her heart singing with joy, had no sooner told that whited sepulchre about her third and latest message, than he took her gently by the hand and led her into his chapel.

"Madam," he said, "you must leave your beautiful daughter here."

"In a *chapel*?"

"Your daughter and I will begin praying," explained the hermit. "Then God will tell us what to do."

"And you will do it?"

"Of course."

The widow went away.

When the hermit found himself alone with the girl, he made her strip naked, as if he wished to baptize her for a second time.

However, he did not baptize her.

In due course, the news spread that the daughter of the widow woman was pregnant by the holy hermit of Walsingham, and that it had been revealed to them by the angel Malvolio that their son was to be Pope.

So – when the poor girl gave birth to a fine, bonny, bouncing – DAUGHTER! – then the sparks really flew!

The widow woman died of shock and grief.

The hermit ran away.

The girl made the best of her situation, living quietly, and bringing up her child. Because she was beautiful, and gentle, and good, and did not lose her faith on account of one man's wicked deceit, she found in time a husband to help her in the world.

And her child prospered and grew up even more beautiful than the girl had been in the days when the hermit had her.

'I know this for a fact,' concluded Pistol, with a flourish of his cloak. '*Since she was my mother!*'

We were all suitably impressed and astonished.

Well, I was not so astonished.

The news that my ensign was the son of a bastard Pope of the wrong sex did a lot to explain his bombastic and thrasonical manner of speaking. Which manner, incidentally, I have not attempted to emulate in recounting the substance of his story, simply because it always bored and irritated me. He could not say anything as simple as 'the sparks really flew', for example, which I have employed above, haven't I, Worcester? What Pistol actually said, as I recall it, was 'the world was fracted and corroborate.' No one would want to hear too much of that kind of stuff.

LXXXIII

About the siege of Harfleur

Our King went forth to Normandy, as it says in the Agincourt song, as we sing in the Agincourt song, us veterans of Agincourt, followers and companions of that King, Henry, by the grace of God King of England and France, the 5th. And the day we went forth was the 11th day of August, 1415 of God's Death, which day was a Sunday.

Swans.

White swans all around us on the silver sea as we fared forth for France.

We left three heads on spikes behind us in Southampton. Cambridge, Scrope, and Grey. (This Scrope my stepson Stephen's cousin.) They had plotted to kill the King. Henry saw their heads chopped off before going on board his ship, the *Trinity*.

6000 men-at-arms, knights, knights bachelor and esquires.

24,000 archers, yeomen, cross-bowmen, pikemen, spearmen.

25,000 horses.

1500 vessels.

O swords. O swans. O trumpets.

We sailed like a moving city. And in that city, within that great and glorious fleet, it was easy enough for one loyal subject of King Henry 5 to observe the strict condition of his banishment, and keep himself 10 miles from the same Majesty's person.

I joke, Worcester. (That was an excellent pestle pie. You may even mention my approval to that bugger Macbeth. He must be drunker than usual, or improving.) I joke. That ten-mile-limit was a thing of *form*.

I stood for something which Harry the Prig had to reject.

Would he have been a greater King if he had not rejected it? I don't know.

I do think he might have been a better man if he had not felt

359

the *need* to reject it.

But, then, I am biassed – hey now, was ever a man so biassed and with such a belly of obliquity before? And, besides, it gives me the toothache talking about this man or that being 'better'. You have to take your fellows as they come. And, for a final *besides*, I was soon to find that shrewd King Henry 5 had stipulated ten ENGLISH miles! *Id est*, he had no intention of disallowing himself my military services at closer range on foreign soil. I was expected to be the thick of things as usual.

It was hot. Those ships stank. We'd waited 18 days for a wind to France. There was a shortage of sack. My shirt made me itch.

Porpoise playing beside us in the pride of the tide.

Light on the water like diamonds scattered. Or a blade, cutting drowned fire.

We cast anchor next day, at noon, at a place called Chefde Caux, about three miles from Harfleur. There we sat. There we rode. There we creaked. There we waited. All afternoon, all evening, and all night.

Next morning, before daybreak, Sir John Holland, Earl of Huntingdon, was sent with a small company to reconnoitre. Then, when morning dawned and the sun shone clear, the King moved in with the main part of the army, effecting our landing in little boats and skiffs, taking up position on a hill overlooking Harfleur. I remember three things. There was a wild wood running down to the estuary of the Seine, on our right hand. There were green fields, with farms and orchards, on our left. And coming up out of my landing craft I trod straight in a cow turd, which made Bardolph laugh until his nose turned normal. I kicked him to wipe my foot.

Standing on that hill, the larks ascending, I sniffed success as I looked down upon Harfleur. I sheathed my sword in buttercups and drank burnt brandy. I reflected, not for the first time, but more keenly than ever before, how fine a thing it is to be alive and to be a man of parts.

As for the cow-shit, I counted that lucky. Caesar stepped in some before Pharsalus.

Henry sent a herald to demand the surrender of the town.

This was consonant with his position. He presented himself to Harfleur as a sovereign demanding no more than his rightful inheritance. He was the lawful Duke of Normandy. Harfleur owed him obedience. He promised death to Harfleur if Harfleur refused him what it owed.

Harfleur did refuse.

The defences of the town were strong. Its garrison consisted of 400 men-at-arms, who with their attendants must have made up a force of about 3000. Further, Harfleur had ditches round it, and walls with high towers, plus three gates, before the biggest of which the Frogs had erected a defence called a barbican, with great trees bound strongly together, leaving only a number of chinks and crevices through which they could shoot at us.

Nasty. Like a fortified pie. Bristling with knives. And surrounded by gravy.

Henry began with orthodox siege tactics. He set up his heavy field-pieces, with shields of wood and iron to protect the artillerymen. Then a cannonade began, with us shooting stones from the guns, using ignited powder. This went on for seven days and nights. Our gunners directed most of their attack against the barbican, battering it with the stones, and three times managing to get the wood on fire. But the enemy did us as much damage as they could, with their guns and crossbows, and as the walls and towers were broken by day, they heaped up in the breach by night logs and tubs filled with earth, and great piles of sand and stones. They also built up mounds of thick clay – a clever trick, for these took the stones from our cannons. It was like shooting plums into a pudding. Very frustrating.

Henry sent the miners in. They dug long trenches to undermine the walls.

But the Frogs dug counter-mines, and baffled us.

Then the King sent a party in close, to fill up the ditches with faggots, with a view to taking the town by storm. But the French met us with a fusillade of stones and arrows, pouring vats of quick-lime and burning oil on those who got through, and finally scotching *that* stratagem by dropping burning torches into the faggots, so that they burnt harmlessly all round the foot of the walls.

I stood between our siege guns, observing operations.

The King's Daughter, we called the major engine. The others, her Maidens.

Ah, war! Kiss my arse!

I smell it. The stench of the tunnels, which kept flooding, and the corpses floating there.

I hear it. The mighty whang-whang-*whang* of the siege guns. The whistle and hiss of arrows. Peto lost an eye. But he was lucky. The King had made regular provision for the medical and surgical treatment of our wounded. Mr Nicholas Colnet, physician, and Mr Thomas Morstede, surgeon, together with 12 assistants, manned our ambulance service. Peto owed his life to Morstede's skill.

I touch it. The casings of steel on your arms and legs and chest. The prickly shaven sides of your skull, where the hair was cut to the roots, so that your head should keep cool and comfortable inside your helmet. Here is the helmet I wore at Harfleur and Agincourt. A salade. Covers all the vital parts of the neck. A little old-fashioned now, of course, but a vast improvement on the old heaumes I can tell you.

I see it. The flags opposing. The glint of the sun on the King's Daughter and her Maidens. The barbican burning. Those obstinate towers.

Harfleur proved obstinate all right.

As fast as we made holes in their defences, the French filled them up.

Then it began to rain. It rained and rained. It would not stop. It got inside your armour and your boots. It turned the ditches into moats. It made our banners look like wrung-out rags. It made the horses cough, and stand all the time on three legs, hindquarters turned into the wind, eyes shut, like creatures in a dream. And, worst of all, I think it was this sudden access of unseasonable wet weather which caused the vile epidemic of dysentery which swept through our ranks. Conditions around Harfleur made the place a breeding ground for such disease, I daresay. The countryside was one long swamp now, with the breath of decayed and decaying flesh on every breeze. Rotting corpses. The offal of slaughtered animals. And when at last the rain stopped, and steam rose from the broken ground, the flies came, and the very summer sunlight seemed infected with the flux.

2000 of our men fell victim to the dysentery, and died. Prince Thomas, Duke of Clarence, went down with it. He did not die. But he had to be carried to a ship and back to England.

For the first time, I suspect, with the departure of his brother Thomas, it crossed Henry's mind that Harfleur was maybe *not* his for the simple plucking. That was enough to make that eagle eye flash bright, unconquerable. He proclaimed by trumpet through the camp that the whole army should prepare to storm the city at dawn. It was to be an all or nothing attempt. We had, he said, to 'imitate the action of the tiger'. I was never a great tiger man myself. Lions and elephants are more my style. (Though I know that Bacchus liked to travel in a chariot drawn by tigers.)

However, what is interesting here, in any case, is not the animal chosen by the King as symbol, but the fact that he was still talking of *acting* and *imitation* at a time like this. I think for Hal the whole world was a stage, and all the men and women merely players. He was himself now playing the part of King to the utmost.

All night the King's Daughter and her escort of Maidens kept up that fusillade. Whang-whang-*whang*. Pistol strutted in his scarlet cloak, careless of danger under a full moon, shouting of Sir Acolon, Sir Ballamore, Sir Beaumaris, Sir Bors, Sir Ector, Sir Eric, Sir Ewain, Sir Gaheris, Sir Galahad, Sir Gareth, Sir Gawain, Sir Kay, Sir Lamerock, Sir Lancelot of the Lake, Sir Lionell, Sir Marhaus, Sir Palamide, Sir Pelleas, Sir Peredur, Sir Sagris, Sir Superabilis, Sir Tor, Sir Tristam, Sir Wigamur, and all the other Knights of the Round Table, comparing them on the whole unfavourably with his own performance as planned for the next day. Nym and Peto diced. Bardolph kneaded his nose. I sat on some dead French (the ground being damp), and drank sherris sack. A good sherris sack has a two-fold operation in it. It ascends into the brain, making that organ quick and apprehensive, full of fiery shapes. The second property of your excellent sherris is the warming of the blood. Under the moon, that night, my cups of still white wine from Xeres lit up my face, until that face was like a beacon giving warning to all the rest of this little kingdom, man, to arm. And then the vital commoners, the inland petty spirits, mustered my whole being to their captain, my heart. Which heart, great and puffed up with his retinue, was ready to do any deed of courage in the morning. O it was like drinking white fire, moonlight, Samson's honey blood. And all this valour came of sherris. If I had a thousand sons, Worcester, the first humane principle I would teach them should be to forswear thin potations, and to addict themselves to sack.

Morning came. We prepared to charge.

But something –

Harry Monmouth doing his best to imitate a tiger?

Pistol astride the King's Daughter discharging?

Myself, red roaring drunk on the green hill?

– SOMETHING, at any rate, made the inhabitants of Harfleur suddenly aware of the hopelessness of their position.

A man with a white flag slid down the barbican.

It was an envoy from the commander of the garrison. He came with a promise to capitulate, surrender, and give up the town completely to us, unless Harfleur should be relieved by the French King or the Dolphin before the first hour after noon of the Sunday following. That was, within three days.

Harry agreed to the terms.

It was now (I think) the 19th of September, and the siege had lasted exactly 30 days.

And, of course, neither mad King Charles nor his equally empty son showed up before the Sunday.

And in the afternoon of that day, our King Harry, clad in gold armour, seated on his throne in a pavilion on the hill, with Sir Gilbert Umfraville on his right, bearing on a spear the crowned helmet of the King, received the Lord of Garcourt, accompanied by all the other chief inhabitants of Harfleur, making a formal surrender of the keys of the city.

'*God for Harry, England, and St George!*'

The King kept the captain of the garrison, and his council men, all garbed in the grey shirt of penitence, with ropes round their necks ready for hanging, – kept them kneeling in the evening air, a touch of autumn in it, on their bended bones. . . .

Then, with a nod, he spared their lives.

And when the moon came up that night she saw the banners of St George and the King of England on the gates of Harfleur town.

And Harry Monmouth, barefoot, walking through the streets to the church of St Martin, where he offered up a thanksgiving for his success.

And me, Fastolf, barefoot also, upon the barbican, astride the three sweet daughters of the Lord of Gaucourt – a different form of thanksgiving, but no less sincere. I had the satisfaction of hearing those three virgins cry out with pleasure one after another and *thank* the English milord for his puissance in their siege. *Merci!* – or was it *Mercy!*? Their hymens vent, we devised several new geometries as the night wore on – theorems not in Pythagoras – in discovering ways for those three girls to have their breaches simultaneously filled. – (Madam! Well, since you ask: my cock, my tongue, and my big toe. . . .) – Their English was no better than my French, but I have found that problems of communication can always be solved by your prick erect. There is nothing like it, whether for explanation, explication, or interpretation of meaning.

LXXXIV

About Bardolph's execution

Henry sent a challenge to the Dolphin, offering to submit his claim to the throne of France to the issue of a single combat. No answer. Not even one tennis-ball. The King then decided on a march to Calais, leaving 500 men-at-arms and 1000 archers to garrison Harfleur, and taking 900 men-at-arms and 5000 archers with him on the march. Our prisoners, our booty, our wounded, and those still incapacitated by the quickshits, we sent back to England. Also the engines of war. The last had served their purpose, and the King had other military ambitions now. We fought our way through Picardy, crossing the River Somme near Nesle, where there was a ford where the water was little higher than to a horse's belly. The French troops now fell back quite deliberately in front of us, massing to post themselves in force across the road to Calais. You could see the highway all broken up where they had retreated. *Their* march was miles wider than ours. By which we knew that they had a very much larger army than we did. And Bardolph stole a pyx from the church at Corbie, and the King had him hanged for it. He was strung up on a tree, right next to the church, in sight of the whole army. Pistol pleaded for him, but to no avail. The pyx was worthless, made of copper gilt, which Bardolph had thought gold. I was not permitted to speak to the King myself. I saluted my hanged man with the hilt of my sword as we marched under him. His nose was executed, and his fire was out.

The attentive reader – if ever I win one, that ideal reader suffering from an ideal insomnia, reading my every word with eyes in search of a waking dream – the Attentive Reader will remark that although I have got myself to France (and that no mean feat of seamanship and engineering, given a womb like mine, and the fact that none of our ships was more than 500 tons), still, I have not, as promised, handed over my narrative to Peter Basset.

Dear Attentive Reader, the reason is Basset. Looking over his Latin got me to sleep for seven nights in a row. To set Scrope and Worcester to serving up this gruel again in translation would do no service to the richness of my days.

I am a banquet, or I am nothing.

Besides, I would miss my Days – which is to say, the time I delight in most (aside and apart from certain slippery interludes with my niece) in every 24 hours that pass. Which time I spend in remembering. And then dictating and discoursing and descanting. And generally spurring my secretaries to set down in these pages my exploits and my rages and my jests and my opinions.

As for this matter of my temper – let it be said once and for all that I have a parcel of rogues about me, and that the Devil himself could not manage my estates with a grin on his face. Besides, if an Englishman is not permitted to kick the arses of his secretaries then whose arses can he kick?

To let these bone-idle dogs get away with translating Basset into English would be to pay them good money for nothing. Not that I pay you in cash if I can help it, eh, my pretty twins? Patience: you will be rewarded in heaven, no doubt. St Michael was always on my side, and ever ready to lend a friend a pound. And before that, lads, if you are good lads, and write straight, there has to be the matter of my Will. Not that I intend to quit this my huge companionable outfit of flesh for 19 years yet. I shall live to be a hundred, just as I served in the Hundred Years War, and shall tell my tale here for a Hundred Days, and as the Hundred River goes on flowing, flowing, flowing, until it meets the sea.

It is my plan, then, Dear Attentive Reader – (and I trust Gentle too, for that is how clerks call you, is it not? yet for my part I should not object to fierceness in you, Reader. . . . Go on, kick the cat, you bugger!) – It is my plan, Sir, it is my design upon you, Madam, to use this hound, Basset, as the merest guide, or prompting ghost, the thinnest starkest skeleton to my history in France. Oh, the Basset's records are fair enough, so far as they go. But they lack – what shall we call it? – a certain *tone*. . . .

Having Hanson read over to me the choicest passages of these *Acta* to date – more especially the final minutes of that Day when I had Miranda from behind while she bade the Pastons goodnight, O how she wriggled, and how our naughty Christopher's voice went up and down in the recital –

And having Bussard fart again to remind me of the rosy flavour

366

of that 22nd chapter, not to say its intricate music of punctuation –

Yes, and making Luke Nanton read aloud the version stewed out of Mrs Quickly's fertile fancy, of what I did with my late lamented wife in the snowy nuptials of St Hilary –

All these simple pleasures have brought before me an immediacy, a zest, an abundance I rejoice in, and which I fear I would lose if I let my bastards earn their keep by copying out 10 pages of Basset's wretched scribble every day.

Yet the Basset's notes are history. (Hail Clio, *ad infinitum*, *ad interim*, *ad libitum*, *ad literam*, *ad nauseam*, *ad quod damnum*.) These were the jotting of an honest soldier, moved to record and recall the deeds of his captain and comrade, me. They must therefore be kept before the eye in this, my telling. Be sure then, Fierce or Gentle Reader, that when you read a chapter concerning my adventures in France, you are hearing *my* voice NOW – here, in Caister Castle, the year of Our Salvation 1459, and a very good year too, though England's nearly gone to the dogs for ever, and nothing is what it used to be, save only my belly and my phallus, and even the latter may be a shade –

No! By cock! Miranda's not yet complained. Or asked for you two to come in and help me out, eh?

What you are hearing, Dear Guests, is Fastolf on the day at each Day's title, Fastolf *here* and *now*, remembering *then* – which is to say, at present, that autumn in Picardy, when, to quote Basset 'his march with King Henry led him through the villages of Peronne, Albert, Bonnieres, and Frevent, until on 24 October he reached the village of Blangy, on the River of Swords, where our army crossed, and coming to the top of a hill we saw the French, in three great companies, about a mile in front of us, filling the whole plain like an innumerable multitude of locusts, their headquarters somewhere behind the village called Azincour or Agincourt.'

In my remembering, then, I shall have Peter Basset's chronicle of my wars in France before me. And you will be getting the benefit of Basset's ghostly voice and my live one.

Put it away, Hanson.

I knew a dago called Iago once. He went blind through doing that as much as you do. Bit *less* than you do, as a matter of fact. Every time I so much as mention Miranda, out it comes, and you sit there in the corner so reflectively spinning off your distaff that a man could hear a garter drop without bothering with a *Honi soit* . . .

One day, if you're a really good boy, I'll get her to play with it for you. . . .

There: that's finished him off.

367

LXXXV

About the Battle of Agincourt

The 7 Sorrows of the Blessed Virgin Mary

All night it rained.
We were camped in some orchards.
I remember the smell of apples rotting underfoot.
I picked two apples up – to juggle. But they were soft and squashy, and put me in mind of the knobs on Bardolph's face. I threw them away, and sat with most of me in a huge hollow oak, eating my Cerne Abbas figs and spitting the pips. I ascribe no supernatural portion to these figs. There is no superstition in my swearing by them. But when princes as redoubtable as Thomas, Duke of Clarence, fell quaking in their breech with the abomination of the swamp disease, the appalling action of this fevered flux, I ate my fig a day and went quite clean.

We were encamped so close to the French that, when darkness fell, we could hear them calling to each other. Word passed along through our lines that they were feasting on the other side, and already casting dice for us as prisoners. By the King's command, there was no such merriment in the English camp. Not that there *could* have been. Harry, after all, was offering the Frogs incredibly good odds on a victory. There were about one hundred thousand of them, well-conditioned and well-appointed, to our emaciated five thousand nine hundred. Correction. To our emaciated five thousand eight hundred and ninety nine, plus me. Even allowing for me, things looked extremely favourable to the French.

Not a cry from our camp all night, as I say. That was the order. We were promised that any gentleman who broke the rule would lose his horse and harness, and any common man would lose his left ear.

We kept quiet.
We listened to the rain.
And in the early hours of St Crispin's Day, in the dark before dawn, Hal went about among our men, encouraging them, and himself.

One of the officers, warming his hands at a brazier, remarked to the King that he rather wished some of the brave fellows now safe asleep in England were here to help us.

'No,' said the King. 'I would not have one man more. If we are defeated, we are too many. If God gives us the victory, we shall have the more honour.'

I reckoned this a superb reply – and will not even quibble over that word *honour* in such a context.

The King sent a Welsh captain, called David Gam, to reconnoitre. When he came back, and the King asked him how things looked in the French camp, Mr Gam replied: 'There are enough to be killed, enough to be taken prisoners, and enough to run away.'

These sayings passed in whispers through our army until, about an hour before first light, you could sense a strange *excitement* growing in us. Perhaps it was *because* our chances looked so hopeless, and we all knew that we could rely on each other utterly, to fight till we dropped down dead, because there was nothing else to do. Perhaps it was because the King had infected us – not so much with confidence that we were going to win (which would have been a mad confidence), but with faith in ourselves, as *a band of brothers*, who might just be capable of rising to any occasion God was going to allow. Perhaps it was also because of the rain and the enforced silence. There is nothing like listening to the beating of your own heart, and some consistent adversity of weather, to make a man determined to prevail.

Doing his rounds, the King did not confine his conversation to the officers. Observing this, from my throne in the hollow oak, I reflected with no little satisfaction that it was at *my* court in Eastcheap that Hal had learned his manners and the common touch.

Thin light grew.

Crows began to fly from tree to tree, between the woods of Agincourt and Tramecourt. Your crow does not discriminate between English eyes and French eyes, when battle is done, and it comes to dinner time.

I did not expect Hal to speak to me, and he did not.

I was a ghost to him now. A fat phantom. A great lubberly wraith. An amplitudinous vision. A memory.

Not, though, a memory he had quite forgot.

As he strode back to his tent to arm himself for battle, I knew and he knew that he could choose either to walk in front of the hollow oak or behind its back, and that if he chose the latter path he would not even need to be seen not seeing me.

He chose to walk straight in front.

His eyes did not stray from the way he was walking.

'God save the King,' I said.

Without breaking step, without so much as a glance in my direction, he lifted his right hand as he passed the hollow oak, and flicked something small and bright and round at the unmissable target of my belly.

I clapped my hand to it, and caught it there.

My eyes filled with tears. The sun was just below the rim of the horizon. The King disappeared into his tent.

I knew what it was, of course, before I opened my palm and looked into it, before it even hit my belly. . . .

The seal-ring. Given to me by my uncle Hugh, the admiral. Picked from my pocket so long ago while I slept behind the arras in the Boar's Head tavern. The same seal-ring which the Prince (as he then was) never tired of telling me was only made of copper. And which I once under-valued at 40 pounds. In fact, as I realised, blinking at it in the early light of Agincourt, copper or not, that ring was worth about a million.

After the rain all night, the dawn of the 25th day of October, 1415 of our Lord, came bright and clear. It was the feast day of St Crispin and St Crispinian.

Henry had learned from a prisoner that the arrogant French intended to ride our little band into the ground by repeated cavalry charges. They were drawing themselves up in three thick lines, a forest of horses and lances and plumes and shining helmets. We learned later that the first line alone, under the command of the Dukes of Orleans and Bourbon, consisted of some twenty thousand men. Behind this came another line, unmounted men-at-arms. And behind this again, a third, chiefly cavalry like the first, commanded by the Duke d'Alençon.

Our English army consisted of one single line. The men-at-arms were posted in the centre. To their right and left, Henry positioned his archers. Each archer had a sharpened stake, which he planted in the ground in front of him, pointing outwards slantingly towards the enemy. The baggage was placed at the back, under my command. Don't laugh, Madam. This turned out to be a more important factor in the battle than you would expect.

Henry was not one of those kings who go into a battle disguised. Or perhaps I should more truly say: Suddenly, here was Hal, disguised as a King, displaying himself conspicuously in the centre of our line. He rode a small grey horse while seeing to it that we were all in the correct positions. He wore a surcoat suitable to his claim to the thrones of England and of France, for it was complete with our leopards and their lilies. His helmet was circled with a crown of gold.

The job of marshalling done, *the King dismounted*.

I stress this point because it is an unusual one, and because in my opinion it played a significant part in what was to come.

Bear in mind two things:

First, it had rained very heavily for more than twelve hours, and the ground was soaking wet.

Second, we were positioned in a narrow space, as it were at the bottom end of a funnel, with trees to our right and our left. Here, I will draw the shape of it –

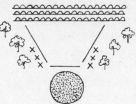

In this representation,

Now, I think what would strike any great general or captain of the Art of War, looking at this diagram, is that the force superior in strength and number (i.e. the French) is placed at a considerable disadvantage *unless the smaller force comes to it*. The further the French advanced down that funnel of trees, the less their overwhelmingly larger number of men was any use to them. If we had gone up at the French, and spent ourselves in attacks upon *them*, it would all have been over in half an hour, and instead of talking to you I should now be a biggish quantity of Christian dust at the position marked

Further, consider the heaviness of the ground – all that rain, all night – and the trees and tall hedges and wilds of briar and brushwood which made the sides of our funnel for us. And *further* consider the fact that the field sloped *down* towards us. . . .

Harry Monmouth, who had learned a thing or two that night on Gadshill, taking into account all these aforementioned factors, had issued the unheard-of order that *his knights were to fight on foot*. He had perceived the worse-than-uselessness of horses on that sticky pitch. His task now was to persuade the French to come thundering down the funnel at us.

This he achieved by the simple actor's stratagem of waving his sword above his head, shouting

'*St George!*'

and moving forward. . . .

All those silken Frenchmen in the first line needed no more excuse or encouragement. Supposing that we were on the way, and keen to start winning, they set spurs to their horses and charged.

Henry, meanwhile, and the whole English line with him, had taken no more than a dozen strides up the field.

He halted.

We all halted.

He signalled to the archers. The archers stepped across in front of us, driving their stakes into the ground, and then knelt down, kissed the earth, and springing to their feet shot arrows sharp and straight into the French line as it came.

Such terrible rain of arrows! Such a snowstorm!

Your English longbow can be used to fire twelve arrows in a minute when the right hands hold it. (The French crossbow, admittedly more powerful, fires never more than two in the same time.)

We had the right hands at Agincourt.

All the same, the sheer weight and ferocity of that first French charge nearly carried the day for them. In one or two places they burst through. But then our men-at-arms, led by the King himself, and all on foot, moved about nimbly cutting the horses down, pounding at the French with axes, encircling little clumps of them and slaughtering them.

Stage two.

The archers pluck their stakes out of the ground and again, with the King conspicuous at our head, bang in the middle of the line, we feint to advance up the field.

Snap!

The fool Frogs, the second line, the unmounted men-at-arms, come rushing at us!

Once more, the archers halt, stick their pikes in the ground along our front, and pour forth another deadly hail of arrows.

I'll say this for the French – they kept on coming. . . .

Stuck through with arrows like hedgehogs with prickles, or pin-cushions with pins, so it seemed, they kept on coming down the field. . . . The charge was so sustained, and there were so many of them charging, that it might be thought that nothing could have stopped them.

What stopped them was themselves.

And the mud.

And the clay.

And all those horses dead or impaled upon our pikes.

And all their own knights, fallen in the first charge, who were floundering about on their backs like topsy-turvy tortoises, the weight of their armour making it impossible for them to get up.

That second French line found itself in dreadful trouble. Apart from the unceasing rain of English arrows, it had to contend with the fallen underfoot, and what remained of the first French line of cavalry, now trying to wheel about in the narrow space between the trees. I have heard it said that more Frenchmen died of suffocation in the press than were killed by English swords or English arrows. That is an exaggeration. But it gives you some idea of the heaving mass of men and horses, dead and alive and dying, which was Agincourt, so far as the French were concerned.

Only those in the very front of their attack, you see, were able to lift their hands to strike a blow at us.

And all the time the archers kept on firing, firing, firing. . . . It must have seemed that the skies were spewing arrows. French corpses lay in mounds at the bottom of that funnel. They mounted higher and higher, so that you had the spectacle of their soldiers having to try to scale the ramparts of their own dead to get at us.

There remained the French third line, under the command of the Duke d'Alençon. You will remember that this also consisted of cavalry, so in the circumstances it was powerless to press down between the trees and come to the aid of its predecessors. Alençon, who was no fool, sized up what was already a desperate situation for his side, and decided that the only thing which might reverse the day for them was to kill the King himself. He fought his way bravely to where Henry was, using a small company of men-at-arms, avoiding the morass of mud and dead and horses. He succeeded in thrusting the King's youngest brother, Humphrey, Duke of Gloucester, to the ground, and getting his sword into his groin below the metal plate-armour which covered the Prince's torso. But then Hal rushed forward and stood astride Humphrey, and fought the Frenchman off again. A slice of Henry's coronet was cut right off by a battle-axe. But he fought over his wounded brother like a man inspired, and Alençon soon fell dead, cut down before he could get in another proper blow at either Henry of Humphrey.

Alençon gone, that third French line seems to have split up into three separate factions.

The first, taking its defeat for granted, decided that its position in the rear was ideal for a little exercise in the old art of Running Away. So it did just that.

The second, braver, or more foolhardy, depending on how you look at it, managed to thread its way down the side of the funnel, through the orchards, and come in to make a final desperate charge at the King *behind* the line of our archers. This party, consisting of about a hundred men-at-arms on foot, under command of the Lord of Fauquemberg, fought very fiercely. But Hal was not to be denied or conquered now. He hacked and he thrust and he swung his sword round and round so that he looked for all the world like a star falling headlong on those French. Fauquemberg's faction were killed or made prisoners to a man.

Which left the last third of that third line.

Under whose command? I don't know. But I do know that just as Alençon had decided that if he could kill the King then maybe the day might be retrieved for France, so whoever directed this last remaining segment of the French army evidently realised that if he could kill ME then perhaps the tide would turn their way.

The notion was not so preposterous. Being so large, I suppose I appeared the most ransomable or murderable Englishman in sight. And, besides, I was in charge of the baggage, *and the baggage contained the King's crown.* (He didn't wear *the actual thing* to fight in, Madam. He left it to me to look after. The sliced one on his head was second best.)

What remained of the third line of cavalry, therefore, craftily rode right round the outside of the woods of Tramecourt, and came thundering at me full-tilt just as the day seemed in our grasp!

DO? What do you *think* I did?

I baggaged them!

I stood alone, with that heap of spare hauberks and helmets and jaques and gauntlets and metal plate and lances and battle axes and iron darts and several hundred bags of jewels. And as those six, or twelve, or eighteen French fry came rushing at me, I advanced my belly forward, with a mighty belch of old –

'Fastolf! Faust off! *Faust off!* FASTOLF!'

– and I pelted them with

hauberks and

helmets and

gauntlets and

metal plates and

lances and

battle axes and

iron darts and

SEVERAL HUNDRED BAGS OF JEWELS!

The effect was tremendous. In a trice, they were all off their horses and scrabbling for the jewels in the grass. It was then an easy matter for me to spike them up the bum as they were bending, or knock their heads together, or generally boot them into Kingdom Come.

Unfortunately, it was this singular engagement which provoked Hal to the assumption that a whole new enemy host had appeared behind him, where it was engaged in competition with a small *party* of our men. The general safety of the army seemed in that case to require immediate and decisive action, for if the enemy host succeeded in fighting its way to the French prisoners we had taken, those noblemen might yet effect some retrieval of the day.

Accordingly, the King issued orders that all the prisoners were to be killed. An order which was carried out without enthusiasm. A cut throat meant no ransom money.

But when Henry heard who had been in command of this rearguard English action, and who had comprised the entire company which had taken part in it, and won, and how, he stopped the slaughter of the prisoners, and then I believe he smiled the only smile which was ever smiled upon the field of Agincourt.

The day was done. It had taken three hours.

The victory was England's.

The French losses were enormous. Their dead included, besides Alençon, two brothers of the Duke of Burgundy, the Dukes of Brabant, Bar, and Charles d'Albret, the Constable of

France. Also the Great Master of France, Sir Guichard Dolphin; the master of the crossbows, Lord Rambures; and the lords Grandpré, Roussi, Foix, Beaumont, Marle, Vaudemont, and Lestrale. I mention only the most illustrious. Their own chroniclers – who are inclined to under-estimate such things, of course – put the number of noblemen dead at *no less than ten thousand*. We took as prisoners the Dukes of Orleans and Bourbon, both princes of the blood-royal. As well as the Earls of Richemont, Vendôme, and Eu, with the Lord Boucicault, and a few thousand others. No one counted the common dead, of course.

As to our own dead: there were nine. Our principal loss was the Duke of York, who was crushed to death in the shambles, and the young Michael de la Pole, the Earl of Suffolk. Humphrey, Duke of Gloucester, was badly wounded, but recovered, thanks to Morstede the surgeon. Besides the nobles, we lost one squire, four men-at-arms, and twenty-eight common soldiers.

The last figure – that 28 common soldiers – is absolutely reliable.

I counted them myself that afternoon. (After retrieving every one of the King's jewels, of course, and packing them back in the baggage.)

28.

Morbid of me?

No, Sir. I was looking for honour.

I knew he would be there.

Among that 28.

I found him too, Madam.

His name was Mr Gam.

LXXXVI

How the King came back in triumph to London

And when we landed at Dover, the people rushed into the sea to welcome us. Especially the women.

It was always like this after a great battle. Mars and Venus seem to tickle each other up, as I've noted before.

Not that Hal took any hot girls to his bed. He was saving the royal sperm for Katharine of Valois, youngest daughter of the mad French King, at that time fifteen years old and busy learning English from her mother. Katharine was said to be very beautiful. I hope that English was all the French Queen taught her. Ysabeau, since her husband's madness, had lived a life of extraordinary scandal even by French standards. She kept a whole retinue of lovers, as well as a pet monkey which she liked to masturbate in public while conducting boring affairs of state.

There was nothing like that about our Henry now. After resting for one day at Dover, he made his way slowly up with us via Canterbury to his manor of Eltham. He sent heralds to announce that he intended to enter London on the Saturday following. Elaborate preparations were made to receive us conquerors.

We were met at Blackheath by the Mayor of London, with 23 aldermen in scarlet, and the rest in red with red and white hoods. These came at the head of a procession of (I should suppose) about 20,000 people, all on horseback, and bearing the insignia of the various guilds and crafts they represented.

We crossed London Bridge at ten o'clock in the morning.

And all the bells of London rang for us.

And on the tower at the entrance to the Bridge I saw that they had set up a great statue. This statue, in the shape of a champion, bore an axe in his right hand and the keys of the City in his left. And on the other side of the arch stood a statue of a woman dressed in scarlet. And all around were the royal banners.

The trumpets and the clarions sounded.

CIVITAS REGIS JUSTITIAE was written on a banner right across between the statues.

And every tower of the Bridge had been painted or emblazoned in some way to celebrate our victory at Agincourt. Thus, one little tower was painted to look like green and marble jasper. And on the next was an antelope with the royal sceptre in his right foot and the arms of England round his neck. And on the next a lion erect, bearing in his claws the King's standard unfurled. And on the next a statue of St George with a laurel wreath studded with pearls, and on his right hand hung his helmet, and on his left his shield.

And as we marched over the Bridge, the people leaned down and showered us with rose petals out of the windows of the many houses on the Bridge. And we were suddenly met by a great number of boys all dressed in white, who walked all round the King, singing to the sound of organs from the thrown-open doors of the chapels and churches around and on the Bridge. And what they sang was that greatest of English canticles, the Agincourt song:

> *Deo gratias Anglia redde pro victoria!*
> *Our King went forth to Normandy,*
> *With grace and might of chivalry;*
> *The God for him wrought marvellously,*
> *Wherefore England may call and cry,*

DEO GRATIAS!

and so on. All six verses of it. Which never fail to bring a lump into my throat and tears to my eyes. Complicated tears, you understand. Since when I hear that song I see Bardolph hanging on his tree also, and David Gam face-down in the Agincourt mud, his brains in his cap beside him – as well as the more obvious things.

I marched at the back of the procession, which by now was so long, what with our army, and the choir, and the aldermen, and the guildsmen, and the prisoners-of-war in chains, that I daresay I was not infringing upon the limits of that ten-mile banishment.

At Cornhill, the people set free from their cages a vast number of sparrows and other little birds, which flew about the King, some resting on his crown and on his shoulders.

At Cheapside, he was met by a company of maidens, all dressed in white, playing timbrels and dancing and crying:

'Welcome, Henry the Fifth, King of England and of France!'

And as he passed round to St Paul's, there were a number of little pavilions lining the streets, and in each pavilion, like a statue, a girl, with a gold cup in her hands. And each girl blew out of her cup and showered leaves of gold upon the King's head as he passed.

And the crowds the whole way from Blackheath to St Paul's were so thick that we had to proceed very slowly, since we could scarcely get through them. And from every window, every tower, every house, every rooftop, every crevice, people cheered us, and shouted, and hailed, and hurrahed, and sang, until the whole of the streets of London seemed to reverberate like one great drum beating to the slow triumphant music of that song:

DEO GRATIAS ANGLIA REDDE PRO VICTORIA!

And the conduits ran with wine.

The King heard Mass sung in St Paul's, and then passed on to his palace of Westminster. He wore a gown of purple, simply cut. With the great crown of England on his head.

I wore a suit of buckram, simply cut. With my uncle Hugh's seal-ring on my little finger. I heard Mass too, since the doors were left open and it was possible to make one's devotions standing in the middle of the crowd in the streets.

Then I passed on to the Boar's Head tavern.

LXXXVII

How Sir John Fastolf drank the elixir of life

18 September

Dame Milicent was in Yarmouth, spending her pin money. (£100 a year, if you want to know.) My stepson Scrope – then just big enough to cut a sorry figure on his hobby horse – no doubt skipped behind her in attendance. The strings would have dangled from her apron, and he would have wanted them in his fingers.

Caister could wait.

I was back from the wars.

We were back from the wars, King Henry 5 and I – and while that cold fish might be content to save his Plantagenet sperm for the French princess, I saw no harm in learning a trick or two in London to take home for my wife's delight in due course. Be sure, Uxorious Reader, my dear brother, all the various dalliances and pranks and pastimes I describe in these pages I have practised also with my wife. I brought everything home to her in the end. Yet to tell you true, Dame Milicent was never so wild a body in bed as I would have wished. She suffered my embraces rather than enjoyed them. All the same, her eyes and thighs widened an inch when I taught her the ways I brought back from London after this celebration at the Boar's Head following the English army's triumphal return from Agincourt. I remember that she was so pleased with the new game that her greed for it threatened somewhat to interfere with my supervision of the unloading of the 130 tuns of Gascony wine which I had at that time as ransom for the Lord of Soubooze – which fleet of sheer intoxication made a valorous sight as it came wallowing up the Hundred River I can promise you. And now, in any case, Dame Milicent dead, I have my niece to keep me warm in bed at Caister of a night. Miranda is a lovely lively girl, loveliest liveliest, like a wave of the sea with the sun catching its underlip as it turns upon a golden shore –

and there is nothing I have been able to teach this wise and innocent niece of mine which she does not love, and want to do again twice in the morning. Oh I know there are some who say an old man should not wear himself out between sheets in this way, when he stands on the threshold of eternity. But the way I look at it is this:

If heaven is unendurable bliss infinitely prolonged then we had better start learning how to endure it.

Besides, such foretastes, carnal and imperfect as they are, cannot harm me, nor deflect me from my last great voyage. I was ever a voyager, an Odysseus, an explorer of new winds across old seas. I must rejoice, at all events, that my member has not lost puissance or appetite with the years – rather on the contrary, to Miranda's pleasure.

Besides, *my* shadow on the threshold of eternity is 19 years long. I shall live to be a hundred. I had it of a certainty from a sybil.

Worcester, my Cyclops, where was I?

Ah yes. Ha! The Boar's Head. What! That naked dinner.

Nell Quickly was there, and Pistol her spouse, and my dear adorable Doll. And we drank and we sang. And I can tell you that it was not the Agincourt Song that we sang in the Dolphin chamber of the Boar's Head. No. It was this:

> *I cannot eat but little meat,*
>   *My stomach is not good;*
> *But sure I think that I can drink*
>   *With him that wears a hood.*
> *Though I go bare, take ye no care,*
>   *I nothing am a-cold;*
> *I stuff my skin so full within*
> *Of jolly good ale and old.*
>   *Back and side go bare, go bare;*
>   *Both foot and hand go cold;*
>   *But, belly, God send thee good ale enough,*
>   *Whether it be new or old.*

I love these old English songs as much as dim chalk cliffs or wild bells at midnight or mist or drenched roses or roast beef. All the English things. The shifting hedgerows in the fog.

We'd sung a verse or two together, and shared a few firkins, and I had untapped a basket of my figs sent up from Cerne Abbas on the usual mule, when Nell (or was it Doll?), ever ready to avail that bawdy establishment of the newest fangled and most intricate comforts, enquired if we martial gentlemen had heard of what the Romans were doing now.

'Poping each other,' suggested Pistol.

I confess my own imagination flew to some of the classical – or I suppose I had better say sub-classical – scenes conjured up for me in my schoolboy days by my tutor Ravenstone. I must have launched into a description of one of these, for Mrs Quickly said:

'No, Jack! None of your naughty whippings. A fine feast.'

'A feast?'

'A feast,' said Nell. 'An unusual meal on an unusual table.'

Pistol pulled at his moustaches. 'Ambrosial?' he enquired. 'Or nectarine?'

'Figs if you like,' said Mrs Quickly. (Well, Mrs *Pistol* now – but Quickly sounds quicker than Pistol, don't you think?)

'Now your fig –' I began.

'Figs or fish or fruit or gumbo,' said Nell Quickly-Pistol. 'Pies or jams or plums or puddings.' She winked in the firelight. 'Anything you fancy,' she said.

I shrugged. 'It doesn't sound so interesting to me,' I said. 'I can eat my figs any time anyway.'

Doll giggled.

'That's as may be,' said the inventive Nell. 'But your Roman mischiefs, O Jesu, they serve this meal up on an unaccountable table, as I say.'

'What unaccountable table?'

'*The naked body of a girl!*'

Pistol started to sing again:

'*Back and side go bare, go bare. . . .*'

I popped a handful of figs into my mouth.

We were in business.

When in Rome, do as the Romans do. And *quantum libet*.

When in the Boar's Head, do what Mrs Quickly tells you. And *ditto*.

Doll! Tearsheet stripped.

She lay down on the carved couch in the firelight.

Nell then brought in fruit and sweets and pastry so thin you could see through it, as well as liquorice and creams, sauces and sweet wine.

She employed the jams and syrups to stick some of the food to Doll's firm flesh.

I dined first.

I nibbled cherries dangling from Doll's nipples.

I gnawed the veil of pastry from her breasts.

I ate to the hilt a banana which Mrs Quickly pushed between her thighs.

I licked the cream from her lovely little belly, and returned with teeth and tongue to the stick of liquorice now inserted in her crack.

Doll, for her part, grew so excited by the action first of the banana and then the liquorice stick that her own love-juices began to flow. She tasted delicious. Her legs were tight around my head. When I got to the last bit of the liquorice, I gave her little bud a gentle bite. She had been fooling around with my cock while I licked her and slicked her. Now she tossed me off wildly as I drank her oyster. I teased her and tickled her with the tip of my tongue. Then I drew back my head. Nell Quickly poured a thimbleful of sherris sack into her friend's dearest bodily part. I sucked out every last drop of it, and a good deal else besides. Doll came and went beneath the ministrations of my busy tongue and lips. It was like seven great waves breaking on a virgin shore.

Virgin, you will say, Madam, is a foolish word to apply in the cunt of a whore.

As you wish. But then Doll had never been brought to her seven tidal waves in quite such a manner as this before. It was her initiation in the art of being eaten. She was all in ecstasy on that couch before the sea-coal fire, urged on by cries and whispers from Nell Quickly, and by toasts to the vanishing food from the excited Pistol.

For my part, I kept my tongue as stiff as my sword at the crucial comings. I licked her up and I licked her down. And when she was most velvety and defenceless, I thrust away with my tongue until she was quite quenched.

Later, we went at it top-to-toe.

Nell had baked a pastry, a great pastry, in the shape of a penis. I had to fit this over my weapon, and Doll nibbled it and ate it, first the pastry, and then the flesh, while I took cream from her exquisite little clack-dish. I shot my cream into her sucking mouth at the precise moment of licking out the last curds from her cunt. We stayed for a long while like that, by the light of the fire, with my tongue in her tail, and my prick in her mouth. It was all very sweet.

Meanwhile, Nell had sprinkled soft cheese over her own

nipples, with onion shredded in it, and her husband Pistol was doing his duty gobbling it all up, every bit, and tickling her splendidly about the tits with his waxed moustaches while so engaged.

The alchemists turn base metal into gold, and in so doing they find the universal solvent, and the elixir of life.

O Muses, Sacred Nine, and Memory most of all, mother of all of them, and they our mothers – I was Doll Tearsheet's alchemist that night, and by gamahuche turned her base metal into gold. And found myself solved in her universal solvent. And drank the elixir of life from the quivering goblet of her cunt.

What did it taste like?

Eternity, Madam.

Or chestnuts.

LXXXVIII

About divers minor charges, costs & wages owing to Sir John Fastolf

(*3rd Note by Stephen Scrope*)

St Matthew's Day

Where are his sons then?

Of all the lies in this book of lies, I think that none will give more offence to sober men than his lies about what he has done with women.

Owing for divers charges and costs borne for the time that he occupied the office of the Constabulary of Bordeaux, the sum of ...
£227. 15s. 3½d.

These are monstrous filth.

These are the ravings of a devil.

There is even the chapter which he has entitled 'about the ***** of Sir John Fastolf'. I have not read it. I will not read it. No right-minded person would be seen looking for an instant in that direction.

Owing for wages in his service done to the King, and to the Duke of Clarence, being the King's Lieutenant in the Duchy of Guienne, the sum of ....
£200. 10s. 0d.

But I have read his lies about my mother.

Which insult *me*, Scrope.

In that case, for reasons best known to himself (but shame would not be among them), he chose to attribute the disgusting narrative to his 'Mrs Quickly'.

Owing for costs and charges that he bare when he was Lieutenant of the town of Harfleur, in Normandy, as shown by a debenture ...
£133. 6s. 8d.

I say that as certainly as there never was a 'Mrs Quickly' or an 'Ancient Pistol', so he never did those things to my mother in the snow, or anywhere else. He neglected my mother, and me, wasting our money on drink in London.

That he wasted money on whores too, I can believe. Only a whore would tolerate such a beast. Whether or not he did with his whores the filthy deeds which he has said he has done, I neither know nor care.

Owing for the keeping and vitalling of the Bastille of St Anthony in Paris, as shown by the creditors of Sir John Tyrell, late Treasurer of the King's house, in a bill remaining in the Westminster Exchequer, the sum of ....

$£43$. os. od.

He gives the game away in that 'Day LXXXIV', where he rejects Basset's narrative of his petty adventures in France . . .

In the first place, he rejects Basset so that he can lie and lie and lie in giving his own versions. (As if so great a battle as Agincourt hung upon an attack on the baggage!)

In the second place, in that chapter you will notice him teasing and taunting those pathetic toadies, Hanson and Nanton, with more of the disgraceful fantasies about his niece Miranda which have disfigured and dirtied his book from its beginning.

Owing for the safeguard of the town of Pont Meulent, the sum of
$£39$. 10. 4d.

I, Scrope state for a fact that it is all lies and nonsense.

I, Scrope, state for a fact that this crude animal, my stepfather, is *impotent*, and has been so for many years.

Indeed, there may well, *never* have been a time when he was capable of fathering a child. Consider for one moment his immoral praise of sherris sack in that 'Day LXXXII', where he has put it on record (in Worcester's hand) that if he had a thousand sons he would teach them to addict themselves to drink.

A man betrays himself in what he says.

This great Lucifer betrays himself here.

All his tales of doing the deed of darkness with so many women are untrue.

'If I had a thousand sons. . . .' he said.

He has no son.

He has fathered no child.

Yet if he was only a thousandth part as potent as he has made himself out to be in these obscene boastings, then surely he would have been father to many children?

I, Scrope, write facts.

Over all this, owing for wages of him and his retinues being in the King's service in France and Normandy, as well as for sundry expenses borne in the safeguard of the fortress of Alençon and other fortresses abroad, the sum of ....

£13. 13s. 3d.

He speaks sometimes of a bastard son, in Ireland, who became a monk. No one has ever seen this 'Dom William Fastolf'. He does not exist.

He told in earlier chapters of a stepsister, called 'Ophelia'. I never heard the name before in heaven or earth. Just as there never was an 'Ophelia', so you can be sure that he never did with an 'Ophelia' any of the secret things he said that he did.

As for his niece Miranda – she is my cousin, and a sweet and kindly girl. I play chess with her. She helps me when he sets me to absurd and demeaning tasks, such as piling logs for him as if I were his slave. I, Scrope, write facts. I swear that this same Miranda is as chaste and ignorant of his filthy dreams as the day is long. He chooses to imagine for himself all manner of wanton occupation with the dear Miranda. And out of fear and their own lewd longings, titilated by his, those henchmen write it down. I tell you none of it takes place outside his head.

Why does he tell such lies?

Why is the Devil damned?

He writes a kind of requiem for a life he never lived.

He tells you lies about himself.

I, Scrope, tell you the truth about him and about his book.

This is a work of fiction.

Sum total owing of ....

£657. 15s. 6½d.

LXXXIX

How Sir John Fastolf went to the wars again, &
about the siege of Rouen

Michaelmas Day

I was suffering once more from consumption of the purse. There seemed no remedy but a return to the wars. Besides which, peace palled and appalled me. My spirit languished in its stews. My lance grew rusty in the hat-rack. I turned my thoughts again to France.

This was Hal's second great voyage of conquest.

First, the Earl of Huntingdon was given the job of clearing the English Channel of the enemy's ships. This he did. He met nine of them, all hired by the French King from the Republic of Genoa. The first three he sank, the second three he put to flight, and the third three he captured – together with their admiral and a large sum of money.

We sailed from Southampton on 23rd July – which meant that I had time to keep the Feast of my dear St Mary Magdalene the day before embarkation.

Fair stood the wind for France.

Our army consisted of –

1000 pioneers and miners;

25,528 combatants;

1500 ships of all sizes.

Of the 25,528 combatants, there were 17,000 men-at-arms. 17,007, if you count me. It was a sunny showery morning, with blackbirds on the cross-trees of the masts, and I was in quest of my knighthood, though I did not know it.

The beaches were deserted where we landed. Banks of pebbles stretching as far as the eye could see, and not a Frog in view. The disaster of Agincourt had so broken the courage of the French, we soon discovered, that they had very little intention of meeting an English army again in the field if they could help it. Their plan

388

of campaign was to garrison their fortified towns as strongly as possible, so that we would exhaust ourselves gradually in the effort of taking them. That plan failed. Henry was better furnished for siege warfare than he had been before (all those pioneers and miners). It did not rain, and we did not fall foul of the quickshits. And I was in an invincible sort of mood. I could have knocked towers over with my belly.

Touques, a royal castle, fell first to us. Then Damvilliers, Harcourt, and Evreux. We took Caen after a short siege, in which Hal demonstrated how much he had learned from the experience at Harfleur. Our miners got right up to their walls, which were battered by cannon at the same time. We did this by mining first on one side, while the cannon attacked the other, and then reversing the *modus* of attack. We ended up by entering the town on both sides, simultaneously, and with a loss from first to last of less than 500 men. Henry treated the inhabitants of Caen with clemency, so long as they acknowledged his right to the French Crown. Other neighbouring towns at once offered to capitulate.

This is the list of the towns, castles, cities, and abbeys that fell to us on that second tour of France: (I follow Basset) –

Falaise, Argenton, Bayeux, Alençon, Fresne-le-Vicont, St Savers de Vive, St Jakes de Beuron, St Jakes de Burvam, St Low, Valence, Averence, Lisieux, Everose, Counsheux, Vire, Karentine, Cherbourg, Vernoile, Morteyn, Esey, Powntlarche, Dounfrount, Pountedomer, Turve, Costaunce, Galion, Caudebec, Mustirvilers, Dieppe, Vernoile sur Seine, Mawnt, Towk, Morvile, Cursy, Gundy, Vermus, Garcy, Eu, Vileine, Egyll, Curton, Fagernon, Chamberexs, Ryveers, Bewmanill, Bewmalyn, Semper, Trace, Groby, Tylly, St Denise, Bonvile, Perers, Asse la Rebole, Tanny, Antony, Balon, Mountfort, Tovey, Lowdon, Noaus, St Romains in Plaine, Daungell, Peschere, Bolore, Keshank, Turre, St Germaine, Bomstapyll, Croile, Bakuile, Bellacomber, Likone, and Ankorvile.

Most of these surrendered without a fight.

At Falaise, we simply sat between the French and their relief, waiting for shortage of puddings to do what swords do quicker. It took three weeks only.

Amid the welter of mere names, the Benedictine abbey of Bec-Hellouin remains in my recollection vividly. The French had kicked the monks out and commandeered the place to use as a fortified strongpoint to arrest our progress. After we had smoked them out, and hanged a cowardly captain for the blasphemy of posing as an abbot to save his skin, we spent a little of the winter resting there. Why not? Our force was under the command of Thomas, Duke of Clarence, which meant that the Benedictine wine did not have to stay unbroached. That was a warm and welcome winter, in a vine-bright country, with drink in plenty, and roaring fires where we could toast our bums, bake nuts, and sit and dream of home. It was there that I began to make my plans for investing all my profits of war in good fair English land. I laid plans also for the creation of Caister as it is now – my dream, my castle, and my home. When stores ran low, we had only to send out a few men to fill up the cellars again from what they could find in the neighbour castles.

Spring came. Harry came. He took command. We left Bayeux and marched up the southern bank of the Seine. Our destination was *Rouen*.

Rouen. I dare to say that there has been no greater siege in the history of the world since Troy and Jerusalem were taken.

This is the story of it.

Hal's first object was to possess himself of the strong position of Pont de l'Arche, a bridge about eight miles above the city, and commonly known as the Key of the River. This bridge was held by the French, and our scouts reported that it was so constructed and so thickly manned that to force its overthrow would inevitably involve us in a great loss of our own men. The King accordingly marched us some three miles lower down the river, to a place where it was divided by an island.

The Frogs, curious, followed us.

Why were they curious?

I'll tell you why, my little Pigbum.

Because dancing along in the rear of our party, mounted on a vast horse, a lovely Suffolk, *I came*, with a small group of followers, including my Ancient Pistol, *all kitted out and caparisoned for the fox hunt.*

The hunting of foxes was unknown in France at that time. We had started the sport in England, and it was in its infancy. But I was already a devotee of the art – despite the impedimenta presented by my belly – and liked few things better than to flush foxes from the coverts round the Hundred River, and pursue them across this pancake county.

Now the countryside round and about Rouen had put me terribly in mind for Caister, and with a night's riding and a bellyful of burnt brandy inside me, I was brimming over with nostalgia as we made our way down beside the Seine away from that Pont de l'Arche.

I resolved, therefore, on a little spot of innocent fox-hunting.

Or not so innocent. . . .

For I had, of course, required the King's permission to indulge my whim. And he, the sly fox himself, had seen in this bizarre request an opportunity for an ingenious stratagem. Hal was now an old hand at war, and he knew that in the battlefield so much depends upon what men *expect* to see, and then what they *do* see. If the two things fail to match, then a soldier may behave unpredictably. Those Frogs guarding the Key of the River Seine expected to see the King of England ride past, carefully beyond the reach of their crossbows. They expected to see the huge force of pioneers and men-at-arms in his wake. They expected the drummers and the banners and the priests and the baggage. In short, all the usual retinue and panoply of an army on the march.

But they certainly did NOT expect to see the rear guard in command of an inebriate fat gentleman on a great grey shire horse. A gentleman dressed in scarlet and blowing on a silver horn. And surrounded by a small party of other chaps similarly accoutred.

So, as I say, hey diddle diddle, they turned curious, and about half of them followed.

Perhaps they thought I was a carnival.

Perhaps they thought the King would by-pass Rouen, and they had orders merely to see us out of sight.

Perhaps they feared some necromancy.

I don't know.

What they *got* was a full-blown fox-hunt! For it was my luck, just this side of the island dividing the river, to flush a splendid creature from the brushwood. He came up out of the grass like a red flame suddenly lit in clear morning air.

'Tally ho!' I cried.

And we were off. . . .

My little fox-hunting party, that is, and the foolish Frogs. For, momentarily, *the idiots followed us*! They had dashed across seven fields and some of them fallen off their horses and into the ditch, before serious shrill trumpets from behind them warned them that their frivolity had not gone unobserved by the general garrison remaining on the Pont de l'Arche, and that the commander there was hopping mad at this diversion.

But by the time the runaway French had mustered, and

gathered their wits, and rejected the novelty of this red-coated English game of pursuing foxes to the death – our King had swung round with the main body of the English army, occupied the island with a small force of gunners, and thrown up such a sudden cannonade that all the enemy troops left to guard the passage were put to flight.

Those French novices of the fox-hunt withdrew in dismay and some disarray to face the fury of their commander.

I caught my first French fox. And I caught the French.

I had a fine brush despatched to the King, via Pistol.

I drank burnt brandy sitting on top of a haystack.

Henry, now holding both banks of the Seine, constructed a bridge of boats to join his two camps, and went on pounding at the Pont de l'Arche from these powerful positions, bombarding it night and day for three days, until it capitulated.

'Qu'est ce que ceci *Tally-ho*?' was all the garrison's commander had to say.

And I took pleasure in instructing him in the mystery of how we English had declined (or elevated) it from the old Norman hunting cry of *Taillis au*! ('To the coppice!'), which my ancestors had heard their overlords employ after the Conquest, when William's men went after English stags. So the wheel had come full circle. And the French had been led a dance by our new English version of their own old game.

Rouen was now isolated from the rest of France.

We held command of the river. We had invested all the country round about. Every way the French looked out from the walls of Rouen they must have seen the sun shining on the armour and the banners of the English army.

The story was only beginning, however. Rouen was very strong. Its walls were high and well supplied with artillery. I suppose the whole must have been five miles in circumference, having some 60 towers each armed with guns and catapults, and reinforced by a deep ditch running round it. The garrison within was uncommonly large. There was a local militia numbering at least 15,000 men, and a force of not less than 7000 regular troops and artillery. A spiked jewel. An iron maiden.

Hal made no assault upon the town. He simply made it impossible for the French to get out. He even had a heavy iron chain strung across the river, in case a ship should try to run the gauntlet of our guns. The French were well and truly trapped, and they knew it. Besides which, in addition to their large garrison, Rouen was packed with a multitude of countryfolk who had flocked in from the neighbourhood to avail themselves of the shelter of its walls.

I remember the Duke of Clarence pointing at the haystacks in the fields and saying: 'My brother is getting as skilled as Caesar in these little matters. He's got this city under siege *before* it had the chance to secure a harvest for the winter. They've had it!'

I think we all knew that, English and French. For our part, you see, we could afford to send off marauding parties to obtain provisions from the towns round about, whenever we needed them. But Rouen had to wait for help from the King of France. And the King of France could not help himself, let alone his city of Rouen.

We heard as winter set in that all bread was used up in the city. They had nothing but water and vinegar to drink. The only meat they had left was horseflesh. The citizens of Rouen were driven to the eating of their cats and their dogs, as well as rats and mice. A quarter of a horse, fat or lean, sold for one hundred shillings. The head of a horse was worth a half a pound. Dogs went for ten shillings, cats for two nobles, while a rat cost 40 pence and a mouse 6d. Not that there were many mice left. The people were compelled to eat roots and bark and moss, and any grass they could find growing within their walls. And then they began to die in that rich city, and they died so fast every day that they were left unburied.

Towards Christmas time, its governor was driven to attempt to relieve a desperate situation by expelling from Rouen 12,000 non-combatants.

Women and children.

I think that this was one of the most pitiable things I ever saw.

For Henry said he could not allow these refugees through our lines, and after we had given them a little bread, and done them no harm, he ordered us to drive them all back again into the ditch below the city walls. Some of them lingered there until the very end of the siege – but most did not. They died, and lay there, unburied in the waste land.

Henry relented a little from the severity of his order on one day only – Christmas Day itself. On that day, a few priests from our side were allowed to venture into the ditch, taking food to the starving women and children who lay there. I asked to go with them, and was given the King's gracious permission to do so. It was when I was in the ditch, with our priests, giving bread and wine to the starving, that I saw a baby born there, of a French woman expelled from Rouen pregnant. So terrible was her suspicion of us, that she refused to let any of our priests baptize it. The child was accordingly hoisted up in a linen basket to the top of the walls, duly baptized by a French priest, and then let down again to perish of hunger no doubt. I left that woman with enough burnt brandy to see her out of her misery in the cold.

It snowed.

Between two dead men in that no man's land, you might see one still twitching.

You would see a woman still holding in her arms her dead child, and singing to it.

And you would see a living baby in a dead woman's lap.

King Henry the 5th has been much blamed for the inhumanity he showed in this siege. I have nothing to say on the subject. It none of it surprised me. Hal was not cruel, but he was a King. He believed that France was his by right, and that Rouen belonged to him. He treated those besieged French as rebels. He was a soldier, and he was determined that the city should fall to him.

As for the refugees dying in the snow in the ditch. . . . I suppose he was determined to make an example of them, and to make things harder for Rouen by not allowing them to pass through our lines to freedom. Rouen had to watch them die, as we did.

In the face of that death, who showed the greater inhumanity?

Rouen, by its obstinate refusal to surrender, which would have brought immediate release to the poor people trapped between the armies?

Or Hal. . . . ?

The issue is not easy. I do not presume to judge it. Neither do I intend to applaud or criticize myself for a foolhardy action undertaken some few days before the siege finally ended, when I could stand the crying of a particular child no more – and crept down into the ditch and brought it out with me.

It was a damnfool thing to do. The baby died in my arms as I came back into the English camp. I was arrested instantly. I expected that I would be hanged in the morning. Instead, I was brought before the King, who gave me a good cold dressing-down in his usual style, then asked if I had anything to say in my own defence.

'Nothing,' I said.

'Kneel down,' he ordered.

I did. 'Arise, Sir John,' I heard him saying.

It was all like a dream. It is still.

He knighted me as matter-of-factly as a man might wash his hands after doing a job which has made them dirty. He turned on his heel and was gone before I could say a word. Not that I had a word to say. I felt nothing. No joy. No grief. No triumph. I remember that I suffered an imagination for a while that I could still hear that child crying. And the newly knighted John Fastolf found the first task of his knighthood in digging a grave for the child, and finding a priest to give it Christian burial.

Rouen surrendered three days later.

On 22nd January, King Henry entered the city by the wide gate of Caux.

Without pride.

Without pipe.

Without drum.

Without blast of trumpet.

Riding on a black horse clothed in black damask, with a breast-plate of gold, and pendants behind him so long that they hung on either side to the ground, dragging as he rode.

And those in Rouen who had never seen him before knew by his look which was he.

And it was noticed – with much speculation as to the meaning of the symbol – that a page rode behind him, and the page bore a lance to which a fox's brush had been attached after the manner of a pennon.

XC

How Sir John Fastolf was made Captain of the Bastille, & about the marriage of King Henry 5th & the Princess Katharine

(*4th Note by Stephen Scrope*)

After that fraud of his death in London, he cheated me out of my inheritance.

My mother had bequeathed to me money and land, by a deed signed with her first husband, Sir Stephen Scrope, my father.

How this Devil persuaded my mother to set her signature to a new deed, which made over all her estates at Castle Combe to him, I do not know.

But he did.

And then, while I was still his ward, he handed me over to the Lord Chief Justice for a sum of £500.

The deal was that I was being sold to marry one of Gascoigne's daughters.

I had to go and live in Gascoigne's house.

I was treated like a serf.

I fell into a melancholia.

It was there, in Gascoigne's house, that I contracted the sickness which laid me low for 13 years, and left me crippled as I am.

Gascoigne did not even marry his daughter to me then.

He tried to marry me off to a girl of inferior rank.

My friends protesting, for such a marriage would have disparaged me, the Lord Chief Justice proceeded to sell me back to this Devil for another £500.

He bought and sold me like a beast.

Like a slave.

Against all right and law.

He cheated me out of more than a thousand pounds.

As a consequence of which, I took that sickness, by which I am disfigured in my person, and shall be until I die.

These are facts.

I mention the little lies – the figs and the potatoes and the slugs – that you should perceive the big lie of the whole.

He bought me and he sold me like a beast.

It would be charity to suppose him mad.

He is not mad.

XCI

About the capture of Meaux, & the death of King Henry the 5th

The King took Katharine back with him to be crowned in the Abbey Church of Westminster. He left the Duke of Clarence as his Lieutenant General in France, and with a special charge as Governor of Normandy. Paris was under the care of the Duke of Exeter, as I told Scrope yesterday, with the Bastille my particular responsibility.

Worcester, at last you have the advantage of me. You have one eye. But it seems that I am to have none. This morning I picked up the notes I gave to Scrope concerning the divers small charges borne by me in my service in the wars abroad. (These are mere crumbs – but to be added in due course to my great Bill of Claims against the Crown, which is now nearly ready for dictation.) Do you know, my Cyclops, I couldn't make out a word that Scrope had written? Though I saw the sums there more or less, with underlinings where the totals came.

I am blind, Worcester. My eyes have almost gone. The light is dying.

Does he write a fair hand, stepson Scrope? Has he got it all right? Not just about those wages, but about Queen Ysabeau's behaviour in the Church of St Peter at Troyes? About the murder of the Duke of Burgundy at the Bridge of Montereau? Dragged down. Overwhelmed. Stabbed (to death). Queen Ysabeau was in tears. But she could have had the Duke, her lover, killed, and cried disconsolately when the deed was done.

Henry was hardly gone, when the Dolphin took the field again. He'd bought the service of 7000 Scots, under command of the Earl of Buchan. My old master, Clarence – the one who'd told me we owe God a death, while hanged men thumped the wall – he was dining when the news came of these reinforcements marching to join the French. He left a perfectly good meat pie, with gravy, to go and get them.

'Up them, gentlemen!' they say he said.

He was not in time to prevent the junction of the enemy's forces. He met two armies at a bridge across the River Coesnon. A terrible battle took place.

2000 of Clarence's troops were killed, among them the Lords Ross and Gray, and the Earls of Huntingdon and Somerset.

Clarence himself, in rivalry or emulation of Hal's style as usual, wore on his casque his ducal coronet. One William Swinton, a Scot, attacked him and dismounted him. Clarence got up to fight on foot, but Buchan brained him with his mace.

This was a bad reverse for England, and the King knew it. When someone asked him if he was planning a tournament among the festivities to celebrate his marriage, he answered that they should have tilting enough, but that it should be tilting in earnest. On 10th June, he embarked from Dover with an army of 4000 men-at-arms and 24,000 archers, arriving at Calais the same day at noon.

He came first to relieve our difficulties in Paris. This was quickly done. Indeed, by this time, Henry's name and fame stood so high among the French that his mere presence was enough to make our cause seem plausible again, and to make the Frogs start hopping in the opposite direction. He went down to Chartres, which the Dolphin had beseiged while the King was in England, and the French retired without fighting a battle as soon as they saw the English army approaching across that long flat plain. I marched with the King to Chartres, and heard Mass sung in the cathedral there, and knelt before the fragment of our Lady's dress which that most wonderful of churches is a house for.

It took Hal just 10 weeks to regain all the territory lost during his absence.

The Dolphin and Buchan kept out of his way, collecting what forces they could as they went along. They retreated as far south as Bourges.

Henry let them be there, for the moment. He lay siege to Meaux, since as long as this fortress remained in the hands of the Dolphin, Paris was not safe for us.

Meanwhile, on (I believe) 6th December, in the year of the Second Adam 1421, while that village in Dutchland was being drowned by a flood in the night, Queen Katharine had given birth to a son. This event took place at Windsor. I heard from the

King's chamberlain that Hal was thrown into a strange fit of gloom when the news was brought to him. He said:

'I, Henry born at Monmouth, shall small time reign, and get much. This Henry born at Windsor shall long, long reign, and lose all. But God's will be done.'

Meaux held out for seven months. It was ruled by a barbarian who went by the name of the Bastard of Maurus. This Bastard was *such* a bastard that he had no hope of any pardon should he capitulate – so, of course, he did not capitulate. He had broken every law and common usage of war. His allegiance to the Dolphin was the merest excuse for butchery. An elm grew outside the walls of his fortress. It bore a crop of bodies, winter and summer, of people he had murdered for the plunder's sake.

By April we had occupied a small island in the river, from which we were able to smash their walls down with our cannons. Before ordering an assault, the King invited Meaux to surrender. His invitation was answered with an insult. We went in then through the breach in the walls, and fought with them hand-to-hand for seven long hours. It was a particularly nasty encounter. When their lances were all broken, that garrison at Meaux fought with iron spits.

Night was falling. Henry again offered terms.

I find this worth mentioning, Worcester, since I want to be fair to his character as *king*. This offering of terms – when he could just have killed the lot of them in the morning – was a kingly act, seeing that Hal had been personally insulted during the siege. It shows that his temper was under absolute control. He showed neither anger nor pity. Which is what one should expect of a king, perhaps.

Also: the terms offered (and accepted) were not unduly severe.

Four persons, among them the Bastard of Maurus, with all English mercenaries, Scotch and Irish soldiers in his pay, were excepted from the King's clemency. The rest were to be kept close prisoners until the end of the war.

On 11th May, or thereabouts, – I remember it was pissing down with rain anyway – Meaux was in Henry's hands.

I saw the Bastard of Maurus beheaded, and his body hanged up by the ankles on the elm tree where he had hanged so many others.

It was my responsibility to march the captured English mercenaries, plus the Scotch and Irish, to the Bastille in Paris, where they were executed after proper trial.

This capture of Meaux was the last military exploit of King Henry the 5th.

At the end of the same month of May, Queen Katharine landed at Harfleur, with her infant son, and accompanied by her brother-in-law, John the ox, Duke of Bedford. They journeyed from Harfleur to Rouen, and from Rouen on to Vincennes, where Henry met them.

I witnessed their entry into Paris.

It was magnificent. Katharine came with two mantles of ermine borne before her carriages, to symbolize her twin royalty now as Queen of England and of France.

I had charge of the small command of foot-soldiers lining the route where the procession passed the Bastille.

I knew that Henry knew that I was there.

I brought my men to attention as he went by, and with one accord they cried the words that I had schooled them in:

'*God save your grace, King Hal!*'

And, for myself, I cried as I had cried before:

'*God save you, my sweet boy!*'

But as I said the words, I knew it was too late. God was not going to save him now. God had other plans for Harry Monmouth. The King's face was drawn and sunken in. He was plainly dying.

I don't know whether he heard the words my soldiers shouted, or my own words. On reflection, now, I rather hope he didn't. I would prefer him to have taken to the tomb – if I ever crossed his mind at all in those last days – the fact that on the night before Agincourt I had said more circumspectly, 'God save the King!' Or even, that on the occasion of my knighting at Rouen, when I had half expected rebuke or worse for what I had done in the ditch, and he had asked me what I had to say, I had answered, 'Nothing.'

GOD SAVE THE KING or NOTHING might well be better as words for King Henry the 5th to remember me by.

But, then, GOD SAVE YOU, MY SWEET BOY, were the words I felt again compelled to say.

In any event, the matter is problematical only in my own heart. For, true to form, King Henry the 5th gave no sign whatsoever of having heard a small party of English soldiery salute him with an unusual mode of address, or of having even noticed an old fat English knight by the side of the road, his cap in his hand, and tears blinding his eyes.

Blinded now indeed, Worcester. My age and my blindness began in that Paris street, as the King's death rode by me.

Henry Monmouth died about two months later, on the last day of August, of a sharp fever with vehement dysentery, having just completed his 34th year on earth. He had demanded the truth of his physicians, and when they told him that it was impossible for him to live for longer than another two hours, unless it was the will of God to decree otherwise, he sent for his confessor, made his confession, and received the last sacraments of the Church. I heard that he then asked his priests to recite the 7 penitential psalms, and that when they were chanting the 51st and came to the words, *Build Thou the walls of Jerusalem*, he interrupted them and said that he had intended, once peace was restored to France, to conquer the kingdom of Jerusalem. I heard also that when the priests went on with their devotions, he cried out once again, in the midst of them, 'You lie! You lie! My part is with the Lord Jesus!' But nobody knew who he might be speaking to.

XCII

How Sir John Fastolf was installed a Knight of the Garter

St Faith's Day

Pigbum, there was a lot more History.

It doesn't seem important any more.

With Henry the 6th in his cradle — and at the height of his significance as a king, you might say — John Beaufort, Earl of Somerset, and Richard Plantagenet, Duke of York, had a great quarrel in the riverside gardens of the Temple, each of them plucking a rose from the bushes growing there, to serve as his badge. Somerset plucked the red rose. Plantagenet the white. I always liked white roses.

I was made Master of the Duke of Bedford's household in France. That was in the January of 1422. I think. O royalty. O responsibility. I remember a little shit-faced runt, Guillaume Raymond his name was, governor of Pacy. This Raymond agreed all the way to the bank to pay me 3200 salutes in gold by way of a decent ransom. My lord the royal ox of Bedford did me out of this prize. Very disgustingly, he claimed the same piece of French excrement as *his*, and carted him off on a shovel. May I say, little farter, that I regretted the duplicity of one who was a brother and uncle to Kings, now himself Regent of France, seeing fit to stoop so low as to cheat a soldier of his due.

Miranda sucked me off last night. She made me put on my blue hood of the Garter, and lie back on pillows of red velvet. Then she took my weapon in her mouth. She tickled with her sweet little prickly tongue — like a vixen's, it is — round and round the head of my cock. Then she started moving with her whole mouth up and down on me, and sucking, and pumping like mad. Her eyes blazed like meteors. Plainly, she was loving every moment of it as much as I was. She sucked and sucked. She put her fingers up my bum-hole too. Then, when she felt me starting to come, she squeezed at my balls as if she wanted every last drop of the precious stuff, and got as much of her mouth over my organ as she could, so that the head of it was rubbing against the back of her throat, and she could swallow the whole lot down in one go.

It was exquisite.

Most refreshing.

Reminding me of the night before Verneuil, when a French girl called Jessica did the same office for me – only that was in less comfortable environs. I had to lean against a wall, and this little carroty-headed mamselle knelt down before me.

'*He eez too beeg, milord!*'

But we managed, somehow. And, afterwards, I fucked her fore and aft against the selfsame wall. And there were no more complaints regarding the size of the English milord's battering ram.

At Verneuil, now, in that great battle, an August it was, and stinking hot, with flies everywhere, but I forget the year – at the Battle of Verneuil, I took the Duke of Alençon prisoner. (That is, John II, son of the Alençon who fought so bravely against us at Agincourt, inheritor of his father's title and a great part of his courage.) I agreed with him on the sum of £26,666. 13s. 4d (Twenty Six Thousand Pounds, Thirteen Shillings, and Fourpence) as a right ransom. This was paid – though it took three years for the money to come through, and Alençon meanwhile lived here at Caister at my expense, I having seen to it that he was safely shipped home on my own little vessel *The Blythe*.

Now, then, Bussard, put this down clear. The money was paid, but I never saw my proper share of it yet. Lord Willoughby (that cheap paederast) and my lord the ox of Bedford got every penny of it between them. Such nervous gratitude! *And* I'd just agreed to provide 80 men-at-arms and 240 archers to help the Ox win his campaign in Maine! Ah well, the numbers will at least give you an idea of how your author had risen in the world – or fallen? –since those days when he took only 10 and 30 to the fight at Agincourt.

My niece Miranda is different from that Verneuil girl in one respect. She likes to drink it all down, to swallow it. She sucks me off as though I were a sugar stick.

After Verneuil, and Mons, and St Ouen d'Estrais, and Beaumont le Vicomte, and Silly-Guillem, I was installed a Knight of the Garter. I have my Garter, my collar and George, my lesser George and ribbon, and my Star. All very nice, though they don't keep out the cold.

Move those curtains.

We should have more wax on those curtains.

I want more wax on those curtains.

HONI SOIT QUI MAL Y PENSE.

Full circle. I had to wear garters in the service of the Duchess of Norfolk.

As for my own coat-of-arms. . . .

Bussard, I cannot see. It would give me pleasure if you would draw them for me on the page before you. Draw boldly. I might be able to make it out.

That motto, ME FAUNT FARE, means *I must be doing.*

Doing, Pigbum.

Oh, I know the local translation of it, don't worry!

So then, now then, I had honours and dignities and responsibilities. I also had money to invest. It was impossible for an English soldier not to make money out of the fortunes of the war in France. Where I differed from others like me was only in my dream of Caister. I was determined to invest my profits in good English land.

Item, 23rd January, 1426, I entrusted 8000 gold crowns, equivalent to some £1333 (One Thousand Three Hundred and Thirty Three Pounds) to Sir William Breton, the bailey of Caen, and to Jean Roussel – for them to forward to England on my behalf. That money was paid to John Wells, alderman and grocer of the City of London, and to John Kirtling, clerk, my receiver-general on this side of the Channel.

Breton was not my only basket.

Item, 26th April, 1430, from Bartolomeo Spinola the Genoese, Wells and Kirtling took delivery in London of a sum of £333 (Three Hundred and Thirty Three Pounds), which I had deposited with another Italian merchant in Paris nearly nine months previous.

My Paris banker, Spinola's colleague, was Johannes d'Franchis Sachus. I called him John Sack.

This money – and much else besides – came here to Caister. To build my dream. This castle. But more of that anon. I shall reserve a Day for it. For an inventory of my castle and its building. And how I had in the end a licence from the Crown expressly for the purpose of bringing my own fleet of six ships with building materials up the Hundred River.

Caister Castle is my dream, my craze, my maze, my embodiment in stone, my pleasure dome. And all that, and the glory in France, is very nice. But what really counts in the end, little farter of mine, is the state of your soul and your prick and the number of figs in the barrel.

The sun on the wall.

A girl.

A cask of wine.

That's what remains.

Sap rising. Miranda. And sack.

That's all the facts. That's what remains.

Sap rising. Miranda. And sack.

XCIII

A fancy of Sir John Fastolf's concerning the marriage of Joan of Arc & the Marshal Gilles de Retz

St Dionysius' Day

Joan of Arc. Joan la Pucelle. Joan the Maid. Joan the Puzzell.
Gilles de Retz. Gilles de Laval. Marshal of France. Bluebeard.
The story of those two.
Father, I wish that I could tell it.
There is a very great mystery here. I was a witness to the edges of it.
I saw half France in flames, and the Dolphin's hopeless cause suddenly alive again, and all because of a virgin in a suit of white armour, bearing the sword with which Charles Martel was said to have vanquished the Saracens.
I saw the same girl burned as a witch in the market-place at Rouen.
And I saw her heart afterwards, in the hands of the executioner. It would not burn.
'We have burnt a saint!' he told me. And he threw her heart in the Seine.
What are we to make of this? What are we to make of the whole tale of her 'voices' and her victories? And the fact that every single one of her judges, starting at the top with Peter Cauchon, the Bishop of Beauvais, came to some kind of violent and cut-throat end? And that from the day of her burning – it was on the 30th of May, in the year of our Lord 1431 – nothing went right again for the English in France?
Was Joan a saint?
I saw her three times – once at Orleans, once in the flames, once at Patay (more of that last time later). She died crying *Jesu! Jesu!* She was a short, stumpy, ugly girl, with a dark complexion. She came from the marches of Lorraine, a place called Domremy, in the Vosges Mountains. There were several prophecies that a

virgin would come out of those oak-forests, and be the salvation of France. Yet this Joan was a strange sort of salvation, severe and spotty-faced, and the Dolphin made no effort to get her back when Burgundy captured her and sold her to us.

> *Relapsed heretic. . . .*
> *excommunicate catholic. . . .*
> *apostate, idolatress, divineress and sorceress. . . .*

I remember the words on the paper they hung round her neck, and the cap they put on her head. For years I had this jingle in my memory, whenever I thought of her:

> *A thing in the form of a woman*
> *By name of the Pucelle*
> *Was burned by the soldiers at Rouen*
> *After a proper trial.*
> *She was a relapsed heretic*
> *And excommunicate catholic,*
> *Apostate, idolatress,*
> *Divineress and sorceress;*
> *A devil from Lorraine*
> *Whence devils come* ›
> *In the dress of women,*
> *As everyone knows.*

Not *my* jingle, father. I have stooped low, but never so low as to verses. Nym was the author. That humorous Nym. He was hanged not long after, for an offence similar to Bardolph's.

But – I confess that Joan the Puzzell worried me, and worries me. Sometimes I've thought her bitch, witch, and murderess. Sometimes – something else. And then, three years ago, Pope Callistus III accepted the findings of that commission which he had appointed to investigate the whole matter of her trial, and declared her rehabilitated. O for God's sake, I've no doubt there were political motives behind *that* little move. But the Pope's the Pope, and the politics aren't really relevant. The rehabilitation of Joan's memory just expresses what a lot of people felt who saw her die. There was a soldier of my company who made a cross out of two sticks and held it up in front of her eyes even as she was burning. A witch would have flinched from that, or spat, or just ignored it. I never saw such love as came in tears from that girl's eyes as she fixed her last look on those two crossed sticks in the smoke, and cried out *Jesu! Jesu!*

But then there's Bluebeard's shadow on the story. . . .

The man she chose, the general she selected, her comrade-in-arms, the captain of her captains – and not so very long after we burned Joan, this same Gilles de Retz was arrested, and brought before the Bishop of Nantes by his own people, and accused of witchcraft, and sacrilege, and the murder of little children. Threatened with excommunication, he *confessed* to the crimes. And the details of that confession were so vile that the Bishop of Nantes got up and threw a veil across the crucifix. It was obscene, atrocious. Bluebeard had burned the bodies of most of his victims – but I heard that they found sufficient remains to indicate that 46 children had been murdered for his pleasure at Chantocé, and 80 at his castle at Machecoul. He was executed after a trial which lasted a month. Strangled. Then burned. There are records of that trial in the archives of the Chateau at Nantes. It is a mercy that no one has ever been required to read them, save those judges, who got up and *veiled the cross* as the tide of De Retz's filth swept over them.

Father, I am haunted by these images of contradiction. . . .

Joan in the white armour.

De Retz on the black horse.

The saint.

The devil.

Is it so simple? *Can they be separate?*

Father, I say some ceremony must be found. . . .

to marry the Maid of Orleans to the Marshal of France!

Last night I dreamt of it again –

The cathedral at the bottom of the sea, where the organ sounds the *Gloria in Excelsis* backwards –

Bells and bright light in a garden at noon –

Blue streams of smoke among leaves –

White flames curling upwards –

Joan at Patay, in ridiculous armour, and waving her sword like a flag, but sovereign all the same, a wingless Victory riding down upon us –

Gilles in that dark tower at Poitou, the cracked winter landscape, the smell of myrrh and cinnamon –

The Marshal's dogs with blood on their paws and muzzles –

Snow falling, falling –

A nightingale singing in a black tree at the wrong season –

And that cross made of serpents twisted, hung upside-down above the pit –

The huge ivory phallus –
The air beating –
Beaten –
As if with the wings of eagles –
Flutes! Drums!
THE DANCE BEGINS!
Christ dances!
Jupiter dances!
Apollo dances!
Venus dances!
Mars and Mercury, Juno and Minerva, Neptune and Vulcan,
Ceres and Diana!
Bacchus dances!
Saturn and Proserpine!
Isis and Osiris!
Taramis, Teutates, Esus, Belinus, Ardena, and Belisarna!
Up and down, and in and out, arm-in-arm, and round about –
Love makes them dance!
And my heart dances to that tune.
But now –

O

My Eros has been crucified!
Lord –
The Marshal with the whip.
Lord Jesus –
Fire and shit and flesh and a single drop of blood in his beard
burning like a blue jewel.
Lord Jesus Christ –
Fire and black wine and flies buzzing in that inner chamber
hung with cloth-of-gold from roof to floor.
Lord Jesus Christ, Son –
FIRE and Joan again rejecting him, accepting him, rejecting
him by accepting him, that stake in the Rouen market-place her
answer, her meaning, her love, her martyrdom.
Lord Jesus Christ, Son of –
They say that wicked man died with much peace, having made
his confession and asked forgiveness of the mothers of the chil-
dren he had murdered.
Lord Jesus Christ, Son of God –
Joan did not die in peace. She died in agony in the flames. But
she cried *Jesu! Jesu!* at the end.

Lord Jesus Christ, Son of God, have –
Their story was not my story.
Lord Jesus Christ, Son of God, have mercy –
I was the fat man in the crowd, who came to watch the witch Joan burn, and thought at the time of the price of decent brandy and how to get more money up to John Sack in Paris and how his feet itched in ill-fitting boots and whose stomach was vaguely disgusted by the present stench and a memory of Badby burning in his barrel.
Lord Jesus Christ, Son of God, have mercy on –
Their story was not my story.
Lord Jesus Christ, Son of God, have mercy on me –
But is her story my story?
Lord Jesus Christ, Son of God, have mercy on me a –
Or is his story my story?
Lord Jesus Christ, Son of God, have mercy on me a sinner.
How many stories do you think there are?
I got piss-absolute drunk that night, and fell into the Seine, and would have drowned, only I was fished out by the executioner on his way to kill himself.

XCIV

Sir John Fastolf's great Bill of Claims against the Crown

(With Notes by Stephen Scrope)

Translation of St Edward the Confessor

Billa de debitis Regis in partibus Franciae Johanni Fastolf militi debitis

These are the injuries, losses and damages that the said Fastolf has had, as well within this kingdom of England as in other parts:

First, it is to be considered how the said Fastolf has been vexed and troubled since he returned to England by the might and power of the Duke of Suffolk, and by the labour of his servants in divers wises, as in great oppressions, grievous and outrageous amercieaments and many great horrible extortions, as it may appear more plainly by a roll of articles thereupon made, the damages of which extend to the sum of ....

£3333. 6s. 10d.

(The said Fastolf is also so stingy that I was obliged, on coming of age, to sell a manor which was part of my inheritance and take service in France with Humphrey, Duke of Gloucester. It was my hope by this to obtain favour with the Duke, and restitution of the Lordship of the Isle of Man, which belonged to my uncle the Earl of Wiltshire in the days of King Richard II.)

Item, the said Fastolf has in particular been greatly damaged and hurt by the might and power of the said Duke of Suffolk and his councillors, in the disseizing and taking away of a manor of the said Fastolf, called Dedham, in the county of Essex, to the value of £66. 13s. of yearly rent thereby lost for three years, to his great hurt, with £133. 6s. in costs expended in recovery of the same, the sum in all ....

£333. 6s. 10d.

(The said Fastolf, when he heard of my possibilities with Duke Humphrey, wrote to my mother, his lady wife, and by some hold over her got her to insist that I give up my engagement with the Duke, and serve instead with *him*, the said Devil, in France. Which I did. To no advantage whatsoever, except to the said fiend.)

Item, there was cast into the King's hands by untrue forged offices and inquisitions, supposed to be found by divers escheators in the counties of Norfolk and Suffolk, three certain manors of the said Fastolf, to the value of £66. 13s. yearly, which said offices and inquisitions were never duly found, but forged by untrue imaginations and means of certain persons wishing ill to the said Fastolf, as has now been confessed by those that were appointed and named to be upon the inquests; and by the malicious labour of his said evil willers, the said manors have been troubled and put in jeopardy for the past four years, to the damage and cost of the said Fastolf, the sum......................

£333. 6s. 10d.

(The said wickedness not only cheated me out of my wages in his service in France, but when a dispute arose between me, Scrope, and the Marshal of Harfleur, the said scoundrel took the latter's part, and I was forced to return to live upon my mother's charity in England.)

Item, the said Fastolf having the right to the Baronies and Lordship of Silly-Guillem and Lasuse, in the county of Maine, to him and to his assigns for ever, the which were gotten by the said Fastolf, and at no charge to the King, bearing a value of £500 of yearly rent, he was commanded by the King's letters to deliver up the said baronies and lordships to the King's commissioners, promising him, by the King's commandment, recompense therefor, as the said Fastolf has those letters to show, and he not recompensed nor rewarded nothing for the levying of his said baronies and lordship, to the damages of the said Fastolf of the sum of...

£1666. 13s. 5d.

(The said villain, with me his stepson returned home, presented me with *A bill for my food and drink in my mother's own house!*)

Item, whereas the said Fastolf had a prisoner of his own taking, called Guillaume Raymond, which was ransomed, and agreed to pay him for his ransom with the sterling equivalent of 3200 salutes in gold, the prisoner, without knowledge or licence of the said Fastolf, was taken away from him by the Duke of Bedford, then being the King's Regent of France; and with the said prisoner he caused the town of Pacy, then lying in the governance of the French party, to yield itself to the King, and to his said Regent in his name; and the said Fastolf, after long pursuits made to the King and his council, was recompensed only to the value of 1600 French gold salutes in the form of lands in Normandy, when these fortuned to fall into the King's hands, (which lands he has now unfortunately lost). And also the said Fastolf has lost the residue of the said ransom, beside the said lands, to the sum of...

£2666. 13s. 5d.

(The said traitor 'unfortunately' lost the King's lands overseas by reducing their garrisons to next to nothing in lining his own pockets and smuggling the money back to England to build this fantastic folly of a castle, amongst other extravagances. Further, he was *not joking* about that bill for my meat and drink in my mother's house, and in order to pay it, I, Scrope, was driven to contract a marriage which was not the most advantageous for myself. However, my wife died. However, *the said monster then brought an action against me by means of which I was deprived of all the little property that my wife had brought me!*)

Item, the said Fastolf still has outstanding to him his portion and part for the recompense and reward that should be due to him for the taking of John, Duke of Alençon, at the battle of Verneuil, which ransom amounted to £26,666. 13s. 4d. Part of this ransom being claimed by Lord Willoughby, and part by the Duke of Bedford, there still remains, after the usual deductions by the Crown, that part due to the said Fastolf, to the sum of...

£2666. 13s. 5d.

(After living in poverty for three years from the death of my wife, I had to sell my daughter to meet my expenses. I got a very low price for her, too, since the buyer knew I *had* to sell, and the girl was so young.)

Item, being due to the said Fastolf, by the execution of the last will and testament of John, Duke of Bedford (whose soul may God absolve from sin), for the said Fastolf's expenses and other charges for safeguarding and keeping of certain fortresses, castles, and towns, and for other costs, wages, and charges borne by the said Fastolf in the said Duke's service, as it may appear in certain articles written in a roll particularly of the same, the sum of...

£3066. 5s. 6d.

Summa totalis, or *Grand Total* of ....

£14,066. 6s. 7d.

(Owing to me, Scrope, by the said Fastolf, another *SUMMA TOTALIS* or *GRAND TOTAL* of ....£14,066.

He can keep the 6s. 7d.)

XCV

About the Battle of the Herrings

There have been seven great and *decisive* battles in the history of the world. These battles are, in chronological order:

> *The Battle of Marathon*, B.C. 490.
> *The Battle of Syracuse*, B.C. 413.
> *The Battle of Metaurus*, B.C. 207.
> *The Battle of Chalons*, A.D. 451.
> *The Battle of Tours*, A.D. 732.
> *The Battle of Hastings*, A.D. 1066.
> *The Battle of the Herrings*, A.D. 1429.

I come now to the last – the peak, the zenith, the pinnacle, the utter acropolis of my military career. Yes, little Cyclops, my son, the moment you've been waiting for. I come to the famous Battle of the Herrings.

The time was the season of Lent. The year 1429. The place of this celebrated action: Rouvray.

Orleans, you will remember, was under siege by us. The occasion was critical. The city was hemmed in by English forces, and the fortune of the French was at its lowest ebb. But our gallant besiegers were fainting for lack of food.

The Regent dispatched me to Paris to get provisions.

I went. I got. I came back.

I went to Paris.

I got barrels of herring sufficient to occupy 400 waggons.

I was coming back when the French got wind of the matter.

Your herring, your authentic *Clupea harengus*, that abundant fruit of the salt sea, is very suitable Lenten eating, and cheap besides. Unfortunately, he also stinks.

A very great number of the French got wind of our coming.

An enormous force of the French army was dispatched to

intercept us. The Puzzell and the Marshal knew that if they could prevent that consignment of vital fish from reaching our troops, then the siege of Orleans would fail, and all England's glory in the Hundred Years War come to nothing. Everything hinged on the herring.

I fear that we presented an easy target to those Frogs.

We were 400 waggons, weighed down with barrels and crates and creels and cradles full of herrings.

We lumbered.

We bumbled.

We came plodding and heavy with the funeral of all those fish, moving at a snail's pace in early Spring sunlight towards the village of Rouvray-St-Denis. I remember I lay sprawled atop a heap of barrels, with a basket of my figs to hand, and a flagon of sherris sack – it being, though Lent, a Refreshment Sunday. Skylarks hovering briefly overhead, in the clear February day, like the dark specks in the eyes of my Dame Milicent. I felt, I confess it, sick for home, seeing the opening blossoms of the blackthorn along the way, and the early buds here and there in the hedgerows, and remembering days of the year like this in Caister, when I would go a hunting after squirrels as a boy. That countryside down towards Orleans was not much like Caister – no snows to melt that year and put long leagues of flat land under water. But from the general *feel* of the month, and the disposition of the high clouds flying, and the primroses, and the cabbages, not to speak of *the Yarmouth smell* of all those herrings, under and around me, and my great nostalgia bred of the figs and the sack, I was not in a martial mood as we rolled down from Paris, and that's the fact of it.

We feared no attack.

We anticipated none.

Discipline was (shall I say) lax. A Refreshment Sunday in Lent is precisely the moment whan an army realises that it marches on its stomach. I had permitted my company the small dispensations I was allowing myself – that is, in their rank, cakes and ale. We trundled along comfortably enough with our waggons, the sun low but very bright and burning on the horizon, with a certain amount of singing which I tolerated. No, Madam, your English soldier actually on the job does *not* sing the Agincourt Song. We were singing, if I recall it right, a certain speculative ditty regarding the number of balls possessed by a) the Dolphin, b) the Duke of Burgundy, c) Joan of Arc.

It was all very jolly.

Luckily for me, for England, and for History, your average French army smells rather worse than 400 waggons laden with herrings. Luckily, again, this particular French army massing to attack us was of a vast and therefore *stinking* character.

I sat on top of my herring boxes. I brought the column to a halt.

'Gentlemen,' I said, sniffing at the February air, 'I smell France! I smell Frenchmen! I smell trouble!'

And at just about the same moment, my scouts reported that astonishing forces of Frogs were coming up through the villages to our east and to our west, bent on waylaying us, and pinching our cargo.

This information filled me with much fury.

I saw in a flash, you see, that this French army intended the DESTRUCTION *of my herrings*. They could have no hope of taking the fish from us, and making their own way into Orleans thus encumbranced. They would not get through our troops circling the city. Nor was it likely that, having won a battle, they would then sit down and open up all the barrels and just *eat* the herrings. No. They would destroy them. They would waste them. They would over-throw and scorn my herrings. How disgusting. Unconscionable.

I resolved on victory.

Like Harry in the night before Agincourt, I surveyed my men, and visited them, and drew them up in an order consonant with both the terrain and our advantages and disadvantages, militarily speaking.

The terrain was flat as a bowling green.

Our advantages were 400 waggons of herrings.

Our disadvantages were the same thing.

Now, the French, with their fetid allies, the Scots, chockablock with black puddings as usual, were under orders not to attack until the Count of Clermont, their leader, had elected to join them. Clermont (known to his friends as Cordelia) was a nancy, a pathic, a male varlet, a masculine whore. He wanted the pleasure of riding to an easy victory with his puce gloves on, and no danger of getting them wet with any of his own blood. This French fairy was jealous as all hell of Joan of Arc.

These intricacies gave me precious moments in which to prepare.

I grouped my 400 waggons to form an enclosure, two lines deep. Shown opposite:

This enclosure will be seen to be open at two points only – so long as Worcester has drawn it exactly as I have told him. At one of these points, the larger, – mark it with an X – I stationed my

English bowmen. At the other, – mark it with a Z – I put my French mercenaries, who always fight most enthusiastically against their own kith and kin. Both archers and mercenaries I arranged behind two palisades of sharpened stakes, and the odd barrel of herrings with the lid off. O Hal. O Agincourt.

Now then, fig me, what do you think happened?

The Scots and the French fell to quarrelling as to what we were up to. The Scots, because of Agincourt, were fascinated by Point X, but determined not to fall foul of the same fate that met the various cavalry charges on St Crispin's Day. Hot as ever in the head and the stomach, they got tired of waiting for the Count of Clermont to prance up in his puce gloves. Leaving their horses behind (because of Agincourt), they rushed at my archers on foot, with swords and staves and clubs and daggers and suchlike apparatus. A few French idiots followed them – Scots and French alike to be met by a hail of well-directed English arrows. But for the most part, the French, still wavering, still without the perfumed benefit of the Count of Clermont, decided to attack our other entrance, the one marked Z. They came on their horses in deliberate defiance of Agincourt, and in scorn of the barefoot Scots.

All this was just as I had hoped, and indeed planned.

The Scots attack was well repulsed by the archers, firing from behind the safety of their palisade, up and over the stakes and down into the faces of the enemy as they came running.

The French attack – their usual magnificent cavalry charge – ended with a great number of horses spitted on our spikes, and many more losing their feet and tumbling their riders vulnerably to the ground on account of the multitude of slippery herrings we had shovelled out of the barrels and cast about in the grass.

But the beauty of my enclosure, from the victory point of view, lies in the proximity of Points X and Z, *and their complete irrelevance.*

What I mean by the latter is that the enemy was fascinated by the openings. So fascinated that they concentrated their attack upon them, when if they had simply charged at any other segment of the circle no doubt they might have over-run us and destroyed us.

What I mean by the former is that the proximity of Points X and Z, – which a less brilliant general, admit it, Sir, might have arranged at diametrically opposite sides of the enclosure – allowed my eager mercenaries, to nip out quickly as soon as the cavalry charge was spent, and skip up round to their right and come up the backsides of those Scots who had got past the arrows and the stakes and were now engaged in hand-to-hand fighting with my bowmen.

A keen and bloody battle ensued at that Point X.

My archers, like Harry's at Agincourt, threw down their bows and fought with their staves and their swords, to deal with the Scots who got through.

My mercenaries came suddenly like thieves in the night, and *since they then came shouting in French* (because they WERE French, Madam, really you have no head for these affairs of war!), the Scots were thrown into much confusion, not quite knowing if these were their allies or not.

They soon found out.

For my part, I directed operations from the top of the waggon on the Z side of Point X. (Mark it with a herring-bone arrow will you, Worcester? For the Lady Reader's benefit!)

From this position, my contribution to the victory was several thousand herrings thrown with devastating and demoralizing accuracy in the faces of the Scots.

What a day! What a strategy!

It was all over in fifteen minutes.

Then the waggons rolled on. We proceeded down to Orleans with our Lenten glory.

Laugh if you like. I tell you that your laughter betrays your ignorance of the details that usually go to win a glorious battle. We *used* our resources (*id est*, herrings). The French and the Scots used nothing except their capacity for falling into a properly baited trap.

And the Count of Clermont?

Cordelia came late, Madam. When she saw what had happened, she burst into tears. I hadn't the heart to kill a pretty little thing like that. So I had my men strip her (save for the puce gloves) and shove her half-pickled in a barrel of herrings, her head sticking out of the top, do you see, and her hands and arms out of the sides. Thus carapaced in fish, and with holes in the bottom of the barrel for her legs and her feet, we drove the Count of Clermont down the road to Orleans before us.

That is the true story of the Battle of the Herrings.

My finest hour. Well, fifteen minutes.

XCVI

An inventory of Caister Castle

(Compiled by Stephen Scrope)

St Luke's Day

~~An Englishman's castle is his home.~~
No!
I wrote down what he said.
I will not write down what he says!
I, Scrope, am none of his ghosts. Let him say on. I shut my ears to him. I am deaf to the old fool. I ignore the ancient Devil. Scrope is no part of his pattern. Scrope is outside the cobweb.
All that nonsense about herrings.
As if there was ever a battle in France calling itself the Battle of the Herrings!
It is all lies and stories.
It is all things that are not.
I tell you things that are.
I tell you the truth.
Worcester says that I must write at his dictation. Worcester says we are to humour him.
I'll humour the monster! Worcester misses a vital difference between me and the rest. I am not a servant in this house. Scrope serves no man.
Friar Brackley says he may be dying.
Him? *Die?* That Devil?
I'll believe it when I see him in his coffin, and that coffin planted deep in the earth, and an anchor on it.
The Devil is not capable of death.
I think.
Yet tonight, being St Luke's Day, I am pleased to report some change in his condition. These days of hectic fever, during which he has scarcely once stopped talking, have left him looking like a hodge-pudding.

A bag of flax.

A puffed man.

He is old. He is cold. He is withered.

His intolerable entrails must be giving him the Hell he deserves.

Tonight, also, being St Luke's Day. He has called me in here to make an inventory of his goods. This could be construed as the act of a man growing conscious that he stands on the edge of the grave.

I shall prepare as much of an inventory as interests me.

I shall ignore his self-interruptions on the usual themes – of fornications, and taverns, and sack, and wine, and metheglins, and drinkings, and swearings.

(What is 'Sack'? It is like his 'potatoes'. It does not exist.)

How can a man claim to have spent his life drinking a drink which does not exist?

That would be alchemy. Or witchcraft.

Who is he?

He is staring at me!

But his eyes are blind now. He cannot see me. He cannot see what I write. He cannot see anything.

He pribbles and he prabbles about his Tower which is 90 feet tall, and the 26 chambers here at Caister, and the Chapel with its gilt candlesticks, and its pyx and its cross, and its ewers and its chalices, likewise all gilt, and its images of St Michael and our Lady. He chatters about his six acres of gardens.

Enough of all this.

It is a trap.

It is the Devil's trap.

He is not going to shut me up in the fiction of his castle.

I will confine my inventory to what defines *him*.

I will confine my inventory to facts.

For instance, his clothes. . . .

Togae remanenciae hoc tempore in Garderoba Domini

First, a gown of cloth of gold, with side sleeves, like a surplice.

Item, another gown of cloth of gold, with straight sleeves, and lined with black cloth.

Item, half a gown of red velvet.

Item, one gown of blue velvet upon velvet long furred with martyrs, and trimmed with the same, sleeves single.

Item, one gown, cloth of green, three yards long.

Item, one side scarlet gown, not lined.

Item, one red gown, of my Lord Cromwell's livery, lined.

Item, one chammer cloak of blue satin, lined with black silk.

Item, one gown of French russet, lined with black cloth.

Item, one buckram suit.

Tunicae Remanentes ibidem

Item, one jacket of blue velvet, lined in the body with linen cloth, and the sleeves with blanket.

Item, one jacket of russet velvet.

Item, one jacket of black velvet upon velvet.

Item, one jacket of chamletts.

Item, one jacket of fustian.

Item, one doublet of red velvet upon velvet.

Item, two doublets of deer's leather.

Item, one pair of hosen bound with leather.

Item, one pair of scarlet hosen.

Capucia et Capellae

Item, one russet hood, without a tippet, of russet satin.

Item, one black velvet hood, with a tippet, half damask and half velvet.

Item, one hood of deep green velvet, the tippet black.

Item, one riding hood of red velvet.

Item, one tippet, half russet and half black velvet.

Item, two beaver hats.

Item, one knitted cap.

Item, one blue hood of the Garter.

Aliae res necessariae ibidem

Inprimis, one canopy of green silk, bordered with red.

Item, five pieces of scarlet for horses' trappings, with red crosses and white roses.

Item, one piece of St George's livery.

Item, one piece of red satin, embroidered with *Me faunt fere*.
Item, one piece of green worsted, 30 yards long.
Item, one dagger.

For instance, his pillows. . . .

Inprimis, five pillows of green silk.
Item, one white silk pillow embroidered with blue lilies.
Item, five pillows of red velvet.
Item, one little green silk pillow, full within of lavender.
Item, one pillow of purple silk, and gold.
Item, two pillows of blue silk, with a shield.
Item, 7 long pillows of fustian.

For instance, his tapestries. . . .

Inprimis, one cloth of arras, called the Adoration of the Shepherds.
Item, one arras of the Assumption of our Lady.
Item, one new banker of arras, with a bear holding a spear in the middle.
Item, one tester of arras with two gentlewomen and two gentlemen, and one holding a hawk in his hand.
Item, one tester of arras with a lady crowned and a great roll about her head, the first letter N.
Item, one cloth of 7 conquerors.
Item, one cloth of the Siege of Falaise for the west side of the hall.
Item, one arras cloth with three archers shooting a duck in the water with crossbows.
Item, one cloth of arras with a gentlewoman harping by a castle in the middle.
Item, one cloth of arras for a bed, with a man drawing water out of a well in the middle.
Item, one red banker, with three white roses and the arms of Fastolf.

For instance, his pots, *et cetera*. . . .

Item, three great brass pots of French making.
Item, one great brass chamfron for a war-horse.
Item, 38 arrows swan-feathered.
Item, one wicker basket.

Item, 7 feather beds.

Item, one bolster, covered with green satin, and a scene depicting an upstart who shakes a spear.

Item, many blankets.

Item, many curtains.

Item, sheets.

Item, a pair of tongs.

Item, carpets.

Item, a pair of bellows.

Item, quilts.

Item, one iron bar.

Item, 15 steel crossbows.

Item, 25 spears.

Item, one green chair.

Item, 7000 pipes of red wine.

Item, dishes.

Item, carving knives.

Item, trencher knives.

Item, silver cruets.

Item, goblets.

Item, spoons of silver, with their knaps gilt like pearl.

Item, 7 great silver basins, gilt borders inscribed *Me faunt fere*.

Item, missals.

Item, one cauldron.

Item, one dripping pan.

Item, spits.

Item, one flesh hook.

Item, vinegar bottle.

Item, a lure for hawks.

Item, the Bible.

Item, the encyclopaedia of Bartholomew the Englishman.

Item, *Vegetius on Chivalry*.

Item, *The Dictes and Sayings of the Philosophers*.

I, Scrope, translated the last, for his 'Contemplation and Solace.'

He made me write that at the end.

In fact, I translated it because he stood over me with the dagger and one of the 25 spears above mentioned. It was his vanity that wanted it. In himself, he has always preferred the stroking of girls' spines to the stroking of the spines of books.

And yet, tonight, St Luke's Night, he begins at last to look dry and yellow and broken, and every part about him blasted with antiquity.

So?

Shall we see the Devil young again?

Fie, fie, fie, Sir John!

To Hell with you, where you belong!

XCVII

About the reverse at Patay, & the fall of France

St Crispin's Day

Damn it all, Worcester, the fall of France was not my fault.

Jack Napes, the Duke of Suffolk, sold us all along the line. I am too old and tired to recite his manifold villainies. Suffice to say that he was never much of a soldier. He got the quickshits at Harfleur, and came home before seeing two swords crossed in anger. He danced about at Verneuil, but some distance to the rear. After Salisbury's death, he succeeded to the chief command of our English forces in France. God and the Duke of Bedford alone know why. Jack Napes it was who captured Margaret of Anjou, and quickly bedded her, and then arranged for her to marry prickless Harry 6th and remain his mistress.

What a shit. There is nothing to compare with your Suffolk shit. Here was a prime shit out of Suffolk.

He lost our castles and our garrisons in France.

He threw away Anjou and Maine.

Worse, it was Suffolk who had Humphrey, Duke of Gloucester, murdered, and his wife Eleanor banished to the Isle of Man for sorcery. Poor Humphrey. He was a bit of an idiot. He only ever wanted to be like Hal. The resemblance is now complete, since both are clay.

Damn Suffolk! He cheated me out of my property at Dedham.

He got what was coming to him, that Jack Napes, when the pirates caught him off Dover – *Nicholas of the Tower*, the pirate ship was called – and beheaded him at sea.

His body was washed up headless on Dover Beach.

Henry, our holy wonder, goes and has it buried at Wingfield.

May God have mercy on that Suffolk for his villainies. I cannot.

In the days before Suffolk, in the days about the time of my finest hour –

O glory. O herrings.

We were young lions.

I've burnt more French haystacks than I've had hot dinners. And drink. . . .

I remember a session in Bordeaux. Myrtles, lemon-trees, and ilex: why not? I captured this castle and had the pick of its cellars. They had to set me for seven hours head-down in a waterfall to cool me off from the sampling session. And then my head made the spring boil like a volcano, and steam came hissing out of the green growing wheatfields in the valley below.

I had my licence from the crown also. I took much wine by way of ransom, and shipped it home here to Caister in my private fleet. It was not all building materials came wallowing up the Hundred River. France has fallen, and God rot the so-called Englishmen responsible for that, but we can still drink the glory of those days. It lies in the pipes in the cellar beneath our feet.

Here's to the Lord of Soubooze, and all his kind!

So.

A glory was gone out, or going.

Packets of jewels. My best the spear-pointed diamond set in a collar called in English a White Rose. This was bought by Richard, Duke of York, for £3000 (Three Thousand Pounds), and given to me in part repayment of a loan, in part as recompense and for my labours and vexations when he was the King's Lieutenant in France. That is the most valuable jewel in England outside the royal treasure. The collar is too tight for me to wear. Sometimes I wear it round my wrist. Sometimes I let Miranda wear it when we are in bed together.

I have also from that time, of course, this cross and chain. Inside the cross is a piece of the Holy Cross Itself embedded. I never take that off.

Tell Bartolomeo –

No, no. I know. He is dead now.

They are all dead.

John Sack is dead.

Was the Count of Clermont queer? Madam, *any queerer and he would have been a Lesbian.*

Worcester, you bugger, I remember another party of French lads that I captured in the Côtentin. Very pretty lads they were. I made them strip. They were all a-tremble with anticipation. What could the gross English milord desire or require of them?

'Madamoiselles,' I said, 's'il vous plaites – *fart!*'

'*Pardon?*'

I demonstrated.

They thought I was joking. Till I got my little chopper out, and had them all standing on one leg, and trying very hard indeed.

'C'est difficile, milord!'

'FART!'

They did. A hard little, pert little, prissy little fandango of farts in the French morning.

Those were the days.

I marched. I marched vastly all those years. I was worn out with marchings. For an Englishman – and it is my content that no man ever lived more English than I am – for such a man, I have spent too many of my days under a foreign sun, biting on outlandish foods, drinking inferior ale. Yet the French harvests of the vine had many good years in those years. So from all that marching at least I have the bottled sunlight in the cellar as a token of my triumphs.

I refer only briefly, little Cyclops, to the talk which buzzed at my reputation for a time. Regarding, that is, the surrender of certain of my towns and castles when disaster beset the armies of England under government of my lord the Shit of Suffolk. Gossip is the biting of so many little fleas. I returned my castles to the French only when their return became inevitable. I have always been a firm believer in the inevitability of the inevitable.

Besides –

Home –

Home is –

Home, my home is –

England.

This day is called the feast of Crispian.

England.

Crispin. Crispinian. Those were their real names, those two saints. They were cobblers, martyred at Soissons. There's an altar bearing their name in the parish church at Faversham. The shoemakers round here still keep up the feast of their patron saints. Keep it, indeed, with such a fierceness that there's a rhyme:

> *The 25th of October –*
> *Cursed be the cobbler*
> *That goes to bed sober.*

I have other reasons for remembering it, and for not going to bed sober.

This day is called the feast of Crispian.

Thus Harry, before Agincourt, when he promised a band of brothers, of which I was one, that those of us who outlived a particular St Crispin's Day, and came home safe, would stand a tip-toe when this day is named, and rouse him at the name of Crispian.

I do. I do indeed.

Old men forget, but I have not forgotten Crispin Crispian yet.

And today, for my sins, Worcester – it would *have* to be today – it so falls out in these my *Acta* that I have to tell the story of my latest and my last defeat. I refer to the most unfortunate matter of the slight reverse at Patay.

It was as a result of this that certain unjust accusations were made against my courage. I still taste bitter in my mouth from the memory of them. I am going to set down here nothing but the facts. And let the truth speak for itself.

In June of the year of our Lord's harrowing of Hell 1429, responding to a request from John Talbot, first Earl of Shrewsbury, I was dispatched from Paris with a force of about 6000 men. Our object was to relieve the English besieged in Beaugency on the Loire. We joined with Talbot, only to learn that Beaugency had already surrendered. We were now uncertain what to do. Rather, Talbot was. For my part, I had no doubt what I thought we ought to do.

Seven weeks before, Joan of Arc had ridden into Orleans. She was at the height of her strange career. The French, red with success, were rushing in all directions behind her banner. Now we had word that Joan, at the head of an army numbering between 20,000 and 23,000 men, was marching down to meet us.

We held a council of war.

'We are out-numbered nearly four to one,' I said. 'Yet allowing that one Englishman is worth about three Frenchmen, the odds are not so bad against us. However, there is the matter of the Maid.'

'You mean the Witch?' said Talbot.

'If you like,' I said. 'Maid or Witch, Pucelle or Puzzell – she is very hard to understand.'

Talbot bit his nails and looked at me impatiently.

'I make her out clearly,' he said. 'She has inspired the French by some sorcery.'

'You may well be right,' I said. 'It depends what you mean by sorcery. I have seen her just the once. She rides in company with the Marshal of France –'

'De Retz? A gallant soldier!'

'He has other attributes,' I said.

Talbot scowled. 'Meaning?'

'I don't know what I mean,' I confessed. 'All I know is that there is some strangeness we are faced with here, over and above and beyond the usual encounters of war. I don't know what happened at Orleans. It seems the siege was relieved by the Maid. A siege which by all the known rules should never have failed. *Could* never have failed. The Marshal de Retz and the Maid together turned that siege of Orleans into something else. It was as though Orleans became their private trysting place.'

Talbot snorted. He was a furnace of a man. The Bastard of Orleans liked to call him 'the fiend of Hell', and I've heard that to this day when a nurse or a mother in France wants to frighten or pacify a fractious child she will say 'Be quiet, or Lord Talbot will come and get you!' But with this fieriness went a certain scepticism also, an impatience with anything that could not be explained in terms of the here and now. I should tell you that Talbot had been imprisoned by Henry 5th on suspicion of Lollardy tendencies, owing to his being a friend and companion-in-arms of that disreputable Sir John Oldcastle, the heretic burnt alive in chains at Welshpool. He had survived such suspicions, and distinguished himself in Ireland and in France as a good soldier. But 'good soldier' about defines his limits. He could not see for the life of him what I was driving at in regard to Joan of Arc.

'We must face the French,' he said stubbornly.

'No doubt,' I said. 'But be sure it is not only the French we are required to face.'

'You are frightened?' he sneered.

'Yes,' I said. 'But not of the French.'

'Of the Witch?'

'Something like that.'

'Of some power she possesses?'

'Or which possesses her,' I said.

At this point, our debate was concluded by the arrival of a messenger who informed us that the avant garde of the enemy – some 1500 Frogs on horseback – were approaching at speed.

We took up improvised positions. It was the best we could do in the circumstances, but to someone who had fought at Agincourt and the Battle of the Herrings you will understand that our lack of proper tactical array was somewhat shocking. The vanguard, the baggage, and the artillery were all drawn up in higgledy-piggledy fashion alongside the hedges. The main body of our chaps tried to fall back to take up their stand between a bosky little wood and the fortified church of Patay. It was a difficult manoeuvre. To be frank, Talbot did not much help by charging and blustering about, and urging contradictory orders upon us all. The upshot of these orders was that we were to prepare ourselves to die. Now that has always seemed to me to be the wrong thing to tell soldiers going into battle. Better to tell them to prepare themselves for a fine old age by fighting like wildcats to give themselves a chance of attaining it.

Talbot reminded me of Pistol, if you want to know. A different quality of man, no doubt. But a similar fire-eating bull-headedness. A similar absurdity.

He had command of 500 archers. These were excellent archers, and it was his job to hold the road along which the Frogs were coming at us. This road was as narrow as a good nun's cunt. We should have held it.

We did hold it, for a brief while. But only because the French could not locate in growing dusk exactly where the main body of our bowmen were positioned. Then it was their good luck to start up a white roe-deer – as it seemed, by accident.

And it was our bad luck to have that ass Talbot in the front line, for he immediately ups and betrays our position by shouting out, 'A stag! A stag!'

Think on these things.

In warfare, as in life, there are really only *incidents*.

The French happened to start up a roe-deer. That need not have been to their advantage, or our disadvantage. But in the revelation of human character epitomized by Talbot hurling himself stupidly forward down that lane, crying 'A stag! A stag!' you see a battle lost.

Foolhardy impetuousness is not courage.

The French horsemen fell on Talbot. They came at us suddenly from both sides, now certain where we were, outnumbering us completely. Even so, the battle raged for three hours. Talbot was taken prisoner. I fought on. The Lord Scales was taken prisoner. I fought on. The Lord Hungerford and Sir Thomas Rampston were taken prisoner. Still, I fought on.

When I say *fought* I do not mean hacking and smacking about with swords on the ground like any common butcher.

I was a captain, remember. I was conveniently positioned in an oak tree, from which I directed our English operations.

Hopelessly outnumbered, with all our other captains captured, we might still have saved that day, but for the following incident.

Darkness fell. The moon came up. Our archers kept firing, firing. Our men-at-arms fought as bravely and as well as at Verneuil. The French came at us in one long wave after another. And with each wave, it seemed that *now*, surely, we must be beaten. But we were never quite driven back beyond the fortified church. We were holding on. . . .

And then, in the moonlight, I saw Joan of Arc for the second time.

She was standing on a little hill about two hundred yards from the tree where I was hidden.

The moon shone down on her, and on De Retz beside her.

She was standing as if exhausted, leaning on a short sword half-buried in the earth, her head bent down. Not a very beautiful or remarkable posture. But in that moment it was not so much that a light shone about her. For a second or two, *she was the light*. And De Retz disappeared.

It was the latter evil, rather than the former marvel, – if it is proper to speak in these terms about things which must remain speculations of mere vision – that caused me to fall out of the oak tree.

When I looked up from where I had fallen, the moon had ridden behind a cloud.

I stood up.

I dusted myself down.

I put on my hat.

And then I saw the white roe-deer coming towards me.

Unlike Talbot, I did not leap into a hunting stance. But I dare to say that I was more astonished than Talbot had been, and had more cause for dismay, since I saw more than Talbot had seen – or more than he would ever after admit to being possible, when I brought the subject up very tentatively with him years later.

I saw a white roe-deer with the face of Joan of Arc.

Some of the French historians say that I ran.

That is untrue.

I turned round, and I walked.

But I walked fast, and I took my men with me, and I got them out of that place alive.

Joan did not pursue us. Heaven knows why. (It probably does, yes, Madam, I mean it.)

Talbot was ransomed.

He reported me for cowardice to the Duke of Bedford.

I was deprived of my Garter.

I asked for a private audience with the Duke, and was granted it. At that audience I told him the story which I have now told you, and which I have told no other living soul. John, Duke of Bedford, was a block of a fellow, a bit of an ox, a slow mover and a slow thinker, not at all like the other brothers in that family of princes, as I've had occasion to remark more than once in these memorials. But he was no fool and no Lollard, and he knew me well enough to know that I was not lying to save my skin.

'Do you think the woman is a witch?' he said, when I had finished.

'I wish I could think that,' I said. 'Sometimes I do. And when I do I can think that God will still allow England's right to France, and our cause to prosper.'

'And when you don't?' Bedford pursued.

'Then I think she might be something else.'

'A saint? Surely not! Surely you don't think she can be a saint?'

'I think that for a moment she was the light itself,' I said flatly, 'and after that a deer. A white roe-deer.'

Bedford insisted that she must be a witch. But in the circumstances he was prepared to give me back my Garter. Talbot never understood why. And when I vaguely hinted at a certain peculiarity in what I had seen coming towards me under that oak tree, his blank incomprehension made it clear that he would never understand even if I tried to explain it to him.

So I did not try.

Reader, if you doubt my story, reflect on the fact that after my secret interview with the Duke of Bedford history will tell you that I was fully restored to his confidence, and enjoyed his unmitigated favour.

Yet to this day – St Crispin's Day – there are those who believe the French version.

I am not surprised. A soldier learns that his enemy's version of events will readily find believers at home, since men who do not fight are always ready to find fault with the actions of those who fight for them. Cowardice is a mighty quickener of tongues.

A man learns slowly from what he sees.

Talbot saw a white stag, at Patay.

I saw a white roe-deer with the face of a girl, at Patay.

I see now that I saw also in that white roe-deer with the face of a girl, at Patay, the subsequent inevitability of the fall of France, and the end of our English dominion.

Joan of Arc. Joan the Puzzle. The Church in her wisdom will know in the end whether the woman was truly a devil or truly a saint.

For myself, Worcester, for myself?

I wished the deer no harm.

I wished the white creature no harm.

That's why I turned and walked away.

XCVIII

*The Last Will & Testament of Sir John Fastolf**

Feast of St Simon and St Jude

In the name and the worship of the holy blessedful Trinity (in the year) of our Lord Jesu Christ 1459, and in the 38th year of (our sovereign King) of England and of France, Harry the 6th, the 28th day of the month (of) October, being the Feast of SS. Simon and Jude, apostles and martyrs, I, John Fastolf, of Caister, by Great Yarmouth, of the county of (Norfolk), Knight, being in good remembrance, albeit I am sickly and through age enfeeb(led), bringing to mind and often revolving in my soul how this world is tra............and how, amongst all ea(r)thly things that are present or to come, there is nothing in this unstable world so certain to creatures of mankind as is departing out of this world by death, the soul from the wretched body; and nothing earthly so uncertain as the hour and time of our death – Therefore I, willing and desiring that of such goods of worldly substance, movable and unmovable, that God of his bounteous grace has sent me in my life to dispose and occupy, that they be disposed as it may be thought best for the health of my soul and to the pleasure of God, and also for the relief, succour, and help of the souls that I am most obliged and bound to purvey and do...............for, as the soul of John Fastolf, my father, Dame Mary, daughter of Nicholas............my mother, and the soul of Dame Milicent, my wife, the daughter of (Sir Robert) Tibetot, Knight, and for the souls of other of my.................kinsfolk and special friends hereunder written, – I ordain and...............this my last will in form and manner following:–

First, I will and ordain that, if it please our sovereign lord King Harry the 6th, or his heir Kings, for the long continued service by me in the days of the strength and health of my body, to him and to (the noble) King Harry the 4th and Harry the 5th, his progenitors, and to his (noble) uncles John Duke of Bedford,

436

Thomas Duke of Clarence, while they were in the wars of our said sovereign Lord and his (noble) progenitors foresaid, in France and Normandy as in countries and other places, considering my many great labours, pains, and perils in the said service of our sovereign Lord and his (noble) progenitors foresaid, and his plenteous grace without any other..............of my executors named in my testament, or else for a reasonable sum of (money) which our said sovereign Lord owes me, or in some other wise, or by any other means, so as my executors therein shall accord with our said sovereign Lord and his council, or with his heir Kings and their council, to licence and grant to them that be fieffed to my use in my own lordship's manors, lands, tenements, rents, services, with their appurtenances, or to their assignees after the effect and form of the law, by the advice of my executor, to ordain, found, and establish, within the great mansion or dwelling place late by me newly edified and moated in the town of Caister, by Great Yarmouth, in the county of Norfolk, which mansion or dwelling place goes commonly by the name of Caister Castle, a college of a priory of 6 religious persons, monks of the order of St Benedict, and a prior, and to immortize and grant to the said prior and 6 religious persons, or to their successors, the foresaid mansion or dwelling place, with all the appurtenances and other sufficient and clear lifehood of the foresaid lordships, manors, lands, and tenements, rent, and services, with their appurtenances, for the sustenance of the said prior and 6 religious persons and their successors, and for their other charges and reparations, and for the maintenance of 7 poor men in the said college in perpetuity, by the advice and discretion of my executors (hereinunder named) and that then the foresaid fiefees or their assignees if they..............grants of others having interest in this to be halved lawfully as requisite, and they shall make, found, and establish, in the said college, with the said prior and 6 religious men, ever to endure, for to pray for my soul and for the souls of my father and my mother, and for all my kinsfolk and good doers, and for the souls of the blessed memory (of the) Kings foresaid, Harry the 4th and Harry the 5th, and the said (noble) Dukes, and for the good estate and prosperity of our sovereign Lord during his lifetime, and after for his soul, and for all Christian souls, therefore to sing and say daily divine service and prayers in perpetuity; and to be of the orders, profession, obedience, and governance of the Order of St Benedict, and of the same order and profession as are the monks of St Benedict's at St Benet

Hulme, in the county of Norfolk, and shall be established by the good advice of my executors. And to that prior, and to those 6 religious men, and to their successors, I bequeath the foresaid mansion and dwelling place, with the appurte (nances),...........sufficient, sure, and clear livelihood of the foresaid lordships (and) manors............rents, services, with their appurtenances in Caister foresaid, and in all other places...............all for the sustenance (of the) said prior and 6 religious men and their successors, their servants, and the (said) 7 poor men. And for the charges and reparations foresaid, to the yearly value of £200 (Two Hundred Pounds) sterling over all charges, to have and to hold to the foresaid religious men and to their successors for ever, (provided always that the said prior and religious men and their successors be bounden and compellable sufficiently in law by the discretion of my said executor), to sustain the foresaid 7 poor men continually, sufficiently, and conveniently in all things within the said college for ever, and to pray for the souls aforesaid.

(It)em, I will and ordain that all and singular lordships, manors, lands, and tenements, rent(s), and services, and their appurtenances, in which any person or persons are fieffed or have estate and possession to my use, in whatsoever counties or towns the said lordships, manors, lands, and tenements, rents, and services are within the realm of England; and that all the foresaid and singular lordships, manors, tenements, rents, and services, with their appurtenances, in which any person or persons are entitled to my use by the law, shall be sold by my said (and sole) executor (Stephen Scrope), except manors, lands, and tenements, rents, and services, with their appurtenances, as shall be required for the said college (if the foundation thereof take effect). And that the money of the sale or sales coming be disposed by my said executor (Stephen Scrope) in the execution of this my last will and testament, and in other deeds of alms as my said executor (Stephen Scrope) by (his) discretion shall seem best to please God for the health of my soul and for the souls foresaid. (And that should the foundation of the said college not be established, nor the said college founded, then all aforementioned lordships, lands, and tenements, rents, and services, with their appurtenances, be assigned to my stepson Stephen Scrope, and to his heirs, to be sold by him, or by his heirs, and all moneys thereof coming be his, or theirs)..........and in other deeds of mercy, pity, and alms as shall seem best to my said (sole) executor

(Stephen Scrope) for the souls aforesaid and the souls under-written.

Item, forasmuch as it is said that divers persons of divers descent pretend ....
........................at this day to be next inheritor(s) to me after my decease, where ....
........................know that no creature has title or right to inherit any ....
........................lands and tenements, rents, and services that ever I had, or any person or persons........................have to my use. Therefore I will and ordain that no person nor persons as:........................me for no doubtful or obscure matters contained in this my present will, nor for none other, shall take any manner of advantage, benefit, or profit by any manner, means, or ways, of any manors, lordships, lands, tenements, rents, services, goods, or chattels that were mine at any time.

Item, I will and ordain and grant that my executors (before named), shall have the declaration and interpretation of all and singular articles, sentences, clauses, and words in this my last will and testament, in which articles, sentences, clauses, and words should any doubt or doubts, darkness or diversity of understanding befall or happen to be found, then shall no person or persons by reason of such articles, sentences, clauses, or words have or take any profit or advantage otherwise than after the manner and form of declaration and interpretation of my said executors.

Item, I will, ordain, and command that all debts owing by me (after due examination) be fully paid to the creditors; and also that all wrongs, trespasses, offences, and griefs by me done or committed, if any be, that any manner of person has been hindered or damaged wrongfully, if any such be that can sufficiently (and lawfully) be proved and known, I will first before all other things that my executors do make amends, restitution, and satisfaction to those persons or to their executors by me damaged and hindered as conscience and good faith requires.

Item, I will and ordain that in every town in which I have lordships, manors, lands, and tenements that the poor people of the tenure of the said town have 2 years to gather in re-ward........................the 10th part of one yearly value and revenues of the said lordships, manors, lands, tenements, and rents, half to be given to...........parish churches for works, ornaments, and other things necessary to the said churches, and half to be given amongst the said poor people that are tenants of the said lordships, manors, lands, and tenements............(but so to be disposed after the discretion of my executor before named)............after my will approved, and my debts paid.

. Item, I will and ordain that the prior of the priory of the parish church of Yarmouth for the time being, and his successors, observe and keep yearly and perpetually to endure an anniversary in the said parish church for to pray for the soul of my father, John Fastolf, Squire, that lies buried there in the said church, with *placebo* and *dirige* and Mass, noting the vigil and day of his obit, with the number of priests and clerks according in such a cause; and to sustain the keeping of the said anniversary, I will that by the advice of my executors (before named) that lands or teneme ....
.......................to the yearly value of.................(20 shillings)............sure to the said priory or parish church, only to sustain and bear............and charges of the perpetual keeping and sustaining of the said anniversary.

Item, I will and ordain that if I have any relics of Saints, also such ornaments for the church, that I have left as vestments, garments of silk or velvet, or robes, and my gowns, that parcel of them be given to the said monastery church of Saint Benet Hulme, where I shall be buried, to remain for ornament of the chapel there by me late edified; and also part of them to be distributed amongst the parish churches that are in such towns where I have any lordships, manors, lands, tenements, and rents, provided that a reasonable and competent part of the said relics and ornaments be kept and given to the said college to be made at Caister, and this to be done by the advice of my executors (before named).

Item, I will and ordain that such of my consanguinity and kindred which are poor, and have but little substance to live by.......................having consideration to those that be nearest of my kin and of..
Also of her good disposition to God-ward and to me always my dear niece..other of my friends............that a consideration be had and given to the relief and preferment of.......................for his good, true, and long service done to me.

Item, I will and ordain that the holy place, the monastery and abbey of our Lady's church of Langley, in the diocese of Norwich, for my soul to be more specially recommended, and also to keep and sustain, one day in the year, my anniversary solemnly, by note the *dirige* and Mass of requiem for ever to endure for the health of my soul and for the soul of Dame Milicent, my wife, (the daughter of Sir Robert Tibetot, Knight), which was of the consanguinity and kin of the founders of the said monastery, and she owing a singular affection and love of devotion to the prayers of that place, that the Abbot and his convent have a reward and a remuneration of my (moveable) goods (at the discretion of my executor before named).

Item, I will and ordain that (by the advice of my executor before named) provision and ordinance be made that the obit and anniversary may be yearly in perpetuity kept with *placebo* and *dirige* and Mass of Requiem for the sould of Dame Mary, my mother, in the church of Attleburgh........................(at the discretion of my executor, my well-loved stepson and good-doer Stephen Scrope).

Item, I will that a convenient stone of marble and a flat figure, after the fashion of an armed man, be made and graven in the said stone in Latin in memorial of my father, John Fastolf, Squire, to be laid upon his tomb in the chapel of St Nicholas, in the parish church of Yarmouth, and with my escutcheon of arms, and his, and our ancestry, with a scripture about the stone making mention the day and year of his obit.

Item, I will that in similar wise a marble stone of a convenient.................made to be laid upon the tomb of Dame Mary, my mother, in the.........founded in the parish church of Attleburgh, and that a figure.........of a gentlewoman with her mantle, with a scripture made of Latin in on...............escutcheons of arms of her several husbands, as the escutcheon of Thomas Mortimer, Knight, (John) Fastolf, Squire.....................and of John Farewell..................... and the day and year of her obit to be written about.

Item, I will and ordain that the executors of John Wells, alderman of London, who had great goods of mine in his governing while I was latterly in the countries of France and Normandy, and never returned to me open declaration to whose hands my reservoirs had been given, or to which servants of mine the said goods were delivered particularly, and for that cause as well as for the discharge of the said John Wells's soul, his executors and attorneys may offer (to my above named executor) a full declaring of my said goods according to the truth and their conscience.

Item, to be provided, if it be thought commodiously that it may be done (by my executor), that a chantry may be founded in the church of St Botolph's, by Bishopsgate, in London, to pray for my soul and for one unnamed soul continually.

Item, my breviary to be buried with me.

Item, the prior and 6 religious men of my college established to pray by name with *dirige* and *placebo* and Mass of Requiem one day of the year in any year, in perpetuity, for the souls of certain friends and companions of my youth and age, and of my time in England as in France and Normandy, to wit, – the oblate Duncan, Bardolph, Nym, my ancient Pistol, Peter Peto, Robert Shallow, Robin my page, mine hostess Nell (Helen) Quickly of the Boar's Head tavern in Eastcheap, and..............Doll (Dorothy) Tearsheet.

Item, I will and require that it be known to all people present and for to come that where before this time while I dwelt and exercised in the wars in France, Normandy, Anjou, and Maine, as in Guinne, having under the King, my sovereign Lord, offices and governances of countries and places, as of castles, fortresses, cities and towns, for 30 years and more continued, by reason of which offices............many seals of my arms graven with my name written about......officers being in divers such places occupied under me, the seals and signets to seal safe-conducts and billets of safeguard, and other writings of justice belonging to such offices of war......and I believing that some of the foresaid seals of arms and signets on monuments, charters, deeds, letters patent, blank charters in parchment or paper, or other evidence forged and contrived without my knowledge or assent, might so be sealed against all conscience and truth and rightwiseness; and for these causes, and for fear of any inconvenience that might fall by this my writing, I certify for truth and affirm on my soul, I swear and protest that since I came last out of France and Normandy, 19 years past, I never sealed writing of charge, use, or grant with any other seal of arms or signet than with this same seal of arms and signet affixed (to this my present will and my last testament). Wherefore I require all Christian people to give no faith nor credence to any private writing not openly declared nor proven in my lifetime, nor to blank charters sealed in my............whereof I remember well that one John Winter, Esquire, late my servant, had in keeping a blank letter in parchment enseesaled under my seal, and never delivered it me again, but said he had lost it at his confession, as writing under his own hand makes mention or he did.

Item, I will and ordain that my household be held and kept with my servants for the space of at least one half year after my death, so as they will be true to me (and obedient to my executor) and their wages for that time paid, and that in the meantime they purvey themselves for other service as they like best.........; but if any servant be not well behaved and holds against my......(or against my executor) to break my good disposition, I will that he shall be removed, and that he abide no longer among the fel........................truly avoided without any reward from me (or from my executor).

Item, I will and ordain that amongst other lords, friends, and kinsmen that I desire, for the discharge of my conscience, be put in remembrance of prayers for the good affection I had towards them, and therefore to be prayed for, is the soul of that ~~sweet prince~~ (great King) ~~my royal Hal~~ (his Majesty King Henry the 5th); also the souls of John Farewell, Squire, my stepfather; Dame Ophelia, my sweet stepsister; Dom William Fastolf, of my consanguinity, professed in the order of St Benedict in Ireland; Francis Pickbone, Esquire; George Barnes (Esquire); John Doit; John Sack (?), merchant of ~~Black~~ Paris, my trusty friend and servant; and of those yet living ....
....
(chiefly my well-beloved and right trusty stepson, Stephen Scrope, as aforesaid my sole executor in this world).

Item, I will, ordain and straitly charge that no one shall sell, or cause to be sold, any part of my lands and tenements, jewels of gold or silver or of other kind, or any chattels, or any vessels, or any vestments of silk, linen, or woollen (or velvet), or any other utensil, to my person or to my household pertaining, nor any other goods of mine, movable or immovable, quick or dead, generally or specially, without........................(the knowledge, pleasure, and assent of my singular executor, before named).

Item, I will, I ordain, and I heartily desire, seeing that every mortal creature is subject to the limits or marks of mutability and changeableness, and any man's life and living is a story of sins known only to God, therefore on the behalf of Almighty God, and by the way of an entire charity, I exhort, I beseech, and I pray ~~all~~ my (sole) executors, in the virtue of our Lord Jesu Christ, and in the virtue of the aspersion of His holy blood, shed out graciously for the salvation of all mankind, that for the more hasty deliverance of my soul from the painful flames of the fire of Purgatory, that in the following manner, in the year of my burying, after all my other bequests and endowments have been effected, ~~they~~ (he) divide(s) the sum of ~~£14,066. 6s. 7d.~~ (£140) into as many portions as there have been years of my life, and that

the portions be taken into the streets of the City of London, and upon London Bridge, and given ....
....
(at the discretion and mercy of my sole executor, Stephen Scrope, Esquire).

These are the articles, 22 in all, concerning the intent and purpose of my last will, now put into the hands of my executors, and which I pray, beseech, and charge ~~them~~ (him) entirely, faithfully, and straightly to execute, as ~~they~~ (he) will have help of God and of his holy Gospel. And so I require ~~them~~ (him) as wisdom, justice, and conscience to do for me as ~~they~~ (he) would I should do for ~~them~~ (him) in like case. In token and witness whereof, to this my last will, I, Sir John Fastolf, above ....
....
....
....
....
....
....
....

PS: and 2d for bread for the ducks on Thrigby Pond.

* This document is printed from the original draft in William Worcester's hand. Passages within brackets have been added by Stephen Scrope. Words and letters have been crossed out by Stephen Scrope. Dotted spaces represent mutilations in the manuscript.

XCIX

*Sir John Fastolf's confession to Friar Brackley**

All Hallows Eve

Bless me, father, for I have sinned.

I confess to God almighty, to blessed Mary, ever-Virgin, to all the Saints, and to you, father, that I have sinned very much in thought, word, deed and omission, by my fault, my fault, my most grievous fault. Especially since my last confession, which was last Good Friday. . . .

I made up a fanciful account of my begetting and my birth, to the dishonour of my mother and my father. This was a sin of pride, father. I always delighted to imagine myself a giant. In fact, I am only a fat man.

I told certain lies to my man Worcester, about the extent of my relations with two ladies of Windsor, out of lewd imagination, and out of boastfulness, and to excite him and impress him. On that same occasion, I insulted you, father, with a lewd joke, and by going on with the story of my imaginary excesses even when I knew you had come into the room and would be offended by the recital.

I made up stories about my ancestors, again out of pride, and to prove to myself my own glory.

I constructed a false mysticism upon the number 7.

I have been many many times drunk.

I have sometimes prayed carelessly.

I have seven times broken the Church's rule of fasting before receiving the Blessed Sacrament.

I have used oaths, and taken God's holy name in vain.

I have sometimes used the practices of devotion out of ostentation.

---

* This exists in the following notes in Fastolf's own hand. It is not suggested that Fr Brackley broke the seal of the confessional.

In my lifetime, I have failed to give alms according to my means. I do not and cannot justify this by mentioning that it is in my will and testament just made – to leave Caister Castle and a good revenue of all my estates – to Holy Mother Church. I have all my life found it easier to give to the dead than to the living, unless it was in moments of drunkenness and abandonment. Father, I have all my life found it easier to sin than to be good. I failed to keep resolutions which I had made, I disobeyed those in authority over me, I was discourteous to my servants, I found fault unfairly with those set under me, I have used abusive language to them and to others.

Father, I struck my servant John Bussard in anger.

Father, I have borne malice, and been sometimes spiteful in these memoirs I have written of my life. But mostly my sin in these has been again to consider myself a giant, a hero, when really I am only a fat old man, who was once a young man, and as self-indulgent then as now. I have been quarrelsome and refused to be reconciled with others. I have taken delight in hearing evil spoken of others. I have spoken evil myself, and made my secretaries write it down.

I owe Mr Mumford for those three venison pasties. I was not going to pay him.

Father, I unlawfully as you know, and for some time past, have felt carnal attraction towards my niece......But also, father, I have lied and made waking dreams about the same soul, to no harm to her person, no violation, but to the wicked excitement of those I made to believe the stories, and to write them down. All my life, father, all my long life, I have found lust easy, and love difficult. You know of my relations with my wife. It was because I loved her – so far as I can tell, before you, father, and before God, and before our Blessed Lady – that my necessary lust for her was not what she might well have wished it to be. I could waste my flesh on my whores in London, and there was one whore that I loved. But always, where love came into my dealings with women, there was a temptation for me to put them on a pedestal and to lose them. I cannot explain this. I do not wish to explain it. I am confessing to the sin of impure thoughts and impure deeds with myself alone, and in my imagination. Some of these impurities were cruel and perverse also.

**** That time in Yarmouth. . . .

XXX Twice in this very castle.

**** On the shore. The swans. By the Hundred River.

**** Lies about my whole life. But try & explain: some *true* lies?
Father......
self-willed & obstinate. . . .
only myself *sometimes*, father – my great failing. . . .
Hal: ingratitude rankled. But my fault was. . . .

These are past sins, and already confessed and forgiven, glory be to our Lord Jesus Christ, but I mention them again, in this confession, since I have revisited in my imagination in these past 100 days the times when those sins were committed.

Father, I am a vain man, and conceited, and all through these memoirs I have sought, however curiously, the admiration of my secretaries and whoever should one day cast his eye upon them. These tricks were mostly through fictitious immodesties. I always cared to picture myself as a great man. I was only ever a fat man, father.

I boasted that my member and my other parts were. . . . – But I am only the same as any other man, – no more, no less. The same.

I have been too fond of money. . . .

O father, I have sinned against heaven, and before thee, and am no more worthy to be called thy son. . . .

make me a clean heart, O God, and renew a right spirit within me.

HAVE MERCY UPON ME, O LORD, FOR I AM WEAK.

For these, and for all my past sins of drunkenness, and adultery, and lewdness, and theft, and above all my unconquerable pride (that demon, that deadliest of the 7 Deadly Sins) – he bestrid my life – my Pride was like my belly – for these and for all my other sins which I cannot now remember, I am very sorry, firmly resolve not to sin again, and humbly ask pardon of God – and of you, father, penance and absolution . . . etc.

In the name of the Father, and of the Son, and of the Holy Ghost.

Amen.

C

About the death of Sir John Fastolf

(*7th Note by Stephen Scrope*)

All Saints Day

He is dead!
  I told him what I had done.
  It killed him.
  The Devil is at long last dead.
  He talked a lot before he died.
  It made no sense.
  He said that he was someone called Arthur, and then he said
something about a little girl in a linen basket. All stuff and
nonsense.
  He is dead.
  'This world is a place of exile,' he said.
  I asked him what he thought of my betrayal – of my refusal to
write down the filth of his life.
  He gave me some answer that had nothing to do with what I
had said.
  'Madam, my mother,' he said, 'forgive your son.'
  (His mother has *of course* been dead for more than half a
century. I mention this rigmarole to demonstrate the way his wits
wandered at the end.)
  I told him what I had done to the will only when I heard the
death rattle begin, and knew that he could do nothing to prevent
or alter it now.
  He cried out for water.
  Water! Him!!
  He cried out that he didn't intend to be damned for any King's
son in Christendom.
  (I report the more amusing nonsense.)
  It was just between twelve and one, even at the turning of the
tide.
  I watched him fumble with the sheets, and play with flowers.

448

(There were no flowers. I mean, he *thought* that he was playing with flowers.)

He spoke of a plume of butterflies over his shoulder, and of running through cornfields, and suchlike sentimentalities.

It was when I saw him smile upon his fingers' ends, that I knew that it was safe to tell him, to kill him, to destroy him.

'Stepfather,' I said, 'your sybil got it wrong.'

And then I told him.

His nose was as sharp as a pen.

He begged me to wash him in wine.

Of course, I did not.

Then he cried out for his uncle to carry him along the shore.

I told him that his uncle was long since clay.

Then he babbled of green fields.

Then he called out in a great voice:

'*Kyrie eleison.*'

Then he cried out:

'*Benedicite.*'

I told him that he blasphemed.

He farted!

(In the same breath that he cried out to God, he farted!)

(Thus I knew he was a devil. But not *the* Devil. That was my mistake. He is a mortal devil. He can die. He is now dead.)

He spoke of sun and moon and showers and dew and fire and heat and dews and frosts and ice and snow and light and darkness and seas and floods and whales and fowls and beasts and cattle and priests.

Then he pulled himself up on the bell-ropes that hang by his bedside, and he shouted out his own name. But the name choked in his throat and it sounded like:

'Faust off!'

He fell back in his pillows.

I told him he owed God a death.

He looked at me.

I am sure that he could not see me. He has been blind for months. But he kept on staring at me.

I told him that I had killed his rat.

Then he said:

'The fields are green. The woods are green.'

Proving that he was mad, for it is winter, and All Saints Day.

Then he said:

'I can hear the chimes at midnight!'

(But it was past midnight, as I tell you, and nearer to one
o'clock.)

He asked me to lay more clothes on his feet.

I did not.

Then he said nothing more, after that.

And after a while I put my hand into the bed and felt his feet,
and his feet were as cold as any stone.

And then I felt to his knees, and his knees were as cold as any
stone.

And so upward and upward, and it was all as cold as any stone.

I turned away.

He was dead.

I am sure, that he was dead.

I, Scrope, write facts.

I, Scrope, tell you the Truth.

I, Scrope, say that it is a lie that I heard a voice like his, and
that voice saying:

'Remember me.'